Bequest

Ian Thomas

Manor House Publishing Inc.

National Library of Canada
Library and Archives Canada Cataloguing in Publication data:

Thomas, Ian, 1950-
Bequest / Ian Thomas.

ISBN 0-9781070-1-2

    I. Title.

PS8639.H56B47 2006   C813'.6   C2006-903038-3

Copyright 2006-10-30 by Ian Thomas.
Published October 30, 2006
Manor House Publishing Inc.
www.manor-house.biz
(905) 648-2193
First Edition. 288 pages. All rights reserved.

Book cover design: From an original painting by Darrel Duchenes (www.dduchene.com). Special thanks to the artist for his kind permission to reproduce his etching, *A la Frontier*.

Printed in Canada.

We gratefully acknowledge the financial support of the Government of Canada through the Book Publishing Industry Development Program (BPIDP), Dept. of Canadian Heritage, for our publishing activities.

Bequest is a work of fiction. All content is owed in its entirety to the imagination of the author. Any and all characters and situations are solely the creation of the author. Any perceived resemblance to real people/events in the pages of this novel is purely unintentional.

For My Father

Dr. John Edward Thomas (1926-1996), a "boy from the tips" whose passionate inquiry led him from the mines of South Wales to the universities of the world and into the hearts and minds of many. I learn to love in absence after the luxury of loving in presence.

Acknowledgements

A few good friends and creative spirits were very encouraging with early versions of Bequest.

To these souls who enrich my life with their presence and friendship I offer my thanks: Rik Emmett, Keith Reid, Tom Salter, Stewart Farago and most importantly Catherine Thomas, my reality check, and I confess, a well of inspiration for much of what I do… daydreams included.

Additional early editorial input from Jane Christmas and Catherine Marjoriebanks was greatly appreciated.

A special thanks to the wonderful Canadian artist Darrel Duchenes (www.dduchene.com) whose front cover graphic design, based on his etching *A la Frontier,* invites people so wonderfully into this book.

I have savoured Canada coast to coast through the warm amber of a single-malt with Murray McLauchlan. His presence in the Foreword to this book is particularly meaningful to this old sentimental fool, especially considering he usually gets the last word.

I would be remiss if I did not add to this list publisher/editor Michael Davie, who has been encouraging, steadfast in his support, gentle with his input, and extremely patient with my neuroses… quite a feat really!

Manor House Publishing
(905) 648-2193

Foreword

Ian Thomas is of Welsh and Scottish background and so has a long cultural tradition of being quite at home with things that go bump in the mind. There are people wandering around his house who, quite frankly, have long since shuffled off this mortal coil.

I play in a band with Ian and we have a hell of a time. I end up tours with such a case of face-ache – from laughing at his ongoing dissertations on the state of everything – that I have to eat through a straw when I get back home. Ian is a very bright and funny guy with a unique take on life and how it should be lived.

Imagine my surprise when he announced he'd written a novel. What? Not content with writing hits for Bette Midler and America, now you have to be inked with the stamp of cultural and literary credibility? Surely everybody knows songwriters can't make a compound sentence.

Then he asked if I'd write a foreword for it and sent me the book in manuscript form. I got the five-pound FedEx box and set out to perform what I thought would be a chore. I guess if I was honest, I'd admit I wondered what I could say to be encouraging: "Alright... first book... new writer... jitters... finding your own voice... blah, blah, blah!"

I finally finished it in my bed at 4 a.m. because I hadn't been able to stop reading. I couldn't put the damn thing down. I never expected that the guy could actually write!!

Well, what we have here is a tightly crafted, little, ecologically based, metaphysically oriented whodunit with lots of pithy observations on life, sexual relations, ethics, morality and politics. It's even action-packed and fast-moving. I wish I owned the movie rights.

Ian's writing is informed, as those who know him understand, by his relationship with his father, a philosophy professor, Baptist minister and medical ethicist, who recently passed away; and by Ian's marriage to his high school sweetheart, an enduring bond that contrasts sharply with the up-and-down relationships of others he has known. Ian mines a deep and rich mother lode of experience in the creation of this, his first novel.

You, dear reader, are about to enter a realm where the realization dawns that ordinary people are a lot more comfortable with and accepting of the paranormal; where ordinary folk collide with the lowest venalities of corruption in corporate and political life. Enjoy the ride.

- Murray McLauchlan C.M., author, ***Getting out of here alive*** (Viking)
Murray McLauchlan is a Member of the Order of Canada (C.M), winner of over a dozen RPM and Juno awards; and singer/songwriter of hits **Farmer's Song, Little Dreamer, Child's Song, Whispering Rain, On the Boulevard, Honky Red,** *and* **Hard Rock Town.**

Contents

About the author

The son of a Welsh philosophy professor at McMaster University and a Scottish mother, Ian Thomas was born July 23, 1950 in Hamilton, Ontario, Canada. His brother Dave is an actor, famous for his Second City and Strange Brew movie character, Doug McKenzie.

At age six, Ian was taking piano lessons, and 13 he took up guitar. A year later, he began writing songs. Still in his teens, he arranged music for the Hamilton Philharmonic orchestra. He's also performed with the Hamilton orchestra and the Toronto Symphony orchestra.

By the mid '60s, Ian formed a group that became Tranquillity Base and in the late '60s he penned the hit single *If You're Lookin'*.

After the band broke up, Ian worked as a CBC Radio producer in Toronto. In 1973 he signed with GRT Records, releasing the self- titled album, *Ian Thomas*, and hit singles, *Painted Ladies* and *Come the Son*.

In 1974, he earned a Juno for Most Promising Male Vocalist. A string of hits followed through the '70s and '80s, including *Long, Long Way; Liars; Pilot; Hold on; Time is the Keeper*; and *Right Before Your Eyes*. Hits *Hold on* and *The Runner* were recorded by Santana and Manfred Mann. Chicago featured *Chains* on their come-back album.

Ian also teamed up with his brother Dave in 1983 to record some music for the soundtrack of Dave's movie venture, *Strange Brew*. Also featured in the recordings was Rick Moranis, the other half of the Bob & Doug McKenzie hoser team.

The '90s saw Ian form a new band – The Boomers – and release a string of albums to worldwide critical acclaim.

With the break-up of the Boomers in the new millennium, Ian met up with old friends Murray McLauchlan (*Down By the Henry Moore, Whispering Rain*), Marc Jordan (*Marina del Rey*) and Cindy Church. Ian released a live CD and DVD of a performance titled; *Lunch at Allen's* and the friends continue to perform together.

With several decades of song-writing experience, Ian Thomas is a superb pop artist, a star of the first magnitude in Canada, with an uncommon melodic flair and lyrical sensitivity. The Toronto Star has described him as "a fine craftsman-like songwriter."

Ian likes to call himself "an anti-star," and lives quietly in the rural town of Winona, outside Hamilton, Ontario, with his wife Cathy. He says, "I'm still in business, still creative. I've been fortunate that I've been allowed to do what I want to do."

Bequest is his first novel.

A word from the publisher...

Ian Thomas is beloved around the world as the singer/songwriter of such smash hits as *Painted Ladies; Hold On, The Runner,* and *Right Before Your Eyes.* His more recent solo and collaborative efforts are also finding an appreciative audience, and he's written several screenplays.

Now the creative force that gave us so many classic hit songs has turned to novel writing – and what a novel: ***Bequest*** tells the story of a Canadian university professor filled with inner turmoil; an ordinary man beset with visions, of dire things past, present and future; of death and tragedy and dark secrets hidden in the American countryside.

Filled with touches of humour and personal observations on the human condition, ***Bequest*** also draws heavily on the author's own experiences with love and loss. Thomas breathes life into his characters, makes us care about them and keeps our heart rates soaring as he skilfully takes the plot through unexpected twists and turns and masterfully builds tension to the breaking point.

Manor House Publishing is privileged to have the honour of bringing this important "new" writer into the public domain with a truly superb novel that's destined to join the author's hit songs as an enduring classic. This is an intriguing book that will have readers hungrily consuming page after page of well written prose.

Ian Thomas has proven adept at subtly raising important issues while creating a fictional world that can seem all too real. ***Bequest*** is his first novel, and it's hoped, the first of many more literary gems to come.
- ***Michael B. Davie***, *president, Manor House Publishing Inc.*

Manor House Publishing Inc.
www.manor-house.biz
(905) 648-2193

1

The Big One

George had just wanted to sleep but there was far too much activity going on in the cosmos for even the most peaceful of minds to avoid. Only the increasing light of morning would slowly burn off the voices in his head.

He looked over at Joan, envious of her slumber, then rolled out of bed and padded down the hall to the bathroom. It was pretty gloomy in there. The light filtering through the blue-grey sheer curtains made the grey marble countertop look even more ashen than usual.

The mirror was screening a deteriorating black-and-white feature that had been held over for many months. Some pale-skinned old coot with white stubble on his face stared back as he moved in for a close-up.

That particular morning George had the look of a prisoner after a long interrogation, an expression made even more vivid from a lack of sleep since the middle of the night.

Suddenly a waft of dizziness fell on him like a mist and... he *knew*. He knew he was avoiding *something*, pushing some *incoming* back from a conscious mind that wanted no part of it. He gripped the counter until the event subsided a moment later. He then returned to the daily salute to masochism... a morning glimpse of himself.

George flipped the light switch on and it was even worse in colour. "Oh God... good thing I don't have my glasses on." The words hit the air then submerged into the depths of other unspoken horror stories of vanities stolen by time.

Glasses were the latest reminder of the twenty-year difference in age with Joan – and George felt like it was increasing. He wasn't so much pre-occupied with his own demise as he was annoyed that it had to be so bloody apparent. He didn't feel fifty... well... come to think of it he did, that landmark having already gone by. He felt he was sitting squarely on the slide to the big dirt nap.

A gaseous puree of toast and coffee was wafting upstairs from the kitchen. He tried to fluff his hair up – "yeah right," – then smiled at the thoughtfulness of his love, Joan, rising early just to have a few minutes with him before he left for an early class.

Joan was at the partially refinished antique maple table nursing a mug of coffee. The outline of everything naked under that T-shirt she called nightwear made him forget pretty much everything... for a moment. He leaned over and squeezed some of the most rewarding flesh he could hope to squeeze, then kissed her on the back of the neck. She went up on her toes as she snuggled her soft, dark hair into his face.

George smiled. "God, you're a pretty girl."

A prevailing socialization designed to have him seek some cheerleading, blond streaked, dream-girl with big breasts had not taken root. The societal trend favouring implants of course had defeated gravity but they had also made breasts dangerous protrusions – things moms warned their children about because: "They could poke your eye out!" But there she defiantly sat – relatively short with an athletic sturdiness that exuded good health – while sporting her own beautiful imperfections. She had an unaffected appearance that made him weak and very aware of an inner bio-diversity program that steered him away from girls named Mandy, Randy and Brandy.

"Thanks for making breakfast," he said. "Sweet of you to get up."

"Hmm," she murmured as she sat sipping coffee and staring into her mug. "You know, I've been thinking about going back to school."

George couldn't believe his ears. "Why would you want to do that? You're already making twice the money I am." Joan and a computer-wise school friend by the name of Jim Grayson had a very successful marketing research company. It had been a couple of years since Jimmy emigrated to the United States and the US contracts they were now pulling in, once converted to Canadian dollars, made George's academic salary look like chump change.

"I think a PhD would look better on my business cards than an MBA, and maybe even attract some contracts that appear a little out of our reach at the moment," Joan mused. "Letters impress some people... yours really impressed me Dr. Moss, enough to follow you home."

George looked at the clock, stuffed too much toast into his mouth and washed the mulch down with coffee.

"If only you could love me for the inner me and not some academic veneer... how shallow," he huffed with feigned indignation, pulling his green oil-cloth jacket off its hook.

George opened the back door to the drizzle of rain only to be snared, spun around and grabbed by the buttocks. "See you later, old-timer," Joan grinned. Then she kissed him sensually enough to make him want to call in sick. It was one of those deep and somewhat wet kisses resplendent with germs and wonderful promise. But Dr. George Moss was above all a responsible man, a punctual man. Okay, somewhat overly punctual. He squeezed her buttocks, and kissed her neck.

"Lunch?" he asked hopefully.

"I'll be here – hurry home," Joan purred with a sensual tone that may have ended many a war a little sooner than expected. But that day, the pull of responsibility would drag him out of the door.

George was never late and had a low tolerance for people who kept him waiting. Lateness demonstrated, in measurable units, the self-centeredness of a person. His theory was that the farther away from zero or an agreed-upon time, the more self-centered one was. He knew a fellow back in Lincoln, New York, who, on one occasion, was exactly on time with the small exception of being an entire week late. They all thought he did the brown acid at Woodstock and never made it back to this reality in his entirety. Only a selfish and distant part of him returned.

Of course the opposite also applied. People who measured in negative integers and arrived a little early, were, very often, quite humble and selfless. But once again, if they got too far away from zero, if they arrived way too early, something could be clinically wrong. George surmised that serial killers probably showed up way too early, unless of course a previous murder kept them late; like some poor victim who kept getting up, blow after sickening blow, in a painfully pathetic testimony to the tenacity of life.

The rain had been light but persistent in most of Ontario that week and the Hamilton Bay area seemed to be getting more than its share. The ten-minute walk to the McMaster University campus felt like the outer envelope of survival for a wet April day.

George loved the Gothic architecture of the original part of the university that had been run by Baptists until the 'fifties. In those early days of course, and true to good Baptist thinking, there was hardly any sex on campus because it could have led to dancing. George had found the place comfortably familiar having attended an old rural Baptist church in his childhood in upstate New York. Even without the surety of life made simple and safe by the blinders of dogma, the campus still had the feel of a less complicated world. For him Academe was a haven from a real world for which he didn't much care.

The ivy-covered Arts and Humanities building was now before him.

But as he jogged up the stone steps, the sensation suddenly hit him again. The hair on the back of his neck stood on end followed by another waft of dizziness. He stopped, spun around and stood frozen, connected now to the morning occurrences that awakened him at 3:05:53:27 a.m. according to his sports watch. *Watches now offer too much information. In the middle of the night, a clock that said three-ish would suffice nicely, thank you very much. But no-ooo, it's the new millennium and everyone must know where they are in hundredths of a second. As a directionless social evolution increased in speed, so too did the need for smaller and smaller measurements of time. I woke up at 3:05:53:27-ish. The "ish" left room for even more annoying technological growth....*

It was an odd feeling that had awoken him that morning. It was as though a vortex behind the bed's headboard was trying to suck him in. The hair on the back of his neck had stood on end accompanied by the usual dizziness but he resisted the pull. It would have been easier to let go but George wasn't going there anymore. At times it took everything he had, but with years of practice, resistance was getting easier…

The sensation subsided. George pulled one of the mammoth oak doors open and walked down the hall to his office. Dark paintings stuck to the walls like windows to another dimension. Former chancellors and professors peered out from their gold-framed cells with a look that appeared sinister in the dim light. It was as though they knew something he didn't know or didn't want to know. He tried to shake all such thoughts from his mind, seeking only some kind of normalcy as he entered his office.

After hanging up his coat and quickly scanning the day's junk mail, he headed to class. He couldn't help but notice how much younger the students looked every year. It had only been five or six years since Joan was one of them. It was just after his divorce from Margaret.

Margaret was what they now refer to as a starter marriage. They had known each other for about eight years, thought the convenience of casual sex might become love, and got married. Their marriage was like an old car. It got them around but neither one seemed willing to invest much in it so they drove it until it broke down. It sputtered to the lawyer's office where they handed over the keys, got out and walked away. The attempt to squeeze love from a friendship had summarily killed the friendship. After the divorce, whenever they saw each other, the most they had to offer was a nod of reluctant recognition.

George first noticed Joan in his second-year class a couple of weeks after the divorce papers were finalized. She used to stare at him during lectures, making him both nervous and a little self-conscious. His jokes never made her laugh, but on the other hand, when he was being serious, she would smirk. She later told him that whenever he spoke passionately, regardless of the subject matter, it turned her on.

"Weird, huh? Yeah, well, thank God for weird!" He mumbled, striding down the hall. He would often defensively point out, to anyone who cared, that he didn't date her until he was no longer her teacher. And those "dates" consisted of her precociously sitting at his table to talk whenever he ate lunch in the cafeteria.

She was so bright, funny, and... the other thing, which he tried to ignore, not wishing to be accused of being a dirty old man. Why would she want him anyway when surrounded by muscular young bucks in their prime? But he was so glad she did. They became friends long before they kissed a year later. *Jesus, just thinking of her gets things stirred down below.*

"Dr. Moss?" A voice came out of the abyss behind him. When he looked up he realized his reverie had caused him to absent-mindedly walk right past the lecture hall. A first-year student held out a book that he had borrowed. George thanked him for the rare occurrence – the safe return of a book – and continued back in the right direction toward the classroom. *Now, if I can just keep my mind off of Joan long enough, I might be able to get through this damn class.*

The room was chaotic as usual – the rustle of coats, the clunking of books as they hit the desks or the floor, a few mating rituals in progress, and jocks talking about the game last night. It was one of George's pet peeves; no matter where you were on campus, no matter what time of day or year, there was always "the game last night." He rolled his eyes, gathered his thoughts, though his mind was clearly not fully with him.

Things seemed to quiet down a little quicker than usual. There was a general air of enthusiasm, at odds with the norm for a generation that considered the world – its soil, water, air, rainforests and ozone – "all fucked, dude!" George delighted in this particular batch of students, who offered a strange glimmer of hope for the species.

An engrossing discussion sprang from a recent college publication about the holocaust, and how the Nazi extermination of the Jews was more than an isolated example of man's dark side. The writer asserted it was symptomatic of a flaw in humankind, citing recent evidence in Bosnia, Zaire, East Timor, and France where a political party was calling for the expulsion of immigrants.

The province of Quebec entered the discussion with what was called a linguistic version of ethnic cleansing. One student felt it frighteningly similar to other historical attempts at racial purity.

The lecture hall was electric with spirited debate when, suddenly, the hair stood up on the back of George's neck, again. *Oh no, not now!*

Something was terribly wrong on the other side of the lecture hall door. A fuzzy red head in the front row, noticing his distraction, stopped dead in the middle of a good rant with a more-than-curious expression on her face. George was aware the entire class was watching, but whatever was pulling him toward the door was too powerful to ignore. The room fell quiet with the exception of the hum of fluorescent lights that buzzed like an electric razor in his ears. He opened the door, and there was Joan with a curious but ominous expression on her face. The sensuality of her lips had disappeared into a tight, quivering line.

"What is it Joan?" George went into the hall, quietly pulling the door shut behind him.

Joan gathered herself but clearly did not want to speak. Her eyes filled, she put her head down unable to look at him, then finally pushed the words out: "Somebody named Doctor Harris called. Your father had a heart attack and is... he's... he's dead George." She started to cry, and buried her face in George's shirt.

He felt an odd sensation. Why was Joan crying? She didn't even know his father. He had thought about such a moment, pictured it in his mind and how he might deal with it. He had more or less imagined the perimeter, but then the floor started to fall. *Oh shit, the floor, I forgot about the floor!* His father had always said: "The presence of those who love us is like the floor on which we stand." Presence didn't have to be proximity, just the knowledge that somewhere in the world... a piece of reality, security, a floorboard, actually existed.

A sick feeling started in the pit of his stomach and moved up and across his chest. He felt like he was in an elevator plummeting to the ground. His father, it appeared, contributed more to his sense of well-being than he could ever have anticipated. Hitting ground would have been merciful; at least there would have been an end to it. The ground, his ground, ground taken for granted, no longer existed.

The pain felt larger than life, far worse than he had ever conjured in his occasional futuristic mental meanderings. He couldn't cry, and he gasped for air with the realization that he was even forgetting to breathe.

A morbid stoicism covered him like armor, completely out of sync with the pain inside. *I'm not crying. Why am I not crying? Am I such a cold heartless bastard that I can't cry? I want to cry! I want to cry like Joan! Oh Jesus, my father is gone! Oh Jesus!*

But the anguish stayed locked silently inside the recesses of his mind. Joan's words continued to echo, sobbing words that had brought a sickening verbal confirmation to what he had felt, and had chosen to deny, since 3:05:53:27 a.m.

2

Lincoln

The train rides from Hamilton, Ontario, to Lincoln, New York, seemed to take forever. George stared out the window not seeing anything in the impressionistic blur of colour on the canvas streaking by. He tried to picture his father's face.

He could hear the old man's voice: "Come here, boy. What's the matter, boy? You know what your problem is?" There was so much he wanted to tell him, words now forever lodged in his throat. Yes, he had been a lousy son. He didn't want the family farm and hadn't been back for three years. Oh sure, he called him at Christmas, Thanksgiving, and his birthdays. *But come to think of it, that stubborn old bastard never even called once! It takes two to tango God damn it! He could have called me, once in a while!* The internal voice raged on.

The absolution he sought in various rationalizations eluded him; he was judging himself a lousy son. It didn't matter if George Moss senior had been a lousy father – *he* had been a lousy son. Now his father was gone, along with any hope of redemption. Without hope, George felt like he was slowly becoming nothing more than a life support system for the beast of grief.

When his mother died George was only nine. It was bad but it sure didn't hurt like this new inward excursion. Maybe it was because he didn't have enough time to burn as many bridges with his mother as he had with his father. So much had been left unresolved, in the valleys that separated them. Maybe it was the new status of being an orphan. His mind sought answers to an infinite stream of questions.

He glanced at Joan asleep on his shoulder. Her shiny hair had lost some of its lustre, or maybe his eyes were refusing to see it. She didn't know what to do for him, so she just held onto his arm. Even Joan didn't appear to matter to him at that moment. His father's death reduced the entire world, everyone and everything in it, to complete insignificance.

Somehow his mind gave up and allowed a glimpse of sleep, afloat in the sound of distant steel wheels clattering over tracks. Off in some other reality he smelled coffee, and thought of Joan in that T-shirt. His eyes opened and there she was, with two cups of coffee. *Oh Jesus, I'm on this train. I'm going home to bury my father. Oh Jesus, reality. To hell with reality, I want to dream!* The internal turmoil raged on.

Joan's face came into focus. "Thought you could use a coffee."

George grunted as he straightened up. "How long have I been out?"

Joan handed him the one with the R scrawled on the lid in magic marker and sat down. "About two hours."

"Two hours?" A fatigued stone had made it feel like two seconds.

"I was so glad to see your eyebrows unfurl when you closed your eyes. How are you feeling, honey?"

George shook his head unable to provide an answer, and then resumed his post, staring out the window at the irrelevant blur while Joan resumed her position at his side, helplessly holding his arm.

When the train pulled into Lincoln station, it was early morning. Joan didn't have a license, George was in no shape to drive and flying wasn't a good option, so they found themselves without transportation on arriving at the old Lincoln train station on the outskirts of town.

Lincoln, New York, was a previous life. George was born there and lived there until escaping to Canada to avoid the draft and Vietnam.

When President Gerald Ford granted conditional amnesty to draft dodgers who had fled to Canada, George had returned for his first visit, overwhelmed by the row of white crosses in the graveyard with names he knew, lives lost to a foreign policy that more closely resembled missionary zeal than politics to George. *Guilt? You bet. Anger? Oh yeah.*

From Canada, George had become a member of an audience staring south across the border in amazement at the world's largest stage. These Canadians around him were an odd bunch, hard to define in their moderation. They were like Australians without the sense of adventure, Americans without the ammo and nationalism or Brits without their aristocracy and bad dental plans. He did sometimes feel Canadian; but often not. And he was often embarrassed to say he was an American, dismayed at the myopia of an America that was going to presumptuously save the world from its own evolution by righteously exporting its values while the marine choir hummed. It was going to spread freedom by depriving other countries of the freedom to find their own way.

America couldn't see it was really at war with itself and that the American dream was becoming a nightmare.

Rows of white crosses were the deficit of the empire and the true currency of fear mongers professing to have the answers and an inner knowledge of God's wishes. God's wishes it seemed always managed to be connected to power or huge profits – perhaps mistakenly spelled "prophets" on ancient goatskins. As a history professor, George Moss could only shake his head and mutter: "Some things never change."

Lincoln, New York, was one of those things. It had only been three years but it could well have been fifty. Lincoln was an average farm town whose population never fluctuated much. Pretty much everything in Lincoln was named after Abe after the assassination. Even underwear from the old cotton mill bore his name, as though the ultimate way to honour the deceased President was entrusting the man's memory with one's privates...

George and Joan grabbed belongings, got off the train, and walked down the cracked concrete platform to the pay phone stuck on the dark brown wooden clapboard wall. They stood, staring like two lonely refugees, at the train that continued on to happier destinations. Scanning the scene, without a soul in sight, everything was as George remembered it: A rinky-dink little whistle-stop classic H.O. gauge train station built in the 'twenties. In the distance, watching over the town sat the old water tower, the only thing for miles more than two storeys in height. The name Lincoln, once a vibrant red scrawl on the tower, was now quite faded, leaving the top part of the second L almost invisible. At first glance it looked like Lincoln.

Pushing a quarter in the pay phone slot, George called the only game in town – Al's Limousine. The phone rang a good ten times before someone finally realized whoever it was, just wasn't going to go away. It was a gruff female voice that answered struggling through what sounded like vocal tissues scarred by countless cartons of cigarettes and bottles of Jack Daniel's: "Yeah?"

"Yes, I'm looking for a ride into town. Is Al there, please?"

"Who the hell is this? Do you have any idea what time it is?"

"It's George Moss, I'm at the train station, and it is 6:28:13-ish." The hundredths were moving too quickly for his tired eyes to even approximate – anyway, he figured, people in Lincoln probably didn't "do" hundredths.

There was a bit of a muffled conversation, some hushed whispers, the rustle of bed covers and then... Al. "George, is that you?"

"Yes it's me Al. Can you come to the station?"

Al's voice cleared and took on a totally different, reverential tone.

"Oh George, I am sorry about your father. If there's, you know, anything I uh, can do..."

"How 'bout a ride, Al?"

Al's voice changed again and was now back to business. "I'll be right over." There was more rustling as the receiver got handed back to the mystery woman who George heard say in a fairly annoyed tone, "Doesn't that fuckin' jerk own a fuckin car yet? It's the fuckin' middle of the fuckin' night for fuck' ss ... " The phone crashed back on to the cradle and the dial tone clicked in. George assumed her last word was "sakes." It seemed rural New York State had replaced "land sakes" with "fuck sakes" in honour of the new millennium. However the number of "F" words one could cram into a sentence remained about what he remembered for a certain element of Lincoln folk, maybe even lower than the benchmark of his high school days.

Joan was sitting on the luggage, half asleep. They waited in silence with the exception of a few rather happy sounding birds that obviously hadn't heard the news.

Five minutes later a very "previously owned," light-green Chevy wagon crowned with a magnetic roof-sign that read: "Al's Limousine," skidded to a halt in the gravel parking lot. Al got out looking much the same as ever. Al was one of those guys who never gained weight. George assumed coffee and cigarettes must have been keeping his metabolism working at an elevated level. When they were teenagers the already chain-smoking and coffee-addicted Al never got sick. George and his best friend Bill McDonough had concluded that the main reason for Al's imperviousness to disease was that no bacteria or virus could survive in a tar-based host.

Al was wearing filthy, ripped-at–the-knee old blue jeans, a faded and stained blue jean shirt, a filthy and threadbare blue jean jacket and le piece de resistance; he even had what looked like filthy mock blue-jean shoes, one of which had a sole that flapped as he walked. George hadn't seen shoes like that since the 'Seventies. Al sucked back on the last inch of a freshly hand-rolled cigarette and headed toward them.

Al had always rolled his own smokes. Over the years, he must have saved a fortune because nobody ever bummed smokes – they were usually wet with saliva and took way too long to light. Al had dropped out of high school the year he got his license, bought a wreck, and started Al's Limousine service, which is pretty much where Al's "bio" levelled off. His friends used to razz him, sometimes quite mercilessly, about what he tried to pass off as a "limousine." They were usually cars that would have been scrap metal if Al hadn't rescued them and slapped his sign on the roof. To Al, they were limousines, things of beauty.

"Hi Al," George said pointedly, interrupting Al who was busily giving Joan the once-over. Al's eyes snapped on to George's face with a somewhat guilty look, having been caught in the unconscious act of sniffing Joan with the animal section of his brain.

"Hullo George," he shrugged, sweeping his grey-streaked dirty blond hair under a Home Depot baseball cap. This was followed by silence as he stood there slowly nodding his head as if affirming George's identity. Joan stood up and offered her hand.

"I'm Joan." Al shook her hand strongly causing her to rub some blood back into her fingers in the aftermath, then he resumed nodding his head uncomfortably, saying nothing.

George knew Al well enough to realize he could stand there for hours if not given the assistance of some kind of direction. "Al, could I trouble you for a hand with the luggage?" Al jolted to life, scooping up the luggage in one swoop and hobbling toward the wagon.

"Al, don't hurt yourself. Let me carry some of that."

"This is nothin' George, all part of the service!" They could hear him puffing with exertion and by the time he reached the car his face was beet red with beads of sweat accumulating on his forehead. He was clearly winded and actually looked a little sick as he chucked everything in the open back window of the old wreck. Years of smoking hand-rolled non-filters, or "rollies," as he called them, had taken their toll.

The winded limo driver and his passengers all piled onto the front seat. Ashes spilled on to the floor from an ashtray that counted on decomposition, fire or spillage to make room for incoming.

Al cast a sideways glance: "Are you goin' home or are you goin' to view the, I mean, your dad's, uh, well... oh shit, you know."

Al never was much with words. In fact, a consummate professional, he usually sat in silence waiting for a destination before starting his car. This of course saved fuel. It was all part of a fiscally responsible protocol he had finely tuned over the years. George spoke the words he had feared for many hours with dread and resignation.

"Take us to Brown's Funeral Home, Al, and then, if you wouldn't mind waiting, we'll be going to the Hotel. I don't think I can face the farm today."

Al started "her" up, and in three or four manoeuvres the big boat was facing the right way. Beer bottles clanked under the cracked vinyl of the front seat as Al peeled a little gravel for his passengers to make them aware there was quite the "mill" under that hood.

The trip into town felt surreal to George. The memories were too strong for the moment and all too familiar except for one thing: the person who would no longer walk those small town streets.

Al drove with one hand, and rolled a smoke with the other. Joan, despite her fatigue, was fascinated with such a feat of dexterity and watched him with an interested smirk. They passed Annie's Variety and turned left at the white Shell station on to the main drag. The old store facades were like a set from a 'Thirties film... Walker's Hardware,

Sandfield's Country Cut and Curl Hair Salon, The Lincoln Town Hall, Patterson's Real Estate, the old Lincoln Post Office. With the smell of morning dampness, cigarette smoke and the vintage vinyl of Al's Chevy, George was transported back to another time. He was in his teens on his way to high school... until the sign for Brown's Funeral home snapped him back to his new reality like a stiff smelling salt.

As they pulled into the parking lot, George began to shake a little. The ache in his chest increased exponentially with the proximity to his father's body... his "father's body." What an awful sound that phrase had. It wasn't his father any more; it was, as they say, *the* body, the corpse, the stiff, the cadaver, an organic casing that once housed a soul.

Al shut his limo off and got out. George's legs were not ready to move, both knees felt squeamish like they wouldn't hold him. He sat looking at the wall through Al's cracked windshield while Joan stared patiently at his pathetic face. He was about to make his move when the door swung open and there was Al, rollie in mouth, looking serious and sympathetic.

George sighed. "Thanks Al."

Al gave him a sweet nod. "Okay buddy," he offered as though there were fraternal bonds that couldn't be denied in such times.

George accepted the sentiment and got out, standing motionless and staring at the buildings, until Joan grabbed his hand. As they approached the side door, Mr. Brown's face scowled through the window.

Mr. Brown was expecting them. His breathy voice had sounded strangely comforting over the phone, even though the words and tone were his well-practiced bread and butter. Never had there been anyone more physically suited to the role of undertaker. George's father used to say Mr. Brown was born looking like an undertaker. Suits that were a couple of sizes too small accentuated a lanky and slouched posture, forged from years of leaning over bodies and caskets. He was one of those guys who liked his clothes snug and high off of the shoe in case of flooding. Maybe baggy suits represented wasted material to his Depression-era mentality.

As a professional in death services Mr. Brown was amazing. He could hold up one side of a casket while supporting a fainting widow with his other arm with no sign of discomfort. This was not so much due to his strength as it was to the tremendous stability offered by his huge feet. When the door opened there they were... the huge feet. It was a good thing his arms were long or he'd never have been able to get close enough to the door to open it. As the group entered the funeral home, a hand attached to a Muppet-stick arm reached out to greet George.

George looked into the Basset-hound face.

"Hello, Mr. Brown."

"Oh George, what a terrible shock to us all." He looked at Joan with a puzzled but polite expression.

"I'm Joan Parks, Mr. Brown." Joan stated simply. Mr. Brown offered one of his practiced, sincere smiles.

"It is so nice to meet you Ms Parks." He immediately swung his gaze back to George with an expression that had grown even more serious, which was quite an accomplishment.

"George, there is something I must tell you before we move into the viewing suite. Your father has been dead for more than twenty-four hours now, and there may be some unsettling physical deterioration. He may not look the way you remember him."

"I understand." George said stoically. He prepared himself for the worst. His chest felt like it was going to explode. They moved down the floral-patterned carpet to the doorway with the adjustable marquee overhead. There on the black grooved board, newly arranged white letters spelled his father's name, Mr. George Moss. It was the same room his mother had been in. It was the same room where his entire Grade 12 class had filed tearfully by Doug Braxton's appropriately closed coffin, after he was thrown off his motorcycle, head first on to pavement – sans helmet. Of *course* it was the same room: It was the *only* room – or as they say in the trade, *viewing suite*. Joan held his arm tighter. He took a deep breath, and crossed the threshold.

The room was a pukey-green color, punctuated by cheap landscape art in even cheaper-looking frames. The walls went away as George's eyes were drawn toward the polished wooden casket floating in the pukey-green void like a warning beacon. There lay, slightly uplifted in a funereal pose, the pale grim face of his father. George was pulled closer by duty, morbid curiosity and an unfamiliar dark force of gravity. The pain in his chest began to slowly convert into silent convulsions.

Contrary to Mr. Brown's warning, George's father looked much like he always did. He was such a pale man in life, that death wasn't much of a cosmetic stretch. In fact, George Moss Sr. looked like he could he could sit up at any moment and say: "Boo!" – as though this was all some elaborate joke to get the wayward son home for a visit.

George's stoic front crumbled. Silent convulsions now increased in intensity until the ripples broke through the surface where they manifested into heaving sobs. He reached out to touch cold skin and kissed the wizened forehead that he could hardly see for the tears. Joan, somewhere in the distance, cried for him while he cried for himself, his father, mother, the end of a generation, and what at that moment felt like the end of the world. The crying didn't make the chest pain go away. That, he thought was to be his life long companion.

George needed to hold his father's hands. Years of labour and arthritic knuckles couldn't hide the gentleness those hands still exuded. They always had a spiritual quality to them – the were his heart. To shake his hand, was to feel the transmission of a sub-dermal data stream. It was warm, gentle, loving information. The physical appearance of his hands offered a strange blueprint for the gentleness within. Now they held only a memory of warmth – transmitters with no power. The pain of never-to-be-resolved differences was unbearable. George wanted to die, reluctantly gasping for air between sobs.

Al, ever dutiful, was still in the parking lot waiting to take them to the hotel when they finally came out. The radio played a sad country tune while he sucked on a rollie and stirred the ashes in an attempt to put out a fire in the ashtray.

There was some traffic in the street. A yellow Bluebird school bus went by, leaving a ghostly face of diesel exhaust that hung in the air as if to momentarily view as much of the sad scene as it could before its molecules were spread too thin to look into the more compressed human dimension. A police cruiser swerved away from the front of the Deluxe Restaurant and headed at a slow ceremonious pace toward the intersection of the road that led to the train station and highway. It was the beginning of just another normal day in Lincoln... for some.

Through the night, George memorized every detail on the walls of the room in the Lincoln Hotel. They had walked back to Brown's where George spent most of the day just staring at his dad while Joan stared at George. They returned to the hotel sometime in the afternoon and attempted to sleep. George laid there, eyes fixed on the ceiling, in too much agony to give in to anything resembling slumber. They slipped out again in the evening to see the body for the last time – George Sr. still looked the same. There still was no visible deterioration except for a blue-red discoloration in the ear lobes. At dusk, they walked in silence to the Deluxe Restaurant for a club sandwich. Fortunately, the waitress was new and didn't know George, so the only words they had to deal with were: "Are you ready to order? Do you want fries with that?" And, the ever sincere: "Bye now. You take care."

Back in the hotel room Joan stayed awake as long as she could while George further inspected the walls and ceiling from a cranberry velour wingback chair. The hotel hadn't had a makeover since the tacky '70s and the velour wasn't the worst of it. George hadn't been in such a room without wearing bellbottoms and clogs – sailing gear for the deep seas of shag rugs.

At first light, Joan stirred, got out of bed and headed to the washroom. George's eyes followed her pretty feet, nicely shaped calves, thighs, and his mind continued on up under her T-shirt where he knew she wore nothing. There he was, dumb struck with grief and still thinking about sex. He scolded himself for bringing dishonour to some unwritten rules of mourning, but no matter how hard he tried he couldn't chase the notion away.

When Joan returned from the washroom she saw a hint of something familiar behind the mask of pain. When she leaned over to give him a kiss she saw he had a bigger problem. She pulled back and caught his eyes fixed on the hanging neck of her large T-shirt that offered a rewarding and somewhat pendulant view.

With a smile of half affection, half sympathy, Joan pulled her shirt off and straddled him on the chair guiding his head gently to her breasts and other parts to the warm shelter of her femininity. It was a strange passion, as though nature was trying to offer a reminder of how wonderful life could be. The shadow of death was powerful, but so too was the power of life. Somehow George and Joan ended up in the bed, and drifted off. Her soft fragrant hair on his chest soothed his soul in the closest thing to rest he had experienced since "it" happened.

The phone rang from far away. Groping in a frustrated stupor his hand finally landed on the receiver. It was Mr. Brown.

"Are we running a little late, George? I'm sure the church is full by now. The service was for ten if you recall." The pain flooded back into George's chest through the open hatch of consciousness. George looked at his watch; it was 10:01:13... ish. The velour curtains had effectively suppressed sharp strains of daylight. It was his father's wish to be buried next to his mother the morning after his death. In his usual no-nonsense style Dad had made most of his own funeral arrangements with Mr. Brown right down to a half-up-front payment. They were already a day late. Mr. Brown, ever aware that funerals were for the living, and not the dead, had allowed the extension of time.

George snapped to attention. "We'll be right there, Mr. Brown!" He turned to Joan who was already mobile and scrambling into a dress.

"Shit," he hissed. The church would be full of friends and neighbours. His being late and grubby would just confirm what some of them might expect from a draft-dodging, oddball, history professor.

Joan looked great without doing a thing; one of the perks of youth. With white stubble on his face, George resembled a rummy and would need more time to resurrect a presentable rendition of himself.

Fifteen minutes later, they appeared, luggage and all, like a couple of tourists, late for the grim tour o' death. The hearse was parked in front of the funeral limousine. A young driver in a black suit saw to the door of the limo while Mr. Brown scurried back to the hearse.

The drive out to the old Baptist church on Four Side Road was an introspective one. Grief, it appeared, was a slow, painful, solo flight. Yes, Joan *was* there, but not where George was. That was, after all, *his* father, a piece of *his* life in the box in front of them. Mr. Moss had once said that following his father's box was a pain worse than he had ever known or imagined. He was right. The emotional elevator continued to plummet while the search for some resignation to life with his absence in perpetuity drove George deeper and deeper inside. Infinity, he felt for the first time, lay as much within as without.

His father had always said death forced spiritual evidence on humanity. The evidence resided in the ability to love in absence after the luxury of loving in presence. Mourning was the bridge between those realms. Love's existence in absence was indeed a spiritual thought, but at that moment, all such lofty thoughts offered little comfort. George saw no bridge, only the gorge. He sensed his father's voice prodding him to look for evidence and not to dismiss what transcended three-dimensional criteria. He was conscious of loving his father at that moment more than ever, and, for some reason, sensed his father's love for him was still alive. His mind skipped over ripples of thought like a flat stone.

"What is this madness? Okay, okay, thinking I'm mad, was a judgment based on what? Based on the crude scientific stance that a dead person no longer does anything. So no normal person should admit to thoughts otherwise. Maybe the sensation of dad's voice was a reflection of myself. And yet, I sense that I am still being loved by this person who supposedly no longer exists. An empiricist would probably offer hyperactive memory cells as an explanation but that would merely be a conclusion based on what? A fairly shallow perception of a rather deep data stream? Is it merely the limits of a primitive scientific method that rule out or marginalize what I feel? "

Then he heard his father's voice speak quite loudly. *"Don't judge an infinite universe by the inch you know!"*

"I'm sorry!" The words were out before he knew it. Joan looked at him, puzzled.

"What for?" she asked.

George just shook his head and mumbled something about talking to his father. He probably should have made a more Earth-bound statement about how sorry he was that she had to go through all of this because her expression only acquired more concern. He just didn't have the energy to lie or elaborate. But he had heard his father's voice as he had heard his mother's after she died.

News spread fast in Lincoln. Cars and trucks were lined up along the road, well before the hill crested. Just beyond it stood First Baptist Church, a humble edifice of crumbling brick and peeling paint. George glanced reluctantly at the old cemetery and the freshly dug grave as the

24

funeral cortège crackled over the sparse gravel to the front of the church.

It was all like a set from some low-budget horror movie. There were a few people smoking outside. The heavy branches of the giant spruce trees swayed in slow motion. The memory of snow lay on the matted grass in the adjacent field. Sanding icy roads in the winter left a dirty film that nature hadn't rinsed off with late spring rains.

There was an all-knowing sound to the breeze that purred through the tops of the spruces. That sound was forever entwined in George's soul when, as a child, his mother had called it "the whisper of God." He loved the status that her metaphor bestowed on those towering, wizened old trees. It seemed insulting that the ones at the back of the building sheltered the outdoor johns, well into the '60s. In those years, the whisper of God was destined to be drowned out by a cacophony of human flatulence, at least once a week.

The youthful limo driver, who looked vaguely familiar to George, opened the door. Mr. Brown had already hopped out of the hearse and sprung into action recruiting bodies to act as pallbearers, making the wayward son painfully aware that he hadn't attended to any details. Mr. Brown was on autopilot and George felt useless, thinking of nothing other than his own grief.

All of a sudden a wave of dizziness swept over him – all sound around George fell off into a distance. It was much the same sensation as on the steps outside his office, except this time extremely directional. He knew the feeling well but had not felt it with such intensity in a long time. George grabbed the roof of the funeral car to steady himself as his eyes were pulled in the direction of the back of the hearse. It appeared as though it had been in an accident. The bumper was bashed in and a piece of the left tail-light was laying in pieces on the ground. Joan's voice called to him from somewhere… miles away…

"George… are you alright? George?" He moved back up the tunnel toward her. The dizziness disappeared as his eyes slowly refocused on the back end of the hearse, which… was not damaged. It had been years since he had experienced a visual manifestation to accompany one of those dizzy spells. Mr. Brown eyed him with concern.

"I think you had better move your hearse, Mr. Brown." George said with a flat, matter-of-fact tone.

Brown looked at him, torn between duty and what he knew to be a suggestion from the son of George Moss. He had learned to take such suggestions seriously. However, he had a funeral to tend to and it was running late. He acknowledged the warning, too conflicted to act on it.

George followed the casket down the aisle through a sea of faces from his childhood. Some stared with overdone sympathy, others simple curiosity. Mr. Walker, who owned the hardware store… Where was his wife, Millie? Doc Harris and his prim 'better-half' were looking as spry and well dressed as ever. Patricia Sandfield wasn't even looking at George; she was too busy eying George's Canadian girlfriend, as potential new grist for the gossip mill. George's father's old war buddies stood with medals on blue jackets, grey pants and berets. Ned Patterson had become his father with the addition of a few extra pounds and the phoniest look of sympathy in the crowd. Al, God bless Al, nodding his head continually, and next to Al, the woman who was very probably the voice on the phone. She looked pretty rough yet familiar, and then George realized who she was – Christie Adams: When they were teenagers, the boys unanimously agreed Christie had the best body in town. The body seemed relatively intact. The ubiquitous push-up bra was pushing up a little too much for a funeral. Despite her efforts, George was more drawn to her face, which told a silent, painful tale.

She was supposedly carrying Doug Braxton's child when he took his swan dive off his motorcycle on to the pavement. She had disappeared for a while and the rumour was she had a child that was adopted before she had really made up her mind. This apparently led to some time at the funny farm before she came back to Lincoln. Life had obviously not been kind to her but at least she had found Al. He was a little thick, but he possessed a good heart, and appeared to dote on her. As George passed by, he wondered if Christie smoked Al's rollies. If she did, it was love for sure.

Mrs. Harrison was playing the piano. She used to lead the cub pack when George was a kid, and was now close to ninety. She played okay but that old Heintzman piano was so out of tune, Horowitz would have sounded awful. They never kept the church heated during the week and so over the years the wood holding the tuning pegs had grown pulpy and loose from condensation. A good tuning job only lasted a few hours before the strings would slip. The remaining congregation of about twenty had chipped in for a new furnace, a new piano being too much of a challenge for their dwindling numbers. The smell of the oak pews and oxidized paint when combined with the sound of that old piano provided an odd comfort, sensory connections to more secure days when George's family attended services there.

The box finally reached the front of the altar where Mr. Brown had cordoned off the first pew, herding his charges like a masterful sheep dog into the pen. The minister was young and a little green. He was a student minister covering for the Reverend Bertrand Jackson, who had a very fast-moving version of Alzheimer's disease. The Reverend had been moved into a full-care facility shortly after he was found delivering an impassioned sermon at the Post Office wearing only his wife's housecoat and an army helmet. As the story goes, Sheriff Williams didn't make a move until after the Benediction when the Reverend flipped back the housecoat exposing himself while passionately asking everyone to join him in a pee for the Lord. George had heard all about it in a Christmas phone call to his father, who spoke with an obvious fear of the disease and its hideous erosion of dignity. He didn't have to worry about that anymore.

My father, oh Jesus, my father. He screamed inside: *Do you have any idea how much I love you?* There was an immediate reassuring affirmative that could have just been his mind except it clearly felt as though it was from somewhere external and internal at the same time.

He was unnerved about the abrupt nature and clarity of the feeling. This was not a slow comprehensive acquisition of consciousness working through all the problems between them, just an overwhelming flood reducing anything that stood between them to its own level of insignificance. This new consciousness held within it precious time lost to insignificant differences... a lesson learned too late. He loved his father even though the small stuff of human interface made him a pain in the ass...

The young minister stoically attempted to impart some meaning to the farewell, a difficult task when you don't know the deceased. Every other sentence was punctuated with, "So I'm told," or "If I had known Mr. Moss, I'm sure I would have... blah, blah." There was some poor metaphorical poop about plucking a flower in full bloom for God's beautiful garden that everyone could have done without, followed by a closing prayer. As Mr. Brown got up to gather his impromptu pallbearers, George forced himself to his feet and grabbed the old man's elbow.

"Mr. Brown, I think my father's friends should carry him out." The always-deferential Mr. Brown nodded.

"I'll ask them immediately," he said in a smooth but hushed tone.

"No, I think the request should come from me."

The prayer had ended and everyone now looked on as if to say, "What the hell is going on with the fruitcake?" The church came alive with whispers as George walked to his dad's old war pals, Jack Klager, Rudy Barnes, Wilf Roland, Al Maitland, and John Freeman. Even they had a look that read, "What the hell is this poor, bereaved nut-bar up to?" It was a look with which George was all too familiar.

"Gentlemen, I wonder if you would do me and my father the honour of helping me carry him to his grave?"

On the last word his voice cracked and his eyes filled uncontrollably. Jack Klager took one look at George, puffed out his chest, took a deep breath and said sternly, "Ten-shun!" The other old warriors clicked their heels to attention and moved to the coffin with the dignity and ceremony of a well-rehearsed manoeuvre. George whispered under his breath, "Your lousy son has at least done one thing right."

They lifted on Mr. Brown's command to the strains of *Abide with Me*, played tenderly by Mrs. Harrison, and proceeded down the aisle. Tears poured from George's eyes as he passed a familiar smear that was Joan's empathic face. She fell apart, helpless, as now even his arm was unavailable to hang on to.

That old hymn cracked George the rest of the way open. It caught him totally unprepared – yet more of his Dad's evidence of "something bigger than us all." That melody, that day, held the exquisite pain of a million passages and the sweet sadness of childhood memories, all oblivious to an out of tune piano.

Mr. Brown, of course, ran point and tried with great difficulty to get the amateurs to place the coffin properly on the canvas straps running out of the stainless steel funereal hardware surrounded by phoney grass. It was only after the third attempt George realized that some of his father's war buddies were pissed drunk. On closer inspection... *all* of them were! Jack looked up at George with a sheepish expression of apology, "We were drinking to you father's memory most of the night and had a couple of bracers this morning."

There was a terrible splintering crack as Rudy Barnes lost his balance, causing his side of the coffin to slam into the Cartwright's huge pink granite memorial. These rank amateurs had nearly dropped, and may have actually broken, one of Mr. Brown's boxes. Mr. Brown's cool façade briefly crumbled, revealing what appeared to be a different expression, before returning to the sad stone bust that usually sat, forever unchanged, on his shoulders. No one had ever seen him look worried. George sensed his father would have loved it – a sombre moment of ceremony, broken by the random uncertainty of life. Such surprises, he had often said, made life worth living, or at least interesting.

By the third attempt everything was lined up to Mr. Brown's satisfaction and relief. He tried in vain to cover up the scrunched bottom corner of the coffin with some phoney grass, but gave up with a sigh of frustration as mourners approached.

Joan found George's arm again as everyone assembled around the grave. The minister began the internment ceremony, ending with the old favourite, "Ashes to ashes, dust to dust." followed by the mandatory Lord's Prayer.

But the final solemn drone of "lead us not into temptation" was punctured by the sound of skidding tires on gravel, metal on metal and breaking glass. The prayer stopped abruptly as heads turned. George realized what it was; He had seen it before entering the church.

There it was, Billy McDonough's Cadillac parked a little too close to the hearse... okay, it was parked *in* the hearse somewhat, broken tail light lying on the ground. Billy, all 6-foot-3 inches of him, slicked back red hair, over-fed and stuffed into his best suit, got out to survey the damage.

George had warned Mr. Brown to move that damn hearse. Joan looked puzzled for a moment then turned to him for an answer – she was on to him. Mr. Brown glared in George's direction with an angry expression. He sought to blame but realized he had not heeded a warning from the son of George Moss and therefore the blame was his alone.

Mr. Brown abruptly spun around and took off with the fast paced walk of an Olympic speed-walker. Running of course would have been undignified; his speed-walk however couldn't have been more comical. Many of the mourners cracked a smile and covered their faces; hoping amusement might be mistaken for grimaces of grief. Mr. Brown's hushed voice cracked into a spot-on imitation of Don Knotts from the old Andy Griffith show.

"Just what the heck is the matter with you young man? Have you no respect for the dead?" George saw Mr. McDonough, Billy's Dad, sitting embarrassed in the passenger seat shaking his head. Billy quickly assessed the damage as not too big an expense and curtly responded to Mr. Brown.

"I got plenty of respect for the dead, which is why we're going to take this little altercation up later! You know where we live!" Billy looked George's way with a pained smile, then strode to him with real affection in his eyes. Over his shoulder, George watched Billy's father open the door and hobble over to apologize to Mr. Brown for his son.

Billy was George's best friend and neighbour for years. They grew up together, lived apart, but never grew apart. They knew each other too well to attempt any type of pretence. It was an unwritten pact neither one had consciously created, but nonetheless, they both knew of its existence and that there could be no negotiation around it. Billy was the closest thing George had to a brother. Even though they didn't share the same genetic material, they were brothers. George's father had often said, "Relatedness without relationship was no cause for celebration."

The wish in Western culture for some kind of ideal TV family like the Andersons of *Father Knows Best* or the Cleavers from *Leave It To Beaver*, created tremendous expectation with certain disappointment not too far behind. Maybe it all began with those idealistic Norman Rockwell pictures. Some people are clearly born into families with whom they have nothing in common, no meeting of mind or soul. For this they feel a lifetime of guilt as they struggle unsuccessfully to apply the Norman Rockwell brush to their family portraits or to squeeze into a picture that just doesn't fit.

Billy, stinking of vintage Vitalis hair cream and breath mints threw his arms around George and wept. He loved Mr. Moss and had been helpful to him over the years. In some ways, he'd been a better son to George's father than George. But he had also been a better son to George's father than he was to his own. That, of course, was due to that wonder of wonders many know but will never understand – family dynamics. Loving intensely with no ability to communicate without pushing all the wrong buttons is real family life for millions of people.

"I'm so sorry, George," Billy sobbed. George was suddenly aware of how cold he felt. There was no emotion left in him. He had seen this at other funerals where widows or children accepted the tears of friends but had none of their own. There was a passing thought of one-upmanship that said "You think you're sad, well I'm in hell, what do you think about that?" But George's, schooled mind reasoned that the brain must have been be secreting some type of chemical depressant. The organism sought survival by attempting to sedate a brain that felt no respect for its own life at that moment.

Billy's sadness was real and deep. He kept his arm around George and nodded his head at Joan. "You must be Joan."

Joan, still preoccupied with George's prediction of the hearse incident graciously found a smile and responded. "You must be Billy."

Billy reached for her and a three-way embrace resulted. The minister cleared his throat and geared up to restore order.

"Ladies and gentlemen, to conclude this interment perhaps we should start the Lord's Prayer over again as its words are a complete thought and we owe this much to Mr. Moss."

"Our Father, Who art in heaven..." Everyone began the autonomic drone again. George stared at the box, picturing his father inside. Joan supportively held his arm while Billy wept. The ceremony drew to a close. These would be the last words spoken in the proximity of George's father's ears. George felt finality without the closure that the ceremony was supposed to bring.

"Amen." That was it. The end. No closure, just loose ends and emotional threads reaching out into infinity. The young minister approached with a pious but sincere look and reached for George's hand, which he held in both of his while offering words of sympathy. Old Mr. Walker was next up to bat.

"Millie sends her love, George. She couldn't attend due to her health." He paused and shook his head. "We're sure gonna miss him, we owe him so much."

The line worked its way by in a recessional spotted with some folks George had grown up with but never really liked. Ned Patterson of Patterson Real Estate was a sweaty as ever. Joan's smile morphed to disbelief when he passed his business card to George. "We make selling your home look easy!" was written in bold letters underneath his name.

His face was puffed up from a genetic predisposition to obesity, one buffet too many and mid-life metabolism. He combed his hair up from the back and sprayed it in place to cover his cue-ball head. His father had done the same, which was a source of amusement for many in Lincoln. Ned for some daft reason must have believed his "do" wasn't as obvious as his father's.

Patricia Sandfield from Country Cut and Curl, the local beauty salon, approached, and as anticipated, was more interested in Joan. Her average frame of sixty-odd years was always covered in pastel shades of violet or rose with a matching tint in her hair and lipstick. She had one of those faces that just pissed people off, even when she was trying to be nice. Her husband knew only two words: "yes dear." Townsfolk had two words for him: "poor bastard." As a chronic gossip she unabashedly got right to work.

"So sorry about your father, George. We can never repay him for everything he's done for us – and this is the new Mrs. Moss I presume?"

"No, Patricia, this is Joan, and she is my friend and lover. We currently live in sin." Joan smiled graciously and put her hand out.

"Nice to meet you Mrs. Sandfield, George has told me so much about you." Patricia's expression froze as she realized her reputation preceded her. She moved on, making her way past drunken pallbearers.

Rudy Barnes on point, apologized for nearly dropping the box, and the others looked repentant in an "all-for-one" kind of way. Jack Klager was the last, and was so grateful to have had a role in seeing his buddy to his final resting-place. Jack's tears were tears of real affection. George's stoicism seemed to have a few cracks but something quickly filled them in. Al, who had already lit a rollie, just nodded and didn't say a thing. Christie Adams held his hand tightly and followed. Her eyes were filled with tears as she muttered something, with breath that could've preserved fruit, about "how fuckin' awful you must fuckin' feel 'cause I fuckin' know, I've fuckin' been there, man… fuck." George appreciated the sentiment and fought off a smile.

Mrs. Harrison just held his hand and nodded knowledgeably, saying nothing. At ninety, hers was a deep knowing, from the experience of surviving the deaths, one by one, of an entire world that no longer was. Her look seemed to say it doesn't get easier; it just goes deeper and becomes a constant companion like an emotional version of arthritis.

It was a parade of familiar faces that had been either friend or acquaintance in the lives of George's parents. Some were genuinely moved by his death or had been helped by Mr. Moss in some way, a frequent sentiment that caught Joan's attention. George knew an explanation would be needed, all too soon.

Finally, it was just Joan, Billy and George, waiting for Billy's dad, while he made his way to the grave with the rhythm of an old steam-powered farm machine. It was a slow laborious step, synchronous with the wheezing of his emphysema. His skin hung off of him like a melted clock in a Dali-esque rendering of a man last seen as a relatively healthy farmer only three years before.

"George, he was a good man," he huffed on arrival. George held Mr. McDonough a little too long. It was an obvious parting hug never given, and long enough to make the old man's machismo uncomfortable. Mr. McDonough turned to Joan and tried to lighten things up a little, even though his eyes were moist and his voice unstable.

"Well now they grow 'em good up north of the border don't they?" The old man still loved a good flirt. Billy saw George staring into inner space, and leaned in. "You want a lift home, George?"

"All our stuff is in that funeral car, and I think I'd rather just sit in the back of that damn thing and face the farm by myself Billy."

"Hell, you might as well get your money's worth with what Mr. Brown charges." Billy took no offence and after saying good-byes, he was cornered by Mr. Brown for insurance particulars regarding the damages to the hearse.

Mr. McDonough started on the long step-by-step journey back to the car. Through the limousine window, George watched a black cloud of diesel exhaust burst upward, spitting the excrement of combustion into a pristine blue sky. Moments later, a greasy old red tractor with a backhoe emerged like a spider from its hidden lair behind the church.

3

The Long Road Home

M r. Brown's young assistant drove slowly in silence along the dirt road to the farm. At George's request, he stopped at the end of the long driveway. George and Joan got out before the kid had a chance to open their doors. There was something familiar about him as he retrieved bags from the trunk. He placed the bags on the dirt, shrugged his shoulders at the sight of the long driveway and got back in the car.

George and Joan stood with their luggage staring at the empty Moss farm. Behind them, the crunching of the departing funeral car on the gravel road faded into a sombre silence that fell with the last of the dust.

The old combine sat to one side of the driveway, bleeding rust from the mortal wounds of obsolescence.

Peering at the old farmhouse, George saw images of his parents waving good-bye from the porch as their child climbed the steps of the school bus. He saw his father standing there alone after his mother died and again, later, when George left for Canada in a beat up Chevy Corvair; mental pictures that saddened him in the taking. Imprints; that were burned into optical memory, tore at his heart.

Imagining was one thing, but once again, real knowledge came with physical manifestations.

George picked up the bags and started up the driveway. Joan grabbed her valise and purse with one hand and hung on to his arm with the other. He was aware she was watching him but couldn't respond, distracted by memories that stabbed at him again and again.

All fell respectfully quiet while the pathetic little processional passed. The sound bites in George's head were cacophonous: His mom calling after him: "You forgot your lunch!" His dad wondering where the hell he thought he was going before the chores were done; his grandfather laughing at an attempted moustache; Lady, the old, blind retriever, barking halfway up the driveway until she caught a familiar scent. And, his father's lecture when he and Billy were caught smoking pot in the barn. He called them idiots for smoking in such a firetrap, then damned if he didn't try a little of it before shredding the rest under his worn-out work boot.

The dilapidated windmill began to move as if driven by the shadows of the past that played all around. The conspicuous emptiness of the place weighed heavily. Grief was layer upon layer of an endless onion whose fumes every once in a while would waft up and sear unprepared eyes. After watching George stand and stare at the front door in silence for a couple of minutes, Joan finally spoke.

"Do you have a key?"

"No."

"No? So what do we do, break in?"

"No, the door's always open at the Moss house."

"So why don't we go in?"

George stood paralyzed except for the index and middle finger of his right hand that gently rubbed the cracked paint on the door as though it carried a Braille message. After a few moments, courage was found to turn the knob, and the door swung open in response. Joan walked in followed by the prodigal son.

The living room looked just the same: drop desk, sofa, threadbare rug, his father's armchair next to the chrome airplane ashtray. The guy never really smoked; he just liked the chrome airplane: It had reminded him of the DC3 he jumped out of over France in World War II.

Joan entered the kitchen, then seconds later let out a loud expletive on finding life forms growing in the fridge. Mr. Moss was never the tidiest person in the world and used to joke about calling the fire department every so often to wash down the fridge with high-pressure hoses. As a widower he delighted in watching interesting fungi and feathery moulds grow on leftovers in faded pink, green and robin's egg-blue Tupperware containers.

A welcome bottle of Scotch was discovered in the china cupboard next to the televisions, one on top of the other. One was the old 26-inch floor model from the early sixties that Mr. Moss couldn't throw out, what with such a nice wood cabinet and all. When that TV quit, he just put the new plastic 12-inch on top of it, but still turned the old one on with no picture because the sound was better. Every once in a while he'd find himself unable to follow the dialogue in a movie because he had the audio from one channel and the picture from another.

Joan found some canned tomato soup and managed to turn on the front element of the Westinghouse stove that looked as though it had been assembled from the chrome dashboard parts of a 'fifties Desoto.

Bequest

The off-white linoleum floor in the kitchen was worn and cracked around the legs of one chair where a lonely occupant had eaten his meals. A black rotary-dial phone sat on the chrome-framed, red-marbled Formica kitchen table next to the recently upgraded roam-phone.

Nothing in the house had changed much since George's mother died. It was pretty much a 'fifties anthropological time capsule. Whenever someone would crack to Mr. Moss that he ought to update the décor a little, he'd reply that there was plenty of wear left in everything, adding: "You just don't throw stuff out because it gets a little old – God damned disposable society!"

The water line on the scotch bottle had dropped considerably by the time George finally found the nerve to wander down the hall. His old room looked exactly the same as the day he left home. Old school books sat gathering dust: *Living Latin, King Lear, Tess of the D'Urbervilles, Anthology of Great Poems*, and the old *Encyclopaedia Britannica*. He took a rain check on that particular excursion down memory lane and continued on.

The last rays of a dying sun angled through the open door of "the" room onto the hall floor. Reluctantly rounding the corner at the end of the hall, George came upon the bed his father had died in. Next to it were some work clothes lying in a heap where they had been dropped at the end of another lonely day. George stretched out on the bed and stared at the ceiling that was probably his father's last sight, trying to get some sense of him. He pictured his face and smelled Aqua Velva wafting up from the pillow. Mr. Moss had been a convert since the commercial with the pointy-breasted woman peering out from under a beehive hair-do sensually cooing, "There's something about an Aqua Velva man." The "something," George later decided, was that an Aqua Velva man was undeniably cheap and smelled it.

A wave of nausea suddenly rolled over him and the ceiling began to spin. *Oh no, the whirlies*. He hadn't had the whirlies for years. It must have been that damned Scotch, but it wasn't just the whirlies. There was also the distorted sound of feet in the hallway and whispering voices, then everything went deathly silent. The bedroom door burst open, slamming the doorknob hard into the wall. Two guys with black ski masks ran in.

"Jesus! What the hell is going on?" Fear sucked the moisture out of George's throat reducing the words to an inaudible squeak. Before he could get up, each man grabbed an arm, pinning him down. George kicked hard sending the shorter guy flying against the wall, knocking his parents' wedding picture to the floor, shattering the glass. While George flailed at the other guy with his fist, the short guy got back up and dove on the free arm. Pinned again, heart pounding, George thought about trying to protect Joan, but where was she?

A third man came in and spoke in a strangely calm and polite voice.

"Good evening, Mr. Moss. This won't hurt a bit." Something snapped. George broke free, sat up and screamed.

"What have you done with Joan?" The words hit a dimensional wall and ricocheted back in his face. There was no one there; George was covered in sweat.

A groggy voice called out of the darkness beside him. "What has who done with me?" Joan squinted through an open eye. George surmised she had found him out cold from a little too much single malt and crawled in beside him.

"Sorry honey, I guess I just had a bad dream."

"Mmm," she responded, satisfied enough to drift back to sleep. George fell back on his pillow, shaking from an ordeal he knew was much more than a nightmare...

Morning arrived with an intrusive chirping. George regretted having left the window open. At first light, birds, just so damned ecstatic to be alive, started in on their songs of ignorant joy. An Uzi with a hundred round clip might have bought a few minutes of silence. Badly hung over, George opened bloodshot eyes and scanned the ceiling down the wall to the dresser and his parents' wedding picture. The picture wasn't there!

George bolted from bed. He looked behind the dresser and found broken glass on the floor. The shattered remains of the portrait lay nearby. The wall behind the door bore an indentation from the impact of the doorknob. Powdered plaster trailed down the wall to the floor.

"Jesus!"

Joan came close to consciousness and muttered: "What now?"

"In my nightmare last night I dreamed this picture got smashed, and here it is, smashed!"

"Mmm," she droned sleepily while squinting with a look of complete exhaustion. George went to her and stroked her hair. The last two days had been hard on her as well. She at least deserved some rest. As he pulled the covers up around her, she murmured her gratitude.

While the sun sifted through lace curtains in the living room window, George shuffled out to the porch where the light was new and pure, like the air. He'd forgotten how satisfying good air could be. In the city, his lungs wouldn't allow a deep breath in a vain effort to stop PM 10s from embedding themselves in the few remaining pink inner lobes. Ten city breaths he figured might contain the same oxygen value as one country breath. Whatever, it felt right; he breathed deeply. What testimony to a twisted social and technological evolution that something so basic and essential to existence as good air should become so rare. It was like he was dining on hors d'oeuvres made from endangered life forms, just one greedy gobble away from extinction.

As he scanned his surroundings from the vantage point of the porch, his eyes were drawn to the crude "running horse" weather vane he'd made in metal shop in Grade 8. It was still sitting on top of the barn, defying both taste and skill. His father had clearly believed encouraging creativity was more important than the homestead's property value.

George stumbled on a moment of self-pity as his eyes filled. That stupid tin horse was a reminder of how he had been loved. The tears went away, but the current beneath felt like boiling magma looking for a weakness in the crust. It was unsettling, not knowing when it would bubble to the surface or what might set it off.

Out of the corner of his eye he saw something scurry behind the barn. He strolled over cautiously to investigate, but the closer he got, an odd ringing in his ears increased in intensity. There it was again, something moved. This time it was accompanied by the sound of metal on metal. As he rounded the corner of the barn the ringing in his ears approached pain. There was someone... a little girl playing horseshoes.

"Who are you and what...?" He couldn't finish the question. The sound grew so intense it made him nauseous. George's legs crumpled under him and in that last second of consciousness he managed to break the fall by rolling off to one side. As a child his father had taught him how to fall without hurting himself when overcome by the curse. Even though it had been years since an incident of that magnitude, he was grateful the reflex remained.

Moments later, when George regained consciousness, the little girl was gone and so were the horseshoes, the sandpits and the metal shoe poles. In fact, the old tractor was right where he saw the kid playing. *Of course the old tractor is there – we've never had a horseshoe set up!* George wobbled to his feet, dusted his clothes off, and stumbled back to the front of the barn. Damn it all, it was back, the reason he left the place and rarely returned – and it appeared to be getting stronger.

The old barn door groaned as it open a foot or two on begrudging rusty rollers. Shafts of light streamed through the cracks between the boards, like focused spotlights slicing through a fog of barn dust, onto an old tarpaulin. Her smooth lines lay underneath, waiting, in stasis. George carefully removed the tarp and there it sat, gleaming from a recent coat of wax. He walked around her, and when he touched her shiny skin he could see his grandfather. Grandpa Moss loved that old Fargo truck and babied the thing. After his death, George's father became just as fanatical about it. He stood staring, mesmerized by the gleaming metal that exuded a strange nobility.

The barn door complained again at another intruder. Joan slipped through wearing only a long T-shirt with one of George's father's old work coats draped around her shoulders. Steam rose into the damp air from the two mugs of coffee she carried.

"There you are! I thought you could use some coffee. Sorry it's only powdered creamer, but it's hot." She clomped across the boards like a Clydesdale in a pair of his dad's work boots and handed George the hot brew. Then she paused a moment.   "What a beautiful old truck!"

"It was my grandpa's. He used to say it was like my grandmother: stubborn, finicky, and responsive only to politeness and affection."

He walked around to the driver's side and there, swinging in the ignition, was the rabbit's-foot key chain. George hopped in and turned the engine over. Old pistons sprang to life pushing a blue puff from the exhaust before settling into a smooth throaty rhythm. Holding that steering wheel made him smile for the first time in what felt like years. He could feel the memory of his grandfather's hand during a hair-raising driving lesson. Whenever George got uptight his grandfather would reach for his knee with a reassuring touch and say, "easy does it now, boy." After he died, George would often come out and sit in the Fargo and feel the phantom touch of that consoling hand and the whisper of those words. He revved the engine a couple of times, turned the ignition off and got out. The engine continued to sputter causing Joan to remark.

"Needs a little tune up," She yelled.

"No, it's done that for years. It started doing that after my grandfather died. My Dad said it was my grandfather's spirit controlling the last thing he had any power over. It will only do things when it's good and ready, just like grandpa!"

"Do you believe that stuff?" Joan asked with a smirk.

"We should learn to respect possibilities and not dismiss evidence."

Joan's smirk was replaced with a puzzled look. "That doesn't sound like the old sceptic I've been living with for the last few years."

"Jesus, you're right. Those were my father's words. Maybe I'm just a little unsettled by the last couple of days. They say when someone close dies; people have a tendency to think in more spiritual terms as a way of coping. If you can believe life goes on in other forms you don't have to deal with the finality of death... you know... that kind of thing."

"So do you believe life goes on in other forms?" she yelled. The truck finally quit sputtering and shut off as if awaiting an answer.

"I don't know, Joan," George shrugged in reply. The look on Joan's face said she suspected otherwise, but seemed willing to give George a day or two's grace. She was dying to inquire about the back end of the hearse and why George thought Mr. Brown should move it. That conversation would hit the air, all too soon, for George.

4

Tending to Business

It was around noon when the city slickers finally scrubbed up and headed into town. Billy McDonough waved from his porch as George and Joan passed by. The Dobson farm next to Billy's lay abandoned. In one of his last calls to his father, George had learned of Ernie Dobson's passing some months ago. His wife, Elida couldn't see very well and without Ernie to care for her she ended up in a senior citizens' home on the other side of town. Their only daughter had married a guy who worked in Detroit. So much for the farm – no farmers!

George figured on a couple of days to put things in order. He needed to settle up with Mr. Brown for the remaining funeral costs and see Ned Patterson about selling the farm. Joan wanted to get a few groceries to feed them both until the details were settled. George was anxious to get back to campus and away from painful memories ASAP. He also wanted to leave before any more clues dropped at Joan's feet that there was something unusual about him. Like a couple of locals, they pulled the Fargo up in front of the grocery store and got out, patiently waiting for the sputtering engine to finally give up.

"I'll go to Neddy's office and we'll meet back here," George advised as he turned and started down the street.

Joan called after him: "What if I'm finished first?"

George stopped and looked back in her direction somewhat taken by the appeal of her profile. "Then, uh, come and find me at Patterson's Real Estate – this isn't exactly New York City." He was staring at her behind when she turned for the store. She saw the look on his face, the same one she had seen in the hotel, the same one he had given up trying to conceal a couple of years ago. There was no point; he was a bad actor.

Joan put extra wiggle in her walk as she neared the store, then did a quick U-turn to catch George frozen in a libidinous state. She did her Groucho eyebrow thing accompanied by a knowing grin, and went in.

George headed to Patterson Real Estate feeling like a dirty old man. Grief seemed to be just making him even more of a one-track-minded, mid-life lusting fool than he was before, if that was possible. He chalked it up to the weirdness of emotional overload and fatigue.

Across the street at COUNTRY CUT AND CURL, Patricia Sandfield's face peeked through the Venetian blinds. George waved like he always used to and the blinds dropped as quickly as they always used to. Up ahead, sweeping the sidewalk in front of his hardware store, Mr. Walker, resembled a more hard-nosed version of Gepetto from the Pinocchio story.

"Good morning, Mr. Walker," George opened.

Mr. Walker looked up with a smile, then the colour suddenly left his face.   "My Lord George, I thought ya were yer father. Ya sounded just like 'im. Oh dear, wasn't the most sensitive thing to say was it?"

"That's okay Walker," George said, changing the subject as quickly as he could. "How's Millie?"

"Oh, still in the hospital like I told ya"

"What's the matter with her?"

"Well, now, I don't know that I should be blabbin' it 'round town, but between you and me, she's in there with well, you know, woman problems."

The term "woman problems," George had ascertained, was a Victorian version of the Bermuda Triangle. It represented a zone of health issues into which a generation of women vanished mysteriously without a trace. The mere mention of such problems, in turn-of-the-century Britain, must have resulted in a jail or banishment to Australia.

"I'll head over as soon as I'm done in town"

"Oh, she'll be thrilled, George. All she's done is pester me about how ya look now and how y'are about your Daddy's passin' and all."

"Well, have a good day, Mr. Walker. I better get moving."

Mr. Walker took no offence at the dismissal. His head again peered down at his fairly meticulous sweeping as he responded. "Good day to ya, George."

As George walked up the two steps into Patterson's Real Estate he turned around quickly just to piss off Patricia Sandfield. She of course was spying through the Venetian blinds and snapped them shut on having been discovered yet again. How she ever found time to cut hair was anyone's guess. Fortunately most of her clients were as interested in the gossip as their hair and willing to pay dearly for the information in more ways than one. Back in the days when monks held a virtual monopoly on the written word, people like Patricia had to have been the precursors to the newspaper. She pretty well had all the bases covered with the exception of a sports section.

When George entered Ned's, he was on the phone in an inner office that was partitioned off with dark stained wood and corrugated opaque glass. There were two empty grey steel desks in the outer area and on the wall, a corkboard with about a half dozen listings, most of which were pinned with red "sold" stickers. The place couldn't have had a coat of paint in twenty years, and it smelled musty. George closed the front door rather loudly to announce his arrival, causing Ned to whisper as though he was passing top-secret information to a code-named superior. Ned always had a flair for the dramatic. He concluded his call quickly, after all, this was a small town and he had a customer creating vibrations on the outer reaches of his economic web. He emerged like he was running for election, hand extended, full of himself and ready to kiss a baby.

"Well, well, George, so kind of you to drop in. What on Earth can I do for you?"

"Nice try Neddy, but you ever so tactfully gave me your damn card at my father's funeral. You know I'm here to ask you to sell the farm."

The words stuck in George's throat like his body was about to have an allergic reaction to such a crude utterance. Ned saw him struggling internally and tried to head off any uncertainty that might lead to a loss of commission.

"Kinda figured you'd need me George. I mean, what the hell does a professor want with a farm? You never liked this one-horse town too much anyway and I can't say as I blame you, you know I…"

"Ned, spare me the analysis!" George snapped. "Will you put everything together for me and call me with the details; how much we should ask, how much you think we'll get. You know the drill."

"I can get an estimate ready and bring the paper work out to you."

George wanted out fast and opened the door. "Fine, Ned, that's fine." He turned and left feeling physically ill. In an effort to regain control he had to breathe deep. As he headed back toward the Fargo his head finally cleared and he remembered his promise to stop in on Mildred Walker at the hospital.

Stopping off at the florist shop, George saw an older woman behind the counter with reading glasses and coifed hair. She looked up and spoke as he came through the door and that's when he realized she wasn't older. She was the same age as him!

"May I help you?" she asked politely.

"Ann Jameson?"

"Oh, my God, George."

"Ann, how have you been? I haven't seen you in years.

41

"Of course you haven't. You ran away. Remember? Some of us just stayed in this nothing place with our nothing lives looking forward to nothing. Wasn't that about how it went?"

"Ann, I'm sorry, I..." George's discomfort changed her posture immediately.

"No, George, I'm sorry. I'm sorry about your dad. My son told me about the funeral. I can't do funerals; they're too hard on me so I don't attend them anymore. I meant no disrespect to your dad. My thoughts were on you all day, yesterday."

"Thanks. You said your son told you about the funeral?"

"Yes, he works for Mr. Brown. He dropped you off at the end of your driveway."

"I thought he looked familiar. He sure has some of you, Ann." Wheels turned internally. The son of his old girlfriend drove him home: Such occurrences inflicted an awareness of age with the subtlety of a well-aimed jab from a professional boxer. Ann put her hand on George's, giving it a sympathetic squeeze. He knew she loved his father and knew also that when he left town years ago he had hurt her. She was a good soul but not "the one." *Hmm, neither was my first wife for that matter and I married her; so much for that theory...*

"Ann, I... " At that moment Joan came through the door and saw the two of them holding hands. It was ridiculously uncomfortable for George but Ann broke the ice with her usual directness.

"You must be Joan, the sweet young Canadian thing, who is twenty or so years younger than George, probably a former student, currently lives in sin with him, wears expensive perfume and has no idea what she's got herself into!"

George looked at Ann puzzled. She'd never met Joan before. Then it dawned on him. "Patricia Sandfield?" he asked.

Ann nodded affirmatively and chuckled. "Just had the hair done this morning! Hi, Joan, I'm George's old girlfriend, Ann, and you've nothing to worry about. I'm happily married – and have been for twenty years."

Joan laughed. "Well, Ann, it's a pleasure to meet you."

Ann rounded the counter and gave Joan a hug. "Welcome to Lincoln and the good ol' U.S of A. I don't imagine anybody's been particularly friendly to you thus far. I just want you to know we're not all as bad as George may have made us out to be. We just take a little while to warm up."

"Oh, that's where George gets it from," Joan replied playfully.

"You mean you actually got George to warm up?"

"Okay, okay, before you two start comparing notes," George objected, "I'm here to get some flowers for Millie Walker."

Joan and Ann looked at George and Ann again broke the silence.

"You know Joan, he's absolutely right, we should compare notes when we can speak more freely, you know, when he's not trying to steer the conversation. You want to have a coffee together before you head back to Canada?"

"That would be nice," Joan responded as if it was the proverbial done deal. They chatted for a few more minutes, and Ann had them both laughing with her sarcastic and disarming wit. That being said, George felt lucky to get out of there alive. He had forgotten how direct Ann was, though Joan clearly took to her honesty immediately.

Driving the old Fargo to the hospital was a surprisingly rewarding sensory experience. The feel of the steering wheel on country roads, the pleasing shiny curves of automotive metal sculpture, and the crackle of Chopin on the tube radio all conspired to convince George there was some joy left in life.

The hospital on the other hand brought back memories of parents sick with worry, fretting over their son's broken arm. Hospitals, like old schools, somehow manage to resist time and change. The parade of life and death there operates at such a high frequency it occasionally synchronizes into the phasing pulse of twin engines – the cry of the new born in rhythm with the faint strains of an old soul's last departing breath. People coming out of hospitals are often like passengers leaving giant interstellar ships immediately aware of how much the world has changed in their absence. In keeping with Einstein's ideas on general relativity, it is as though they had been circling the rim of a black hole at the speed of light only to return to an Earth that had aged a thousand years in but a few of their days.

After a parade of IV poles, housecoats and slippers, and one glimpse of a fairly saggy backside revealed by the dignity-robbing design of the hospital gown, they finally found Millie's room and walked in. She looked up and started to cry. George put the flowers on the floor, and sat on the edge of her bed and hugged her, rocking slowly, stroking her coarse white hair.

"Oh, George, let me look at ya." She pulled back and looked him in the face.

"You need a hair cut even though you're thin on top. Don't tell me ya went to yer father's funeral lookin' like that!" She looked over at Joan with a mischievous smile. Then she looked back at George with a wordless request for a formal introduction.

43

George complied. "Millie this is my friend, Joan."

"Well, Joan, if yer a friend to George I'm proud to know ya! Now tell me, are you two livin' together?"

"Millie, you shouldn't..." George started to object...

"Why yes, Millie," Joan interrupted, "we are."

Millie smiled at Joan's relaxed confidence. "Do ya love 'im?"

Joan chuckled, then answered firmly: "Yes, I do Millie, I can't seem to help it."

Millie smiled sweetly at Joan, then her face clouded over as she looked back at George with a familiar look of parental disapproval.

"Still afraid to make a commitment, George? I woulda thought you'd grown up b'now. You know yer just as stubborn as yer father."

Joan burst out laughing. George was a little peeved. But, that was the Millie he knew and loved. What was unsettling though was how wonderful Joan's public declaration of love for him felt. He sensed somehow that was Millie's purpose. The words were important and in the presence of others there was a heightened awareness of their worth.

"I brought you some flowers, Millie"

"Did ya kill 'em?"

"No, Millie," George said, reaching for the pot of tulips on the floor. "They're still alive."

"Good boy for rememberin'. They are livin' things like us all and deserve what time they have. You know yer father was in here the day he died braggin' 'bout ya. Oh, George, what are we gonna do without yer father?"

She crumpled into tears. George held her old bones in his arms again and kissed the top of her head. There was a warm and good familiarity in holding this old soul who had been like a mother to him.

Joan's smile left her face as she sat in the chair next to the window and began to cry. George wanted to cry with them, but nothing came. He was stuck on the notion of his father bragging about him. *Bragging? About me?* Where the hope of reconciliation used to reside, there now lay a gaping hole in his being that might never have a chance to heal. It was as a cancer created over the years by the constant irritant of his own idiocy – his pride.

5

The Deal

Back at the farm, Joan was clacking away on her iBook via modem to Jim, her marketing research partner. They were designing a new survey for a Canadian grocery chain while George prepared one of his exotic stir-fry chicken dinners: The canned pineapple was how he got away with the word "exotic."

It was odd being in that kitchen using his father's stuff without his presence. He felt like a little kid dressed up in daddy's suit. It was part of his dad's past, but not his; it was tailored to his father's life. When it was the family home, and George was a member of the family, there was the innate feeling of ownership that a child has when he asks someone to "come over to my house to play." With both parents gone he was aware for the first time that the house was a remnant of their dream, one that he had only inhabited for a preciously short period of time.

Joan had no sooner gone off line and plugged the phone back in when it rang. She picked it up and handed it to George, who already knew who it was.

"Hello, Neddy, what's on your mind?"

"George, I have all the paperwork ready and I've got some very good news for you regarding a buyer. Can I come over?"

George thought for a second about spending one of his last evenings at his father's farm with Ned Patterson and it didn't sit well.

"Ah... Ned I'm a little tired. Can I meet you at your office tomorrow morning around ten or so?"

"Well, I guess so, George. I just thought that uh... yes that's fine."

When he hung up, Joan had one of those looks that said: "Well?"

"Neddy has everything ready, including a buyer."

"Boy, that was fast! How did you know it was Ned when I handed you the phone?"

"Just a lucky guess," George lied, serving the stir-fry. After postulating a little over why a buyer for his father's farm might have appeared so quickly, they pretty much ate in silence. Joan worked off-line on her computer in between bites while George searched inside of himself for some elusive reassurance that selling the farm was the right thing to do. He was selling off his childhood, severing the few decaying fibres of a worldly umbilical cord that connected him to his family.

George wandered into the living room. Joan followed moments later sitting next to him, running her fingers through what was left of his hair. She kissed his cheek then stood up and spoke with a quiet sensuality.

"You look like a fella who could use a little distraction. I'll be down the hall waiting, and I'll be somewhat scantily clad." She did the Groucho Marx eyebrow thing and headed down the hall. She wouldn't be waiting very long.

George got up immediately. "This isn't mercy sex is it?"

"Oh, no, not at all Georgie. I will show no mercy!"

They laughed as he followed her into the bedroom. She felt so good when everything else around felt so strange and sad.

Afterwards, sleep arrived and brought with it a re-run of the night before. It started with the nausea again and the feeling of being wide-awake. As before, the door crashed open and two men burst into the room and held him down. The struggle ensued, the picture got broken then the third man entered and spoke in that pretentiously calm voice.

"Good evening, Mr. Moss, this won't hurt a bit." His eyes were as cold as his tone. He raised a syringe, flicking air bubbles out though the needle before injecting the contents of the glass reservoir into George's arm. Instantly his chest felt like it was going to explode, thrusting him back into the reality of consciousness and a crippling pain across his upper body that was unbearable. A more powerful wave of nausea rolled over him as he felt a great weight pushing down on his chest. Joan stirred, squinted out of the corner of her eye, then shot up with a look of horror as George held his chest grimacing.

"George, what is it, why are you holding your chest?"

"I don't know. I think I'm having a damn heart attack!"

Joan jumped to her feet. "I'll call 911. Oh, God, don't do this, please don't do this!" She ran down the hall to the kitchen phone crying. By the time she got there George's pain and the nausea were gone. He got up, gingerly, but somehow knowing he was fine. Joan was in the kitchen, half-crying; half-talking to an emergency operator who didn't have much information and had not yet dispatched a response vehicle.

"Joan, I'm all right," George said firmly. "I don't think we need any help." She couldn't speak, so beside herself with fear. George took the receiver from her gently and spoke to the operator.

"My chest pain is gone; I appear to be back to normal." The operator asked a few more questions, and when he assured her an ambulance wasn't necessary she told him to head to county hospital anyway, as these things were very often warnings of things to come.

George hung up and found Joan deep breathing to pull herself together. He sat next to her on a kitchen chair gently rubbing her back.

"I guess this is the sort of territory that comes with loving an older guy hmm?" she mumbled.

After convincing her all was well enough for the night they went back to bed and he watched her fall asleep. George remained awake, fearing a replay of that damn dream, and once again watched the sun rise. He got out of bed as quietly as he could and headed down the hall.

As he approached the living room, a familiar squeaking sound was coming from the porch. He leaned back in the darkness of the hallway and looked out the front window on an angle. It was that little girl again, the one he had seen playing horseshoes. Now she was on the porch swing, gliding back and forth oblivious to the world in her coveralls and bare feet. She sang a nonsensical song, staring off into the place little girls go to for such funny little reflections of their own creativity. That fragile wisp of a voice warmed George's heart with its undeniable sweetness and innocence. Long, shiny brown hair obscured her face but not the presence of an endearing little soul. Once again as he attempted to walk to the door, a high-pitched sound painfully attacked his hearing.

George stopped in his tracks, then backed up. The sound decreased in intensity. When he leaned forward again the pain increased. He backed off a second time and tried to make some sense of it. It appeared that he could only observe this phenomenon, and from a distance. He couldn't think of any physical law that says one cannot approach someone else without excruciating pain, nausea and unconsciousness... lawyers excepted, so what was going on?

The squeaking stopped. The little girl was now looking in George's direction with an odd expression as though she sensed his presence but couldn't actually see him. Was this vision one-way he wondered?

George was looking into her familiar face when she suddenly jumped off the swing, as though someone had called her, and disappeared. He moved forward carefully, one step at a time with no pain. He took a couple more tentative steps, then cautiously, one foot after the other until he was out on the porch. She was gone and the swing was gone. Of course, the swing was gone, there never was one! He looked at the ceiling; there were no hooks to hold a swing, nothing. Why did a squeaking swing on the porch sound familiar when it didn't exist and never had?

George sat on the steps, head in hands as his body began to shake uncontrollably. He hadn't had that kind of an experience since his last stay on the farm. George's father had them and his father before him. They considered it a blessing. George considered it the family curse, and fought it. He just wanted to be like other kids, but apart from Billy, most other kids wouldn't let him. He was the Moss boy, the son of those weird people on the outskirts of town who had visions and the like.

The front door opened and Joan came out in her T-shirt.

"You okay?" Her voice was groggy. George snapped out of his funk figuring she'd had enough for one morning and pulled himself together.

"Yeah, just taking in the morning. Come on let me make you a coffee." Over breakfast Joan insisted on a check-up at the hospital as a favour to her. George didn't know how he knew that it would be a complete waste of time, but agreed anyway.

They were headed into town to meet Ned when the Fargo started to sputter and stopped dead in front of Dobson's farm. George got out, lifted up the hood and heard Joan laughing.

"What's so funny?"

"Oh nothing, history professors look right at home underneath the hood of a truck. Do you have the foggiest notion of what's under there?"

"Yes, as a matter of fact I do. Granted, it is a foggy notion, but a notion nonetheless." He proceeded to look for loose wires while Joan got out, went over to the fence and surveyed the Dobson farm.

"Whose place was this?" she asked. George banged his head under the hood and came out rubbing the sore spot as he walked over.

"That was the Dobson's, Ernie and Elida Dobson. I used to help Mr. Dobson out once in awhile for pocket money. This was one of the best farms in the county!"

They stared quietly for a few minutes at the abandoned house, barns with missing boards and fields growing wild from neglect.

George sighed. "Mr. Dobson farmed less and less property every year. Dad said it was a curious metaphor for his ebbing life."

"Kinda' looks sad, doesn't it?" Joan said with a wistful tone.

"Oh, it's sad all right. This is very fertile soil, you could grow anything on this farm and it'd be bound to win something at the county fair. No, you don't get much better than this except for our place."

Joan laughed. "*Our* place? Why George, you old farmer."

He headed back to the truck and shot back over his shoulder. "That was eighteen years of programming speaking. Don't worry you're safe. You don't need to invest in any coveralls yet."

George tried the ignition. The engine fired up right away. He jumped back out to close the hood and then they both got back in.

Joan had a puzzled look. "What was the matter with the truck?"

"I haven't a clue."

"So how did you get it going?"

"I don't know, it just started." George laughed it off but he had some odd thoughts about the Fargo just stopping like that. It was his grandfather's style to place George into a situation, and wait for him to draw his own conclusion. This of course would provide the basis for a decision. If that conclusion was the same as his, you got a pat on the back. If not; you would have to suffer through an interminable lecture. This is where his grand father's skill as a teacher ended and his powerful urge to preach began. George learned over the years what responses could avert the big lecture. Grandpa Moss knew his grandson had him figured out, and would just smile and give a synopsised version of the lecture anyway. They learned from each other. The gains were patience and diplomacy for one, and attempted brevity for the other.

George longed for what had annoyed him about his grandfather. He used to say that when you love somebody "you love em' warts and all." George thought it kind of funny how sometimes it was the warts he missed the most. The "warts," in a way, constituted the little abrasions that made one aware of another's existence, a part of a defining signature, where one soul rubs another.

A few minutes later the Fargo pulled into a parking spot in front of Patterson's Real Estate. Ned watched from his window as George and Joan approached the door. He called them into the inner office and stood behind a desk so tidy it was obvious he'd been waiting for some time with nothing better to do than draw an ornate doodle on his note pad.

"Well, well, if it isn't the luckiest person in the county. Have a seat, George. I've got quite a pleasant surprise for you!" He pointed to a beat up office chair in front of his desk. Pre-occupied with selling his father's farm, George sat down on automatic pilot. Joan stood behind him and put her hands on her man's shoulders as Ned slid the papers forward.

"You'll see here, at the top of the paragraph, the purchaser, New World Developments is offering... "

"How'd you do this so fast, Neddy? Nobody's even been out to see the place. I just told you yesterday I was selling." Ned was clearly a little uncomfortable: He had only expected smiles, not questions, from those acquiring such wealth.

"Uh, sheer luck, George. I've been dealing with a developer who bought a couple of other places in the area, and I talked him into your place as well. You'll notice the price is more than fair, well above market value."

"What do they develop, Mr. Patterson?" Joan asked dryly.

"Oh, uh, you know, beautiful executive homes with large lots, that sort of thing."

George looked at the contract and couldn't believe the money involved. "This seems like quite a whack of dough for a run down farm in the middle of nowhere, Neddy."

"Like I was saying George, you're a lucky man."

Joan grabbed the documents and stood up.

"Well this is wonderful news Mr. Patterson. We would like to talk this over and get back to you tomorrow."

Ned looked really flustered like someone fumbling a ball.

"Ms. Parks was it? I was talking to George, and you know, George, I'm not sure how long I can keep these people on the line."

Joan clearly wanted out of there and didn't like Ned's dismissive tone. Something wasn't right. George was even able to feel it over his monumental guilt from entertaining the idea of selling one of the last earthly ties to his parents. He could take the money and run, he had run from that town before. Joan's instincts and immediate action however, were a little surprising.

"You know, Ned, Ms. Parks is absolutely right. This is a big decision. We'll talk it over and get back to you tomorrow."

Ned grew even more flustered and had one more kick at the can. "I really think you should..." He stopped his pitch, not wanting to appear too eager, which was obviously far beyond his powers of self control. "Okay, uh, tomorrow then. Will that be in the morning again, George?"

"We'll call you," George replied. Joan was already up and on her way to the door. Once outside George wondered what made her so anxious to get out of there.

"What was that all about, Joan?"

"Your body language."

"My body language?"

"I have never seen you look so awful as you did at that desk. You kept wriggling in your seat. You never wriggle. You always exude so much self-control. Then it dawned on me."

"What dawned on you?"

"What he was saying made no sense to you, or me for that matter."

"Well, my mind was mulling over some obvious questions like, where the hell are the executives going to come from to live in those expensive executive homes? The nearest city of any consequence is seventy-five miles away. Then, add to that how much they're offering."

"Could I be in love with a wealthy guy?"

"Look at the second paragraph."

Joan looked and her face lit up. "Oh dear, now I really, really love you. I was just kidding before. Did I ever tell you how handsome you are? To Hell with how creepy Ned seemed, I could shop on the jewellery channel for years on this, well a few months anyway."

They both started to laugh, until Joan got serious again. "So what's a farm like your Dad's worth?"

"I'll bet it's no where near this offer. Let's go see Billy."

On the way to the truck Joan had that "bursting-at-the-seams" look again as though she had something more to say but was considering the ramifications first. George could have signed those damned papers and been the hell out of there but for Joan. He was so glad for her intervention and now curious. Joan grabbed his arm. She had made a decision to say what was on her mind.

"George, we don't need the money you know."

George looked at her with obvious affection, nodded in agreement and leaned over to kiss her cheek. Money was a funny thing. He had never thought of somebody giving him a cheque for such an outrageous amount. In a world where the ultimate dream was to be monetarily well endowed, the offer seemed like manna from heaven. But what did he need? Nothing, really. Unlike most divorces, he and his ex each took what was theirs and called it a day. Both left financially stable keeping what lawyers usually extracted by escalating vitriol. Now, with his love of Joan he really wanted for nothing, except for physical capabilities more in line with the measure of his lust.

A yapping dog in need of a Valium, welcomed them into McDonough's driveway. They always had yapping dogs. Mr. Moss used to say the McDonoughs subscribed to the psychology of irritation and noise as a first line of defence. Instead of a "CAUTION! GUARD DOG" sign, he always thought McDonough's sign should read, "BE PREPARED TO BE IRRITATED TO DEATH BY YAPPING DOG". The honesty of such a sign might prove effective against most salesmen and maybe even two Jehovah's witnesses.

Back in Hamilton, George had made peace with the local Jehovah's Witnesses, in his own special way. He told them that they could have all of his stuff on their Judgment Day, a day that kept getting pushed back for some unknown reason. The idea of eternal life on Earth sounded insufferably boring. "And besides," he'd added, "it's going to get a little chilly for you folks when you've risen from the grave, kicked all your dirt off, and the sun eventually burns out."

George and Joan endured the dog and drove up to the porch where Mr. McDonough sat bundled up in the sun looking pasty and unwell. It was a little cool but the fresh air probably made it easier for the old bugger to breathe. Billy came bounding out with his usual energy.

"Geeze, it's about time you two came over. I was beginning to think you'd already skipped town. Come on the porch and sit a spell." Mr. McDonough made an attempt to get up out of respect for Joan; his face lit up when Joan went over and kissed his cheek. George shook his hand and the old man held it strongly looking him in the eye with one of his no nonsense looks.

"We'll never forget what yer Daddy did fer us. Never did think he'd beat me to the Pearlies though, George." He started to wheeze and gasp for air causing Bill to spring into action. He rushed over, grabbing an inhaler on route that he plugged into his father's mouth like a pacifier.

"Are you okay?" George asked looking at the old man.

Billy butted in. "No, he's not okay! We all begged him to quit smoking and now the stupid old coot has emphysema and can barely leave this house."

Mr. McDonough was clearly embarrassed and sat back eyeing Joan until he wheezed a sentence out.

"Well now, aren't you the pertiest thing I seen around here for some time. Sit down and tell me 'bout yerself." They all sat and had a good old country chinwag. Periodically, the inhaler came out, and Billy, angry at his father's self-created infirmity, dished out painful glares. The beer flowed as it always did on McDonough's porch, and by early afternoon all parties were a little tipsy. They danced around the topic of Mr. Moss's death, instead catching up on local news and solving most of the problems in the Third World. In a lull George brought up the offer on his father's farm.

"So, Ned has some people who have made an offer on dad's farm."

"Oh, really?" Billy looked a little funny and the old man started to shake his head.

"What's the matter with you two? I'm a professor not a farmer."

Billy's Dad wheezed out a sentence. "This poor excuse fer a son sold ours!" The old man huffed.

"You what, Billy?" George asked with a look of shock.

"Dad gave me power of attorney a few months back when he was in county hospital supposedly with a couple of days left on this Earth, or so they said. Then, out of nowhere, I got a ridiculous offer for this place so I took it."

Mr. McDonough started coughing uncontrollably with an awful rattle that came from the depths of his chest. It measured quite high on the disgusting scale, and Joan, for one, hoped that whatever was audibly loose wouldn't make its way out into the world until she was long gone. Even when he stopped everyone still stared. Seeing he had everyone's attention Mr. McDonough entered the conversation right where Billy had left off. "Thought I'd be dead b'now so he sold the damn place!" he snapped in disgust.

George shook his head. "Why would you, of all people, sell, Billy? You love farming."

"Why?" Billy repeated incredulously. "Why don't ya ask the Goddamn government that allows imported and subsidized produce in? Hell, we're all so busy suckin' on foreign teats we can't see our own Mother Earth dying at our feet. So to hell with out-a-touch governments and anyone else who thinks I have some hare-brained moral obligation to keep workin' toward a damn bank foreclosure. The fuckin' banks! Stinkin' rich, knee-deep in profits, layin' people off in droves and foreclosing on farmers; the very same filthy rich bastards who count on what we grow to feed their fat upper class greedy mouths!"

George started to smile; He hadn't heard a McDonough tirade for years.

"Watch yer mouth in front of the lady, boy! I apologize for my son, Joan." Mr. McDonough got the last sentence out before coughing.

"Billy, I'm not sitting in judgment, but I am curious." George offered, trying to cool things off a little.

Joan entered the fray. "Billy, what is real market value for a place like George's?"

"Oh, probably three-hundred to three-hundred-and-fifty thousand."

"And yet, we received an offer close to triple the high side of that," George pondered. "Who are these people, Billy?"

Billy's face got more serious and he looked a little awkward.

"I can't say."

"You mean you don't know who bought your place?"

"No! I mean that one of the terms of my agreement is that I don't discuss it."

Billy and George had never kept anything from each other so there it finally was and it was over money. Money!

George pulled back and decided to push no farther. He understood that the fear of a financially wanting old age does desperate things to people. It's the other side of the American dream. Once age takes hold and the dream of hitting it big is behind not ahead – when there's more past than future – then people start to wonder who the hell will take care of them should infirmity take root. Mid-life can be a real bitter pill on a spoon full of worry.

6

The Revelation

The puzzle of Ned's real estate deal was a welcome distraction from the pain of mourning and the increasing intensity of George's family curse. In the afternoon he decided to look through his father's papers while Joan was back on her computer working online with Jim.

Something about the drop-leaf desk didn't look right. George got the key from its hiding place, a small brass hook screwed into the side panel, but the key didn't go into the lock and the desk just fell open. On closer inspection he saw that the wood around the deadbolt was splintered. The key wouldn't fit because the metal in the lock mechanism had been rendered useless by a crude tool of some sort... the desk had been forced open.

"Hey, Joan, could you come here a second?"

"Be right there," she replied from the kitchen. Well, "right there" was a good ten minutes later. In that time George had become more puzzled. The deed to the property was there and so was a bundle of cash in the amount of $3,272.63, in a small metal cash box. Whoever had broken into the desk was clearly not after money.

"What's up?" Joan stood behind him, crunching down on a cracker.

"Somebody broke into this desk."

"So what's missing?"

"Damned if I know." He was showing Joan the cash box and the deed when the title of one document sent a shiver up his spine. It was a copy of his father's *Last Will and Testament*. As he reverently unfolded it, a tattered piece of paper fell out and floated to his lap. It was written in pencil, in his father's scrawl.

"My dearest son: If you are reading this, you are going through my things and I am physically dead. Of course you know any material possessions I may have owned are yours, for what they are worth. But that isn't what I want to leave you. I leave you with this simple thought. Though we have never seen eye to eye since your mother passed, I love you son, and I love what you are. My most heartfelt wish is that one-day you will too. Dad."

Joan was reading over his shoulder. When George turned, her eyes were brimming with tears.

"Oh come on," George scolded as his lip started to quiver, "how am I supposed to keep it together if you can't?" The floodgates opened again, and more hurt irritated the mortal wound in his chest.

Joan's tearful mood turned to a sympathetic curiosity. "What is it that your father means, you know, about yourself that you don't like?"

"Please Joan, one thing at a time. Can we do this later? I'm feeling just a little too pre-occupied with the steps of this new death dance, to go delving into the cesspit of self analysis, unless of course you would like to see me modeling a new summer line of straightjackets. I feel like I'm teetering on the edge of a colossal abyss."

Joan backed off immediately. They didn't talk for the rest of the afternoon and evening, probably just as well: She and Jim were really into their marketing project with computers humming away for hours. George was first to bed that night and when Joan finally joined him she was a little cold. She didn't wrap herself around him as usual, but kept a safe distance.

George sensed she was probably doing a little re-evaluating. He worried that fear might be seizing her emotional machinery, like creeping rust. Hopefully it was the surface kind, not perforating the very structure that held them together. Not only was she currently playing second fiddle to his significant loss, but also as an added feature, the man she loved was turning out to be a little different in Lincoln than he was back home in Hamilton.

In the middle of the night the dream returned. The nausea first, just to warm him up, then, the door burst open and he found himself struggling again with the two guys trying to hold him down. The portrait shattered as before, and the third guy entered with the syringe.

"Good evening, Mr. Moss, this won't hurt a bit." He injected something into George's arm. George was terrified. *The pain – a goddamned heart attack again! No, this is just a dream! It's just a damn dream!"*

George concentrated on trying to make the pain go away, not wanting to unsettle Joan anymore than he already had. He was reaching the bottom of his brave, suffer-quietly reservoir when something snapped. It was like an elastic connection giving way and the pain vanished instantaneously. He began drifting upward feeling wonderful for the first time in days. *Oh shit, I've had a friggin' heart attack from this damn dream and now I'm dead!* Somehow his demise was of no consequence in the euphoria that enveloped him. He drifted up over his body glancing down at the three men standing over his motionless body.

The guy with the needle held the bedpost with his right hand and leaned over George looking for life signs. *Where the hell is the white light I'm supposed to see? Hey, where the hell is Joan? When did she get up?* The third man with the needle moved out of the way and George mustered up the courage to look down at his dead face in a farewell salute to vanity. *What! That isn't me! It's... my father's face. My father's face? What the... no ... NO, NO!*

George was sitting up; eyes wide open in terror and astonishment.

Joan was shaking him. "George, wake up. Wake up. You're freaking me out!"

His mind was consumed with anger. His father had died needlessly. It wasn't his time. Someone, for some stupid reason had killed him. Sound finally reached the surface scraping its way through his dry throat, the words as unreal as the thought. *The dream was no dream; it was my father's last few moments of life.*

"He was murdered!"

His voice rang off into a smothering silence. Joan saw a rage of madness in his face that she had never seen before, and it frightened her.

"What's going on, George? Joan asked frantically. "You said you had something to tell me and would tell me later. How about now, George? How about now?"

7

The Reckoning

George knew he'd have to level with Joan: He loved her too much to harbour secrets. She deserved an explanation. The problem was that for most "normal" people there could be no explanation. With what he now believed was knowledge of his father's murder, he could barely utter a coherent sentence.

Knowing he stood to frighten away the woman he loved, he needed to find the right words and some kind of emotional control. George made hot chocolate and they sat on the sofa, the air thick with anticipation.

Joan couldn't tolerate his confused look any longer. "Well?"

"All right Joan, all right!" George said with irritation.

"You're angry at *me*?" she asked sarcastically.

"No," he sighed, "I'm angry at the circumstances under which I have to tell you something that might be too bizarre for you to handle. I don't know if I can explain this right now"

"Try me."

"Alright, but understand: You matter about as much as anything in this world can at the moment. God, even that sounds insulting."

"Yes it does, but I'll take it as well-intended."

"There is a thing," George began, "that has run in my family for generations. Folks around here call it *The Sight* – my father had it, my grandfather had it and his father before him…"

Joan swallowed hard. "And you."

"Yes, and me. It's why I left Lincoln. It was even more repugnant to me than the war in Vietnam. Most everyone here knew about the weird Moss family and talked or whispered about us behind our backs. I felt like a freak – oh hell, to them, I was, and still am, a freak! I chose to get away from here and learned how to ignore it, hoping it would wither away like an unused limb."

"And did it?"

"Sort of. I think I really just developed denial into an art. Whenever I had hints of *The Sight* I focused my thoughts on to another subject.

"What did your father do that everyone says they'll never forget?"

"He helped a few people by being in the right place at just the right moment – sometimes he'd know what was coming before it happened. He occasionally helped people to not do something stupid they were contemplating that they might regret later. Once in a while he'd find things that were missing because he'd see where they were."

"So, when you warned Mr. Brown to move his hearse…"

"I saw it damaged."

Joan nodded, adding: "And your dream wasn't a dream was it?"

"Well yes, and no. Somehow I experienced the last moments of my father's life in a dream-like form. Three men murdered him. Two held him down and one injected him with something that caused his heart to fibrillate."

"You really believe that?"

"I *feel* that is what happened. Belief is a little bit more of an intellectual commitment. You know when you dream you see things? Well, I see them, but I also feel them at the same time, and I can sense if the images are real."

Joan's look said it all: This was too bizarre.

"Look," George sighed, "I know all of this is pretty weird, and all you have is my word. This is where I'm asking you to trust me. I'm not insane. Some people are born with musical ability or an aptitude for mathematics. I was born with the goddamned Sight. I feel I love you. I knew you loved me the first day we had lunch in the cafeteria. Can I give you hard proof of that? No, you only have my word and your interpretations of what my feelings are. All the really important stuff I think is at that level. We just have a hard time reconciling our spiritual instincts and feelings with the world we live in. If somebody talks out loud about this stuff, more often than not they're viewed as a crackpot. So, are all those we refer to as "crackpots" really nuts? Couldn't some of them just have talents we can't measure or reconcile with crude rulers of dead wood marked off in black ink at mandatory intervals?"

Joan met his question with silence, then said: "George I, I don't know what to think. I do know I can't deal with being left in the dark by the man I love. So, if you think your father was killed…"

"Joan, I feel in my bones he was, and I've seen how it was done and … he was angry… angry at himself for not listening."

"Angry at himself?"

She had fed his own words back before he had even considered them. He too, only then understood what he'd just said.

"He stayed in bed even though he probably sensed the arrival of the men who killed him. He might have been able to prevent his own death."

Joan shook her head. "Why on Earth would he do that? What's he got, some sort of martyr complex?"

"No, nothing so elaborate, I think he was too tired to get up, and so he dismissed the thought until it was too late." The tear ducts burst open and George began to cry. Surely his father wouldn't have allowed himself to be killed in some pathetic demonstration that there is only death in denial of self. He wouldn't put it past him – the old Bastard!

"Arghhhh!" George's scream was out again before he knew it.

Joan had been watching his eyes dart around in his head before the outburst and stared at him like he was completely insane. George entertained that thought as well. He was after all communicating with a dead man, without sound, oblivious to the physical universe but completely tuned in to a spiritual presence. He tried to get a grip.

"My scream was anger," George explained. "My father might still be alive if only he had done what he had been telling me to do all my life: – LISTEN TO THE INNER VOICE! In a moment of human frailty he didn't listen and now he's dead. Had he acted on instinct, he might still be alive. I could hug him, I could tell him how much I love him, I could kiss him. I could hold those gnarled hands that spoke his heart, and walk with him. We could reminisce about my mother. We could talk about the curse of the damned Sight…"

Thousands of "coulds" surrounded George. He tried to hold on to each one but soon there were so many they slipped through the gaps of his conscious mind and accelerated ahead of him. He struggled to keep up until the whiffs of wishful promise disappeared over the horizon.

Joan looked at him sympathetically for a moment; then her attitude changed dramatically. "Please understand that some of this feels like a crock to me, a bad dream resulting from "an undigested bit of beef" as Scrooge said. If you feel your dad was murdered, then isn't that something you should look into for your father's sake and maybe for the sake of your own sanity. If you have instincts, honey, and you ignore them and keep them from me, I am never, truly going to be a part of your life. I will only be guessing where you are in your head. If it's too weird to share with the rest of world then so be it, *we* won't share it. If it's too weird for me then at least give me the courtesy of deciding that for myself. But, I cannot live with someone who won't let me know who he is or where he is."

Her synopsis sounded reasonable enough. But the reality, George knew, would be far more intense than any hypothetical discussion.

"I don't know if you can live with something I haven't been able to live with myself. My grandfather's brother, Morgan, Uncle Mog as we called him, saw spirits walking around us all, and most people thought he was mad. Do I wish to physically live in one universe and mentally in another? My answer is, no! Do I wish to develop a skill that might allow me to see the dead walking among the living? No! If, as some say, we are spiritual beings having a human experience then Goddamn it, why can't I have my human experience? I will be a spirit soon enough in the overall scheme of things."

Joan looked at him with some distance then spoke slowly and deliberately. "A minute ago, when you were talking about love, you said it was instinctive and couldn't be proven... that sometimes our instincts are all we have. George, through your own words, you already believe in the spiritual elements of your being that you fear and try to deny: You are contradicting yourself."

She's right. She's right – damn it! She's too smart, smarter than me! George chided himself for having thoughts about who was smarter than whom. He got up and walked out the door – stumbling onto the driveway in his bare feet, gasping for air. Tears streamed down his cheeks. He felt like he was falling apart at a cellular level. It was the most despondent moment in his life. He was revealed an idiot and no longer even held the thin façade of being a wise knight in shining armour to the woman he loved. This lofty romantic and mythical status meant more to the man in him than he had realized.

Joan was absolutely right: he espoused philosophies that he didn't live. He believed in things he fought against. He acknowledged there was a spiritual layer to his love for her and yet he railed against things spiritual fearing them to be some deep, dark pit he might fall into that could consume him.

How can I fear what I am? How can I be ashamed of what I feel? Jesus, I'm going mad. I'm not angry with her – it's me – I hate myself!

Joan stood watching through the window as he wandered toward the barn. He did look a little nuts in his father's housecoat, bare feet, tears streaming down his face, wandering around talking to himself like an inmate at yard time. It was sad and somewhat repulsive to her but she didn't want to go to him just yet. Her pragmatism kicked into gear...

Hello Jim, Joan here... the email message began. Jim read it as he sat at his usual post, back in the old Winston-Salem tobacco warehouse in Durham, North Carolina. It was one of those urban renewal projects that converted industrial space into apartments for the chic and artistic.

Jim lived at his computer terminal by the window while his gay lover lived in the flat upstairs. They had met at Duke University where Jim was on the Business faculty and briefly lectured until it became financially feasible to kiss university goodbye. Jim and Randy went through the motions of trying to conceal what everyone knew. Jim was nervous that his sexual preference might have a negative effect on the marketing business he ran with Joan so he did a great impersonation of a macho heterosexual womanizing male. "Harrumphing" still worked in the business world. When he was in his space with Randy, his lover, the mask would come off. He was a sweet man, and more than a friend to both Joan and George. Joan and Jim had often laughed at the irony of not being overly fond of America but madly in love with Americans.

Jim stopped reading her email and picked up the phone: "Joan, what's wrong? It's the middle of the night for goodness sake..."

"Well, if you must know I'm not doing so great. I'm watching George lose his mind, and I don't know if I can handle sticking around for the self-destruct sequence. This sure isn't the man I've been living with for the last couple of years."

"Oh Joan, this is breaking my heart. What on Earth is happening? Is it his father's death? Is he shutting you out? Tell me what's happening?"

"Jim I don't quite know yet, myself. I need a huge favour."

"Anything. You know I'd do anything for you."

"Hold the line one second." Joan ran to the living room desk, grabbed Ned Patterson's real estate contract and returned to the phone. "Can you do a search on a company called New World Developments?"

"Who the hell are they?"

"They want to buy George's dad's farm. They're offering just a little *too* much money. Something smells rotten, and now he's ranting about some dream he keeps having where his father gets murdered."

"Oh my God. Why don't you take the money and get out of there?"

"Would that it were that easy. I think selling his father's farm might be something George would regret for the rest of his life. If we can find a reason for him not to sell, it might be helpful. The question of the day is; why would some out-of-town developer want to build executive homes in an area that doesn't have any executives? Can you do that New World Developments search for me and maybe I'll be able to tell you more once I make some sense out of what's going on around here?"

"Consider it done. I'll call you the moment I have anything."

"Thanks, Jim."

"Love ya," Jim said, hanging up the receiver.

Joan returned to the window to resume her "patient" watch.

George couldn't face her and didn't wish her to see anymore of his pathetic displays so he slipped in through the slightly opened barn door and pulled it shut. A few seconds later, the tarp was off the Fargo and he sat sullenly in the front seat. "All right, grandpa, if ever I needed some input, now is the time!" *Nothing. Absolutely nothing.* The harder he tried to find some of *The Sight*, a hint of knowledge from elsewhere, some comfort or guidance, the more deafening the silence became. Silence was his answer. The message was loud and clear – he was on his own. His father had written in his note that he loved him for who he was, and he hoped George would do likewise some day. Well, there he sat. He didn't like what he saw. And worse, he'd shown an awful side of himself to the woman who loved him. Though Joan thought she might be able to handle *The Sight* if they dealt with it together, George wasn't so sure.

He stared at the chrome grill on the old tube radio in the Fargo until the lines were etched into his optical nerves like a bar code. He was so wrecked that he didn't feel the cold or notice that the windows in the cab of the Fargo were steaming up…

George found Joan on the bed, smelled her hair as she slept. He wanted to make love to her without waking her up. The bedcovers were strewn in such a fashion as to reveal that, as usual, she wore nothing but her T-shirt. What a sight, those thighs, that tuft of hair. He kissed her nipples through the cotton. She didn't move. Gently he moved one of her legs and guided himself into her, rubbing his nose in her soft hair as he very slowly made love to her. So soft, so soft and fragrant. Her smell made him weak. Her softness made him weaker. She took little breaths but didn't stir, uttering a barely audible purr of approval. He couldn't recall a longer orgasm. *Christ!* He jerked awake, still in the truck! *Oh for crying out loud I'm regressing to adolescent dreams!*

George got out of the truck and closed the door gently. The moon sprayed a sheen of silver over the world as he headed back to the house across the cold wet grass of the front yard. His stealth entry was going well until the hinge on the front door gave off a rather loud squawk. His dew-soaked feet squeaked on the hardwood floor to the bathroom. He closed the door silently…

Joan walked in with a curious look: "What are you doing, honey?"

"I fell asleep in the truck."

"If I didn't know better I'd say you've been playing with yourself."

"I guess privacy might be a little too much to ask for around here."

"You're embarrassed – you really *were* playing with yourself."

"No, I wasn't!"

"Then?"

"Alright if you must know what's going on in my pathetic little world I'll tell you. This is about as embarrassing as it gets… you must swear to tell no one! Joan, I, I, I just had an adolescent dream!"

Joan smirked. "So does this mean you're nearly self-sufficient, and as soon as you learn how to cook I'm supposed to pack my things and get the hell out of here?"

"Very funny. This is really embarrassing. I'm nearly fifty-five and just did something that's the domain of a pimpled teenager."

He walked by her to the bedroom and climbed under the covers. Joan followed, and stood looking down at him with an odd expression on her face. "You were screwing *me* in your sleep weren't you?"

"Geeze, I thought dreams were supposed to be private."

"And you were kissing my nipples though my shirt and going really slow and gentle and then you..." She looked at George waiting for an answer as he nodded an incredulous affirmative. *How could she know all this?*

"But I was asleep out in the truck when I had my... adolescent dream – that's what woke me up. I wasn't even in the house with you."

Joan looked stunned. "I don't know if I should feel violated, but I think I consented didn't I?" Then she smiled and giggled. "So, how many people can say: 'I hope my dream was as good for you as it was for me?'"

"You mean you...?" George asked hesitantly.

"No fuss, no muss! It was – you were – great!" Joan sealed the compliment with a kiss and put her head on his chest. "Next time you want to have me in your sleep I would appreciate a little more foreplay or a romantic dinner. Just think, in a dream you could really go virtually over board, and it wouldn't cost you a red cent! If this is what *The Sight* is, bring it on, honey."

They laughed together in amazement. It was so good to laugh.

Once they got past all of the silly stuff there was a realization that something both incredible and beautifully healing had happened.

George smiled at Joan's invitation to "bring it on."

But the smile fell slack on his face as he floated into currents of worry. Joan's welcoming invitation to what *The Sight* had to offer would, of course, differ from the full reality. The chasm dividing things imagined from things manifested was a growing theme in George's life. And it was something he feared.

8

Questions

They slept late and secure in one another's arms. The emotional roller coaster of the previous night had drained them both. It was almost noon when the phone rang causing Joan to jump out of bed.

"That'll be Jim!" She disappeared down the hall, and George snoozed. Sometime later, he felt her crawl back into bed and put her head on his chest while her hands went everywhere. Then everything went everywhere. What a wonderful way to wake up.

When they finally stumbled down the hall for coffee a couple of hours later, George remembered that Jim had called.

"What did Jim want?"

"I asked him to do a search on New World Developments."

"You what?"

"So far, all he's found is that New World Developments is owned by a larger company called Fairchild Environmental and he's having a hell of a time trying to get any dirt on them – he keeps getting wads of glowing promotional stuff."

"So is that as far as it goes?"

"No. He said he thought their mainframe was at their head office in Richmond, Virginia, and was running a program looking for an access PIN, but it was going to take a while"

"I think he's part silicon."

"Do you think New World or Fairchild Environmental, or whatever else they might be called; are the people who bought Billy's farm?"

"Could be."

"So how many acres are we talking here?"

The new detectives-in-love postulated over toast and coffee. They finally showered and hopped in the Fargo for a little information gathering in town. Joan was so quick of mind that George realized how little of his brain he used teaching history. Being a specialist of the past tense, he thought, required much less mental agility. It was a more laborious post mortem way of thinking, a genius of retrospect, which, in the real world, is somewhat of an oxymoron. If she was right, over four hundred acres were of interest to someone who was paying pretty big money for some fairly rundown farms. Usually when a company pays big money for something there has to be the potential for even bigger money at the other end. The question was; bigger money from what?

Mr. Moss's death possibly factored in, and maybe even the broken desk as well. Burglars had left a few thousand dollars in cash, so what the heck were they after? George and Joan quizzed like Holmes and Watson, interchanging roles all the way into town. Joan seemed to think that revenge might provide a welcome distraction from grief. It worked for periods of time, then it would slam George over the head again. He'd gasp for air in the middle of entertaining an unrelated thought. Joan was beginning to know where he went in those moments, when his eyes had the "out to lunch" look. She had seen him slide into that pit of separation and loss repeatedly over the last couple of days, and appeared through repetition to be a little less threatened by it.

For a real whiff of grief, George would play back the funeral parlour memory footage to look at his father's body while accompanying the images with the saddest song he could conjure. It was as though going to that painful moment took him closer to a time when his dad was alive. George returned from all of those dark places with only the pain and emotional fatigue of the journey. He had to quit going there. It hurt too much. It was becoming apparent that one could never understand death, only become conditioned to it. Like a rat in a maze, George realized he too would soon cease the journey to those places of painful thought where there was no cheese.

Once in town, they waited for the Fargo to sputter for a couple of minutes in front of the old town hall before it finally gave up.

The huge limestone block structure looked smaller and cleaner than George remembered – likely from sand blasting or an acid wash. They hauled open the tall oak doors and entered. According to the signage, the County Records office was in the basement. They found the business office at the end of a well lit corridor of large cleaned, newly pointed foundation stones on one side and various office doors on the other.

Behind an oak and hunter green Formica counter were four or five computer terminals and an attractive young woman who looked up from one of them as the strangers approached. Near the back of the room was a pretty stern- looking little guy who glared through two beady eyes set in a shiny, bald, head. It was a confrontational look that said, "Well look here, important people from the city who are expecting us to drop everything we're doing."

George had never met the man, but with so much attitude being exuded, he immediately didn't like him. As kids, Billy and George used to call guys like that, fist-magnets. It was a face somebody was going to hit. Fortunately, the attractive young woman got up to serve them.

"Yes, may I help you?"

"We're looking for some information on real estate transactions." The fist-magnet shot up from his desk and headed over at a quick pace talking loud and officiously as he approached.

"I'll take this, Barbara. The data on the road allowances is ready for you to put together for the executive committee meeting tonight." The young woman, who they now knew was Barbara, turned and gave the man a rather puzzled look as she returned to her desk.

"I'm John Speeks, town clerk. How can I help you?"

"Well Mr. Speeks, we'd like some information on a couple of real estate transactions, in particular the name of the purchaser or new owner." Speeks looked at George sternly.

"I'm sorry Mr. Moss but that information is confidential."

A look of disbelief swept across Joan's face. "Mr. Speeks, how long have you been clerk here?" His curt answer was immediate.

"I don't know of what concern that is to you Miss."

Speeks obviously didn't know that one shouldn't talk down to Joan Parks. Patricia Sandfield hadn't got that far in her gossip, or perhaps Mr. Speeks hadn't had his head buffed lately. George saw the storm clouds, and leaned back to get out of harm's way.

"Well, I think it might concern everyone in this town that their clerk doesn't know the law," Joan retorted. "Once real estate transactions are completed the names of those involved are for the public record!"

Barbara was grinning from ear to ear. Speeks, on the other hand was beet-red. It was clear he was used to talking down to the locals. The tables had turned and, oh pain of all pain, in front of Barbara his subordinate. Add to the mix that the man was an obvious consummate sexist. He must have felt even more pain at being corrected by a woman, *a woman*, for God's sake! The only thing that made George feel bad was Speeks would probably take his anger out on Barbara.

Speeks offered a lame excuse about some backlog of work, and that he would phone with the information when time permitted.

Once outside George saw Patricia Sandfield at her usual post peeking through the blinds at passers by. Joan was seething.

"What an asshole!" she spat.

"Hey, nobody's perfect," George smirked.

"He has no backlog of work," Joan snapped. "He was just being an asshole. And why would anyone versed in municipal law, as he surely must be, try to keep public information from us? That makes him an asshole with something to hide!"

Joan hadn't noticed but he had also called George, Mr. Moss, which struck George as odd, having never met the man in his life.

They hopped in the truck and Joan continued to vent all the way to County Hospital. George hoped that maybe Millie might have some useful gossip. She perked up when they walked in but she looked like hell. Small talk out of the way, George got down to business.

"Millie, do you know what's going on with the Dobson place?"

"I believe Elida sold it to them real estate developer people after she moved into that senior's place."

"This, whatever it is, just keeps getting bigger," Joan muttered.

"Do you know what those real estate people call themselves?" George asked.

"No, but your father did. He told me the day he died they were after his place as well and had made him some kind of big offer. Something about wanting to build beautiful country executive homes out there."

"Millie, what did Mr. Dobson die of?"

"Oh, he had a heart attack. T'was awful. Elida had gone to town with a couple of the girls to play euchre at her sister's. When she came home she found him in the barn. Old Doc Harris said he must have died shortly after she left. He'd been lying there stone cold dead for three or four hours. Elida said he was still holdin' his chest."

George nodded at the confirmation of his suspicions and Millie's jaw dropped.

"Oh, my Lord, you've had *The Sight*! Did ya see it happen before it did? Did ya see poor old Ernie die in some kinda premonition?"

Joan looked at Millie, then at George. Both waited for an answer.

"No," George said evenly, "I didn't see Ernie die, but for some reason I think I know how he died – the same way my father did."

"My Lord, George. I thought you was done with *The Sight*. Yer Daddy said you'd sorta lost the knack of it."

The knack of it. The words sounded odd to George. Maybe he was getting good at it... or maybe it was getting good at him. He was certainly becoming aware of its shortcomings and would soon learn distance was one of them.

9

Have a Nice Day

Jim sat perplexed, head in hands, staring at his computer. Fairchild Environmental represented a bit of a challenge. Jim had found them all right. He had gone to their website and read their sensational promotional material, but the password for their mainframe was elusive.

He began by running names related to their other companies like the names of every last explorer connected with the New World. This seemed like a reasonable place to start for a real estate company called New World Developments.

It was when he went back to their promotional page that he had an idea. He found that the owners were two brothers who had started the company seemingly from thin air. Jim linked to a university library computer and started perusing old newspapers. The brothers' business histories were fairly blank before the formation of the company in 1989. The Peroni family had lived in the area for years. The father had a small trucking firm – one truck – and there were the usual rumours of mob ties due to the Italian surname. During the '70s, when every ethnicity had an anti-defamation league, the mob connection rumours began to dry up.

The sons took over the company from their father and boom; it grew overnight with a mysterious infusion of capital. The youngest brother Lou had a degree in business from a small lack-lustre college. The older of the two, Benito, had worked alongside his father, married young, and had two daughters, Carmen and Rosalie. Jim ran the daughters' names and every variation. Nothing. He searched for Benito's wife's name and found a 1975 wedding announcement: "Christina Mary Dunford and Benito Peter Peroni to be wed." He ran her name, and once again no luck. Jim noticed the girls and mother's initials collectively were CCR and tried that combination once again to negative results. On a whim,

Jim dug up a list of CCR, (Creedence Clearwater Revival) hit songs and started running them when there was a knock on the door.

"Hi hun. Say cheese! Better than that, show me some skin." Randy, Jim's significant other, burst through the door with his new 8mm video camera running and a plate of fruit, cheese and crackers. "So, I brought the appetizers – what's for dins?"

Jim's face said it all. He had been so immersed in his computer search that he had forgotten all about dinner.

Randy looked crest-fallen. "I've been looking forward to this all day, and you haven't made a thing have you? How do you think that makes me feel?'

"I'm sorry Randy. Joan called and she and George seem to be going over some rough ground. I'm doing her a little favour."

"I'm sick of that bitch. If I didn't know better I'd think you were turning into a common breeder."

Jim affectionately held Randy's face and kissed him. "Why don't I just make one of my big Caesar salads and we'll go light tonight?"

Their love for one another was abundant. With a little frolicking out of the way the mighty Caesar was begun. In short order the salad was ready, the table set, the candles lit and... the computer beeped.

"No way!" Jim ran over and there it was, *Proud Mary*. Ben Peroni's wife's middle name, and with a CCR handle – what a fluke! He was in. Randy looked on while Jim got totally lost. Once he was in, he started typing furiously. Randy gave up, knowing full well that when Jim was computer-occupied there was no fighting it.

"Don't worry about me, I'll eat, tidy up, grow a beard and live a lonely life waiting for you, you bastard." He grabbed a little salad and started reading the newspaper while Jim worked.

Jim was looking at all kinds of corporate shells and holding companies. Fairchild Environmental looked huge: It owned companies all over the U.S. and Canada, having grown from nothing in a miraculously short period of time. He tried to enter the company's financial page, but his computer kept requesting "PIN." After five or six tries of re-entering Proud Mary, a large happy face filled the screen with the message: "HAVE A NICE DAY!"

Jim knew his presence had been detected at Fairchild or at least by some kind of security software. Worried about a trace, he immediately shut down his computer and considered changing over to his cell modem to search for the PIN he needed.

"Randy, can you go get me some smokes?"

"Buy em' yourself 'puter boy. It's bad enough I have to eat dinner by myself, I'm not going to be your little gopher!"

Jim grabbed his wallet and shot out of the door, slamming it behind him, angrier at his search being discovered than at Randy's refusal to run errands

"Temper, temper." Randy muttered.

The computer made an odd noise. Randy thought nothing of it; he was so engrossed in the article he was reading. The screen had come back on with the big yellow happy face. It had not shut down or rather some kind of transmitted program had not allowed it to.

Jim ran down three flights of stairs and flew out the back door into the cool night air. The alley behind the building smelled of ripe garbage from a large industrial container that needed to be carted off to someplace else – and soon. Jim headed toward Lee's Variety, chuckling to himself over the stupidity of smoking as his breath hit the cool night air in bursts of vapour. Cigarettes would simply allow him the same reassuring visual but indoors and at a greater cost to his lungs. Rounding the corner, he saw Mr. Lee through the store window and waved.

Mr. Lee had emigrated from Korea to the U.S. in search of a better life, or just a life. Although it was an improvement over what he had, America revealed a disappointing prejudice from more than a few customers toward immigrants. It confounded him to be in a country founded by immigrants, yet prejudiced toward immigrants. Being a gay man, Jim was no stranger to prejudice himself, and so these two diverse life experiences had served to create not only a predisposition to tolerance but to friendship. Whenever Jim came in, Mr. Lee felt like a neighbour, an equal, a friend and – thank you, thank you, thank you, a fellow human being.

"A pack of Camels please, Mr. Lee."

"Hey, Jeemy, house eet hanging?" Mr. Lee inquired as he grabbed a pack of Camels. He began to enter the price into his cash register when it jammed. He tapped the top of it lightly and still nothing.

"Sum of a bee!"

"Reboot, Mr. Lee. You may need a power surge to get that old antique moving again."

"Antique! Thees no antique, onry five yeeah oh."

"In computer land five years is about four generations, Mr. Lee. It's old alright, at least a great great-grandfather"

A dark coloured sedan pulled up across the road from the front of Jim's apartment. In the passenger seat was Robert J. Douglas, meticulously manicured and dressed. His conservative thousand-dollar suits were a disarming camouflage for a trade far more sinister than anyone might have expected. For years he had made little problems go away for the Peroni family.

He spoke softly into his cell-phone.

"What was the exact address again, Joseph?"

On the other end of the phone, Joseph, a young computer dweeb sat at the main terminal in a high-tech systems room. On his screen a light flashed: "LINE TRACE" and underneath it...

JAMES GRAYSON
2350 MARKET STREET
APT. 304.

He read it out to Douglas, who scanned the numbers on buildings. "Beautiful, just across the road. How far did he get, Joseph?"

"He spent some time in acquisitions and personnel then attempted to move over to financial records. He's not in yet but he's very good. Somehow, he got Mr. Peroni's password but not his PIN number. I have control of his terminal. Shall I shut down and trace erase now that the location has been acquired?"

"Yes, Joseph, and I understand there's a nasty virus going around?"

"I understand sir, yes sir, very nasty." Joseph chuckled as he loaded the requested program and hit send.

Behind Randy, the screen on Jim's computer started filling up with numbers and signs that eliminated the happy face line by line.

"Done."

"Good work, Joseph."

Douglas flipped his cell-phone shut, and got out of the car. He looked up and down the quiet street, then, crossed it with a purposeful stride. He turned up the walkway, into the building and up the stairs to apartment 304. Two steel pins were removed from his pocket and the simple door lock gave way.

Randy assumed Jim had returned and didn't lower the thin partition of the newspaper's entertainment section separating him from the intruder. "Well, that was fast Mr. Nicotine Addict," Randy said, without looking up.

Douglas walked right over to him and removed a loaded syringe from his pocket.

An eerie silence caused Randy to lower his paper, look up and see the intruder advancing towards him. As Randy opened his mouth to speak, he was pinned against the back of the couch with brutal force. His shirtsleeve was ripped up and a needle rammed into his arm.

Douglas was already applying pressure and a styptic pencil to the puncture mark on his victim's arm while Randy clutched his chest gasping in agony for the pitiful few seconds remaining in his life. Tears appeared in his eyes as he mouthed the word "Why?" The look on his face was a mixture of excruciating pain and a curious sadness in the realization that he was dying for no reason he was aware of.

When the look froze, Douglas patted him on the head, pleased that Randy's pathetic little struggle had not caused him much physical exertion. "Goodnight Mr. Grayson." He double-checked Randy's arm, wiping off the white residue left from the styptic pencil, pulled the sleeve down and fastened the button. After a glance around the room he walked over to the computer where the happy face and any computer memory were both disappearing line by line. In fact that piece of silicon technology would never work again. His expression was one of reserved self-congratulation at such a swift, effective operation.

Jim didn't see the man sitting in the dark car parked across the street as he sucked on the last of a Camel.

He threw the butt into the gutter and started up the front walk. Before he could pull the door open, Douglas breezed past him and smiled. "Have a nice day."

"Have a nice evening, you mean," Jim responded, but Douglas was already down the walk and stepping on to the street.

Jim started up the stairs to the apartment when it dawned on him. "Have a nice.... oh no, no way!" He ran up the stairs and stopped dead at his open door. He knew he had slammed it when he left. If you tried to close it quietly it would swing open, which was why Jim had been pestering the superintendent to fix the thing for the last week. He had a sinking feeling as he crossed the threshold into his apartment and that feeling sank farther down than the limits of his imagination.

Randy's body sat sprawled on the sofa, paper still clutched in one hand, with an awful expression frozen on his face in a perfect stillness known only to the dead.

Jim's eyes filled with tears as he put his head on his lover's chest. He frantically searched for a pulse in the wrist, then the carotid artery. He tried mouth-to-mouth, but was too overcome with an emotion that quickly evolved into the dry heaves. His peripheral vision caught some movement on his computer screen. The remnants of a yellow happy face were being replaced by gibberish approaching the bottom of the monitor. Stumbling to his feet, he moved toward the computer, remembering he'd shut it off. Glancing out the window, he saw a figure that made his skin crawl. Douglas, looking up from the open door of the dark car, was about to get in when his eyes met Jim's. His stare was evil personified and probed deep into Jim's fear, as if to savour it.

"Well, my goodness, Stanley," Douglas told his driver, "it seems I have a little more tidying up to do."

While Douglas strutted back to the building at a brisk pace, his driver double-checked the position of his mirrors to make sure he could observe anyone who might come down the street.

Jim's heart was pounding so hard with fear he could hardly think. *"Shit, shit, shit!"* He ran past Randy's 8mm video camera on the antique wooden chair by the door, then stopped in his tracks. In a moment of clarity he turned the camera on and focused it on Randy, covering all but the lens with Randy's jacket. Randy's jacket... it smelled of him.

"Oh my God, this isn't happening!" He pushed his nose into the jacket as if to say farewell and saw the end of Randy's key-chain sticking out of the pocket.

He grabbed the keys and bolted out of the door. His body, heavily uncoordinated by the gravity of fear, stumbled almost drunkenly up the stairs to the door of Randy's apartment. Jim frantically tried one key then another, then another. Nothing seemed to enter into the damn lock until finally, a fit.

Closing the door quietly behind him, flipping all of the dead bolts into place, he dialled 911 and pushed a pathetic wheeze through a larynx that barely resembled the sound of a human being let alone his own voice. The voice of Jim Grayson was buried under a sea of adrenaline and some other weird secretions that sure weren't of any use in the survival department.

"Hello, I'm calling from 2350 Market Street, apartment 304. Someone is trying to get into my apartment. Help me! Help me!" Jim hung up and his heart pounded so loud he grabbed a cushion from the couch and held the large sound baffle to his chest. Even restrained breathing felt potentially dangerous at the thought of the door bursting open at any second with a ticket for Randy's current tour.

One floor down, gun ready, Douglas burst into 304 and swept the room. He saw a picture on the fridge. It was Jim and Randy at a Christmas party.

"Well, well... we have a girlfriend. Ah yes of course, the nicotine addict you were expecting." He ripped the picture from the fridge, walked over to Randy, double-checked his pulse and then patted Randy on the head again.

Being the thorough individual he was, Douglas pulled Randy's sleeve up and checked the arm once more for any telltale styptic pencil or blood before rolling the sleeve back down and leaving.

As he calmly surveyed the hall listening for anything unusual, his cell-phone quietly vibrated in the pocket of his jacket. It was Stanley, who, at that moment, was looking out his windshield at two police cruisers approaching from the south end of the street.

"We have visitors in matching party suits out front."

"Thank you so much for your call, Stanley. I'll be right out. Meet me one block south, one block west."

"Yes sir." Stanley pulled away slowly, drawing no attention to himself.

Douglas moved coolly down the stairs and out the back door into the alley. For one who appeared to move so leisurely he disappeared in the blink of an eye and without a sound.

Upstairs, Jim looked through an open corner of curtain as the sedan pulled slowly past the unsuspecting cruisers. He followed it down the block where it made a right turn and pulled over long enough for a man to get in. As the car disappeared into the night, the two police officers began moving up the sidewalk toward the front door.

Jim flew into action, raced down the stairs to his apartment, grabbed Randy's video camera and made it back to the stairwell just as the police were coming up. He quietly went up to the next landing and held his breath as they headed toward his apartment.

Once the fire door shut, Jim took two steps at a time down three flights of stairs and ejected out of the back door into the cool night.

Tears streamed down his face as his lungs gasped for air. Randy, his lover, a man who would never have hurt a living thing, was dead because of him and his damned computer! He knew his life was in danger now.

He could trust no one in a world that could take such a gentle life so coldly. How would they know that Jim wasn't responsible for the murder? Was he strangled or poisoned? Police would have curious circumstantial evidence. Who would ever believe that somebody broke into Jim's apartment and killed Randy in the few minutes it took to get a pack of cigarettes? It just didn't make any sense.

Jim felt he needed to vanish. The police would involve the press. The press would make hiding impossible.

His mind scrambled in a million directions looking for any survival plan, and then it came to him – his home away from home, his only avenue for survival, and his weapon of choice.

10

Pulling on Threads

Joan and George sat sipping coffee in the Deluxe Restaurant when Ann breezed in and sat down. After the small talk ran its course there was a strained silence.

"So this isn't just social is it?" Ann asked, suspecting there was a reason for George's apparent discomfort.

Joan looked at George with concern about this stranger before her.

George smiled reassuringly. "I'd trust Ann with my life, Joan."

Ann's expression changed, instantly matching the severity of tone. "This sounds too juicy for Patricia Sandfield."

Joan looked at her with an affectionate smile then got down to business. "Do you know anything about the company that bought the Dobson's' or the McDonough's' places?"

"Just what Dwayne has told me."

"Dwayne?"

"Dwayne's my husband, and I'm proud to say one of our local town councillors. I've heard rumblings about some developer who wants to build executive homes or the like and a new baseball park, to boot."

"And where are the executives going to come from, Ann? The closest city is at least a good ninety minutes away. Could anyone in Lincoln afford one of these new executive homes?"

The logic swept over Ann's face. "You know I'd never thought about that. Doesn't make much sense does it? So what's goin' on?"

"That's what we'd like to know," George said. "We do know this: They want the property bad enough to play dirty and if our hunch is right the same people who bought McDonough's and Dobson's made an offer on my father's farm before he died. Now they've made an offer to me."

"What do you mean by playin' dirty?"

"I can't say right now Ann; only that we need to be very discreet."

Ann's expression changed to a knowing concern. "You've had *The Sight* haven't you?"

"I don't know which is more spooky," Joan interjected. "A guy who sees weird stuff or a whole town of people who know he's seeing it. What the hell is this – the village of the damned?"

"I knew it!" Ann gloated for a beat, and then continued. "Look, George what say you tell me the details in your own time and meanwhile I'll go shake Dwayne's tree a little for some info which, knowing you, was what you were about to ask me to do anyway."

"You read me like an open book, Ann."

"Well, your face is an open book, George, and always has been. I've got three mouths to feed, I'll call ya tonight." Ann got up, smiled and headed off with a youthful bounce in her step.

George was deep inside his head as usual while they walked to the truck and got in.

"Are you where I think you are?" Joan inquired, sensing distress.

George winced. *Damn my face.* "Oh, I dunno," he replied, "I guess I'm missing my father, but…" Tears welled up uncontrollably. "Even in his death he drives me nuts. I would like to find some time to deal with this grief, but no, that would be too normal! I have to be bloody Sherlock Holmes with my father barely cold in the ground."

Joan just stroked the back of his head with her delicate fingers. George started the truck and the tears subsided. He was growing tired of tears. He was reaching some kind of plateau where tears were beginning to annoy him. He didn't want the attention they brought or the salty dampness of self-indulgence.

He steered the truck toward home. Patricia's blinds were open and of course she watched them pass by. She had her hands in someone's hair and her probes as deep into their private life as she could dig.

Mr. Brown was loading groceries into his car reaching into his cart like he was touching up the makeup on some stiff in a coffin. As George and Joan passed, Brown saw the Fargo out of the corner of his eye and turned respectfully with that programmed subservient demeanour, smiling that sympathetic smile. George waved and once out of sight, he and Joan burst out laughing. It didn't matter that they were having a laugh at someone else's expense – it was a laugh. What a surreal character Brown was, kind of a cross between something Salvador Dali might dream up and one of those Don Martin cartoon guys from *Mad Magazine* whose feet folded over curbs. As George was beginning to enjoy the moment the old Fargo started to sputter.

"Oh, for Christ's sake! What now!" They coasted to the side of the road and George got out to have a look. Joan looked to her right and her laughter muted with an instant realignment of thought. George saw her through the crack between the hood and the engine and thought he should ask. "What is it?"

"This mail box."

"Yeah?"

"It says Mel Harris, M.D."

"Yeah, so?"

"So do you have something you need to talk to Doc Harris about?"

George knew they were at Doc Harris's place but had chosen out of habit to ignore it. OK, the Fargo had stopped because – well, because it just seems to do that whenever he's supposed to stop and smell the roses. These roses, however, were ones he feared: There were details about his father's death to be had and it would have been Doc Harris's signature on the death certificate.

George hopped back in and turned the engine over but it wasn't going anywhere.

"It won't go will it, George? Not until you are finished doing what you are supposed to do here, right?"

"Probably not."

"Well?"

"Well, what?"

"Well, let's go talk to Doc Harris or we'll be here all night while you try to avoid what you're supposed to be doing."

Joan was so practical, coolly assessing even outrageous options in order to determine a course of action. Because the truck was their transportation, she concluded they should see the Doc as a way of achieving their goal, which at the moment was to get home.

"Doesn't this stuff spook you at all, Joan?"

"To be honest, yes, it gives me the creeps, but I also find it fascinating. I've never experienced things like this in my life. You on the other hand, have lived with this stuff since you were a kid and still you choose to ignore it. Either you're really smart or you're a..."

George knew Joan had been pondering for a day or two and there it was... a conclusion.

"Go ahead, Joan; finish your thought. I'm either really smart or ..."

"A coward."

"Hmm, interesting. I've never thought of myself as coward before."

"You're not mad at me for saying that?"

"Mad? Hell, no. I'm just getting a bit cold. Now should we talk to Doc Harris or do you want me to sit on your analytical couch all night?"

George started to walk down the pathway to the Harris's Victorian home when suddenly he felt a sharp pain. He swung around and couldn't believe it; Joan had just kicked him soundly in the backside.

"What was that for?"

"I have a pretty heavy thought and you slough it off like it's nothing. Does that mean you don't take me seriously? Am I just some young piece of ass to you? Is that it?"

"Joan, this is not the place...." But her look said otherwise, so he responded." Oh, alright. I would be a liar if I said you didn't have a great ass and it is indeed younger than my sorry mid-life butt, but just a piece of ass? Hardly!"

"Well, do you have any thoughts about what I just said?"

"Can I get back to you on that? I have a fair list of things to think about right now with some of the biggest bloody items I've ever had to deal with in my life! Why is it when a guy is in it up to his eyeballs a woman figures that's the time to rub salt into open wounds and then offer that old faithful question of insecurity. "Am I just a piece of ass?" Is that like some kind of female trump card designed to make me feel guilty for making love to you? And is that manipulated guilt designed to give you some kind of upper hand so I might patronize you or engage in a conversation I don't want or need at the moment."

"This is about offering me the common courtesy of respect."

"Oh great, now the "R" word! How about some respect for a son who has just lost his father for Christ's sake? How about some kind of prioritizing given the circumstances?"

"What circumstances, George? That you aren't who I thought you were?" George suddenly felt sorry for Joan, and not himself. Her boat was rocking and she was afraid someone might fall out. This wasn't the usual "just a piece of ass" or "respect" argument. George was about to answer her a little more sympathetically when another voice chimed in.

"Are you two going to stand on my path embarrassing me with filthy language and rude talk about your love life, or are you intending on coming in?"

They looked in the direction of the frantic and hushed voice and found Mrs. Harris peeking out of her open door.

Joan went instantly red in the face. Mrs. Harris was the most dignified looking and proper woman Lincoln had to offer. Her expression was a combination of embarrassment and disgust. They had crossed a few of her lines in the sand. Chatter of a personal nature was for padded rooms, not her front yard, and "dirty" language was a no-no. She frantically signalled the combatants to come in, like a mother scolding her children. George and Joan sheepishly obeyed and the door was closed quietly behind them.

"I'm so sorry, Mrs. Harris" Joan cowered.

Mrs. Harris gave Joan the once over and scowled. "Don't you apologize for George's short-comings, dear. George, an introduction might be appropriate at this time. We weren't introduced at the funeral."

"I'm sorry, Mrs. Harris. This is Joan."

"That's nice, George; and does Joan have a last name?"

"Parks, Joan Parks."

Mrs. Harris smiled politely. "Ms. Parks nice to meet you." She shook Joan's hand and then turned to the stairs.

"Mel! We have guests, Mel!"

She looked back, exhausted from having to raise her voice. "Excuse me for calling so loudly but Mel is going deaf as a post, and my arthritis is too bad to chase up and down those stairs after him. Please come into the parlour."

She walked ahead. The grandfather clock clicked away in the corner. As a child, George had often sat on one of the wingback chairs on either side of the fireplace while his mother and Mrs. Harris drank tea on the big puffy floral sofa in front. He would get one cookie and a napkin, and sing little songs in his head to the rhythm of the clock for amusement. Their visits were usually mercifully short, and youngsters were expected to demonstrate self-control by sitting quietly when they should have been running outside.

When his mother died he ached to sit there and just listen to her talk to Mrs. Harris. The memory of her existence was something he often brought up from the cellar like a precious wine for special occasions. He sipped her smell, the sweetness of her voice, the soft skin on the backs of her hands and the way she purred when his father held her. George thought he smelled her perfume in the room and was sniffing at Mrs. Harris before he realized what he was doing.

"George!" Joan looked mortified

"I'm sorry, Mrs. Harris I thought I smelled my mother's perfume. I was just recalling our visits here when she was alive."

Mrs. Harris's shocked expression gave way to sadness.

"She was a grand lady your mother. And I..." Doc Harris entered the room looking a little unkempt. His shirt was hanging out and he was sporting a major bed-head.

"Well, well, if it isn't the nutty professor. I guess I should be calling you Dr. Moss," he cranked.

"Being as I am the one with the real doctorate degree that might be courteous, Doc," George said returning fire with a light volley. The old man's face captured a disgruntled expression for a brief moment before moving on.

"Well, you look a proper gentleman but you're still as impudent as ever, Moss." Doc snapped. Mrs. Harris wasn't about to let things escalate and she cut in.

"Well, at least he *looks* a proper gentleman, Mel. Look at you, you're an absolute sight." She fussed over him, tucking in his shirt, and attempting to push down a clump of hair, determined to stand up.

"Please have a seat, and I'll fix some tea."

"We don't wish to impose, Mrs. Harris," Joan said softly.

The silver tea service was out in a flash, four cookies, four napkins and Royal something-or-other china cups with curly ornate handles that were so delicate they required the fingers of a jeweller. They were designed in such a way as to ensure anyone who tried to actually drink out of the fragile things had no alternative but to stick up their pinky like an interior decorator. They sat, pinkies quietly air-fencing, until Mrs. Harris broke the silence.

"We are both so very sorry about your father, George." Doc said, voice cracking with emotion. "He was a good friend to me. There will never be another like him to walk this Earth." His eyes fogged and George went with him, beating him to the first tear to drop. Mrs. Harris handed George the napkin he hadn't been using, while Doc attempted to speak through emotional impediments.

"I don't imagine you came over here to sit and blubber with me," Doc said, focusing purpose.

"Doc, I know this is going to sound strange, but it was you, who went out to the farm and pronounced him dead, wasn't it?"

Doc nodded. "A trip I wish I never had to make. Billy McDonough found him and called me straight away."

"Did you see any evidence of foul play? Any marks on the ankles or wrists? A puncture mark in the left arm, perhaps?"

Mrs. Harris started fanning herself. "Oh, dear!"

"Well I wasn't really looking for anything like that, George. Your father had some ticker trouble for about a year and I had prescribed a nitro-patch for him. Given the family history and how your grandfather dropped, I assumed he'd had a massive coronary."

"Caused by what, Doc?"

"What the hell is that supposed to mean? Old age, cholesterol, fatty deposits, family history, the usual... I don't know! I didn't think desecrating the body with an autopsy would turn up anything I didn't already know from the tests that we did a year ago. And to be honest, I don't think I could have done an autopsy on your father, he was too close to me."

"Sorry, Doc. What about Ernie Dobson then?" The Doc looked a little shaken.

"Ernie Dobson?"

"A perfectly healthy man drops dead out of the blue."

"Well, Dr. Moss," he said sarcastically." I did do an autopsy on Ernie – for his brother – and found no evidence of anything other than natural causes."

"A heart attack?"

"Well, yes, but given his age... "

"Did you do any blood work?"

"Look, I don't know what you are on about here, but if you must know, I did do blood work on Ernie and found nothing out of the ordinary."

"Damn!" It was out before George realized, and Mrs. Harris ever on guard flashed the evil eye for cursing in her house. The Doc looked at George intensely.

"You suspect foul play, George?"

"Well, maybe I'm just a little stressed and my mind is imagining things. Thanks Doc, you've been very... "

Mrs. Harris grabbed her husband's arm. "Oh, Mel, he's *seen*. He's got *The Sight* like his father. You've *seen* haven't you George?"

Joan thought Mrs. Harris, of all people, would be on the side of sanity, but here was more confirmation that Joan was quickly becoming a minority in the area of reason.

"Don't tell me *you* believe in this stuff, too?" Joan inquired.

Mrs. Harris sat up straight, regaining her composure. "Let's just say, Ms. Parks, we've come to respect it. George's father was right too many times about too many things he had no earthly way of knowing. He was such an honest and gentle man by nature, one could be confident George Moss would never lie about such things."

They left the Doc a little upset. He seemed very disturbed that George had suggested both Ernie and his father might have met a premature and assisted end. He was also feeling his personal relationship might have obscured the inquisitive scientist, or at least tainted his usual meticulous sense of responsibility.

Outside, of course, the truck started first try. Joan and George sat in silence all the way home as thoughts percolated.

When Ann had arrived home, Dwayne was on the couch; their two teenage sons sprawled on the floor, all eyes and minds glued to the basketball game. Chip bags and soda cans lay discarded on the coffee table and no one even looked her way as she entered the room.

"Dwayne, I need to speak to you." Dwayne didn't look up but offered an autonomic "Okay honey."

Ann went into the kitchen and then poked her head back into the room and raised her voice considerably: "Now!"

Barry, the eldest son, looked out from under a backwards baseball cap and cracked.

"Uh oh, look who's in the doghouse. From the Legend of Super Heroes it's… Captain Hen-Pecked."

Dwayne playfully pulled the cap off, whacked him over the head and put it on right way around. Barry grabbed for his dad's foot but Dwayne got away free and clear to the kitchen.

"Sit down, Dwayne – we need to talk." Ann's tone was more serious than usual.

"We'll clean up after the game, honey; I promise it's almost over."

"This isn't about the stupid game. Are the people who bought Dobson's the same people who bought McDonough's and also want the Moss place?"

Dwayne suddenly looked serious and closed the sliding kitchen door. "Just who have you been talking to, Ann?"

Ann looked at him with a disgusted look. "Oh no – you're mixed up in this thing somehow aren't you?"

Dwayne sighed impatiently. "Ann, this is none of your concern. The deal we've made will put money in the town coffers and continue to do so for years to come. These people are on the way up, and well connected politically. Plus, we get a new baseball park out of the deal."

"There are no executive homes are there?"

"Ann, this is council business. It's already a done deal at state level, and anyway, everyone will be clued in to some pretty good news at the environmental hearing in a couple of weeks."

"What environmental hearing, Dwayne? What's this all about? What are you not telling me?"

11

Up the Ante

George and Joan had just put the Fargo to bed and were walking into the house when the phone on the kitchen wall started ringing. "It's probably Ned Patterson," Joan groaned.

George picked up: "Hello?"

An odd silence was broken by a familiar voice. "George, if you know who I am, it's important that you only answer "yes." If the answer's no, put Joan on the line."

"Yes, I recognize your voice."

"Good. Go to a pay phone and call me on my cell." The instructions ended with a click and a dial tone. George hung up and started toward the door. Joan followed instinctively.

"Who was it?"

"Jim." They were now half-running across the driveway to the barn.

"So what did he want?"

"You know his cell number?"

"Of course."

"He wants us to call him from a pay phone."

"Why the hell do we have to call him from a pay phone?" Joan asked as she climbed in the truck after George.

"I've never heard him so serious and he was sniffing like he had a cold. No it's heavier than that. He's been crying."

"I hope he hasn't lost the Loblaw account."

"No, his distress was personal." It suddenly dawned on George. "He, he thinks our phone is tapped, that's why the pay phone."

"Tapped? Are you serious?"

"Yes, and there's something really dark I can't get a hold of."

"You're scaring me."

"I'm scared too, Joan."

By the time they got to the gas station, Joan's curiosity was gnawing at her. She jumped out of the Fargo and ran to the phone booth.

George caught up with her a moment later; she was already talking to a distraught Jim, whose voice was strained from crying.

"No!" Joan's face crumpled into a mass of wrinkles and tears.

"Randy's dead! They killed Randy!" Jim repeated. "They thought he was me and they killed him! They killed Randy!"

Joan swallowed hard. "Who killed Randy?"

Jim sighed. "I was into their mainframe. They must have been on to me long enough to get a fix and send a hit man. They meant to kill me but they killed Randy. They've killed Randy... It's my fault!"

"Who k ... ki ... killed Randy, Jim?" Joan's words were now barely discernable but Jim understood, and George felt his insides sink.

"Fairchild Environmental, New World Developments, whatever you want to call them."

"Oh, God." Joan was shaking as she handed the phone to George.

"Jim," George said soothingly, "I know this is hard, but how did Randy die?"

"I don't know," Jim said, sobbing uncontrollably.

"It's important, Jim. I believe they murdered my father and someone else out this way. Were there any apparent wounds?"

"What the hell do you think I am – some sort of Colombo or something? I'm a marketing researcher, a boring statistician, and I've just lost the love of my life... you insensitive..."

George winced, but pressed on: "Any bullet wounds or blood?"

"No, at least not that I could see."

"Oh Jim I'm so sorry I... "

"Fuck you Moss! If it wasn't for you Randy would be alive."

George looked for Joan and saw her squatting on the ground weeping and shivering. The kid in the gas station kiosk looked at the unfolding drama like he had front seats on *The Jerry Springer Show*. No way was what he was looking at real life or any type of life he could relate to. He checked the lock on his door; afraid the weeping phone-freaks might come over and rob him. George listened to Jim cry for a while and was about to speak when Jim's voice pushed out the words.

"I've got the killer on video."

"You what?"

"When he saw me in the window after he killed Randy I turned on the camera and hid upstairs. The sick bastard who came back for me made an appearance on Randy's video camera. I went back and got it before the cops came."

"Is there a clear shot of him"?

"Yes."

"Jesus, Jim, make copies! Where are you? Are you safe? Can they get to you?"

"Let's just say I'm at my home away from home. Joanie knows where. These guys are dirty, George; they were on to me way too fast. Is there a secure line where you are? I can fax or e-mail you what I get."

"What do you mean what you get?"

"I've been researching on-line for newspaper stuff and I'm looking for information on city and state files. They killed Randy. They're going down, George. These bastards are going down if it's the last thing I do."

George couldn't believe it: Jim was in shock but already working on a strategy for revenge. George started leafing through the phonebook.

"Jim, I'll find a secure fax line and call you right back."

George hung up, found the number he was looking for, and dialled.

"Ann, it's George. Do you have a fax machine? Well, what about at the store? Would you mind giving me that number and meeting us there in fifteen minutes?"

After calling Jim back with Ann's office fax number, George pretty well had to carry Joan to the truck. She was in a place of pain-soaked guilt, not so unfamiliar to him. It was all her fault for asking Jim to search New World a.k.a. Fairchild. Well, almost.

Some anger was now trickling back in George's direction. George was the man who, at the moment, she wished she had never bothered to pursue. He was the aging, complex old fella – old coward in her latest estimation – who had brought killers to the door of her business partner and friend. Why the hell couldn't she have stuck with someone her own age? Someone who passed the normalcy test with no weird family skeletons attached? Her demeanour and body language said it all, like a couple of stiff jabs to the ribs. George wished at that moment that he couldn't read her so well and longed for the welcome harbour of ignorance. Sure, in that harbour, one was occasionally aware of the ubiquitous danger in the raging seas beyond, but also the soothing contrast of the tranquil waters within.

Ann pulled up to the store in her rusting Taurus wagon as George helped a winded Joan out of the truck. Ann headed over smiling, until she saw Joan's face.

"What in heaven's name...?"

"Let's get inside," George interrupted, "and we'll tell you about it."

Ann helped George support Joan by her arms as they walked into the store. The office was tucked in the back of the shop and was appropriately cluttered. George recalled Ann had been a very messy teenager; her bedroom had been an unkempt nightmare. Opening a cupboard or closet had always prompted an avalanche of crumpled clothes. That mess had been a "god-send" the day her mother came home unexpectedly, causing George to seek some cover for his bare adolescent butt. He dove under a pile of dirty clothes and an old duvet on the floor on the far side of the bed. Her Mom had entered the room with a curious look to find Ann in bed alone calmly claiming to have a headache. She gave her a motherly peck on the cheek, found whatever it was that she forgot, and then roared back out of the driveway. George emerged from the pile of laundry, and Ann stared: They had never really seen each other naked before that moment. They always sort of slipped out of their things under the covers with eyes closed. But there he was with the problem of trying to get back to the bed without Ann seeing him. She refused to look away or let him back in bed.

She grabbed George by the privates; it was his first blowjob. Well, one couldn't really call it a blowjob. That was her intent and his wide-eyed expectation. She didn't really know how to do it even though she was acting like a confident old pro. But with George she didn't need any technique. It touched her lips and the damn thing went off like a gun with a hair trigger causing her to run out of the room and spit in the sink. George heard her gargling with mouthwash while he put his pants back on, ashamed of what he had done.

When she came back in the room, she was stark naked, smelling of Listerine and looking fabulous. She caught George staring at her breasts, smiled, quite aware of her power and just stood there letting him take it all in. Then she noticed his pants were back on and blurted out in a commanding tone: "Where do you think you're going? I want to look at you, too. Fair is fair!" George's pants were reluctantly off again, and she stared until he was uncontrollably erect. She stared for such a long time it was intentionally and extremely erotic. They stood; moved closer and stood some more, then stood so close they felt like they were touching even though we weren't. When they did touch, their skin was so hypersensitive in anticipation that everything felt magnified in an amazingly volatile and innocent exploration.

She had been forewarned. It's some of that stuff women talk about when they go off in pairs to washrooms. One of her friends, whose identity remains unknown to George, had counselled Ann in the ways of the first-time, two-second-wonder average adolescent male. George had been pegged for a first timer and Ann was told how to relieve him of that initial round so that he might be more useful to her own needs, which at that moment were only marginally greater than George's. He found out some months later, that was the day Ann had been planning to lose her virginity and had consulted the most knowledgeable of her peers in preparation. They made love all afternoon and the young sixteen-year old George Moss just couldn't believe that he was actually doing "it." *"It" was wonderful and so was the smoke afterward. I was a man, and felt definitively like one for the first time in my life. Some days the smell of cigarette smoke still puts a smile on my face. Some days...*

So, there they were in Ann's messy office. It came as no surprise to George that there was dirty laundry on the floor causing Ann to scurry around in an effort to make the place a little more presentable. There was a sheet of fax paper on the floor, and the machine was blinking for a refill. George saw the box of fax rolls and put a new one in. The phone rang about 20 seconds later, and the machine started spitting out more information from Jim. Joan snatched up the faxes in silence.

"Would someone mind giving me a clue?" Ann asked softly.

George cleared his throat. "Ann, a friend is faxing us some information on New World Developments and its parent company, Fairchild Environmental. They may have been responsible for killing a man – someone who was close to Joan."

"My Lord!" Ann exclaimed in disbelief.

George nodded. "What did you find out from your husband?"

"Well now, Dwayne seemed a little uptight about it all. But you were right, same company – New World whatever – has Dobson's place and a deal on McDonough's. And Dwayne knew they were bidding on your place."

George raised an eyebrow, making Ann a little defensive.

"George, Dwayne is many things but a crook isn't one of them. He's keen on some proposal for a new storage and state of the art re-cycling facility."

"Storage and re-cycling facility?"

"Yeah, you were right, about there being no executive homes to be built. Council has been meeting with these guys behind closed doors, in-camera. Council has already changed the zoning to allow for some kind of storage facility for what the company calls non-hazardous industrial waste. And in exchange for this re-zoning they're going to donate a million bucks for the creation of a baseball park and recreation centre."

Joan looked up from reading the faxes and asked: "Was this zoning change made public? Was it posted or printed in the paper?"

"Gee, I don't know," Ann replied. "It's the first I've heard about it."

"If they didn't run a public notice," Joan said forcefully, "they've already broken municipal law."

"And get a load of this," she added, tearing off a piece of fax paper.

The faxed document presented an uncritical view of Fairchild Environmental as a glowing American Dream story, a little company growing in leaps and bounds in the vanguard of recycling technology.

Ann read over George's shoulder for a moment then remembered something else. "Oh, and also... Dwayne said there's an environmental assessment hearing in a couple of weeks, and the state commissioner himself is coming. Dwayne says these fellas are connected enough in high places to make this a 'done deal' at state level. Council even had a call from the governor supporting Fairchild."

Joan shook her head in disbelief. "A hearing in two weeks?"

Ann nodded confirmation while the last page came through. It ended with the message: "Pick up on the next ring, -Jim."

Joan grabbed the handset on the first ring.

Sensing the two friends wanted to discuss Jim's loss in private, George turned to Ann with a question. "Who is this commissioner?"

"Sam Johnson," Ann answered. "You know, the former Senator? He got his cushy environmental commission appointment when he retired from the senate seat he held for twenty years."

George gripped Joan reassuringly on the shoulder. "Can I speak with Jim a minute?"

As Joan handed him the phone, Ann instinctively reached out her arms. She held Joan while she shook and shivered then unfortunately muttered: "First Mr. Dobson, then George's Dad, and now Randy. These people are sick."

Ann couldn't believe what she had just heard. George couldn't believe what Joan had blurted out, but got right to business with Jim.

"Jim, these boys have to be nailed carefully and publicly. There's an environmental hearing here in a couple of weeks. Can you get me every bit of information on Fairchild, their owners, and former Senator Sam Johnson, who is now the head of the state environmental commission? We should also figure out some way to get press and television coverage. The governor seems to vouch for these guys so there could be some dirt on him, as well"

"I'm on it."

"Be careful, Jim. We can't tip our hand or we could all end up dead. These people don't seem to place any value on any life except as it pertains to their own needs."

"I sure as hell wasn't far enough into their mainframe to warrant what they did to Randy! They've got to be sitting on some huge house of cards. Don't worry about me, George. I have an idea. They will never complete a trace on me again now that I know how they play. Keep this fax line free and loaded with paper."

There was a measure of comfort in Jim's expertise with computers, and George had faith in his assurance no trace could be done. As George handed the phone back to Joan, he found Ann staring at him.

"Is it true about Ernie and your Dad?"

George nodded a stoic affirmative. Ann looked like she had the wind knocked out of her. Her look was a composite of disbelief and fear. She felt like she was in a bad Steven Segal movie where people were dropping like flies for business reasons. The enormity of the scenario was overwhelming. There would be no tall, knock-kneed geek, with sophomoric soliloquies and Buddhist leanings to karate chop everyone to safety. They were on their own.

The pit of despair George was already in over the death of his father made everything else pale somewhat in significance. It even took some of the bite off of the corrupt, violent, corporate greed, they were now becoming painfully aware of. He realized how sheltered the world of academe was, and longed to go back to the university and those moderate Canadians. That longing, however, was not quite as great as a growing appetite for revenge.

Before leaving the office, the trio decided Dwayne should not be made aware that the people he and his council had been dealing with were killers. Ann said he was lousy with secrets and would be uncontrollably angry if he discovered he had been used or duped, or worse, had conspired with murderers. Dwayne might not be the best politician in town but he was a decent and loving man, according to Ann. For the moment, he got the benefit of the doubt. She was convinced he had been led to believe that he was doing the best thing for the town.

As far as strategy was concerned, the idea of having an *in* with the press seemed like an option worth pursuing. Well-researched, public allegation could be a major tool in doing battle against Fairchild. Ann suggested that George call Allan Thornhill. He had gone to school with them and was now editor of the Lincoln Community *News*. It wasn't the New York Times but it was press, and a place to start.

George had to be careful not to link Ann and therefore Dwayne to any stories. Dwayne could be of some use as an insider, if he was clean. What to go with was the question. The murder thing in Ernie and Mr. Moss's case was unsubstantiated at the moment and the guy on video who "offed" Randy was a trump card that needed exactly the right moment to play.

George picked up the phone and called Allan Thornhill. "Allan, George Moss."

"Well, well, a call from a real live history professor. Do you have any idea what time it is?"

"I know it's late Allan, but there is a company moving in on this town that could have a real negative impact on your quality of life."

"We don't really do anything controversial, George. We're known as the good-news community weekly."

"I see," George said sarcastically, "so if a member of your community has terminal cancer, your good-news weekly might report only on how good the weight loss looks."

Allan Thornhill let out a protracted sigh. "This is the George I remember. Always stirring it up, aren't you? Listen Moss, we've done just fine without you around to save us all, believe it or not"

"Sorry, Allan, I thought you might have been aware of the importance of a free and informed press. Sorry to have troubled you, you're absolutely right. You're doing just fine. Goodnight."

"Wait. Wait! Aren't you at least going to tell me what you've got?"

"What if it's too depressing for you and your happy little paper?"

"Okay, I deserved that. What have you got? I can't promise you I can get any of it by the publisher, but at least tell me what's going on."

"Are you familiar with the names New World Developments or Fairchild Environmental?"

"Well, yes I have heard of New World, they have some kind of real estate deal going with council that involves a couple of million toward a park. There's some big announcement coming soon and according to the Mayor we are getting the better end of the bargain."

"Really. Well these guys may have already duped your council into meeting in-camera to avoid public involvement for one reason or another. I'm just asking you to inform the public who their councillors are in bed with, and what the trade-offs might be for the promise of a recreational facility."

"Let's chat in the morning."

"Thanks, Allan; nice talking to you." George hung up the phone a little bit angry. This sure wasn't the Allan he remembered. This guy had forgotten all about the sixties and everything they stood for. Once George got past the anger he realized that maybe his reluctance was from taking a little bit of a beating in life. Allan had always said he was going to be a journalist for a big paper or major network. Here he was, back in Lincoln at the Lincoln Community News. Maybe this was the last stop before throwing his dream away completely. He wasn't about to take any chances with George; after all George was a traitor to the town. He had rejected it and left early for a life elsewhere. Perhaps in Allan's mind, he was being asked to risk what little he had while George had nothing whatsoever to lose.

12

The Real World

The dream was back. There was a strong fear about empathetically experiencing the symptoms of his father's heart attack again. George had never felt pain of that magnitude and didn't wish to revisit it.

This time though, knowing it was his *father's* death he was replaying, he managed to remain detached enough to pass right through the pain and into the out-of-body experience relatively unscathed.

There was the sensation of sinew stretching then snapping as spirit left body. Once again George found himself looking down on the face of his father, distorted with the horrific pain he had felt in his last breath. George wept as the man with the needle grabbed the bedpost and leaned over to check Mr. Moss's pulse.

"There we go, gentlemen. We have accepted a formal apology from Mr. Moss."

One of the two men wearing ski masks seemed nervous. "Let's get out of this dump."

There was something about the nervous man's voice that eluded George, he made note of it as he felt motion.

As the intruders moved out of the room, his father's consciousness drifted with them, George in tow. The man who had performed the injection went to the desk. The calmer of the masked men, with the casual demeanour of an appliance repairman having just fixed the washer, strolled out of the door. The nervous one, looking everywhere but where he was going, knocked over a walking cane rack, sending the walking sticks and umbrellas it contained clattering on to the floor.

"Fuck!" the nervous man cursed while scrambling to put everything back to the way it was. The man forcing the desk open sounded offended at the expletive, and spoke in a condescending manner.

"Please calm yourself. Tidy that mess up and wait in the car like a good boy."

The nervous man fumbled, putting the canes and umbrellas back into the rack. The man at the desk now had it open and found whatever it was he wanted. Placing the document in the inside pocket of his jacket, he opened the door and passed through the silver streaks of rain into the black velvet curtain of night. Meanwhile, the klutz, realizing he was alone, scurried away only to return moments later to shut the door.

It was the sound of the door closing that woke George up. He was seething at the coldness with which these men had dispatched his father. Something told him to let the anger go, that there was more to this dream if only he could remain calm, but at that moment he couldn't. He hated those men with all the hatred he had ever known crammed into a compartment far too small.

The hatred was like acid burning its way through the soft interior tissues, until the remaining hollow shell knew that it too, could kill without hesitation. There was no end too vile or disgusting for those men in the ugly gallery of scenarios he perused. It was when he turned and looked at Joan that he was reminded her life was also in danger, simply through proximity to him.

That's when George knew he had to channel the energy of anger, to transform it from seeking instant gratification to a more methodical calculating process. Oh sure, he wanted to get even, but it had to be a slow, Chinese water-torture kind of getting even. A getting-even that might make a man squirm over having to experience the humiliation of his own low-level actions rather than the quick mercy of a bullet. So why the dream; how could this damn dream be helpful? *Oh yes, Your Honour, as exhibit A, I would like to tell you about my dream. It's a Lulu.* He smirked at the cartoon scenario.

There was so much more to this dream that he needed to know, but uncontrolled anger had awakened him, interrupting the stream. What had he learned that he didn't know before? *The desk!* Before he came to, the calm guy with the needle headed toward the desk and forced it open.

But that wasn't it, there was something more important that he felt he had missed, so he went back over it again and – there it was.

That son of a bitch grabbed the bedpost with his bare hand! Mr. Cool wore no gloves when he leaned over to check Dad's carotid artery for a pulse. George flipped the light on and looked at the bedpost on an angle remembering how it had been grabbed. There appeared to be something resembling a print there, but his eyes just weren't good enough to focus at that moment.

Joan stirred. George turned out the light and got back under the covers. It would wait till morning.

When he awakened, Joan was up and the coffee was on. George remembered where he left off. Her life now depended on how well he could focus his anger and remain calm and cunning. Cunning: Now there's a word he had never seen next to his own name. It was a word though that he could occasionally use to describe Joan. George was aware she had out-manoeuvred many a high-powered corporate executive who tried to put her in her place – that pathetic sexist place ignorant males think women belong. She was a master at gathering data and knowing how and when to use it. She also had some knowledge of law, and there were many similarities in Canadian and American law.

So if George was to get them both out of that jam it meant "I" would have to become "we." He wanted to be her heroic protector but she possessed much of what he needed to protect her. Nothing wrong with knowing one's own shortcomings he concluded, but in the last couple of days there had been an avalanche of them. Joan had even added "coward" to a list that didn't bother George nearly as much as the remorse he felt for keeping his father at a distance those last few years.

It was a judgment day of sorts. If he was to do everything in his power to protect Joan it meant embracing and developing what he had been running from all his life. *Interesting predicament.* He couldn't afford to give anything less than his all and that meant his *"Sight"* had to be included. In that realization, he briefly felt a weight lift off of his shoulders followed by a flash of well-being. Was this as his father had wished? Was this what it felt like to not hate himself for who he was? Maybe it was more about going with his grain and an awareness of how much energy was expended daily trying to go against it. Regardless, he was willing to use everything he had to protect the woman he loved.

After breakfast, they headed across the field to McDonough's place, where their arrival was heralded by the yapping mutt.

Billy was in the kitchen with a beer. It was blatantly obvious he had a drinking problem. It was, after all, barely 9 a.m. – and he already had the smell of beer on him.

"Howdy, you two," Billy said, looking up. "Can I get you a beer?"

George declined. "No, thanks, not for breakfast. Just want to talk."

"Fine, suit yourself but I ain't talkin' 'bout my deal," he snapped.

George couldn't resist. "You don't want to talk about New World Developments because the money is more important to you than the fact they may have killed Ernie Dobson and my father, and now a friend of Joan's? We understand, Billy. We understand completely. Hey how about those Yankees last night?"

"What? Whadda ya mean they killed Ernie Dobson and your father? What the hell are you doing to me, George?"

Joan shook her head in disgust, and spoke in a hushed, angry tone. "What *are* you doing, George? Now Billy has information that could get him killed! If he tells them his source, we're all dead. Really solid game plan, George! Why don't we save everyone some time and aggravation and just call Fairchild to come out here and put us all out of our misery!"

George bit his lip. Joan had given Ann a mouthful the night before but now wasn't the time to squabble or get defensive – *as if there should ever really be a time for that crap anyway.* What really bothered him was that Joan had a meticulous mind and should have remembered she had told Ann. All was not right in the architecture of her well-being.

Billy looked like someone had punched him in the gut as he fell back on an old wooden chair.

"You're serious, aren't you?"

"Deadly serious," George replied grimly. He noticed Mr. McDonough standing by the open screen door having just wheezed his way back from tending the chickens in the barn. Joan saw him and shook her head again. "Maybe we should tell Patricia Sandfield," she muttered under her breath, "just to get everyone in the loop."

Mr. McDonough opened the door and came in. Billy looked peeved and barked at him: "We need to talk in private if you don't mind Dad."

Mr. McDonough glared daggers of disgust at his son. He didn't get angry often but when he did it took everything out of him. His face turned white and he trembled. George had seen it as a kid on occasion, like the day Billy seized the tractor engine by being too lazy to check the oil. They were always one step from being repossessed by the bank, and that year's drought had produced poor crops. Brushing up against bankruptcy because of his son's laziness was more than he could handle, so he blew. He was fixing to blow again and both George and Billy braced themselves for the blast.

"Don't tell me what to do, ya little turd. Ya've sold this place and our souls to the devil. Don't you ever talk down to me! I may have emphysema and be a little weak but I still got more common sense in my pinky than you got in yer big pile of beer-soaked brains. Look at ya, sucking back booze at this hour, you're 'nuf to make yer mother turn in her grave."

Billy started to protest but Mr. McDonough smacked the beer out of his hand. It fell to the floor and rolled under the kitchen table. Mr. McDonough directed Joan and George to sit down. They sheepishly obeyed like a couple of kids getting heck. The old fellow still had some power and authority left in that burned-out shell of a body, his spirit was strong though the physical means were now sadly out of reach.

"Ernie and your father were both friends o' mine, George, and if you're saying these fellas killed 'em just fer their land, then point me in the right direction and I'll blow their damn heads off with ma shotgun. I ain't got much time left on this earth. I'd just as soon go out rightin' some kinda wrong than sittin' here gaspin' fer air, waitin' fer the damn Grim Reaper."

Joan smiled until it sunk in that he was totally serious. George knew him well enough to entertain the idea he'd do exactly as he had said.

Billy started shaking in a demonstration of what appeared to be emotional instability. The old man had seen these little breakdowns before in his son, the lush, and cuffed him soundly over the back of the head.

"Now ain't the time to be gettin' in touch with yer sensitive side, son. Be a man fer once in yer life and see how long ya can hang on to the idea!"

Billy pulled himself together though all present sensed it was temporary.

"Mr. McDonough," George said evenly, "I wish it were as easy as blowing a couple of heads off but if we don't play our hand right, more people than us will be in harm's way."

"So talk to me boy!" Mr. McDonough snapped. "At least have the decency to talk to this old fool. Ya owe me that much."

13

His Weapon of Choice

Joan had informed George that Jim's home away from home was likely the university library or one of the new computer science labs. After grabbing a couple of hours with his head on the desk in a library computer cubicle, Jim assembled a group of a few friends.

They were an odd bunch of people with serious computer skills. Though intelligence may defy a truly comprehensive measurement, some people do look like they are all brains. This look often manifests in nerd-like configurations, which opens the never-ending discussion of what "normal" is. Relative to any mainstream perceptions of "normal," the people that Jim had rounded up had the stuff of the lunatic fringe.

For one of them, sanity had been a battle. For another, sanity was a totally subjective call. For the third, insanity was a word to be proud of when attached to one's name. Sanity for him was an umbrella term for those who sought to be average.

Jim's friends were all beards, tube-socks and Birkenstocks projecting an anti-establishment air. More accurately, they were: one beard; one attempted beard with sideburns; and, three straggling chin hairs with a light moustache. The latter kept the facial hair in defiance of the *Vogue* image of feminine. They were pretty much an anti-everything group except when it came to computers. The power of the computer in the war of good versus evil was their collective passion.

Their hobby was weeding out and exposing political corruption and environmental destruction by feeding relevant information to the press anonymously. They were amazed how little of this information ever actually made it to print. As it turned out, guilty industrial parties usually spent significant advertising dollars with publications, thus ensuring a level of silence. Freedom of the press, and with it much of the public interest, was apparently being quietly sold all over the world. What was once considered payola was currently defended by corporate lawyers as a legitimate method of ensuring the shareholder's stock value and protecting jobs. Journalistic integrity, Jim had said, was being slowly replaced by the illusion of journalistic job security. This distilled down to not pissing your publisher off if he was receiving advertising revenue from someone you had some dirt on. Kind of an editorial form of self-preservation... and self-censorship. As consumer advocate Ralph Nader said after a World trade Organization meeting in Seattle: "The keys to democracy are slowly being handed over to the whims of the multinational corporate world."

With the erosion of the freedom of the press came the erosion of democracy and a slow almost imperceptible loss of individual rights.

Jim had met two in the group at an environmental conference held at Duke, and the third he met on the Internet. George and Joan had met them all at Jim's birthday party in Durham the year before. Martha Lewis was the most passionate environmentalist George had ever met. She was quite knowledgeable about Canadian politics and how the Ontario Ministry of the environment had been all but gutted in the '90s, resulting in former employees getting hired by companies seeking ways around weak environmental laws. Martha's passion was apolitical; the problems were global. She had heard Jacques Cousteau speak a few years before he died about how marine paradises were one by one turning into lifeless wastelands irretrievably ruined by human over-population and the attendant waste. The old Judeo-Christian direction in Genesis to go forth and multiply and be masters of the Earth and everything in it and on it, though doable two thousand years ago hadn't panned out to being a particularly sustainable idea. It was turning out that man was going to be master of his own shit, in her estimation.

Greed continually outweighed the responsibility to leave a reasonable future for the next generation. This was Martha's shame as a human being. It was as though the lust for material comfort sedated the logic centers in the brain like an anaesthetic so all could merrily plant the seeds of death for their own grandchildren – the ultimate consequence of unbridled consumerism. It was deficit financing; leaving future generations only the excrement of irresponsibility, and it left Martha on one occasion in an institution with suicidal depression.

Of course, like most environmentalists she was called an alarmist or a nut-bar, a title she began to wear with pride. Her unkempt appearance resplendent with the faint moustache and three straggly chin hairs didn't seem to help her much in the public-opinion department, so the nut-bar handle stuck. It seemed to her, anyone who went against the desires of industry was painted as such, and often quite viciously.

Various industrial concerns had done a real hatchet job on Martha in the press over the years but Jim knew what he was doing by calling her in. Put Martha on the scent of a company abusing the environment and she was a pit bull. Despite being a little broad in the beam and the hairs on her chinny chin chin, there was something attractive about her. In her case, there was a beauty within that still managed to leak through even though she worked so diligently to undermine it in protest against being objectified.

Bill Monroe was the fully bearded legal nut-bar in the group. He had done contract research work for Joan over the last couple of years, and supported himself as a legal assistant in a major law office, having dropped out of law school. He was always looking for laws that were bent or abused by industrial entities. The practice of payola was his favourite. He had recently exposed a mayor in Illinois by uncovering the property that had been bought for him in a small Florida town by a local industrial conglomerate. The company, in exchange for the Mayor's vote and influence, had purchased the property for close to a million dollars and sold it to the Mayor for ten thousand. Bill had uncovered this old scam through the laborious process of scouring records in every town or city in the USA and Canada. He'd developed a program that searched records on-line while he slept. Of course, he was only lucky if the records had been computerized, which meant much of the world's corruption remained in a state of blackout. But with more and more cities and towns embracing computer technology, Bill was getting lucky with greater frequency in finding information for the public record.

Andy Schumann, 23, was the youngest in the group and owner of the attempted beard with sideburns along with long blond hair, masking a somewhat boyish face. The computer geek had a tall, fairly slender build but his nerdish social awkwardness didn't create a blip on most female radar. Jim once told Joan in strict confidence that Andy had compromised an FBI database but managed to have his hacking traced or rerouted to the FBI's own assistant director. Routing was his thing.

In puberty when Andy started hacking, he was stunned to find himself busted for possession of downloaded bestiality pictures and kiddy-porn shots. It didn't matter that he was a kid too, and the shots were of his peer group. It also didn't seem to matter to the police that the boy was telling the truth, that the pictures weren't his. The pornography belonged to Andy's father. The mother couldn't believe that her husband, a deacon in a fundamentalist Christian church, would ever do such a thing, and rejected her son's confidences. Andy was handcuffed and taken away in front of all the neighbours. The kid was traumatized; the parents received sympathy; and irreparable damage was done.

In the Schumann's church, a lewd thought was a sin, so one could only imagine where that put Andy, accused of having pictures of people screwing animals. Andy was never charged and was released to religious counselling that was relentless to say nothing of unqualified. Apparently even Jesus couldn't cure the boy of his father's problem.

Andy gave up focusing his anger on his own father, and so he directed it towards the police. Big Brother had compromised his life, his anonymity and more importantly to him, his privacy. His mission in life was to never get caught again in anything to do with his computer. That meant of course becoming a master at routing and other elaborate means of confusing anyone trying to run a trace on his activities. He had attached the family religious fanaticism to the privacy issue. He also made his computer unusable to anyone else, particularly his father.

When Jim had told George the night of Randy's death that no one would ever complete a trace on him again, George should have known that meant he'd be in touch with Andy.

Jim walked over to Monroe's first. "No phones" was the rule of thumb when something was up. Not one of them trusted phones. Bill was always harping on about how the rights that everyone thought they had were really just figments of the imagination. Andy would always chime in "Amen!" when Bill said that. They picked up the other two in Bill's old Mercedes diesel, and went to McDonalds for breakfast, which really upset Martha because of the excessive packaging of fast foods. She went along with it, given the shocking news of Randy's death and Jim's obvious distress. He was in pain so if he wanted an Egg McMuffin with a McGrapefruit juice, so be it.

They came up with a plan that involved everyone working from different locations and pooling resources once a day. They knew they had only two weeks until the environmental hearing. Martha had already been looking into the New York Department of Environmental Conservation for irregularities with regard to another matter. The serious environmentalists had started to disappear in the Reagan eighties. As in Ontario many had been bought off to work for the other side. She couldn't tolerate the idea that there wasn't one real environmentalist in her view in the whole damn department. It had slowly become populated with political appointees favourable to industry. That, after all, is the North American way, in Martha's view: Talk big, sound environmentally concerned, and look the other way as industry crosses line after line. "It's all about jobs, don't you know?"

So there they were; Jim, Bill, Andy and Martha working around the clock in an attempt to find anything and everything they could about Fairchild Environmental. The road ahead was a minefield, but passion and purpose were high among the lunatic fringe.

14

What Life Does To People

Billy was a mess. Drinking in high school was something that everyone experimented with for laughs. When the laughs end and some are left uncontrollably imbibing by themselves – oops, there is unveiled: a stumbling tragedy, a booby trap for the undiscovered compulsive-addictive personality.

George once thought Billy could control his drink, but it was obvious it now controlled him. He had been late for the funeral because he was drunk as a skunk. His breath smelled peppermint-fresh that day because he popped mints every couple of minutes to hide the stink of booze. George had thought loose gravel was the reason he skidded into Mr. Brown's hearse, but now he knew better.

As the visit grew longer that morning, the size of Billy's problem grew more obvious. He had a slight tremor in his left hand. He tried to conceal it by nervously putting it in his pocket but was so drunk he would forget a second later and bring the hand back out into the open repeating the cycle.

Billy was once a passionate farmer but as he fed his habit, both his passion and the farm started to decline. He was making bad decisions or no decisions at all. Once again he had become the reason the bank was ready to foreclose. The offer from New World had arrived in the nick of time. It would mean paying off the mortgage and provide enough for him and his father to live on.

George now realized he had judged him unfairly. He thought Billy had broken their bond of honesty out of common greed, but it was alcohol, desperation and survival that placed the unwritten law of brotherhood on the sidelines. George was aware he should have known better. Billy's heart was true despite his weaknesses. He told George that because George didn't know he was a drunk and thought of him only as the Billy he grew up with, it gave him a tiny piece of pride to hold on to, maybe even some kind of hope. Now even this was gone despite reassurances that he remained cherished as a brother. But, he was his own jury and would have none of it.

When asked how bad it was, his father blurted out: "He drinks until be blacks out, the fool!"

"It shuts my mind off!" Billy snapped. "It shuts my god-damned mind off!" There was a cold shiver in that glimpse of hell. Even minimal consciousness was too painful for him to endure at times. What unimaginable torment lay there? George attempted to hug him, which unfortunately led to more tears so Billy wandered off to hide.

Mr. McDonough spoke in a voice filled with parental pain. He had found Billy facedown unconscious a few weeks ago. After a 911 call and an ambulance ride to the County General for a stomach pump, it was discovered he had been drinking cleaning fluids. It turned out Billy wanted to die rather than bring more disgrace to himself and his father. He wanted an exit from what he had become, before all traces of his dignity were gone.

Some reunion of old friends. George's recent loss was no match for Billy's hell. No matter how indulgently George dug into the depths of his own pain, his all-time low waterline towered over the dark desperate pit where Billy languished.

As they stood to leave, George assured Mr. McDonough he would be kept in the loop. Joan gave him a hug and a peck on the cheek that the old gentleman absorbed with warm need.

Once home, Joan hunted in the cupboards for lunch while delivering a lecture on the importance of not tipping their hand too soon. The consequences, they both knew, were severe.

George wondered if he had already gone too far by calling Allan Thornhill at the community newspaper. They both wondered if he should be given any information at all. Randy after all had been murdered because his partner only got *close* to real information.

Joan thought Thornhill should be stalled, or informed there was nothing to the initial suspicions. She was really feeling the gravity of the situation. Silence appeared to be the most prudent option at most every junction. They wished they had reached that conclusion earlier.

What a homecoming. Billy might be lost. Thornhill had appeared to have a real bitter chip on his shoulder with his less-than stellar career in journalism, so George wasn't sure he could trust him at all anymore Neddy was even more of a scumbag than his dad. Christie had becor the mid-life poster child for bad-break syndrome. These were some of the big dreamers, the key players in high school; they were the people who all stood out as exceptional in one way or another. George was almost afraid to bump into anyone else in case they too had been ground under foot by life.

George was feeling rather grateful for his academic existence. At least the university surrounded him with people full of hope and promise, a few neurotic professors excepted. Sticking his head up into the real world was unnerving to say the least. Seeing his old friends worn down by life felt awful. And thinking about businesses that didn't mind killing people for a few bucks was surreal.

The old rationale, "it's business and nothing personal" took on an interesting glow to George as he followed the logic. With billions of dollars at stake, a corporation producing cancer-inducing pollutants doesn't have to reach that far to just go for it and shoot someone.

It all ultimately distilled down to method of execution. Maybe a bullet to the head is kinder than a slow death from a toxin induced cancer. George was so unable to relate to the thoughts of a "business-only and above all" world, that he was beginning to feel like an alien amongst his own species.

15

Conspiring Over Coffee

A couple of brats were running around and screaming when Jim arrived at the McDonalds restaurant the next morning. A chain-smoking woman in shabby clothes, presumably their mother, yelled at them half-heartedly, too fatigued to really care about anything other than the coffee cup she nursed while staring off into space.

Not far from the children's play area and this scene of domestic bliss, Martha, Bill, and Andy sat together, already sipping tea and coffee.

"What have we got? Let's start with you, Andy," Jim said officiously as he sat down.

Andy smiled. "Jim, I've been thinking about how you got traced. I think there is a way to enter their mainframe without being spotted."

"How?"

"Both of the Peroni brothers have computer links at their homes in Richmond." Andy's associates looked at him suspiciously.

"I have friends with a few local servers," Andy explained, "so it wasn't difficult. Anyway, I'm almost certain when they link to the mainframe they're not monitored after their own personal passkeys are verified with their terminal locations. I found out who set up their security systems and made inquiries as a potential customer. I was more or less told how they secure systems from remote locations. The really good news is that the older brother, Benito, has a listed phone number."

They stared at Andy for a moment wondering why this was really good news.

Andy sighed. "Don't you get it? The cable company has no record of him as a client so he must have two lines at his house... one line for phone, one for computer. Now that I know the personal number I can splice the lines and know in a millisecond which line I have. Then I set up a line reader with a thru-port transmitter. He makes one link with the mainframe and I've got everything I need."

"That's illegal," Bill snapped.

Martha's eyebrows shot up with worry. "What if you get caught, Andy? How do you splice those wires without them knowing?"

"They live in an older neighbourhood, all overhead wiring, nothing underground – a van, a utility belt, a phone or cable company hat and bingo. The only awkward part will be getting close enough to the house to monitor the thru-port transmitter."

The silence was all but deafening. Then something hit Bill's fan. "Awkward! Cripes, Andy this isn't *Mission Impossible* you know! We aren't secret agents in some silly game... you... you could get killed!"

Andy looked at him coldly and then spoke. "You can't beat the opposition by playing with a rulebook they don't use. If you want to catch people who break the law, sometimes you have to fight in their arena, or at least with some of *their* rules. I thought you, of all people, would know that."

Jim shook his head. "They have some kind of secondary code as well, Andy. That's how they nailed me."

Andy shrugged. "The line reader would grab that."

"Oh, dear." It was all Martha could say. She looked very pale. Everyone sat sipping respective teas and coffees in silence as minds scurried over various scenarios, all ending with a tragic headline, or an obituary. It was Bill who provided the next step.

"Look. We are all working on this thing in our own ways. We have less than 13 days before the hearing. If we are careful we might be okay. Break-ins and trespassing do not constitute careful behaviour in my opinion. If we advise Moss to move when we have a solid legal case that Fairchild can't wriggle out of, we might be safe. The only way they can get any of us is if we don't expose them enough. They would be crazy to go after someone who exposes them publicly in a big way. I've got some info as to their legal modus operandi."

"Shoot," Jim said, eager with anticipation.

"Their lawyer is Helmut Talmer."

"*The* Helmut Talmer, out of *Richmond?* Martha said in astonishment. "I thought he was one of us."

Bill nodded. "*Was* is the operative word, Martha. The son of a bitch took everything he learned fighting for environmental causes and turned it into a plush retirement plan by selling his knowledge to the other side. He has local and state politicians running scared with his intimidating presence, and he uses SLAPP-suits like they're going out of style."

Andy looked puzzled. "What the hell is a SLAPP-suit?"

"Strategic Lawsuit Against Public Participation." Martha answered. "Big company threatens little person with a twenty-million-dollar lawsuit – little person shuts up and goes away. Voila! Public interest over-ruled by intimidation!"

Bill nodded agreement, then continued: "Even the lawyers in the firm where I work think his heavy-handed tactics are borderline, if in fact they don't cross the line into criminal territory … and the guys I work for are no saints! There is a rumour about some move to have Talmer disbarred but I doubt the law society will do anything too drastic to one of their own; lawyers are a bit like doctors that way; they will only move if the press applies heat, and in this case the local press appear to be in Talmer's back pocket. He's threatened twenty-million-dollar suits on two journalists who now no longer work for their respective papers. One is counter-suing but that could take years. The local paper only prints glowing propaganda about Fairchild, like how two brothers from lowly beginnings have done so well through sheer determination and hard work, and how they've been a boon to the local economy. Talmer is even on the board of directors at Fairchild now, and owns major stock in the company."

"Doesn't Talmer know they're the mob?" Jim wondered.

"How do you know that for sure? Andy asked pessimistically.

"Well, we don't. We only know they got a start-up loan from a transportation conglomerate out of New Jersey, and that same conglomerate has serious mob connections. Talmer knows. He's not stupid."

"In a recent interview he came to the defence of the Peroni family saying anyone with an Italian name unfortunately bears the brunt of racial stereotyping, and he will not comment on such bigotry."

"Nice politically correct way out of admitting you work for the mob!" Martha fumed. "What a snake!"

Jim looked at his three friends with pride. "If anyone needs to drop out for any reason I'll understand. You have already proven yourselves to me in spades, and I love you for it." Mutual eye contact suggested a mental group hug was going on. Andy thought Jim was having a sensitive gay moment and was uncomfortable with such overt affection.

"I don't mean to put a damper on this special feeling but there is more than you at stake here, Jim," Andy objected. "We're dealing with a company and a type of corruption that sticks in our collective craw. So, what have *you* found out, or are we supposed to do all the work?"

"Andy, you could be a little more compassionate!" Martha's tone was somewhat motherly. Jim was peeved but brushed it off accepting that Andy was passionate about the cause.

"Well, where to start?" Jim began. "Fairchild was fined in Minnesota for dumping hazardous toxic waste in a site restricted to non-toxic inert materials. But they blamed it on the employee, whose name appeared on the manifest, accusing him of taking money under the table from the trucking company. There was enough evidence for the employee to do some time in jail, and Fairchild was fined a couple of hundred thousand. I thought to myself, fair enough, maybe an employee screwed up, but then I discovered the same thing happened in Georgia."

"Weasels!" Martha hissed. "And how the hell do you get an employee to go to jail for you? Something's a little fishy about that sort of dedication."

Jim continued. "Well, I thought that was a little odd myself, so I looked further. The employee in Minnesota who went to jail is now out. I got an address and had an old college friend who lives in the same town drive by his rather large, new home last night – pretty good digs for someone with no known source of income that I can find. I'm also running a check on the ownership of that particular piece of real estate."

All three friends leaned forward to hear more. Jim took a deep breath and carried on. "The employee from Georgia had a heart attack before the trial. I found his obituary: He was forty-three, and left a wife with two children. There was also an employee from Texas who was caught dumping liquid waste from his tanker on the state highway at night, but he seems to have vanished into thin air. Fairchild put out a story accusing him of skimming money off them – just like the guy in Minnesota – by forging trucking manifests. They claim he's probably fled the country with the spoils. My bet is he's either part of a concrete foundation somewhere or has become inert non-toxic landfill himself. Well, that's all I've been able to haul out of newspaper libraries so far, apart from the stuff I showed you at our first get-together."

"Alright," Bill offered officiously, "let's convene here again in a couple of days, unless somebody gets something definitive."

Andy, Bill and Jim all got up and started to leave when they noticed Martha was still sitting.

"You all right, Martha?" asked Jim.

"Men. You all sound off, get off and take off. Did it dawn on any of you I may have done some research and could have something to contribute?"

"Sorry, Marty," Jim muttered sincerely.

"Yeah, I'm uh, I'm sorry, too." Bill seconded. Bill and Jim sat back down and they all stared at Andy who conceded with an apologetic look. Martha enjoyed her momentary power, and then reached into her nylon backpack for a few documents.

"This is a picture of the opening of the new Fairchild Environmental head office in Richmond." She passed it to Jim, who shared it with the other two.

Martha then added: "You will note the Mayor of that fair city, three local councillors, Congressman Thompson on the far right, and a rather distinguished looking gentleman standing next to Ben Peroni."

"Of course, these guys would attend such an event," scoffed Bill, who was, as usual, to the point. "They are a major boon to the local and state economy. Nothing damning in that."

"No, nothing damning at all," Martha agreed, "but it's where I started. Here is a wedding photo of Carmen Peroni, one of Benito's daughters. In the background – the Mayor, Congressman Thompson and the same distinguished-looking gentleman."

Martha passed the second picture around, then continued: "And here I have an interesting photo of our distinguished looking gentleman all on his own." She passed the third picture. It was a picture of the man underneath the headline, SENATOR TO HEAD NEW YORK GREEN PLAN. "In the small print that means the New York Department of Environmental Conservation."

"Shit!" Jim sat shaking his head.

"What? What is it?" Andy felt right out of the loop.

"Nothing much Andy, apart from the fact he's the guy presiding over the environmental hearing in Lincoln," Bill sighed dejectedly.

"Exactly" said Martha. "But more importantly, why would he be at a personal event like a Peroni wedding in Richmond unless he was in deep? What's in it for him? What was in it for him when he was a senator in Washington? Probably the same thing that Talmer is after – a comfortable retirement package in exchange for pulling strings and looking the other way while the environment goes to hell. He should never have attended that wedding. That picture led me to this picture, which a friend with a digital mini-cam in her hand bag shot for me in their lobby."

"Whose lobby?" Andy asked

"Fairchild Environmental. She went in under the guise of seeking a donation to the World Wildlife Fund, and shot some pictures that hung on the wall in the lobby while she waited to see someone."

"Ha!" Andy was smiling from ear to ear. He clearly loved the covert stuff. They passed the picture around. It was Ben Peroni with Johnson on either side of a rather large swordfish.

"Was the person she met at all suspicious she wasn't with the WWF?" Jim asked, intrigued.

"No. But that's because she *is* with the WWF and she got a thousand dollar donation to boot." Martha smirked. "You know these Peroni brothers are not the sharpest tools in the box. Bragging about the influence you have politically with pictures in your lobby is really stupid, stupid, stupid."

"Good work, Martha." Andy said with an obvious tone of admiration. It caught Martha off guard but she quickly regained her focus.

"Oh, I'm not done with that picture yet," Martha smiled. "If you look at that picture, it looks like some Caribbean island and begs the question: Who paid for the trip? Which leads to the question, if it was Fairchild, then what else have they bought for Senator Johnson and how does his lifestyle match his income? And what about the Mayor, the councillors and the congressman? You don't stop at a picture, Andy. As Bill said, we need hard evidence to nail these boys. The picture isn't hard evidence, it's only circumstantial, but it does present the questions that might lead us to what we need."

Bill smiled at her and nodded real approval.

"Good stuff, Martha. You won't mind if I work on some of those leads will you?"

"Take your pick."

Jim looked around the table with obvious pride in his friends. "Alright, let's get back to work."

Everyone got up except for Martha, who watched them all leave. But mostly she watched Andy.

16

Silence

Caution had pretty much boxed George and Joan into a corner. At every turn they found themselves ruling out doing anything. Every course of action, once mulled over, was fraught with trap doors that could hurt them, or someone they knew.

They had now moved on to what actions had the least chance of severe consequences. The phone call to Allan Thornhill from Ann's office was so wrong, or at least premature, in retrospect. He was expecting information the following morning and it was afternoon, a day later. They strategized while fearing a call from him before they were ready. Silence that far out from the hearing was the only way they could protect their hand in order to broadside Fairchild with irrefutable evidence while insuring minimum casualties at the same time.

The phone rang.

"Hello, Allan."

"Uh yeah, George. You got call display or something?"

"No, Allan."

"Oh, oh yeah, the old Moss ESP thing still works, huh, George?" he lunged sarcastically.

"Allan, I have decided that the information I have may not be so reliable, my friend Joan thinks we might be fodder for a libel suit – that's why we haven't called."

"Nice try George, but I've been on this since I spoke to you and there is all kinds of odd stuff involving New World Developments. As you suggested, I did do a search on past press and found a pile of stories that just dead end. It's like someone pulls on a thread then the thread is cut before anyone can see what's on the end of it."

"You better be careful, Allan, or your thread could get cut."

"Is that some kind of threat George?"

"Allan, let's get together and talk in person."

"Why?"

"Let's just say I've come to respect my phone."

"You think your phone is bugged? Oh get out! George you're so melodramatic!"

"Are you mobile Allan?"

"Actually I am between cars."

"How about the Deluxe in half an hour then."

"Sure, should I wear a fake nose and glasses?"

Allan hung up before George could respond. Joan looked concerned.

"We've got a loose cannon?" George mused.

When they walked into the Deluxe, Allan was in a booth and waved them over. Something didn't feel right to George. The closer he got to Allan the more his skin crawled but he couldn't pin point the cause.

"Joan, something isn't right here," he whispered.

"Is it your *Sight*, George?"

"Yes."

"So go with it. It's all we may have at the moment." Joan stared curiously at George as they walked over to Allan, who looked up.

"Hey, George, sit down – have I got some stuff for you."

George tried to distract him with a small-talk brush-fire while he figured out what was making him uneasy. "Allan, have you met Joan?"

While Joan engaged Allan in introductory polite banter, George's eyes were drawn to the next booth. The bench seat was too high and he was facing the wrong way but George saw the top of a head and immediately knew who it was. He also knew they couldn't talk to Allan within earshot of that head for some reason.

"Allan, I know we just got here, but come on, I want to show you something."

George left him no option. While Allan was objecting, George just walked out of the restaurant. Joan followed, and after Allan found some change for the coffee he was drinking, he came out looking pissed off.

"Look, I don't have time for wild goose chases, Moss I..." George grabbed his shoulder and looked him in the eye.

"Allan, this is no wild goose chase. You've known my family all your life. Has it ever been the Moss style to waste time on wild goose chases?"

"You were all a little nuts in my opinion," Allan said snidely.

"Alright, I'll re-phrase it: In every action involving my father's little "ESP-thing" as you call it, did you know him to be anything but honest – and secondly, was he ever wrong?"

"So, what did you want to show me out here?"

"Nothing, but there were too many ears in there."

"Back to the cloak-and-dagger stuff huh?"

"Do you have an office where we can talk?"

Allan looked a little irritated, nodding his head in reluctant compliance. As he started down the street George tugged on Joan's sleeve and nodded back to the window of the restaurant. Getting out of the booth behind the one where Allan had been sitting was a funny looking little man. He was a man who should have been at work at that hour. He was a man who previously snagged their interest. Joan's face dropped as she watched the town clerk, John Speeks, put on his jacket.

"Do you think he knew we were...?" He looked their way. George grabbed Joan's hand and they set off after Allan.

"He knew we were getting together with Allan all right. Either Allan is a player and told him, or one of our phones is definitely bugged."

Joan bristled. "He wouldn't give us any information on New World at city hall because he has to be in on it. What other reason would he have for such behaviour? I knew I smelled a rat!"

Allan's office was crammed with boxes, photos strewn around the room and copies of papers past and present. It was a small space. The community paper had come a long way from its hot-type days. It was all laid up on computer and e-mailed to a printing plant in Rochester. Lincoln's paper was one in a chain of small community newspapers in New York State, owned and operated out of Rochester. Individually the papers couldn't make money, so a central sales and advertising department and one press had turned it into a more economically viable operation. Allan ushered them in and rustled up some chairs that he hastily assembled around his desk.

"Allan, do you know John Speeks?" George asked as he sat down.

"Town clerk? Yeah sure, everybody knows that pompous little ass."

"Did you happen to tell him we were meeting at the Deluxe?"

"Hell, no. I was working on an article right up until I ran over there to meet you. What the hell has Speeks got to do with anything?"

"Don't know yet; maybe nothing."

"Well that's a little unlikely given your interest in him. But before you cut me off again, I would like to tell you what I've dug up and then I suppose you will tell me what you think I should do with it. Is that kind of where we're at?"

"Could be, shoot."

"God, you bug me, Moss. Your life and everything in it is always so much more important than anything we mere mortals could hope to aspire to." He stared out the window with a cheesed-off expression. "I don't even know why I stayed at this most of the night, but I did, so here it is anyway. New World Developments is owned by Fairchild Environmental. This company is huge and has friends in high places. It's been up and running for about ten years and went public about eighteen months ago. Everyone loves them because they're involved in recycling. Their promotional stuff says they are able to extract useful chemicals from toxic waste, which renders the waste non-toxic. Only one problem; when I began to look for anything about this wonderful re-cycling technology, there is nothing anywhere about how it works or what it is, not even a hint. No one knows a thing. Fairchild, in an interview with the *Times* wouldn't even talk about it, claiming proprietary privilege. So the way I see it, we have a company making a small fortune hauling waste they are claiming to re-cycle. Because they claim to be recycling, politicians love them and are awarding haulage contracts left, right and center. But what if the recycling thing is hot air, or not all it's cracked up to be? Say they can only recycle some of it, what do they do with the rest? Where do they put it? So they find a nice little hick town near an interstate highway, make big promises in exchange for an inconspicuous site for their latest "state-of-the-art re-cycling and storage facility." Well, that's where I am so far. Now, what did you have for me?"

"Nothing. You already know too much."

"Oh, give me a break! What are you up to, Moss?"

"Are you intending to print any of this in your paper?"

"If I can get my publisher to agree to it."

"And just what will the basis of the article be? All you have is litigious allegation. Have you spoken to any of your town council?"

"I called Mayor Barnes this morning and he said it was a done deal – hard-wired at state level. He also wanted me to keep quiet because it could jeopardize some sensitive negotiations involving a considerable amount of money in tonnage royalties for the town. Apparently, the best option the council had, according to the Mayor, was to see what the town could get out of the deal and in that regard they have some great announcements coming in about a week or so."

"The best option they had!" Joan scoffed. "Don't you just love it when people you elect to look out for your interests, roll over and play dead like that? A done deal is never a done deal until the fat lady sings."

"You've seen Mayor Barnes have you?" Allan chuckled.

"Never met the man," Joan replied, "but as your Mayor he has done his constituents and public process no favours. You just don't do deals behind closed doors and avoid public process unless you are either an easily intimidated hick or a beneficiary of some other agenda."

"Oh, so you know about the in-camera meetings with Fairchild?"

"Yes we do, Allan," George confirmed. "And at face value it all seems like typical political manoeuvring – with a couple of glaring exceptions."

"And those would be? "Allan said with a leading tone.

George looked at Joan; they were now at the point where they had to tread carefully. Joan jumped in.

"Well for starters, there seems to be some confusion over whether the zoning changes for the Fairchild proposal were ever posted publicly. Why would councillors want to keep this thing under wraps, away from the eyes of their own constituents? Historically speaking, in these sorts of cases, public officials are usually bought."

"Oh come on. Barnsie? He'd never do anything like that! And as for the rest of the council, they are ordinary, honest folk like you and me."

"That may well be, Mr. Thornhill, but these ordinary, honest people have broken municipal law. How do you get an ordinary honest person to break the law in favour of a special interest? That's the question."

"I understand the rationale," Allan pondered. "Why don't I start with the circumstances of zoning change and we'll get together again. I doubt very much that you will be able to find that kind of information as easy as I will. Zoning changes are usually posted in this paper. The ones that aren't, are announced at open council meetings, so I can trace the public minutes of those meetings, which are also on cassettes around here somewhere." Allan got up; the meeting was over.

"I don't think you should go with any Fairchild stuff just yet Allan."

Allan's back stiffened. "When I get a complete picture, that's when I go to my publisher, not when you think it's time."

"Watch out for Fairchild," George warned. "They play hardball – and they play for keeps."

"Oooo, that sounds scary. You scared George?"

"Damn right I am. I'm scared for all of us."

Allan's smirk fell when he saw how serious George was. He may have had some doubt about George's abilities versus those of his father, but the fact that George was scared seemed to mean something to him. Maybe it was a chink in the armor of bravado he thought George wore.

As they left the office of the Lincoln Community News, George was puzzled. He had no memory of ever doing any wrong to Allan or being "uppity" toward him. It's a common failing he guessed, not to know how one is perceived in order to compensate accordingly. He had a friend at the university who was so easily crushed as to lead one to believe he was about as sensitive as a human being could be. But the sensitivity was one way; it was only in his receiving apparatus. His words could leave a person devastated – and he could walk away unaware of what he had just done. George hoped he wasn't that unconscious about what he projected. Joan, of course, would give him a straight answer, but some other time. He wasn't in the mood for a new word to add to her mounting "what's wrong with George" list.

They were walking toward the truck when Doc Harris got out of his car and waved at them. His face betrayed an ominous expression that signalled he wanted to talk. George waved back, and Harris motioned for them to come across the road. As they drew closer it became apparent that Doc Harris hadn't been sleeping well.

"George, I've been thinking about what you said the other night and put that in the context of your father's talent, for which I think you have some genetic predisposition. If your father and Ernie Dobson were killed, what was the method? Why were you asking if I did blood work? What do you think you know George? What the hell are you getting at?"

"I'm not sure I should trouble you with all this, Doc. It's probably nothing."

"You Mosses are bad liars. What have you *seen?*"

"I think I've lived the moment of my father's death through his eyes."

"My God." The Doc leaned back on the side of his car, winded. "To see such a thing; what a horrible burden to live with."

"I'm not sure I'm living with it yet, Doc."

"So what was…? I mean how?"

"He was injected with something in his left arm that caused his heart to fibrillate."

"And you think Ernie died the same way?"

"Yes."

"But I did blood work on Ernie," Doc Harris pondered, "so it must be a substance that for all intents and purposes disappears or disintegrates or is absorbed." He turned silent, mulling over possible answers to the riddle. Joan looked at them both with concern.

"You're both on the main street talking about something that needs a detailed and, more importantly, a more private conversation. Can we adjourn to somewhere private?"

The Doc nodded agreement and invited them to dinner that evening with the reassurance that any remote inconvenience would be balanced by his wife's delight in having a chance to get the good china out.

As Joan and George headed across the road to the Fargo they wondered whether to try Speeks out again to see if he had the requested documents. Joan wanted to bug the "sexist pig" so George waited in the

Fargo while she went into the town hall. A few minutes later, she hopped in the front seat and pulled the groaning passenger door shut.

"Well?"

"He was overly nice, and while he said he didn't have a copy for us, he showed me the documents and the Dobson's property was indeed purchased by New World Developments."

"He was overly nice?"

"Yes, as in – all over himself, and patronizing."

"They're on to us."

"What does that mean?"

"It means that Speeks has had his butt dragged over the coals for being anything other than helpful the first time and has received some instruction from Fairchild. They're close to a slam-dunk on this thing and don't want any public awareness or suspicion until it's too late. Did you get anything on the McDonough deal?"

"No, because it's an on-going negotiation."

"Nice trick," George mused. "Keeps you out of the public record!" Billy had told them he'd received half of the total purchase price up front and the other half would be paid when they left the property. This way they wouldn't have to uproot his father before it was necessary.

On the way home, they soaked up the beauty of the land, resplendent with green buds and fruit trees in blossom. George drove conspicuously slow, sweet air caressing responsive senses through open windows. As they pulled into the driveway, he looked over at Joan and watched the sun flicker through her hair and across her neck.

Once he had given the Fargo a pat on the hood, they pulled the tarp over it and headed toward the house, each with an arm around the other's waist. George reached a little farther and managed to hold the side of her far breast. He'd always felt that touching where no one else was allowed to touch was an incredible privilege. They ended up in the grass at the side of the barn for a strange physical encounter. Joan was a little distant, George thought. Perhaps there was just too much going on at that moment for her to deal with, but George feared it was more. They were lying in the grass afterwards with the sun on their faces when the phone rang in the house. George jumped up bare-assed, carrying his trousers.

"Pardon my butt," he apologized, heading to the porch.

"It's not your nicest feature, but it's kind of cute. I'm just glad I got to know the rest of you first." George turned around a little indignant.

"Now, what the hell is that supposed to mean?"

"Well, if I had seen your sorry ass first as an introduction to you I might have kept moving, but as an extension of you, the man I think I love, I like it."

George just shook his head and ran into the house with the notion that most men are so shallow by comparison. He had seen on occasion an ass that he would have died for. Putting up with the rest of the package was the unknown and scary part.

But there were frightening words that halted his usual mental meandering. "The man I think I love," repeated in his mind. His status had deteriorated from her earlier declarations of affection. He got to the phone on the fifth ring.

"Call me from a secure line," Jim instructed, then hung up. Reality was back, in all its splendour. George shuffled into his pants. As he reached the porch he sadly watched Joan getting dressed. Physical longing is such an odd thing. Despite everything going on at that moment he had an odd desire to bite her bare ass and his mind flew. *Now what the hell is this all about? What are the origins of this desire? Oh yes, says the great anthropologist in me, bum biting is really a highly evolved manifestation of a type of mating ritual. The Kumawanadooya people from the Smegma region in prehistoric continental Europe used to bite their women's backsides as a method of selection. An unbitten woman would be cast out and left to die. Conversely, the number of bites on a virgin determined what promise the woman offered the species and therefore how high up in social circles she could expect to move. God, I'm an idiot! Jim just called me on matters of life and death, Joan may be less sure of her love for me, and look what I waste grey cells on."* He began to laugh at himself.

"What's so funny?" Joan asked as he opened the barn door again.

"Nothing really, except when I saw you putting on your pants I wanted to bite your bum and was wondering why anyone would have an urge to bite anyone else's bum. I was creating an anthropological trace of bum-biting in my mind."

"You're really beginning to lose it, old-timer."

"Not as long as I want to bite your ass I'm not!" He shot back while pulling the tarp back off the Fargo. He hopped in and fired up the engine. Joan ran around the corner and looked puzzled. George answered her non-verbal query.

"Jim called. Got to get to the pay phone!"

"Why didn't you say so? Oh yeah, your anthropological study of bum biting." She hopped in.

The gas station attendant looked up with an expression that said: "It's the fruitcakes in the Fargo again!" Their actions the other evening were so "out there" by Lincoln standards. He knew George was from the farm down the road and wondered what was wrong with his own damn phone. The phone call was now in progress, and Jim sounded distressed.

"Randy's name was in the obit..." The phone went silent with the exception of a couple of gasps for air. Jim tried again.

"His name was in... " He didn't make as far as the first attempt.

"I understand, Jim. His name is in the paper. Was there anything written about the circumstances of his death? Is the local coroner involved?"

"I think they are going to do an autopsy, but George, the cops are looking for me now! The apartment has been identified as mine and I am presumed missing. There was a little blurb in the paper this morning saying foul play is not being ruled out. I told Bill Monroe this morning I should take the tape to the cops. I have dubbed it and sent a few copies to friends for safe keeping."

"What did Bill say?"

"He..." Jim was overcome again but fought to regain his composure. "He would like us to hold off until we have a few more bits and pieces of the puzzle to nail this human refuse to a tree."

"Smart plan, Jim. We may have a fingerprint at this end. If it's the same guy, maybe we have another piece of that puzzle. So what else is happening?"

"I'm sending you more stuff by fax but I wanted you to know Sam Johnson may be dirty. We think he's on the payroll somehow along with a few politicians at this end."

"So much for a fair environmental hearing."

"Come on, George. I don't think there has been anything other than token environmental hearings for the last ten years. I bet your local council is in it up to their eyeballs. By the way, I need their names and addresses if you can fax that stuff to Bill Monroe. Joan has the number."

"Consider it done Jim. And there is another person I would like you to look into by the name of John Speeks. He's the town clerk but he seems sleazy to both Joan and me."

"Sure," Jim agreed. "Send me an address if you can find one, or better than that, there should be a copy of his job application at your municipal building. Fax that to me if you can access it. Personnel records are not for public eyes but see what you can do."

"I'll do my best. How are you Jim? How are you coping?"

A moment of silence was followed by an almost unintelligible request to speak to Joan. George stood for a few minutes while Joan consoled her friend and colleague. She hardly spoke but offered all she had – her presence. She didn't recite platitudes or useless equations to her own life experience. She was so compassionate as to sit and just cry with her friend on the phone, unafraid of long pauses and generous in her silence. George went to the truck not wishing to stand over her like the clock was running.

As he watched her, his love for the woman grew in tandem with the realization of his own selfishness and what he sensed had been a lifetime of never really being that responsive to other people's needs or their pain. Oh sure, he could mutter the occasional "I'm so sorry," or other such shallow words, but he never really went too far into other people's pain. It was more often an inconvenience or an imposition on an unwritten schedule. He was observing real heartfelt concern for another human being; perhaps some of the most meaningful interaction one could hope for – a reminder that we are not alone on an often-desolate journey. It was the real stuff, and he felt shame for how little of himself he had offered to others over the years. *Maybe that's what Allan was talking about? Oh God...* George sank a little in the thought.

An hour had drifted by when Joan finally climbed into the Fargo. She was spent. They went home, and George offered to go to the Harris's alone if she needed to rest. He should have known better. They dressed up, aware of Mrs. Harris's love of, and need for, ceremony.

When Mrs. Harris opened the door, she looked like June Cleaver or Donna Reed, decked out in pearls, high heels and one of those slim fifties skirts with matching jacket. Her grey hair had obviously spent some time in curlers, rolled up at the bottom in a perky flip. It was like returning to the idyllic home George had known for such a short window in time. Well, it was how he chose to think of his childhood home anyway, memory having a tendency to guild the lily.

As they walked through the door, the smell of dinner finished the job of transporting George to a different era. Modern kitchens never produced inviting smells like one might experience in an older person's home. Pasta and salads don't exactly have a definable aroma; maybe that was it. The smell wafting out of Mrs. Harris's kitchen wrapped around him like a warm memory and made his mouth water at the same time. The good dishes were out, and the Doc even had a tie on. Mrs. Harris would have no "shop-talk" during dinner, a surprisingly welcome oasis of distraction from the worries and weight of a world gone mad. There was method to her style that fostered a sense of well-being.

George caught a couple of whiffs of his mother's perfume and just smiled a contented grin. He was conscious of no pain in the memories he ruffled through, feeling only the warmth and love of her presence.

The conversation covered everything from the Harris's curiosity for the academic life to "the kids nowadays." They moved on to the Doc's love of medicine and their community of old friends, slowly dwindling in numbers. As they adjourned to the parlour it became clear the Doc was done with pleasantries.

"George, I may have an answer for you regarding a substance that could cause the heart muscle to fibrillate and leave no trace."

George smiled as he sat down. There were no flies on the old guy. He might be a small town Doc but he was bright and still held an on-going inquisitive fascination with medicine. "Shoot, Doc."

"Well, after I left you this afternoon I made a call to a friend of mine who is with the coroner's department in New York City. I posed the question to him about what sort of substance might do as you described."

"And?"

"Potassium injected in solution."

"No way to trace it?"

"The possibility of some surface residue around the puncture mark in the skin, but the rest is assimilated or reacts so quickly on a chemical level as to leave hardly a discernable trace. My friend says there is another way of looking at this. If a dose of potassium large enough to induce death occurred, there may be enough tell-tale imbalances in other body chemicals as to trace a reaction to a dose of potassium."

"So you might be able to prove potassium was responsible?"

"Maybe."

"Could I use your phone, Doc.?"

"Certainly. It's on the kitchen wall."

George got the number from Joan and ran to the phone to call Bill Monroe. He answered on the first ring.

"Bill Monroe speaking."

"Yes, hello Bill, make sure the coroner looks for a puncture mark in Randy's arm and also see to it he's looking for potassium at the source of injection and as the cause of ventricular fibrillation."

"Who is this? Never mind; don't answer. Just never call here again." Bill hung up. George was offended until he realized he broke rule number one – don't trust the phone! As he turned back to the dining room, the Doc stood facing him.

"I wasn't trying to listen in but I heard everything from the parlour. Someone else has been killed apart from Ernie and your father?"

"Yes."

"Oh dear."

"I guess we need an autopsy on my father."

"He wasn't embalmed was he, George?"

"No, he wouldn't have it. He always said he'd like to rot like he was supposed to, so nature could absorb any good he'd have to give back."

"That's your father all right."

"What about Ernie?"

"Embalmed, but we got blood and tissue samples beforehand."

"Why did you need samples from Ernie?"

"He had been in to see me about a peripheral neuropathy. He was losing feeling in his feet. He swore up and down that it was connected to some weed spray he had been using on his driveway for years. I owed it to him to follow through."

"The samples showed nothing out of the ordinary?"

"Well there was nothing that gave us the answers we were looking for but they might hold other evidence, ruled irrelevant at the time. I'm afraid those samples might be long gone but there may be something on file in the analysis work up at the lab."

"No point in digging old Ernie up then, I guess." The Doc scratched his head in thought. "Although if we did exhume Ernie we could look for the injection puncture."

"Wouldn't he have punctures from the embalming fluids?"

"Oh yes, but those shunts leave a considerably larger hole than the small bevel of an injection needle."

"Why don't you two gentlemen join us in here? We're listening to you anyway!" The voice was loud and clear and so very much Mrs. Harris. The Doc rolled his eyes and motioned to George to follow. They went back in to sip tea in elegant cups contrasted by a not-so elegant subject – exhuming bodies.

"The Sheriff will need to be notified in order to exhume," The Doc stated with a somewhat distracted tone.

"Will you need Elida's permission?" Mrs. Harris asked.

"It is more of a courtesy than anything else if there is just cause, but there is a form that she will have to sign... and George, I'll need a signature from you and the Sheriff before we can exhume your father's body. I have the paperwork around here somewhere, being the local coroner and all. I hope you understand that time is of the essence."

"Yes, I do. I don't have to be there do I? For the exhumation?"

"No, and I wish I didn't have to be either." The Doc's face was already pale with the thought of digging up his dead friends. Joan went there immediately with him.

"Dr. Harris, if your friends were murdered they'd want justice for you – and you do them no disservice or sacrilege in seeking the same."

"Thank you dear. Funny how we sometimes need some line of justification, no matter how lame, to do things we don't think proper. I'm not worried about sacrilege and such, I just want to remember them as the thriving people they were and not some piece of rotting organic material for scientific study. But I guess I'm in no position to enjoy that wish, am I?"

17

Andy

Andy had ignored his friends' words of caution. He headed off to splice the wires on Benito Peroni's phone lines about two hours after the meeting at McDonalds. He didn't bother to get a cable company sticker or a hat or, in fact, anything that might disguise him as a service person – he just went for it after borrowing a safety belt and boot crampons from a friend who trimmed trees for the city.

The Interstate 85 from Durham to Richmond was quiet that day and gave Andy a little too much time to worry about the job at hand. He was almost relieved when he finally found Peroni's street in Richmond. The new houses were examples of oversized opulence, each a testimony to excess and one-upmanship. In Andy's mind, some of these people must have liked high school so much they built one to live in.

He pulled up to the curb in front of the Peroni home and took a couple of deep breaths before getting out and strutting to the back doors of his old van like a professional whatever-he-thought-he-was. He put on the belt and crampons, and slipped his tools, a test phone and line reader into a black nylon Nike bag that slipped over his shoulder. He had worked part-time trimming trees with the owner of the crampons for the last couple of summers and found the telephone pole an easy climb.

Once at the top of the pole he found the lines. As he spliced the wires, he ran the test phone with alligator clips to ascertain which line was modem and which line was the listed phone number. He inserted a one-gig reader with a through-line transmitter on the backside of the junction box. Any time Peroni linked with the mainframe at head office his code numbers would enter Andy's reader before heading downstream. He placed a larger unit in circuit in a more obvious location in front of the junction box as a decoy. While Andy was taping up the last splice of the decoy he spotted something unsettling. There was a small red light under the eaves trough of the Peroni house. On closer inspection, he saw the surveillance camera looking right at him.

A sinking sense of doom set in. He surmised that his license plate was probably on tape as well, given the angle of yet another camera farther down. Would anyone look at the tape studiously? Entertaining a hopeful negative response to that question provided the only territory resembling a good immediate future. He checked for a signal with a small receiver he had in his Nike bag tuned to the right frequency. Both his main line-reader transmitter and the decoy spat out healthy solidly lit LEDs – they were officially on the air.

As he climbed down the pole and started toward his van a dark sedan pull over down the street. "Oh, great!" he muttered under his breath. He had only been up the pole for ten minutes at the outside. No way could these two people, who now sat looking Andy's way, have anything to do with Peroni. He watched them in the side mirror as he got into the van thinking how much they looked like rejects from the old FBI TV show in their dark suits. If they were there to follow him, their conspicuousness was either laughable or they boldly didn't care. That last thought sent a cold shiver down Andy's spine.

As he pulled away, they pulled out and followed. Andy's mind raced ahead with a little encouragement from his adrenal glands. Would they have run his license plate numbers? Do they have his name and address? If so, then why not just meet him at home and beat the tar out of him for information there? Then it dawned on him that maybe they wanted to see where he went and who his contacts were. It was the physical version of running a trace.

"So, you want to see who I'm in with, do you?" Andy remembered Martha's pictures. The Mayor and a couple of councillors seemed real close to the Peronis. One councillor Andy recognized as Roger Chaplan, a bit of a grandstander who had sought a seat in congress unsuccessfully. Chaplan also had a high-profile insurance business advertised regularly on a Richmond TV station carried by the cable provider in Durham.

"Time for a red herring or two, my not-so sneaky friends. Divide and conquer!" Andy drove at a slow pace and made like he was unaware of them. They followed close and never let him out of their sight.

After a couple of cell-phone calls for the address, Andy pulled up in front of Roger Chaplan Insurance. He fumbled in his glove box where he found a pen and wrote the councillor's name on the large blank manila envelope that once held the line readers.

When he got out of the van, Andy noticed the two shadows, in the car across the street, watching his every move. He walked into Chaplan's office and gave the envelope to a receptionist who was visible to the men in the car through the lobby window.

As he pulled away, he noticed that one of the men in the car across the road was on a cell-phone. Hopefully, they had bought the bait that he was working for Chaplan. Andy was quite proud of himself that he may have planted seeds of suspicion in the enemy camp. Would they think he was a little fish working for Chaplan? He could only hope so and decided to get back on the highway home to Durham. He could see no one following and felt a sense of relief in the empty length of Interstate 85 in front of him.

Andy rolled into the driveway of his rented bungalow, tired, but satisfied he had pulled off his operation without a hitch. He was enjoying a dash of cocky pride that dissolved instantly in the movement of a shadow across the passenger door rear-view mirror. It was the same dark sedan he had seen in Richmond pulling up across the street from him. He grabbed his Nike bag and walked to the front door as casually as he could, not wanting to appear alarmed.

As Andy put his key in the lock, out of the corner of his eye, he saw a rather well dressed gentleman emerge from the sedan and calmly head in his direction. Andy frantically opened his door and entered the house.

"I'm screwed" he screamed, wired with fear. He ran down the hall and grabbed the computer bag in his office and scrambled looking for the laptop, which wasn't on the desk! On his way to the kitchen in the back of his house he glanced out the front window. The man was now halfway up his driveway!

"No time!" It was either his computer or his life. As he opened the back door he noticed the laptop under a newspaper on the kitchen table. He reached back in, threw his computer in his nylon shoulder bag, and then quietly closed the back door behind him. He scrambled over the neighbour's fence scraping his shins on the rough wood and didn't stop running for ten minutes. When he pounded on Martha's door several blocks away, he was covered in sweat and gasping for air. Heavy exercise to a true computer dweeb was rapid mouse movement. Fortunately for Andy his instinct for survival and a youth, managed to win over a body that screamed from neglect. Martha answered the door with the chain in place.

"What are you doing here, Andy?"

"Let me in quick!" Martha sensed his urgency and opened the door. Andy shot in, slammed the door behind him and locked both the deadbolts and the chain.

Martha looked alarmed. "What's going on, Andy?"

Andy was still gasping when his eyes fixed on Martha's open housecoat. He had a side profile of her right breast in view and just couldn't get his eyes off it. Martha gave him a cheesed-off look.

"It's called a breast, Andy. I have another just like it on the other side." She angrily pulled her housecoat shut. "Now what's going on?"

"I'm sorry, Martha, I.... the... they... they're on to me. They followed me home from Richmond."

"Who's on to you?"

"Peroni's flunkies. I spliced the wires out in front of Benito's home and a surveillance camera got me."

Martha's face morphed from anger to fear. Her mind was considering a flurry of horrid possibilities as she scanned the street through her front window before pulling her drapes shut. She sat on a threadbare sofa partially covered with a quilt while looking through a slit in the curtains.

"How do you know they didn't follow you here?"

"I gave them the slip at my house. I'm pretty sure no one followed me. I ran on foot through backyards all the way here."

"Pretty sure? You're *pretty sure* Andy? These people kill, and you're *pretty sure*? Nice to see you're so considerate of my life. Why here? Why not Bill's place?"

"You were closer – I was on foot."

Martha sat shaking her head. Her considered fears now merged into the solid reality of being flat-out scared. It was seeing the pale and breathless expression on Martha's face that finally brought that reality to Andy. It wasn't a *Mission Impossible* game anymore, and he realized how stupid he was for even thinking that way.

"I... I should go. I'm sorry Martha."

"Where? Where would you go?" Andy shrugged in response as Martha then tried to assess her own danger. What about your files?"

"Everything's on my laptop." Andy responded.

"Well thank God for that. Alright, you're here now, so you might as well stay here and work here. We need all of our resources now more than ever. I've got an extra high speed line you can use and you can sleep on the couch. You probably shouldn't chance going out. I'll have to pick up some things for you so we can at least keep you clean."

Her tone was maternal and comforting. She lifted the living room curtains to one side to scan the street again for anything unusual before closing them tightly.

"Did you get any information before they found you out?"

"No, I had just spliced the decoy line reader when I noticed the surveillance cameras. They've likely found the decoy by now, but… "

"But what?"

"But if they don't know what they're looking for they might not find the other reader. I split the line in an odd place behind the box. I have to go back and check it just in case."

"Don't be silly. You got away once, don't push your luck!"

"Don't you see Martha? It's like Monroe said, if we don't have enough evidence what's the point of all this? An hour on their mainframe could give us everything we need."

"An hour? What if you don't have an hour? What if you only get ten uninterrupted minutes? Who says you're going to get anything at some optimum level? You don't even know if you could get near enough to their house again without being spotted, let alone get into Peroni's computer. Do you have a strategy for a worst-case scenario?"

"I... uh... well, no."

"I didn't think so." Martha felt she had him surrounded, and he was finally seeing the futility and danger of his plan.

Andy felt a bit like a scolded child and spoke quietly. "I don't have to get into their house."

"You what?"

"I don't have to get into the house to access the mainframe once I have the codes."

"I thought you said their security systems would verify codes with source of interface."

Andy's dabbed sweat on his brow. "It would be source of interface. I put a small transmitter on the reader. You can access the line from up to seventy-five feet away and it will still register as the same location."

"And how would you get within seventy five feet without getting nailed, Andy?"

"I haven't figured that out yet."

"You really worry me."

Andy and Martha talked into the night like a couple of excited kids. They strategized while setting up Andy's workstation to link with her wireless Ethernet. They worked on-line, chasing a series of ideas down before giving into exhaustion just before dawn.

Martha hadn't had a guy sleep over before – this was new territory. There was something maternal about it to her, though only five or six years separated them in age. She also had some other feelings that were a little peculiar to her as she got the sheets and blanket onto the living room couch for her guest. After she made sure Andy was comfortable, she headed to her bed where sleep eluded her.

Martha got back up after an hour or so and went to the bathroom. She stared at herself in the mirror, brushed her hair slowly and mustered up her most fetching pose. The spell was broken by the unsightly hairs on her chin. They had never bothered her before as a part of her defiance, her statement against the objectification of women. She rummaged through the drawer for the tweezers, a little baffled by her own actions.

18

Freedom of the Press

There were a couple of days of relative quiet after the initial flurry of faxes. Ann had agreed to take the matter no further with Dwayne until there was some kind of a game plan. From what George gathered about the local council, the corrupt ones had to hold the majority of seats. The Mayor and his cronies were making decisions that, at best, were questionable. When someone takes a corporate interest over the interest of his or her constituents, money is usually in there somewhere.

All councillors' names were sent to Jim as requested, including a copy of Speek's job application that Dwayne had Speek's assistant dig out of the personnel files and copy while Speeks was out at lunch.

Joan and George had a few moments to sift through family pictures and years of family keepsakes in boxes stuffed in nooks and crannies throughout the house. It was sweet and sad. George ached for his father.

Though the intrigue surrounding his death and the deaths of Randy and Ernie Dobson was intense and distracting, it couldn't overshadow the simple physical absence of his father in the world. Grief sat waiting for a pause in conversation, or entered his being on the dust of a few disturbed sentimental keepsakes. He never realized how much of the past resided in the present. This thing called the present is such a delicate transitory weave of the all that has been, all that will be, all that could be, and all that might have been. One thing felt certain – there could be no forward movement until he escaped the gravitational pull of his loss.

There hadn't been much progress from Jim and his crew. They were worried now that Andy had been identified, and feared some trail might lead to any one of them. This, of course, slowed every inquiry down as tracks were painstakingly covered.

Near the end of the week, with the legal end of Mr. Moss's will complete, George and Joan went into town to sign the necessary documents in the office of his father's lawyer and war buddy Rudy Barnes. The farm was legally George's, but somehow he felt it would never really be his. The farm and everything on it, hung sadly on the earth like the garments in the closet, belonging to no one. His father's physical possessions all held a residue of his soul and now, by law, George was in possession of them. He always hated seeing families squabble over the material entrails of the dearly departed and didn't wish to benefit in any way from the death of his father. Mr. Moss never gave a damn about what he had, which wasn't really anything other than a run down farm and the cash in his desk that didn't quite cover funeral costs.

Material wealth didn't mean much to George Moss Sr., except for wanting his wife to have a few of the baubles that other women of that day seemed to think defined their worth. After her death, the only reason he worked was to get his son through university. But no, George Jr. insisted on paying his own way, so much of what he offered was refused. Mr. Moss was saddened that he wasn't allowed to love his son by contributing to his future, but at the same time, unbeknownst to George, he felt a measure of pride in a boy who could stand on his own two feet.

Joan grabbed a few groceries while George sat in the truck staring at the will. It was but a few words of nonsensical legal jargon signed by that big loving hand that was no more. He touched the signature hoping for some trace of something, but of course there was nothing when he wanted it the most. He figured he could never receive a transmission through the static of his own need, which as far as his father was concerned, remained powerful. The door to the truck burst open and Joan hopped in throwing a newspaper on the seat between them.

George glanced down at a headline announcing: LINCOLN WELCOMES FAIRCHILD ENVIRONMENTAL.

The article was pure propaganda citing the great economic benefits Lincoln would reap from the installation of a state-of-the-art waste storage facility. The article was by Allan Thornhill. George thought he had appeared to be genuinely indignant over the information on Fairchild's record that he had dug up, but there wasn't a single thread of doubt anywhere in the article.

"Something's wrong here, Joan. Let's go see Allan."

They walked down the street to Allan's office and unfortunately passed Patterson's Real Estate. Ned must have been watching them approach and timed his exit accordingly.

"Oh, hello George, Joan, how are you two enjoying your stay out in the country?

George forced a smile. "Fine thank you, Neddy."

"Have you given any further thought to the offer?"

"Still thinking, Ned."

"Well, take your time, George. They say the bereaved shouldn't make any decisions too soon after the loss of someone dear. Have a nice day you two." He headed down the street.

"Now that's a change of face if ever I saw one." Joan observed.

"That was confidence, not consideration," George concluded. "Where there is confidence there is a game plan. He has been instructed by someone on how to play his hand."

Allan was in his office throwing a few things in a box. Joan was about to speak when George squeezed her hand. She got the message and they watched in silence for a few minutes while Allan packed and said nothing. Finally, after intentionally ignoring them for quite some time he spoke without looking in their direction.

"Happy now, aren't ya Moss!"

"No, I'm not. You didn't write that article on Fairchild did you?

Joan looked puzzled and George took it further. "In fact, you wrote something completely different didn't you?"

Allan reached for a couple of pages on his desk and tossed them toward the couple. The top line read: TOWN COUNCIL BREAKS ZONING BY-LAWS, FAIRCHILD ENVIRONMENTAL FAST-TRACKED FOR NEW DUMP

"They were waiting for me," Allan said through clenched teeth. "Head office called me no more than an hour after I went on-line with that article. They hummed and hawed, beat around the bush and, well, I'm fired; I have no job. Thanks so much, George! I knew you were trouble, and still I let my curiosity get the best of me."

"I'm sorry, Allan."

"Oh, spare me. It has always been your big important agendas first George, regardless of who or what you leave in your wake!"

"This isn't my agenda, Allan. This is an agenda that is being inflicted on all of us."

"What have you lost George? Nothing! Absolutely nothing! It's only those around you who get hurt and lose!"

George snapped. "Oh, I've lost Allan. And not to understate the importance of your job here, but some might even go so far as to say I've lost more than you have. They murdered my father!"

Allan looked stunned and sat down. "No way. That can't be true!"

Joan pulled up a chair, disbelief and anger etched on her face.

"Great," she moaned. "We're all in it up to our necks now."

Allan's eyes widened. "Tell me you're exaggerating, George."

"I can't, Allan. And how's this for good measure: They've also murdered a friend of ours who was looking for information – and they killed old Ernie Dobson!"

Allan sat shaking his head and muttering. George went over and put his hand on Allan's shoulder.

"I am truly sorry for involving you in this, Allan... I..."

Joan looked up and interrupted. "How could they have got to your publisher so quickly? Did your publisher say anything else?"

"He said he had been threatened with a huge libel suit, over some of the content in my article, by a high-powered lawyer named Talmer... but damnedest thing..."

"What?"

"My article wasn't even published yet and only my publisher had read it. How the hell can you be sued for libel if you haven't uttered the words in contention yet?"

"Strategic lawsuit against public participation, SLAPP... so Fairchild had to know what you wrote before you sent it." Joan guessed.

"I never thought about it like that, but yeah, now that you mention it, sure looks that way," Allan said slowly as her words sunk in.

George looked around the room and thought out loud: "Allan, have you noticed anything out of the ordinary the last few days that might have indicated someone has been in this office snooping around?"

"Nah, nothing really, except... a couple of days ago when I showed up for work, I noticed the door was unlocked. I just assumed I had left it open the previous night."

George raised an eyebrow. "Have you ever done that before?"

"Oh, at lunch a few times, but I don't think I've ever left the front door open overnight."

George went over to the door, opened it and looked at the lock mechanisms. Nothing looked out of the ordinary. "Was it the morning after we met you at the Deluxe?"

"Um... I guess, yes it was."

"Mm," George mused, "*after* you called me. Is there a back door?"

"Of course, but I never use it."

George went to the back door and opened it. Again, there were no signs of forcible entry. Then something shiny caught his eye. There were brass filings that had trickled down the door jam. He looked at the dead bolt; it had some pretty new scratches and one heavy gouge.

"When was the last time you used this door Allan?"

Allan bounded over with a concerned look. "I haven't used that door since I've been at this office and that's over two years."

Closer inspection revealed imprints of a shoe tread on the dirty floor just inside the door. The footprints headed into the office and there appeared to be no prints coming back.

George stroked his chin. "Between these brass filings and those one-way footprints, I'd say you had a visitor who jimmied this dead-bolt open, then left via the front door."

Joan's voice piped up somewhere behind Allan. "Would you have left a copy of your article lying around?"

"Sure," Allan shrugged, "on my hard disc drive."

George picked up where Joan left off. "Okay, so let's assume our burglar is computer literate. How hard would it be to locate an article you were working on?"

"Come on, George, this is Lincoln. It was titled on my desktop and my computer has no access codes or the like. My articles are all on Word files. It's a goddamned community newspaper. The only secrets we ever deal with are the ingredients for Mrs. Local's award-winning rhubarb pie. Besides, how would they have known I was even considering writing anything?"

"Any number of ways, Allan. One, my phone is tapped and we spoke. Two, your phone and computer lines are tapped. Three, we were seen at the Deluxe, and in fact someone was waiting for us there, which might confirm options one or two or both."

"Speeks!" Joan said with a hiss.

"What the hell has that jerk got to do with this?" Allan snapped.

"We think he's linked to Fairchild," George said.

"So he's the burglar?"

"Maybe."

"Like I said before, George, what you're up to is always so much more damned important than anything us mere mortals might be amusing ourselves with."

George shook his head. "You can keep feeding that useless chip you have growing on your shoulder – or consider joining forces with us. If all goes well you may even get your job back."

"And if all doesn't go well, George, what then? Will I get killed like your father? To hell with you, Moss, I'm not dying for one of your causes. I'm outta here!" He gave George a look that said any further interaction was pointless, so George backed off.

"Good luck to you, Allan."

They left Allan the way they found him, throwing things into boxes, except now anger fuelled his resignation.

Joan looked at George and smirked. "The guy moans about never doing anything important, so you offer to cut him in on the most action this town has ever seen and what does he do? He splits. The guy's a loser George. He's not angry with you. He's angry with himself and actually I think... oh, never mind."

"You can't bait me like that, what were you going to say?"

"I think he likes you."

"What, are you nuts?"

"No, you're missing the point George, he *really* likes you. I would go so far as to say he has a crush on you. When he looks at you something else is there. And, his body language when he said you couldn't care less about him... reeked of rejected fantasy."

"Oh, please!"

"Has he ever had a girlfriend?"

"He dated Ann for a while after we split up."

"Camouflage! No, maybe curiosity, he wanted to see what you saw in her. He wants to know you in the biblical sense."

"Don't be ridiculous."

"I'm telling you, George. I've seen enough of Jim's friends to be familiar with the territory."

"If he wants into my pants why doesn't he chat me up nicely, offer to take me out to dinner or buy me something that sparkles."

"He knows you'd reject him. He's probably been rejected fiercely by a couple of heterosexuals already. Besides, in a town like Lincoln, he can't be who he is in any kind of open way.

"Why would he be sweet on someone he knows is a hopeless hetero?"

"Why not? He can be sweet on anyone he wants to fantasize about and never act on it."

"Except for being abusive"

"Well, that's one method of having more than a passing relationship with someone. Emotionally engaging someone, even in a negative way, is a kind of relationship."

They talked about Allan all the way to the hospital. Some of Allan's anger fit the way Joan framed it. Survival is incredibly adaptable.

Millie was in fine form when they got to the hospital and she obviously more than approved of Joan. Seeing the two youngsters appeared to bring forgotten memories to the surface of her mind. Millie had loved someone passionately, if her face was any guide to her thoughts. That someone was in her mind as she spoke. George was just having a hard time thinking of Mr. Walker as a romantic. There had to have been more to that old man, or Millie for that matter, for her to glaze over the way she did.

But there was George, thinking about an old woman's sex life and as usual his new theory began unveiling. *Maybe it's all distilling down to this: We are created by sex. We spend the first few years thinking about what sex must be like. We finally engage in sex, and then we over indulge in the new high. Then some of us move on to the quest for power over others, which might very well be an aberrant expression of sexual behaviour. Some of us try to deny sex in an exercise of mind over matter or to achieve some sense of a man-made holiness revered by idiots – like, ignoring ourselves is to be admired. This suppressed sexuality of course can lead to even more aberrant behaviour like what some priests do to altar boys. For others, sex gets progressively weird, as greater stimuli are required to overcome complacency and familiarity. Then men start to worry about growing old, so they frantically try to get as much sex in as possible before it's too late. This is partially driven by Mother Nature's whip, assuming that if you've lasted reasonably long, your gene pool must be worth spreading around. When we are old and wrinkled and think nobody could possibly want us in "that" way anymore, many retire to just thinking about the good old days when we were able to have sex or we are reduced to speaking suggestively, like we could actually do something about it. When we are completely fucked physically and mentally, we die. Not really a huge amount of spiritual growth in that scenario is there? Life could ultimately just be about sex management. Please allow for at least a ten-percent margin of error in this theory for men, and a much higher margin for women, from what I know of them...*

George was getting ready to move onto another mental tangent when he felt an insistent tug on his arm. Joan had a look that said he was being rude and that his presence was required for polite conversation. His theory would have to be filed away in the back of his mind for the time being.

19

Seeds take Root

The sun streamed onto Andy's face and he began to awaken. He and Martha were burning out on the Net, and both Bill and Jim were simply pulling up variations on a theme. He had decided when he went to bed that the next day he would see if his line reader was still in place. If it was, it was time to attempt to access the Fairchild mainframe. Must be pretty late he thought to himself, given the high angle of the light entering Martha's living room. On his way to the bathroom he passed Martha's open bedroom door and stared at her long golden hair splayed over her pillow.

He had been thinking about Martha a good part of the night in fairly erotic terms. The day before, she had entered the bathroom while he was having a pee and stood there, coolly chatting, as if talking to urinating men was a daily occurrence. She concluded her chattiness with the information that dinner was, in fact, ready, then turned, but only after she had a good look at Andy's privates with a Mona Lisa expression on her face, both knowing and playful. Later that evening, when she was taking a bath she asked whether Andy would mind bringing her some tea, it was quite all right she was safely behind the shower curtain "if he was nervous." But the curtain wasn't particularly well drawn, and Andy caught an eyeful. Martha didn't seem the least bit bothered by his glances, not like she was the day he arrived. Signals? Were these signals? Andy had no idea because; well... he'd never had any signals before. How the heck was he supposed to know what a signal was?

Andy noticed the hairs on her chin were gone and she was wearing her hair down. Martha was a substantial woman in more ways than one and with her recent attention to detail; her attractiveness was not going unnoticed by Andy. However, the idea that he appealed to her was unthinkable to Andy. Although Martha suspected him to be sexually curious, he was painfully shy about such matters, definitely not your average male full of cheap double entendres, turn-offs and suggestive banter... and he was in *her* home. Martha had never really been that close to a guy, apart from her father. Her father had been an abusive drunk so Martha's mother, a social worker, did some social work on her own – she moved her two daughters and herself out of harm's way when Martha was barely a teenager. There generally was a fear of men amongst the three of them but she felt no fear of Andy. Maybe it was his naiveté and the probability that he was still a virgin.

Andy had locked the door for his morning pee. But then, entertaining what was to him some fantastically unreal notion, he opened it again. She must be out cold, he thought, as he disappointedly walked back down the hall and began getting dressed in the living room. Martha appeared and stopped at the kitchen door. She stretched a sleepy stretch that pulled her housecoat open slightly exposing a hint of breast, which she made no attempt to conceal.

"Coffee's on in a minute. How come you're up so early?"

"Early! It's nearly noon, Martha. I gotta get rolling"

"Rolling?"

"I have to find out if my bug is working at the Peroni place."

"Don't be so silly." She walked to him as he pulled on his pants.

"I'm not being silly. I thought Bill could drive me and I could stay out of sight in the back seat long enough to check it out."

Martha sighed. "You know these guys play rough, don't you?" She sat down, intentionally giving Andy a fair eyeful.

Andy's voice started sounding a little funny. "We are at a standstill. We need new information. We need damning information."

"Like what?"

"I don't know yet."

"You need to think things through a little more, Andy. Shouldn't you at least figure out what information we might need, so if you make your kamikaze play, you could reduce on-line time and maybe your chances of getting caught?"

"Yeah, I guess your right."

"Thank you, I know that was hard for you to say."

"Not as hard as some stuff."

"Like what, Andy?" she asked, baiting him.

"You know... stuff."

Martha saw how red he was going and let him off the hook. "Andy, let's meet with Bill and Jim about this. I'll see if they can come over."

When Martha stood up to go to the kitchen phone it wasn't just breast Andy saw. He gulped and could hardly breathe. He was uncontrollably aroused. He was smitten, he was... well... in love, as far as he could figure. He had never been in love before; how the hell was he to know what love was for sure? This had to be a reasonable facsimile at the least – whatever it was, it was strong.

Bill's computer chimed with the cheerful announcement: "You've got mail." There was to be a brunch at Martha's in an hour. Bill and Jim were about to make some lunch so both the timing and the idea itself was perfect. By the time they got there, the pancakes were in the oven and Martha was showered and dressed. Everyone sat around the table.

Martha was fussing over Andy a little while they ate. She was making sure he had a napkin, enough syrup and... cream for his coffee.

When Andy responded with lingering stares of admiration, Jim finally gave Bill a knowing roll of the eyes, which Bill acknowledged. They'd been surprised by Martha's makeover when she answered the door. The first clue for Jim was the missing chin hairs. Martha's beautiful shoulder-length Lady Clairol hair had spent some time in curlers. Jim had only ever seen Martha's hair pulled back into a stringy ponytail. Bill was impressed as well and attempted to compliment her, which of course made her uncomfortable, so he dropped it.

Between gulps of food and swigs of coffee they brought each other up to date on where they stood with their respective searches.

Then, Martha got to the point. "Andy wants to see if his line reader is working. If it is, he wants to attempt to access the mainframe."

"I don't know if that's wise, Andy," Jim advised with a stern tone.

Andy was ready for him. "What other options do we have, Jim? I've been listening to what amounts to a virtual standstill. I don't even need to be seen. I can check if the damn thing is working in a drive-by. Just stop within seventy-five feet of the pole for a few seconds, a minute tops, and I'll know if the line is working. If it is, then we put our heads together, come up with a data-shopping list, and schedule a return visit.

"I already have a list," Bill said somewhat ominously. "I hate to say it but this is our only real chance at the moment. How much time do you think we might need once we are into their system?"

Andy gulped down his coffee. "An hour would be wonderful, two would be better."

Martha blew up. "An hour or two? What are you, crazy? How the hell do you park outside the Peroni house for two hours without them getting suspicious? You were barely down the pole when those guys showed up the last time! What did you have, five minutes? Those surveillance cameras are obviously being monitored around the clock."

Jim looked serious. "There has to be a way. Come on, we have a seventy-five foot radius. How can we get close enough and stay long enough to at least give us some new threads to pull on? Before we invest hours in this plan, let's do the drive-by thing and see if Andy's stuff is even working or still there, for that matter. This whole conversation might be academic"

"I'll take him." Martha offered.

"Alright." Jim responded, "We'll wait for you at Bill's. Good luck. And if you're followed, don't come to us whatever you do. Phone Bill's cell if you can and ask for a fake name to signal trouble."

Once Martha agreed to the arrangements and the group worked out a few final details, Bill and Jim slipped their shoes on and headed out, leaving Martha and Andy sitting at the table.

Martha looked at Andy, smiled, and then leaned over and kissed him on the cheek before she knew what she was doing. It felt surprisingly natural to her.

"Come on, Sunshine," she grinned. "Let's get this over with."

Andy sat for a second, stunned. Her intoxicating touch and smell had paralyzed him.

Then Andy heard the car start.

He grabbed a Nike bag that held a few items Martha had bought for him – and managed to get on his feet.

20

A Corporate World

L ou Peroni had asked for a meeting with his older brother Benito, the CEO of Fairchild, along with Robert Douglas and Helmut Talmer. They all waited silently, decked out in expensive tailored suits with a retail value that could have solved problems in the third world.

The boardroom was a study of chic sterility and power – black leather chairs positioned on expensive dark grey carpet around a huge black Italian marble table with burled-walnut edging. There were no papers or signs of commerce anywhere; just the Fairchild Environmental logo in gold on one mirrored wall.

Helmut Talmer, a tall imposing man with greying hair and a well groomed beard, stared out the window, not wishing to engage the other two men. Lou's initial elegance was shattered on closer inspection by the Mr. T. starter-kit of gaudy gold on his fingers, cufflinks, tie-pin with chain, and Rolex, all oversized in an obvious display of wealth. He attempted small talk with Douglas, but Douglas wasn't having any, smiling politely and saying as little as possible.

Benito entered in his usual gregarious way visually acknowledging all those present before taking his place at the head of the table. He was a rotund man, and the chairs were suitably accommodating. He constantly glanced at the mirrored wall looking for an out of place hair or crease in his clothing that he would smooth over repeatedly. He looked over people when he spoke, but never at them.

"Please gentlemen, sit." He had the tone of humility and benevolence. Those who knew him were aware that such humility was only present when his power was respected. Such benevolence also appeared when he needed something or wished to feed a saintly image that was currently under construction. If anyone had sat down before Benito's invitation to do so, a note would have been made of it. Should such behaviour have occurred a second time, they would be spoken to. Even Lou, his own brother, would only dare to show such familiarity with his brother when no one else was present.

The public image of Fairchild was that of a company owned and operated by two loving brothers. The reality was the "two loving brothers" thing was an image Benito fed to take focus off himself. In public, he deferred to Lou, his university-educated brother, while feigning the pose of a simple man, amazed at his younger brother's abilities. In reality it was Benito's ties with "the boys" that helped build the company, in exchange for a healthy loan that could never be paid back. It was what they called a mortgage, with payments in perpetuity. As long as the payments were made, "the boys" kept their distance, not wanting to hamper the cash cow Fairchild was proving to be.

Waste, industrial and residential was the new gold rush. Organized crime happened to be in a prime position initially with trucking companies all over the continent. Huge profit margins went ballistic as they moved into related industries like garbage collection, sewage treatment plants, plastic and metal recycling and even road building where landfill and aggregate were required.

Fairchild was a working model for the whole sordid mess. It even had a recycling research and development division, the sole purpose of which was propaganda; window dressing to give environmental credibility to their company. Politicians buying into the self-promotion were supporting Fairchild as the way of the future.

The bubble would burst soon. In dumps all over North America, waste was not being processed but simply renamed and thrown into the ground. Mix cyanide in concrete and voila just a bunch of broken concrete – inert waste... until it starts to leach out. Cancers and other health complications, such as respiratory, nerve and autoimmune diseases on the rise in many areas surrounding dumpsites. There was a mounting body of evidence pointing to the toxins in the Great Lakes as being the cause for a dramatic drop in the sperm count in males living in the watershed. In some cases local health officials were being paid off to fudge statistics or suggest data was incomplete or to imply other causes such as fossil fuel emissions or poor dietary habits were the real culprits rather than fellow contributing factors.

So it was a business that was buying time in order to squeeze as much money out of the system as it could. When that time ran out, whenever a dumpsite became an obvious health threat, the company running it would simply go bankrupt and the cleanup became the responsibility of the taxpayer. The system was perfect as far as Benito was concerned. The public was generally unconcerned about where their waste went, just so long as it went away. Benito often laughed at the rationale with which Thomas Crapper had sold the world the flush toilet. The humour in this was priceless to him: Flushing excrement down pipes into bodies of water right next to the pipes that drew drinking supplies. He often said that if God had meant this to be, "our assholes should be right next to our mouths." The reality was: citizens were recycling their own urine and fecal matter by drinking it. This lovely environmentally friendly thought caused Benito, like many of the affluent, to drink only bottled water. Tap water, he thought, should have a warning: "Caution; the fluids you drink might be your own."

Ben Peroni thrived in the wake of consumerism, the backbone of the economic paradigm. So long as people kept consuming products designed not to last in order to keep the machine rolling, Benito knew he had a business fed by a trail of waste, the ultimate renewable resource. He was convinced the world wasn't about to wake up any time soon. The subscription to the UN wartime economic model was nearly complete with China entering the consumer game. Waste, was the New World.

"Mr. Douglas, I understand you have been busy." Benito gave the floor to Robert Douglas, who stood in a somewhat military fashion, speaking in short halting sentences.

"The first indication of a problem," Douglas began, "was an attempt to enter our mainframe. Joseph informed me of the attempt immediately. We dealt with this impertinence and an apology has been accepted. However, the person trying to enter our system has an acquaintance, currently at large. We believe he was involved in the attempt on our security. We consider this a contained and isolated incident not worthy of your time but there are complications."

Benito interrupted. "Before you go any further, do you have any leads on the acquaintance?"

"We are getting close."

"Close? Close doesn't count, Mr. Douglas." The room was uncomfortably quiet until omnipotence turned benevolent again.

"Continue, Mr. Douglas."

"There was an attempt to tap your residential phone lines a couple of days ago and… "

"What?" Benito's face flushed with anger. "My personal phone lines?"

"Yes, sir."

"Why wasn't I informed?" Benito blasted.

Lou cleared his throat and entered sheepishly. "Ben, I uh, I instructed Mr. Douglas to report to you once everything was under control."

"And is everything under control?"

Lou looked at the floor. "Not exactly."

"Not exactly? First I hear Mr. Douglas say he is "getting close" and now I hear you say things are "not exactly" under control and what is worse, I am not informed?"

"That is the purpose of this meeting," Lou offered timidly.

"And were you aware of any of this Helmut?" Benito inquired.

"I am involved in a related matter that has been dealt with effectively, Ben."

"Never answering the question directly, offering only a reply that sheds a positive light on yourself, as usual, Mr. Talmer?"

"It is the same positive light I shed on you as my client, Ben."

Benito huffed under his breath in disgust. He respected honest straight answers. Talmer's entire professional life was testament to an evasiveness that served Peroni's business interests so well it was tolerated.

"Continue Mr. Douglas," Benito huffed. Douglas reached into his pocket and pulled out a small matchbox-size device with stripped wires hanging out of one end.

"This was disconnected from the lines outside your home. It was placed there by a young man named Andrew Schumann. He was arrested for downloading pornographic materials from the Internet a few years ago but no charges were filed. This may not be anything but..." Douglas hesitated.

"Please, Mr. Douglas, spit it out," Benito snapped impatiently.

"Well, after bugging your place he dropped a package off at councillor Chaplan's office downtown."

"Chaplan? What the hell does Roger think he's doing? We've been good to him and his family. Do we need an apology from him as well?" Benito looked at Talmer, who was obviously uncomfortable.

"What is it Helmut?"

"Perhaps I should leave the room for a time if you gentlemen wish to discuss such things."

"Like you have some kind of integrity to protect? Sit still. Answer my question, Mr. Douglas."

"An apology from Mr. Chaplan at this point might be premature. We have paid him a visit and had a delightful conversation. I think the package delivered to him was a smoke screen. There was nothing in it."

"Well, that's one piece of good news." Lou said hopefully, trying to enter the fray with some authority.

"Hardly, sir," Douglas continued condescendingly. "If Mr. Schumann knows we have some connection with Mr. Chaplan then there has already been some research as regards to our promotional programs." Lou's body language recoiled from an authoritative to a submissive demeanour. Benito looked at him with disgust.

"So where are we on this shoe guy?" Benito snapped.

"We have Mr. Schumann's house and his parents' house under surveillance. I think we will have him soon."

"You lost him, Mr. Douglas?"

"I underestimated him once. It won't happen a second time. He is the least of our worries"

Benito's eyes widened. "It gets worse?"

"The gentleman who attempted to access our mainframe, it turns out, was a business associate of a Canadian woman by the name of Joan Parks. Joan Parks lives with George Moss."

"Moss? The man whose apology we accepted regarding the matter in Lincoln?"

"No sir, it's the son who came down from Canada for his father's funeral and has been in touch with the local newspaper in Lincoln."

Benito stood up and started pacing the room.

"And?"

Talmer saw his window of opportunity to pat his own back.

"And I exerted a little legal pressure on the publisher who felt it prudent to relieve the man of his job rather than engage in a suit he can't afford. Nothing will see print."

Benito's face gave way to a smug look of satisfaction. He resented Talmer's opportunistic zeal to appear effective but was still grateful for his quick action in plugging a leaking dike.

"What did they have?"

"Just a couple of minor environmental violations and that the Lincoln council had circumvented a municipal zoning law," Talmer responded coolly.

"Just a couple of minor violations! You, of all people, know the importance of public relations, Helmut. Stay on top of that one and make sure nothing comes out! Do we have the Moss property yet, Lou?"

"He's thinking our offer over."

"Double it. And Mr. Douglas? Find that son of a bitch who tried to tap my phone! Lou, you take Chaplan out for dinner and make sure he's still on the team. Gentlemen, I can't tell you how much this new storage re-cycling facility means to our company apart from being the largest source of income we may ever have! From now on, call me on any new information. We better have this damn environmental hearing moved up. See to that for me, Helmut. Earn your keep. This meeting is over!"

Benito stormed out of the room. Lou and Douglas seemed resigned to their instructions while Helmut Talmer on the other hand was incensed at being talked to in such a manner and huffed himself up and out of the door. He believed in his own illusions of grandeur. However, injured pride was quickly pushed aside by the thought of how much money he was making and how he stood to profit when the Lincoln storage facility went through. The farms were to be dug down in pits sixty to one hundred feet deep. There were already contracts in place to provide fill for new highway roadbeds so there was money to be made from digging the site as well as filling it in.

Fairchild stock would at least double with the influx of the new revenue, which he estimated in the neighbourhood of one billion dollars over five years. Talmer had been given a large chunk of stock in lieu of a huge and accumulating legal bill. As soon as this new waste storage facility was up and running he would announce his retirement for health reasons, sell all his shares in Fairchild Environmental and leave with ten to twelve million.

Douglas hadn't had time at the meeting to voice caution that the interconnectedness of these incidents was the most serious situation Fairchild had ever faced. He knew Moss was linked to Jim Grayson through Joan Parks. He hadn't told Benito he now knew that he had terminated the wrong man and, worse, Grayson had seen him. He also had suspicions that Grayson was somehow linked to Andrew Schumann. It all had the feel of something that was getting out of control.

All of this had Douglas considering a trip to Lincoln and to the Moss farm with the idea that a little investigative conversation might be in order. With no immediate leads in the city, and if his suspicions were correct, this visit to Lincoln might unravel the whole thing. Of course, once the information was extracted an apology might be necessary.

Another termination via the usual chemical means however would appear too coincidental. No, he thought, once information had been extracted a bad car accident or even a fire would provide a more effective tragedy. After all, there was the matter of the woman Moss lived with, so a fire or vehicular mishap would be more prudent when more than one apology was required. The local paper was in need of news so they would soon have the details of a terrible accident to titillate the population for a few days. He pulled his cell-phone from his pocket and dialled a number.

"Please have the car out front in twenty minutes, Stanley, and be prepared for an overnight; we have a small interview to attend a fair distance from the city." He continued down the corridor of the expensively decorated Fairchild office complex, past the huge walnut doors of Benito's office that clicked shut on his way by. The door barely muffled a tirade of expletives as Benito verbally tore into his brother.

At the end of the corridor sat the glassed-in systems room, the heart of the entire operation. Ben Peroni believed in the convenience of technology. It enabled him to play some serious sleight-of-hand. The company's tracking system allowed for quick overviews of what materials were on the road at any given time. He knew how many trucks were out there, what the manifests said, for inspection purposes, and through a coding system, what was actually being carried. Every detail of the company was organized and computerized to the last penny that had crossed a politician's palm. Benito could bamboozle anyone with figures and printouts.

He had figures that could be ready for the IRS on a moment's notice. He had an instant financial position to suit any occasion. It was a wonder of computerization and the purpose of it all of course was to ensure as little money went out as possible. Ben played the inept fool when it came to his knowledge and love of computers. He had a wonderful way of making his systems personnel think his ideas were their ideas. His home computer link had extensive capabilities that, naturally he said he never needed or used and didn't understand. His excuse was that he simply wanted the best technology available and no function was considered overkill. The truth was he used his system to the max and knew it inside out.

Joseph was at his position in front of the security systems, monitoring hits on the promotional pages of Fairchild's web site. This site served the company well with brilliant graphics and environmentally friendly propaganda and even an interactive ecology page for children. Apart from the promotional links, all access to the mainframe by staff was monitored twenty-four hours a day. There were also three monitors from surveillance cameras installed at Benito's house and two for Lou's residence. There was a wall of split-screen monitors fed by two-dozen cameras around the office complex itself. Big Brother was indeed watching. Joseph was always on guard for the likes of Jim Grayson,

Greenpeace or environmentalist hackers. He was also aware of the occasional sweep by what he thought had the signature of the FBI.

There was some thought the FBI might be following up half-heartedly on some of the minor environmental infractions Fairchild had accumulated in a few states. There was also the remote possibility they were interested in looking for any loose ends regarding a missing former Fairchild employee as well as possible links to organized crime. They had attempted accessing the mainframe six months earlier and were detected within seconds. Joseph alerted Robert Douglas and somehow a virus entered FBI systems from an unknown source causing the loss of so much data on criminal investigations around the country that a few heads rolled as a result. The virus was injected when the de-activated terminal that had tried to access the Fairchild mainframe, suddenly came on again in the middle of the night. A large happy face appeared and then, line-by-line it slowly removed itself before the terminal powered down. Meanwhile, the virus continued on tidying up by entering other connected terminals, deleting a large chunk of memory from the FBI system before the alarms went off.

Extraordinary measures were taken by a few programmers who interrupted the virus, stored all remaining un-backed up data in bins, which were then disconnected from the system. They were off line for days before the entire system was swept and the virus removed. Some of the computer system had been rendered useless to the point of replacement. An investigation was begun into the point of origin of the virus but was getting nowhere fast. If they did locate the source it would be an apartment that had been rented by a man who no longer lived there and had no forwarding address. Such a man would no longer use the name on the rental agreement.

Joseph jumped to his feet when he saw Robert Douglas enter. "Mr. Douglas; how good of you to drop in."

"Joseph, I am going out of town for a day or so. I want you to keep your eyes especially wide open over the next few days. If you leave this room for a second, I want only your best people on these monitors until your return."

"Are we expecting visitors?"

"I believe there are a few very capable people expressing some interest in our operations at the moment. I can be reached on my cell. Anything, even the most minuscule thing out of the ordinary, I expect to hear from you immediately regardless of the hour. Do I make myself clear?"

"Perfectly, Mr. Douglas."

Douglas scanned the monitors quickly and was gone. He walked the few short steps to his office and locked the door behind him. He pulled open the top desk drawer, entered a seven digit number onto a small touch-pad of what appeared to be an average looking calculator then hit the plus sign. The sound of an electronic click snapped from behind a classic painting on the wall. The large, ornately framed Rubens depicted a family, hunting dogs and freshly killed game birds, all assembled in front of a glowing fire. The painting began to move laterally to the hum of electric motors slowly revealing a large walk-in wall safe. After spinning in the combination, Douglas hauled the door open and stepped over the high sill. The safe was a good ten feet long and six feet wide with metal shelving and drawers on one side and a modest collection of weapons on the other. He grabbed a small translucent plastic pouch containing syringes from the top shelf. One shelf down, he moved a few stacks of sealed hundred dollar bills revealing a few labelled vials of clear liquids. He selected one vial of the sodium pentothal, one vial of potassium and a few syringes, placing them into the false bottom of a fine leather attaché case. Exiting the safe he went to a tall burled walnut door on the other wall in the office and opened it.

The walk in closet had a half-dozen expensive suits and shirts. He selected two clean shirts and a change of undergarments from the side drawer and packed them fastidiously into an expensive Italian leather bag along with a few toiletries. Douglas always believed he should represent the company well when traveling on company business. Ironically, those he wished to impress would never be allowed the time to comment one way or another. The sodium pentothal, he thought, would provide a nice relaxed range of conversation from the son of George Moss and his lady friend. He was just about to leave when the phone rang. It was Joseph.

"Mr. Douglas, you might want to come in here quickly."

Douglas closed his safe, dialled the numbers back into the calculator and hit the plus sign. The large Rubens painting slid back into place as he left for the systems room.

"What is it?"

"An old Volvo wagon in front of Mr. Peroni's house."

On screen, Martha had the hood open and was looking at the engine.

"How long has it been there?"

"It just arrived, but when it did, there was some guy in the back seat who appeared to be giving the woman instructions, then he ducked out of sight."

Douglas squinted his eyes to observe detail. "She's either talking to her engine or under her breath to the guy in her back seat. She appears quite nervous."

Martha closed the hood and hopped back in the car.

"Can we get a good angle on the plate number, Joseph?"

"I'll try, Mr. Douglas."

As the car pulled away, Joseph moved a joystick anticipating the car's direction.

"Zoom, Joseph!"

Joseph waited a split second, one step ahead of Douglas, ensuring that when he did zoom he would be in the right position. The license was clear as a bell. Douglas grabbed a piece of paper and jotted it down.

"Could you roll back please, Joseph and show me the man you saw in the back seat." The hard disk recording shot back then forward in slow motion as the car approached.

"Hold it right there! Upper right quadrant, and enlarge."

The face was a little blurred but the image was familiar to Douglas.

"Well, well, well, if it isn't our dear Mr. Schumann. Joseph, get me an address for that license will you please, and Joseph..."

"Yes, Mr. Douglas?"

"Good work. I'll be in my office."

"Thank you, Mr. Douglas."

Douglas went back to his office and closed the door. He hesitated for a moment then picked up the phone on his desk and dialled in Ben Peroni's number. After a brief Kenny Gee musical interlude on the office phone system, Benito picked up, still yelling at his brother for a split second to get out of his sight and get busy! Benito cleared his throat and spoke in an instantly calm voice.

"Yes, Mr. Douglas."

"You wished to be informed of progress, sir, so I thought I should let you know that the man who attempted to tap your phone lines was in front of your house moments ago."

"Did you get the son of a bitch?"

"No sir but we have the license of his girlfriend's car and will have an address shortly."

"Douglas." Benito's tone was one of suffering fools none too gladly.

"Yes, sir."

"I know you are following my instructions to the letter but this is micro-management. Call me when the stupid fuck who had the balls to tap my fucking phone, my phone, my residential phone, the place where my family lives for fuck's sake, call me when you have him, not when you are getting close to him! Not when you think you know where he might be, but when you have him! When he has nothing left to fucking say, you may accept an apology! Do I make myself clear, Mr. Douglas?" Benito slammed the phone down hard.

Douglas was visibly annoyed. Peroni had double-crossed him to his own way of thinking. He'd hesitated in calling Peroni as he'd anticipated the outcome of his call. But he wanted the responsibility for his actions to be squarely on the shoulders of Benito. His new instructions were to speak to Benito only when Andy Schumann was dead.

Too many "apologies," he believed, were a result of bad management. An occasional apology was one thing; so many apologies attached to one business venture were another. Benito's impetuousness and bad attention to planning would cause Douglas to accept apologies from half the known population of the world at this rate.

The phone rang. It was Joseph with the address.

Martha was sweating profusely. Andy had hopped back into the front seat once the car was out of range of the surveillance cameras. He was so excited. "My line reader is functioning, they only got the decoy! We're as good as in!"

He kissed Martha on the cheek and she smiled a warm smile. "Don't count your chickens until we are in, and home safely with everything we want to know. We need a strategy session, let's go to Bill's."

"Let's make sure we aren't being followed first," Andy suggested with a not-so-clever motive.

"And how do we do that?" asked Martha.

"We go park somewhere for a few minutes and see if anyone parks near us. Then we move to another location and do the same. Then we head back to the interstate and home to Bill's."

Martha knew what was going on but thought it was sort of sweet in a juvenile way. Andy was a few years her junior and she assumed asking someone to go parking might be the only words he knew for expressing interest. She didn't want to shoot him down.

Within minutes they were in a large secluded parking lot behind a grocery store with the engine off.

Andy looked at her and Martha found the look both powerful and loving. He moved closer to her and kissed her on the lips.

Martha returned the compliment.

Things progressed quite passionately until Martha decided to change course and pulled back for a few reasons, one of which was the need for control. "Andy. I know we have been becoming interested in each other and I want you to know that I quite like you. Don't worry this is not a let-down speech; I like you enough to sleep with you, but... "

Andy looked a little excited and peeved at the same time.

"But what?"

"But I am not going to do it in the car for goodness sake. I want it to be nice and I want some romance, Andy."

"Okay, so what do you suggest?" Andy's voice was a little strained but not nearly as strained as his testicles were at that moment.

"I suggest we cherish the eroticism of knowing we are going to make love, but we go to Bill's first to get the ball rolling then we will have all night at my house to indulge ourselves."

Andy just nodded in the affirmative. He couldn't speak. The thought that this woman had just announced she was going to make love to him all night long was almost more than he could handle.

Martha started the car. "Nobody followed us here, Andy."

Andy just nodded again. He was still lost in the thought of Martha's suggestion. His brain was incapable of entertaining anything else.

Martha pulled out of the lot and began the drive back to Durham.

Bill and Jim were eager for news when they saw Martha and Andy pull in the driveway. They were met at the door and ushered in quickly.

"Well?" Bill looked like he was going to burst.

"They only got the decoy, Andy's reader is in circuit," Martha announced proudly.

"Yes!" Jim formed a defiant fist. "Want to play with us do ya Fairchild? Well you better be prepared to lose big, you cock-suckers!"

Martha looked a little miffed at the language. Bill raised an eyebrow while Andy just stood there catatonically nodding.

"You alright, Andy?" Bill asked in a concerned tone. Andy tried to snap out of it.

"Uh, yeah. We need some strategy now. Why don't we stew on it for a day or so and then get together."

"We're here now and I already have some thoughts to get us going that might serve as a starting point, Bill said. "Then we can split with some semblance of direction."

Bill was quite proud of the strategy he was about to reveal. Andy couldn't have looked more pissed-off if he had rehearsed. Martha gently held his hand and they followed Bill and Jim through to Bill's office.

Jim saw they were holding hands and burst into tears.

"What is it, Jim?"

"Oh just seeing you two hold hands made me think of Randy." Martha dropped Andy's hand and held Jim a little reluctantly as he wept.

Bill looked at Andy. "What is going on with you two?"

"We have become quite fond of each other, Bill." Andy spoke with a strange sense of pride and Martha liked the sound of it. Jim regained control, steering the conversation back to the task at hand.

"I'm not going to mourn Randy until I have his killer behind bars. Let's get to work." Jim sniffled. Bill began unravelling potential plans.

A couple of hours later, Martha and Andy were on their way home.

Andy was still stunned in expectation. Martha thought she was falling in love but didn't want to confuse sex with love. She hadn't been very active sexually. In fact, she had only a few experiences herself that she wanted to forget.

The youthful shyness of Andy and his suspected virginity gave Martha's somewhat-poor self-confidence the extra edge it needed. She thought she would like to make love for a few days and then see if she still felt as fondly for Andrew as he seemed to feel for her.

As they approached the house, Andy's eyes opened wide with fear.

"Stop! Stop now!"

Martha hit the brakes, screeching her car to a halt. The noise alerted two figures in a dark sedan across the road from her house. They turned and saw Martha's Volvo in the middle of the road.

"It's them!" Andy shouted. "It's them! It's the car that followed me to my house. They've found us!"

Martha wrenched the steering wheel as the Volvo's tires squealed the heavy old wagon into a tight U-turn. Pedal to the metal, she pushed the small reliable four-cylinder motor to its pathetic best.

Douglas and his driver buckled their seat belts and proceeded in an orderly manner after them.

"Stanley, I think we can put ourselves into a win-win situation if we get them on to the freeway and in such a position as to favour the third exit." Douglas stated with his usual cool.

"I understand, Mr. Douglas," Stanley replied. He was Douglas's driver for a reason – he was exceptional at what he did.

Martha gasped in fear. "What do we do? What do we do?"

"I don't know, Martha! We try to lose them, I guess."

Stanley was crowding them, forcing them to make a right turn. The dark sedan followed at a safe distance for a few minutes, then pulled up on the outside again, forcing them up the ramp and on to the freeway.

They were no sooner on the freeway than Andy grabbed his cell and dialled 911. He could hardly speak.

"We are being followed by people that want to kill us. Help!"

"Please state your name and location," the operator replied calmly.

Douglas shook his head. "How unfortunate. Mr. Schumann is on the phone, Stanley. However, I believe they are near their exit."

"Understood, sir." Stanley brought the bumper of the company car right up to the tail of the Volvo.

Martha went faster than she'd ever driven in her life.

The approaching exit had a new down ramp under construction with a temporary series of rubber posts that funnelled traffic to the left. The exit to the unfinished portion of the ramp was available to construction vehicles during the day. Stanley waited for the right moment and made his move right on target. He moved the big black car into the passing lane and faked a sideswipe.

Martha over-reacted as if on cue and swerved to avoid contact, sending the Volvo right through the rubber, then wooden barriers on to the down ramp.

By the time Martha saw what was happening, it was too late. She frantically pushed both of her feet to the floor on the brake pedal.

The Volvo flew down the unfinished ramp to a gaping hole where the left front wheel caught a ridge of concrete on the other side of the gap, flipping the car on to its back.

Forward momentum and the ubiquitous force of gravity pushed the vehicle on its roof further down the ramp in a hail of sparks and the shriek of metal on concrete.

Gasoline began to drip out of the gas cap inviting one spark to fulfill the laws of ignition.

The car began to catch fire, as did the trail of gas behind it. Martha screamed as she saw the huge crane that was about to lift the box girder that was directly in front of them.

Construction workers looked on, frozen in momentary disbelief at the scene unfolding almost too quickly to comprehend.

Andy found himself praying to a God that, until that moment, he had never spoken to in his life.

Douglas smiled with a smug sense of accomplishment. "Good job, Stanley. Let's continue on to Lincoln County. It's such a lovely day for a drive."

"T' ank you sir; and yes sir." Stanley plotted a course in his mind to Lircoln County, and reduced his speed to the posted limit.

21
Visitors

Joan and George met with Ann and Dwayne in the back room of the shop. Dwayne had been a couple of years behind in school so George never really knew him. All he knew was that Dwayne was a bit of a jock and, if memory served him well, he was the quarterback on the junior football team, back in the good old days.

Ann was right about him though. He was a good, honest man and worthy of her love. He had obviously been duped into thinking the Fairchild deal was good for the town. With the Mayor and the majority of councillors apparently in favour, he accepted it in the name of democracy. He did have some doubts that were made to appear foolish by the bluster and surety of Mayor Barnes.

George asked: "What format will this hearing take, Dwayne?"

"The usual, I believe. Anyone who wishes to speak simply needs to file a request with the town clerk. Being as the hearing is the last stage for public intervention on this thing, council will vote for approval. Some councillors are actually suggesting that we don't need a hearing, certainly not one with the environmental commissioner."

"So why have one then?" Joan wondered. "If you're Fairchild and can avoid a hearing, it makes no sense to draw attention to yourself."

"The Mayor called for it, saying he wanted the safeguards that public process had to offer in such a matter," Dwayne countered.

"So Mayor Barnes is a straight shooter?" George asked.

"I think so."

"Well, then how did the dump, excuse me, the waste storage facility, get initial council approval without posting the zoning change?"

Dwayne looked uncomfortable. "I'm not exactly sure. I remember hearing the Mayor slough the zoning thing off as a mere technicality."

"One that would alert the public," Joan continued. "If he's crooked, the hearing is probably a necessity by law, and he's using a little smoke and mirrors to appear to be Mr. Concerned-For-Public-Process. Have you noticed anything unusual at council? Has anyone been acting funny? Is anyone looking more affluent than usual?"

"I don't think so," Dwayne replied, looking over at Ann.

"So if you wanted to buy off people like Mayor Barnes and a couple of councillors, how would you do it?" George asked.

Joan beat Dwayne to the punch. "Well," she said, "Patterson is already in a conflict-of-interest situation as he benefits from the sale of the properties in question."

"I never even thought about that," said Ann.

"And if the money involved is inflated," Joan continued, "his cut is even greater. There could even be some more kickbacks after the deal goes through. In fact, there could be kick- backs all round after the fact, over and above the proposed sports facility."

"But how do you snare them up front?" George interjected. "I have to think it would take more than a promise on the back end of a deal."

Dwayne's wheels were turning. "You know, the Mayor *is* driving a new Caddy... nah, never mind. He only leases it, and gets some money toward that lease from the town for expenses. I'd have to say, apart from that Caddy, everything is pretty much the same with everyone on council, that I can see, anyway."

"What about Speeks?" Joan queried.

Ann's look was one of disdain. "He's been here, what Dwayne, about a year?"

"Yeah, that sounds about right," Dwayne agreed. "I don't see anything really out of the ordinary there. He replaced Ray Haroldson who retired early for health reasons. In Speeks' defence I have to say he had one hell of a job making any sense out of the mess old Ray left behind. We were lucky to get him given his qualifications and the money we were offering. He's not such a bad guy, just a little impatient with the business of a small town."

As they began saying good-byes to Dwayne and Ann, George noticed Joan was more than a little distracted. She managed a minimum of politeness to Ann and Dwayne as they headed out of the door toward the Fargo. Rather than breaking her chain of thought up with a verbal question, George decided to see if he could find what she was thinking in the air and, much to his surprise, there it was, at least an inkling of it. There were so many thoughts being sub-processed that finding any single focus was extremely difficult. The moment he began the exercise, he immediately knew he was violating some basic ethical law but he was too fascinated to stop. His *Sight* was getting stronger and somehow he felt in its development he was pleasing his father in some way.

He was amazed at Joan's mind and its attention to detail. In some respects it surprised him how much useless detail was being worked on, not quite as useless as where his mind often drifted, granted, but maybe the merits of details are in the eyes of the one who frames them. What is a catalytic thought to one, could be a complete non sequitur to another. Some of what was going on in her subconscious would probably never surface. When he had the essence of her current quandary he bolted back into Ann's shop.

"Ann, where does Ray Haroldson live?"

"Oh, right in town, in the apartments over Country Cut and Curl. If you go there for a visit you know it will be all over town."

"Thanks, Ann. Oh, is there a back entrance that might be not so obvious to our friend, the all-knowing, all-seeing, all-talking Ms. Sandfield?"

"Certainly is, George," Dwayne jumped in. "There are metal stairs, fire routes that were put in just last year in accordance with our new town by-laws."

"Well thank you councillor and congratulations on a safety issue well taken care of by your council."

Ann grabbed Dwayne around the waist. "It was Dwayne's by-law." Ann beamed. George nodded approval.

"Nice to see you're more than a boy-toy Dwayne." George cracked.

It was sweet to see Ann loved her man. Dwayne's face lit up with her pride in him. Sure it was a small town and the issue of fire routes for a few tenants didn't appear to be major one. Nothing is ever major of course until someone dies. This was Dwayne's logic and his persistence wore down all opposition. Council finally gave in, and the bylaw passed, forcing the landlord to act.

George hopped in the truck and turned the engine over. Joan was still so lost in her own thoughts that George's momentary disappearance hadn't registered. He drove down the street and instead of making the usual turn he turned into the alleyway behind Patricia's shop.

"What are we doing, George?"

"Just a little follow-through on one of your ideas. We're going to pay Ray Haroldson a little visit."

"Ray Harol... How did you know I was thinking about him?"

"I saw you thinking and tried to go where you were."

"You can do that?"

"Sort of, but it felt wrong so I got out."

"Damn right it's wrong! Don't you ever do that again without my permission! I could be working something out that could have an entirely different outcome than what you might conclude. I will not be damned for my process, only verbalized conclusions."

"I understand, Joan. I didn't even know for certain that I could go there; it was more to see if I could do it. The *Sight* is becoming strong and I'm attempting to learn the skill of it… and I guess the responsibility that comes with it. Funny, I wish I could access my own thoughts as clearly as I can others."

"What's it like, George?"

"It's like I am standing at a crossroads looking through someone else's eyes. I feel breathing and the sense of their body. But at the same time I can look at them from above as though I am lifted off their time-line. Sometimes, I am able to see clearly in all directions for a little distance. I sense a field of coagulating possibilities being drawn from past, future, all that could be and all that could have been. I am aware of what is being considered by an individual in order to determine direction. Sometimes, a shadow of a future event emerges in front of the person. I feel what things are being given greater attention through personal biases, which are often the winds of the past. Sometimes these winds are strong enough to blow individuals right past any direction they might have otherwise chosen. For example, you were thinking of the name Ray Haroldson and next to this in importance was the thought "early retirement for health reasons." This is followed by series of "why?" questions attached to many different strings of inquiry that you were tugging on. I got to the first "why" and felt Fairchild Environmental and I think the next "why" was to make room for John Speeks. That's as far as I went, except that your personal biases are constructed from the conclusions you have drawn about Fairchild Environmental."

"As fascinating as this is, I don't ever want you doing that again. If our relationship is going to work there's only enough room in my head for me thank you very much. A woman needs some thoughts to herself." She looked at George with an ominous glare. "Alright, being as we are already on our way, let's talk to Ray Haroldson. Which apartment is it?"

"I think it's the one on the left."

"Is that a guess?"

"Yes."

"I'm fine with that."

They went up the metal staircase and banged on the door. A rather haggard-looking young woman answered. She had just finished feeding her baby and had it slung over her shoulder where she patted its back gently waiting for a little burp or two.

"Could we speak with Ray Haroldson, please?"

"Oh he lives next door."

After a few "goochie, goochies" and a polite retreat they walked across the catwalk connecting the two apartments and knocked on the next door.

"Nice try, George. I guess sometimes the force just isn't with you."

"Damned if I know what just happened. For some reason I had a strong sense that that was where Ray would be at this time of day."

The door opened and a rather timid looking man with a few days worth of stubble on his face gave them a good look over. He was in a threadbare plaid housecoat and some beat-up leather slippers alternating between sniffing and dabbing his red nose with a rather spent looking Kleenex. The face was familiar. George had seen him at church when he was a kid. He may have even been out to the farm once or twice but that wasn't it. He had seen him at his father's funeral. He slipped away apparently not wishing to talk.

"What do you want?"

"I'm George Moss. May we chat with you for a minute?"

Haroldson looked down the stairs, then around as though he was checking for snipers. "I know who you are! Come in quickly, quickly!" He closed the door behind him then looked out the window before turning to Joan and George.

"I'm sad about your father, George. He was good to me, always genuinely interested in what I had to say about things, never talked down to me like some people around these parts."

"I was sorry to hear your health wasn't so good, Mr. Haroldson." Joan said dropping the bait and the opener.

"What? What are ya talkin' 'bout? I'm fit as a fiddle apart from this damned cold!"

"Mr. Haroldson, this is my friend Joan Parks and we were just told that you retired early for health reasons."

"Oh, hell no! I had three more years to go when out of the blue they offered me early retirement, a bonus and pension with full benefits. I would have been a fool to turn down that kind of a deal. But the fella who got my job? It was like they had him all lined up before they even asked me to leave. There's somethin' fishy goin' on around here. Retirement ain't so bad though – it gives me more time with my daughter and grandson. Normally, I would be next door at this hour but I didn't want to give this cold to the child. I've been laying a little low today."

"Well, I'm glad you are in good health, Mr. Haroldson. I just wanted to stop in because I didn't have time to talk to you at my father's funeral. I wanted to thank everyone personally who helped me say good-bye to him."

"There will never be the likes of him again, George. That father of yours was an angel sent from Heaven. The talent he had was surely God-given. I only wish I had been out to see him more. Thought about it many times but well, you know how it is, time goes by and ya still ain't done what you was meanin' to do."

The words hit a raw nerve in George. His eyes welled up. He held his ground unafraid of the tears, which began to make their way down his cheeks.

"I wish I had gotten out to see him more often too, Mr. Haroldson."

"I'm sorry, son. I meant no disrespect."

"Maybe down the road a piece we can get together over some of dad's best Scotch and you can tell me a little more about your memories of him."

"I'd like that, George. We waxed long into the wee hours on a few occasions. Oh, I've got some memories for ya. I'd ask ya to sit awhile over some coffee but I don't want ya to get this bug I got."

"Thank you Mr. Haroldson, we appreciate your thoughtfulness. I'll call you soon."

Mr. Haroldson opened the door. "You do that George. God bless."

As they headed down the stairs, George knew they were being watched and turned to see Mr. Haroldson's face staring through the window. He waved a friendly wave before pulling his curtains shut.

Ray Haroldson's story was another piece of the puzzle. He was offered an early retirement plus a bonus, with only three years to go. So why the big hurry to retire a man with so little time left? And how difficult is getting a bonus from public funds? George didn't think he had ever heard of a public servant getting a bonus. A lot of red tape had been cut to make room for Speeks which begged another question for Joan's legal approach; was the job put out for tender? If not, public interest had been subverted again. Speeks was a plant and obviously favourable to someone's interests, and that someone had to be Fairchild. Unfortunately, that meant someone at city hall might be dirtier than anyone thought.

They got in the Fargo, and George decided to head to Doc Harris's for an update while they were in town. By the time Joan and George were half way up the path, Mrs. Harris was already waiting, door ajar. George couldn't remember a time when she wasn't at the door waiting when anyone came up her path. It was as though there were pressure sensors around the perimeter that set off interior alarms.

"Come on in you two, I'll put a fresh pot of tea on." They went in and she closed the door. "Mel is pretty down. The thought of your father and Ernie being murdered is taking a little bit out of him."

"Now, Mother don't go telling stories out of class," Doc Harris admonished, making his way down the stairs. He looked pale and grim.

"Let's go into the parlour for tea," Mrs. Harris commanded. She was going to have a tea party come hell or high water. The Doc seemed a little peeved but put up no argument. His arm went around George as they walked into the parlour.

"I was just thinking about giving you a call, George. Funny you should drop in, although being a Moss this probably isn't coincidence."

"I'm glad you didn't call Doc, my phone's a little suspect at the moment in terms of the number of people currently listening in. I should remind you to be as discreet and cautious as possible."

"Well now, your phone was a wrinkle I hadn't thought of but generally I'm not as stupid as I look. The word murder usually invokes a sense of caution in me for some strange reason," he said sarcastically.

Mrs. Harris poured tea while they talked murder again. She made sure everyone had a cup, a napkin and one cookie placed ever so hygienically on the saucer with silver tongs. They all wagged pinkies, and spoke of evil things.

"What about Ernie's blood samples?" George asked.

"The lab still has the blood samples but they're not looking like they'll be of any use to us… I guess Ernie's going to have to come out of the ground…"

"Who needs to be in the loop on all this?"

"Well, apart from Elida Dobson, there's the custodian at the cemetery, the truck driver, my technicians at the county hospital morgue, and the lab. No one else knows."

George let out a low whistle. "That's a large group of people."

"And then there was Ted, of course."

"Ted?"

"The Sheriff. The law, for obvious reasons, requires his signature and that he be informed of anything I find with regard to cause of death."

"What have you told him?"

"I said that the two deaths were so similar that I wanted to follow through on a toxicity test to rule out pest and weed sprays. Both men sprayed enough fruit trees in their time."

"And the Sheriff bought it?"

"No. Ted didn't get to be Sheriff because he's an idiot. He knew I was trying to hide something right off the bat. I guess I'm either a lousy actor or Ted just knows me too well."

"Shit."

Mrs. Harris's eyebrows were up immediately.

"I apologize, Mrs. Harris I'm under a little pressure." George offered. She nodded a reluctant acceptance.

"Did he sign the exhumation order?" George continued.

"After I told him you had the *Sight* and saw your father die in an unnatural manner."

"He went along with that?"

"Sheriff Williams believes in the *Sight*, George, and the propensity of the Moss family for it."

"Alright, what's done is done. We'll have to meet with him."

"Oh, he'll be here in a couple of minutes. I took the liberty of calling from upstairs when I saw your grandfather's Fargo pull up."

George smiled at Joan. There were no flies on these people. If George had been more observant he would have seen that Mrs. Harris had an extra teacup on the tray. The sheriff was going to have to wag his pinky just like the rest of them

She went to the door and opened it just as the Sheriff was about to knock, and invited him in. Her ever-vigilant eye had seen the cruiser pull in behind the Fargo.

Ted Williams stood filling the doorframe. He had been the Sheriff for the better part of fifteen years. He came from farming people in the area and George knew him reasonably well. He had coached hockey and used to drive ploughs and school buses for the county before he became a lawman. George's father said he had good instincts and in many ways it was Mr. Moss's endorsement that seemed to put Ted over the top in his first election. He had managed to stay in office simply because people trusted his even-keeled, unexcitable manner. From many years of sitting behind a wheel or a desk Ted had an overly developed middle, if developed is the word. The jackets he wore were always a little on the snug side revealing a shirt that had some difficulty staying tucked into the belt. The belt one presumed was responsible for the line that disappeared into the pudding around his waste.

Ted was one of those guys whose handshake could break bones. He had built up unusual hand strength and not just from constantly pulling up his pants. All in all, he was a good man with a good heart. Mrs. Harris brought him in and they all stood.

"George. I'm deeply sorry about your Daddy." His eyes fogged up – the sentiments were real. George became aware that he had affection for anyone who shed a tear for his father. It was an endorsement of his worth.

"Mr. Williams, thank you. I know my father thought well of you."

Ted teared up even more and sat down in the Doc's big chair.

"I'll be with you all in a moment." He slowly gathered himself together while Mrs. Harris poured a tea for him. His chubby sausage fingers clumsily manoeuvred the overly fussy little English china cup up to his mouth.

"So Mel, what's the scoop?"

"They're going to dig tomorrow morning."

"Fine." The Sheriff spat a little piece of cookie onto the coffee table in front of him. It was a social mistake he would have apologized for in other circumstances, but this was serious business and he was on the job.

"Are we bringing Ernie up as well?"

"The old lab work will more than likely be of no use so I think we should," Doc replied.

The Sheriff shook his head in disbelief. "Who in hell would do such a thing?"

"Sheriff, these two youngsters think they know and someone else has been killed as well," Doc Harris said washing some cookie down with tea.

"Here in Lincoln?"

"No, in Durham, North Carolina," George answered. "He was connected to us."

"Good grief. I'll need to know everything you know George. It's my job and I take it pretty seriously."

"We sort of have a plan we are working on and it is our thought that if we tip our hand too soon we may not get these people."

"More like if we tip our hand too soon we are in greater danger ourselves!" Joan interjected.

"Alright, maybe you two criminologists would be so kind as to accompany me to my office. It sounds as though there is no need to endanger Doc and Mrs. Harris with everything you know."

"I'm not so sure that would be a good idea," Joan said hesitantly.

"What? Now look here Miss?"

"Parks."

"Alright, Miss Parks, there has been a murder in my jurisdiction. Now I can politely request you two to come down for questioning or arrest you for obstruction of justice and cuff you and have you taken down to the office."

"Sheriff," George interrupted, "I think what Joan is saying is we have no problem telling you everything we know, just not at your office.

We have reason to believe there may be an operative in town. If we are seen going to your office and conferring with you, it could cause some alarm that may not serve the outcome we mutually seek."

"I see." The sheriff thought for a second." I apologize for sounding off. I know this is your parlour Doc, but if you and the Mrs. could excuse us for a time I would be very grateful."

"Let's get some air Mother." The Doc extended his hand and Mrs. Harris took it, though somewhat reluctantly.

Once they had left the room the Sheriff was clued in, and he shook his head over and over in disgust. He agreed with the basic strategy. He appeared to subscribe to the theory that you need a strong rope to successfully hang a sturdy criminal on the first fall. Such a rope, he agreed for the time being, was to be found in information gathering. He did make it clear to Joan and George, in no uncertain terms, that he was to be informed of everything they were doing. Anything less would be obstruction of justice and not tolerated.

They concluded their little meeting and found Doc and Mrs. Harris in the kitchen.

After George and Joan expressed thanks for the tea and biscuits, it was a quiet drive home as they both processed the day's events. George became a little dizzy just before turning on to the side road and Joan saw him waver at the wheel.

"You alright, George?"

Something was wrong. In fact, something was terribly wrong if the dizziness was connected to the *Sight*, and he knew it was. His light head caused the loss of concentration and he drifted dangerously over the line towards an approaching car that swerved to avoid what would have been a collision. As that car got farther away from George, the dizziness slowly dissipated.

"I'm fine Joan. Just a weird little dizzy spell."

"You promised me you would get your heart checked and have a complete physical."

He didn't answer. His focus was drawn to the car that had just missed them and now moved down the road towards town. George knew it carried two shadows of significance; he just didn't know why they were significant. He pushed his mind in their direction feeling an ominous negativity, even though their accessible conscious thoughts didn't seem anything out of the ordinary.

As the Fargo passed Dobson's farm, George's mind let go of the two strangers in the car and moved to Ernie Dobson and his unfortunate demise. George was angered with the idea of the Dobson farm being hobbled and prostrate to the whims of a corporate shell that held no love or respect for the land. He thought of Martha and realized Ernie's place was an overwhelming metaphor for a world losing ground to an unsustainable system that only knew how to consume. Martha's environmental sadness was slowly becoming his.

"Not very considerate drivers, these rural types," the driver of the other car sneered.

"So it would seem, Stanley," Douglas grumbled disapprovingly. He had been to Lincoln twice before to accommodate the wishes of his employer. He preferred a defensive rationale when taking life. There was a kind of morality to that in his way of thinking. Actually, it was more logistical than moral; one can simply never kill all the opposition. Stalin supposedly downed forty million of his opponents and still the wall fell in the '80s. This current venture needed to be surgically precise and final.

Douglas had advised Benito Peroni that all other means of changing opinion had not been exhausted before he visited Ernie Dobson for an apology but Peroni wouldn't wait. This property was perfect in its proximity to new highway development. It was out of sight and out of mind and the farmers were old with no interested heirs. Benito wanted everything in place and on his timetable of impatience. Douglas believed such tight timetables very rarely produced lasting solutions.

As it turned out, Fairchild was behind schedule anyway, so Ernie's apology could have waited at least another six to ten months. He probably would have eventually given in and sold, considering his wife's health, but he had been talking to his friend George Moss down the road.

Moss and Dobson were a couple of suspicious old coots, and so Peroni's directive was intended to divide and conquer by assisting one to the end of his life's journey. When Douglas was ordered to return again for George Moss Sr., it was only after he had presented a strong case against doing so. With two properties in place, the digging could begin.

The third property would come on line, in all probability, as soon as the increased trucking and earth removal next door destroyed the pastoral environment that George Moss Sr. so dearly loved.

Benito appeared to be listening to Douglas' argument, but when Douglas had finished, Peroni looked up and snipped: "When I want advice I will ask for it, now go and accept an apology from Mr. Moss, we have a schedule to meet."

Douglas was fuming that day, but as always he didn't let it show. His only consolation was that he thought it was just a matter of time before the egotistical know-it-all and his idiot brother were behind bars. They wanted too much, too fast. This frustrated Douglas's meticulous nature. For the sake of a few months, the foundations of a more secure future had not been laid and cracks were forming in the dam. Douglas was contemplating a future elsewhere.

22

The Horror Hits Home

Bill Monroe was dozing in and out of consciousness when the 11 o'clock news came on. Jim had packed it in for the night fifteen minutes earlier, when Bill normally should have.

Instead, Bill lay there for an extra quarter of an hour knowing he needed to go to bed but far too tired to move. With his last shred of energy, he sat straight up scanning the room for the converter to shut the television off.

His hand slid down the sides of the cushions on the black leather couch and passed over some loose change, potato chip remnants and a stale liquorice all-sort. The hand however was only programmed to grab the desired article; the rest would be left for some anthropological dig in the future. A pain appeared on the underside of his thigh and to his joy he reached under and produced the remote to his TV. The panel that housed the batteries was missing from the back, but that search could wait until the morning.

He held the batteries in place with his thumb and pointed the device at the screen. His attention froze on the remains of a crumpled, smouldering Volvo wagon being hosed down by the fire department. He found the volume just as the *Eyewitness News* reporter wrapped up:

"The passenger is said to be in serious condition at City Memorial Hospital and there are reports that the driver, a young female is in critical condition. Names are not being released until family members are notified."

Bill stared at the Volvo wagon; it looked like Martha's. The news abruptly cut to the next item about a local animal shelter. Bill quickly flipped through the other channels, looking for coverage of the story, and then turned the TV off.

"Nah," he thought to himself. "It wouldn't be them." He started toward his room before deciding to check in on Martha and Andy even though phones were a no-no.

They hadn't been in contact like they said they would. Before he retired for the evening, Jim had said they must be up to some hanky-panky, after observing their behaviour earlier in the day, and they probably shouldn't be disturbed. Bill agreed, but now, in light of the news item, he sought to put his mind at ease. Hell, he had managed to go to all the bother of getting up off of the couch; some peace of mind might be nice before giving in to the beckoning Land of Nod.

He banged in the familiar numbers and waited. After six rings the answering machine kicked in. He hung up and his worries exponentially increased with every second. He tapped on the guest room door. "Jim?"

"What is it?" Jim answered weakly.

"Jim there was a Volvo wagon like Martha's involved in a bad accident."

"There are a million Volvo wagons out there Bill."

"And they said there were two people in the car, and the driver was a young woman. So I'm thinking, same kind of car, woman driving... they didn't call us, you know?"

"So call them." Jim muttered.

"I did, there's no answer. Look, I know you think they're playing with each other's naughty bits but I'm going to call Memorial Hospital and ask to be connected to Andy or Martha just in case."

Bill went back to the phone, looked up the number and punched it into the keypad. He cleared his throat and spoke: "Yes, I was wondering if you could connect me to a new patient by the name of Andy Schumann, please." There was a period of silence followed by a rather sombre tone.

"It's quite late, are you family sir?"

"Uh... yes I am."

"The phone hasn't been connected in his room sir, so I'll transfer your call to the nurse station on his floor."

"Oh man, this isn't happening." Bill could barely talk, and his heart was pounding.

"Four G," a female voice stated officiously.

"Andy Schumann, please," Bill countered.

"I'm sorry, sir, there are no phones in Mr. Schumann's room. Are you related, sir?"

"Uh, yes I am."

"Thank heavens for that. We have been trying to locate Mr. Schumann's parents, would you be his father sir?"

"Actually no, I'm his brother-in-law. How is he?"

"I'm not at liberty to say, sir. I can connect you to Dr. Henderson in Emergency. He was the attending physician."

Bill hung up the phone mid-transfer, immersed in a complex cocktail of emotions and creative conclusions. It was a mixture that produced immediate side effects, a leg began jigging uncontrollably.

"It's them, isn't it?" Bill jumped at the sound of Jim's voice. Jim had come to complete consciousness as the call progressed into the unthinkable, and now stood right behind him.

"Looks like it," Bill said through clenched teeth. "I'm going down there right away. I have to know!"

"If it was an accident?"

"Yeah."

"I'm coming too." They drove to the hospital with the local all-news radio station blaring. There was a reference to the accident, and as on the television report, the female driver was said to be in critical condition. Jim dropped his head on those words and did not raise it until they pulled into the hospital parking lot. They ran to the front desk for directions, found an elevator that took forever and finally approached the fourth-floor nursing station.

"I'm Andy Schumann's brother in law, and this is his family pastor Reverend Grayson. What room is he in?"

"I'll page the attending physician Mr.?"

"Monroe, William Monroe. What is the room number Miss?"

"Well, at this hour I'm not supposed to... " She stopped dead when she saw Jim's distress.

"Room 410, G wing, I'll call Dr. Henderson; he's still on duty."

"Thank you." Bill said, in a short business-like burst.

"He's in the bed closest to the window," the nurse said, addressing their backs. "Please be as quiet as possible, there's another patient in that room." Bill acknowledged the information with a wave of his hand and marched down the hall with Jim at his side. When they got to the room, Andy was standing, gazing out of the window with his arm in a sling, motionless.

"Andy?" Bill whispered.

"Hi Bill." Andy replied in a completely flat emotionless tone. He was staring out the window glassy-eyed. Jim stepped around Andy until he saw the bandage across the top of a partially shaved head discoloured by yellow disinfectant. The stitches, Jim assumed, were under the bandage.

"What happened, Andy?" Jim asked gingerly.

"They ran us off the road. They were waiting for us at Martha's place. They must have found us through the license plate. It's my fault. I thought for sure that there would be no problem with a drive-by; we only stopped for thirty seconds or so. I mean who would track down a car that stopped in front of a house thirty stinking seconds? And now Martha..."

"What's the latest on her condition?" Bill inquired softly.

"She's, she's, oh God, why did I let her take me?" Andy lost it. He sobbed like an abandoned child. The sobbing continued in a jerky convulsive manner. Jim pulled him into a tight hold. Andy pushed his face into Jim's shoulder muffling sobs that continued up from the well of his soul. Jim was about to stroke his head but looked at the bandage and decided contrary to impulse.

A young doctor entered and was about to speak when Bill signalled to him to head outside the door. To Bill's surprise, the doctor complied. Bill thought to himself he was probably an intern, young enough to not feel threatened by anyone telling him what to do in a domain not yet his. Either that or he was just too tired to engage in the scent spraying of some territorial power trip. Or maybe the doctor was just showing consideration for the sleeping patient in the next bed.

Bill followed him out into the hall while his litigious mind was still assessing the nature of the man about to testify. He settled on option two. Fatigue seemed the most reasonable conclusion. Even most interns were already sufficiently impressed with themselves as to think that a patient's sleep couldn't possibly be as important as the all-knowing words of a physician.

Once outside, the doctor looked at Bill with an expression of utter exhaustion: option two was confirmed. Bill was pleased with his assessment.

"What's his condition, Dr. Henderson?" Bill asked noting his nametag.

"Oh, he'll be fine, a rather severe concussion that required a few stitches, and a minor crack in the right radius."

"And the young woman who was driving?"

"Yes, I wonder if you could help us there Mister...?"

"Monroe, Bill Monroe."

"Well, Mr. Monroe, we have no idea where her family is located and Mr. Schumann didn't know, either. They should be notified."

"Of what, Dr. Henderson?"

"Her vital signs are stable but she is still unconscious. There was substantial cranial trauma as well as a punctured lung and fractured femur. Also, her left arm has a nasty compound fracture and she broke her jaw, which has been wired back into place. She took quite a bit of punishment."

"Unconscious as in a coma, or unconscious as in temporarily knocked out?"

"Time will provide the only real answer to that. We are calling it unconsciousness at the moment. Mr. Monroe, can you help us in notifying family?"

"Yes, Dr. Henderson, I will get on that immediately."

"I wouldn't stay too long Mr. Monroe, and keep your voices down. Both of the patients in that room need their sleep."

Bill's eyebrows went up with the erosion of his initial assessment and he smiled a rather forced smile.

"I understand."

The doctor headed back down the hall and spoke briefly with the nurse. Bill assumed it was to make sure he and Jim didn't' stay too long. When they left Andy, they returned to Bill's old Mercedes and sat in the nearly deserted hospital parking lot in stunned silence. Finally, Bill turned the ignition on until the glow plug indicated it was time to engage the starter. The old diesel clattered to life as Bill wheeled his way out of the lot and in the direction of home. Jim suddenly jerked upright and yelled at Bill to take an unscheduled turn.

"Turn right here!"

"What? Where are we going?"

"I need to see Martha's car."

"That's a pretty morbid idea. How do you know where it is?"

"Andy asked the police."

"Why would he even think to ask?" Bill stopped mid-sentence when his mouth caught up with his head." Andy's line reader-receiver?"

"Bingo!"

Adlemen's Towing and Scrap was a large fenced facility on the outskirts of the city. There, out front like some shock value advertisement on the horrors of drunk driving were the remains of Martha's Volvo.

Bill pulled up and they both got out. Jim poked his head in the window and smelled the odour of blackened blood and vinyl mixed with gasoline. The outside metal was badly burned and covered in white fire-retardant. A member of the construction crew fortunately had a large fire extinguisher in his truck and managed to stop the flames milliseconds before they reached the gas tank. When the fire department arrived they covered the wreck in fire retardant foam while gingerly removing its two occupants.

"Where is it?" Bill inquired from the other side.

"Andy's shoulder bag... black nylon with a red Nike symbol."

The car was so mangled it wasn't a question of passenger side or driver's side or even front or back for that matter. Between the collision and the hydraulic jaws used to pry Ann and Andy back into a more hospitable environment, their former metal cocoon qualified more as abstract art than anything one might call a vehicle.

Bill, eyes fixed on the interior, walked around the wreck slowly until the light from the street lamp hit something red. The Nike symbol emblazoned on the bag shone upwards through a veil of twisted metal and the freshly cut gemstones of shatterproof glass. He reached in and grabbed it. "Let's get out of here!"

They hopped in their car and sped off. A tow-truck driver on the night shift heard the sound of Bill's car and poked his head out of the aluminum door of the office trailer that was parked just inside the open gates. His eyes followed the trail of diesel exhaust that disappeared into the darkness. After quickly deciding there was nothing to worry about, he went back inside, pulled by the magnetic force of a perfect night – beer, warm pizza and *The Thing*, on the sci-fi channel. It just didn't get any better.

"So we have Andy's line reader-receiver – now what?" asked Bill.

"Now we figure a way to get close to Peroni's place without being spotted by the security cameras."

Bill looked a little worried. "You can't be serious, Jim."

"Oh yes. I've never been more serious in my life."

"So how do you propose we get within seventy-five feet? Isn't that what Andy said?

"Well, we'll need to know what is around the back of the house, where the closest sewer service is and what is above the house." "What is over the house? What are you nuts?"

"Not at all. Can you take me to my old apartment building? I think the solution to our little problem might just be in Randy's closet."

23

Standing Guard

Joan was sound asleep, leaving George jealous with his usual insomnia. He wanted so badly to shut down and join her in that blissful state. His mind flitted like an indecisive moth from sorrow for his father's demise to fear for Joan's life and then up for the overview of the tragedy of it all. His poor dad and Ernie Dobson... killed for a dump. *A dump, not a waste storage facility, call it what it was: a dump!! Of all the things to die for!*

George wasn't sure when he dozed off but he knew he was back into the dream. It was odd to be dreaming and consciously aware that he was dreaming. *Just how the hell does one get conscious of unconsciousness?* The *Sight* was starting to make more sense the more he let himself go with it. The fear of it that he had dragged along with him all the way from childhood was dissipating. As is often the case with fear, most of it, he was ashamed to admit, was rooted in ignorance.

He shot right through the struggle, the injection and the chest pain to his father's out-of-body experience. Looking down, his dad's eyes had become dark grapes of lifeless jelly that, only moments before, sparkled with the electricity of life. There was a strong feeling of sadness for malevolent creatures that snuffed out life for some temporary material gain. Even in his death Mr. Moss held compassion for those who would kill him. George became aware, for the first time in his life, how highly evolved his father was, which made the loss greater. And of course feeling his own loss only further underlined how selfish and poorly evolved he was by comparison.

The man held the bedpost with one hand and checked the carotid artery for a pulse. All three men moved out of the room and his father's extra corporal consciousness drifted with them. The desk open, some papers, not unlike the documents George had seen in Ned Patterson's office, were removed. A real estate offer on the farm? That was it – the removal of motive. George filed the new information but remained in the stream. One of the other two men went out into the light drizzle to fetch the getaway vehicle, George presumed. The other, looking everywhere but where he was going, knocked over the walking canes in the rack by the front door. He was still nervously putting everything back in place when he realized he was the last one in the house. He gave the room a once over, then grabbed his gloves and took off after the other two. Again there was a familiarity in his demeanour. The sound of tires on gravel disappeared into the night in a long decrescendo that fell under the gentle random rhythm of a light rainfall. In the silence, George, still stuck in his father's consciousness, felt a rush of frustration, slowly displaced by an even greater and overpowering feeling of love. It was a love like George had never felt before. Incredible nuances of every kind of loving thought, woven together in a magnificent tapestry. He recognized from his own life a pitifully small number of loose strands from the weave, but knew they fit into the larger picture.

He no longer felt time was relevant or separated him from anything or anyone. Past tense was also present tense and future.

"Is that you Dad?" he asked timidly. "Are you here?"

"I'm not sure I can help you, George." The sound seemed to resonate in George's chest as though he was doing the speaking.

"Do you know how much I love you?" George blurted out emotionally.

"Of course," he stated with odd abandon.

"No, I mean how much I really, really love you?" George insisted, overcome with emotion. Mr. Moss brushed the question off and appeared to exit George's body facing him with a knowing smile. George understood that love, though unspoken for reasons of human frailty, had never been in doubt between them. His father's face suddenly became serious and he turned towards the window beckoning George to look with him.

George returned to what his father was trying to do in having him look out the window. Was he trying to sell his son on the family farm?

George looked out at the land with him until a light crossed his face. He wasn't looking at the farm. He was looking at the road and the lights of a car approaching slowly. George started to get woozy and the hair on the back of his neck did its little standing-at-attention thing. *Woozy? The hair on the back of my neck? What? These are physical responses!* He turned to his dad again but he was gone. George was sucked back down the hall into his own body lying next to Joan in bed. His eyes opened. "Shit!" He shot out of bed and ran back down the hall to the window where his father had stood. The car was closer. He knew who it was and raced back through to the bedroom.

"Joan, wake up! Wake up!"

"What is it?" she said half asleep.

"We have to get out of here. They'll be here any minute! Get dressed!"

George slipped his jeans on and opened the back window. Joan was sitting up with a stunned expression on her face.

"Now!" he screamed. She jumped out of bed. George knew they were out of time so he grabbed her and lowered her out of the window.

"Wait there, don't move," he said quietly. George looked at the room knowing he had to do something. He wanted their exit to be clean with no clues that they had just fled. He kicked the clothes into the closet, quickly made the bed, scrambled to the window, and climbed out.

Once outside, they heard the car stop halfway up the driveway and the engine turn off. Joan, still a little out of it, started to speak. George covered her mouth with his hand, which made her suddenly frightened, but at least fully awake and aware of danger. He reached up and closed the window quietly then took her hand. They ran through bent straw across the field toward the McDonough farm. The sky was overcast and there was very little light to see where they were going. On one hand, the dark was a godsend; on the other hand, it was a nightmare for two city slickers in their bare feet.

The destination was the light on McDonough's porch about five hundred yards away. The pitch-black night swallowed them whole as they stumbled over rocks and potholes. Their feet slid across a grid of muddy furrows perpendicular to their direction. Joan's feet found the wettest spot in the field and sank in the muck causing her to fall. George hauled her up and they ran on, hearts beating like a rabbits. Joan began running faster than George as he tired and it was she who was pulling, urging him to run faster. He could hardly breathe. His lungs felt like they were bound by bailing wire and couldn't expand enough to let in an adequate supply of air.

The intruders, he thought, must have made it to the porch and were opening the door. They had to hit McDonough's barn before the intruders looked out the window in their direction. They weren't going to make it. Better safe than sorry George pulled Joan down into the long grass and turned to face the house. He looked at McDonough's barn then into his head knowing at that moment they did have time. He hauled on Joan again using the last sprint left in spent muscles. They hit the corner of the barn and spun out of sight milliseconds before a light went on in the Moss house. George and Joan leaned against the wall gasping for breath. McDonough's dog yapped half-heartedly for a moment but fortunately earlier that evening it found an opened bottle of beer and lapped it up after tipping it over. Sleep at that moment held a greater pull for the critter than the responsibility of guard duty.

George walked to the small door sunk into the fieldstone foundation and signalled Joan to follow. They entered the ground level chicken coop to a few beady eyes that bobbed and jerked in their direction with minimal alarm. George pointed to the ladder and motioned for Joan to climb up first. They emerged onto the main floor where the big green John Deere tractor and thresher sat. Then they scaled the next ladder to the loft. George threw himself onto the hay looking out a crack in the barn boards toward his father's place. The light in the bedroom remained on briefly, revealing two figures dressed in black and wearing black ski masks. The light went off a few seconds later. Joan gasped in realization.

"My God, they were going to kill us like they killed your father?"

"Yup," George puffed, between frantic attempts at sucking air, near nausea from the exertion. Then, his knees thought it was time to be remembered – they were throbbing with pain. Two surgeries had relieved George of most of the cartilage while the uneven ground of the fallow field now reminded him of what bone grinding on bone felt like. Funny, he didn't feel much when he was running other than the difficulty his lungs were having in their search for an air supply. The knee pain crept in with a slowing of his heart rate and the influx of available oxygen.

Suddenly, a barely visible black shadow ran from the house to the car parked halfway down the driveway. It was only the contrast with the light coloured gravel of the driveway that allowed them to see the phantom at all. He hopped in and drove a couple of hundred yards down the road to the old tractor path and into the bush. Once the car was stowed out of sight, the figure emerged from the dark near the driveway, disappearing back into the house.

"They're waiting for us to come home." George whispered.

"What do we do now?" Joan said in a voice heavily laced with naked fear. Most people probably never hear the sound of complete and utter fear from a loved one. It made George sad and guilty. He held her and they both shook, realizing now how unclothed and cold they were. Joan was in her usual T-shirt and nothing else, and George just had his jeans on. They froze to the metallic clicks of a shotgun pump.

"Who the hell's up there?" The question was followed by a long and familiar coughing spell.

"Keep your eyes on dad's house, Joan," George whispered.

"Yes, boss." She deferred while simultaneously making him aware that he had just told her what to do, which under most circumstances was a no-no. He kissed her forehead in apology and she reluctantly let go of his hand as he stood up to head to the edge of the loft.

"It's me – George," he half-whispered.

"Who?" Mr. McDonough spat, followed by the rattle of phlegm deep in his chest. Those two little yaps from his dog had brought the ever-vigilant farmer out to his chicken coop, where he had heard more suspicious sounds coming from his loft. George went down the ladder and walked slowly toward him. As he approached, Mr. McDonough backed up, lowering his gun incrementally with each step of recognition. George walked to him holding finger to lips indicating silence was prudent. "They're at my father's place, Mr. McDonough; they're waiting for us to return. We climbed out of the bedroom window in the knick of time and ran over here."

"Is it them same fellas that done in Ernie and your father?"

"I think so, although there were three people involved in my father's death and there are only two tonight."

"Goddamned murderous pricks. Let's head across the back forty, put 'em in the gun sights from the bush and pick the bastards off like grouse. Them kind of folk have forfeited the right ta breathe."

George put his hand on Mr. McDonough's shoulder and looked into the eyes of a deadly earnest man with nothing much by his own estimation to lose.

"No, Mr. McDonough; we need to nail them proper, and more importantly, the ones who sent them."

"Damn you boy, don't ya ever do nothing on instinct? Must that university brain o'yers interfere with everythin' natural?"

He wheezed and began to cough again, which led to a frantic but successful rummage through his pockets for his inhaler.

"Sure I act on instincts," George whispered, "mine are just a little different and maybe more sinister than yours, Mr. McDonough. I seek a richer and more comprehensive revenge. I wouldn't be happy with just a couple of them. I want the whole lot."

A grin came over the old man's face as he sucked comfort from his inhaler. "Yer just like yer Daddy. You always got reasons that can stop people in their tracks."

"Could I trouble you for a coat or something, Mr. McDonough?" Joan's trembling voice caused them to look up to the loft. She stepped back quickly realizing her wardrobe's shortcomings until only her face was visible from below. Old Mr. McDonough's imagination had seen more than his eyes, given the shadows. He muttered something under his breath that sounded to George like "My good Lord," before speaking.

"Land sakes child, you'll catch yer death o' cold. Why don't you come into the house?"

"We need to keep a bird's eye on the people in our house, Mr. McDonough," George intervened. "Could I get something to keep us warm?"

"Don't know if you could find anything, George, even if I told ya where to look. C'mere."

George followed him to the door of the old tack room. He pulled on the rusty iron latch and after a couple of tugs the creaky hinges gave entrance to an even more pungent smell of musty leather and hay than already filled the barn. It was an aromatic time portal that threw George back to the days when the tack room was a hide out and clubhouse for two little kids. Mr. McDonough went for the light switch and George grabbed his hand.

"Better not draw attention to your barn in the middle of the night."

"Catch yer drift," he said disappearing in the shadows. He returned seconds later with two horse blankets and an old quilt over his arm.

"Where's Billy?" George asked.

"Passed out. Couldn't wake the fool up with dynamite. You get these blankets to that little girl o' yers and I'll go see what I can dig up in the house."

"Thanks, Mr. McDonough." The old man coughed, looked up at George in a warm fatherly manner and patted him on the back.

"Gonna get 'em all are we George. Heh, heh. Well we best get that pretty little filly of yers bundled up first."

He hobbled and coughed all the way back to the house. George worried that he might rouse the dog again but Mr. McDonough's cough was a secure sound to that mutt, making him feel a little safer in the stupor of a beer snooze.

George climbed back up the ladder and gave a shivering Joan one of the blankets and the quilt. George covered himself up with the other blanket and they both sat staring through the crack in the barn boards at his father's farm. A good few minutes later the old man's wheeze approached the grassy tractor ramp and through the single door cut into the sliding tractor door on the main floor. George met him at the bottom of the ladder where he produced some wool socks followed by two pairs of overalls, an old flannel shirt and a rather dainty looking sweater.

"The sweater was the wife's, George. I bought it fer her last Christmas on this good Earth. She only wore it but the once... has no use fer it now, God rest her soul. Thought yer Joan might like it."

"Thanks, Mr. McDonough."

"How long you fixin' to hole up here like a couple of thieves?"

"Just the night, I think. I don't know, I hadn't thought about it."

"Well now, never thought I'd live to hear a Moss say that. You get some rest and I'll do likewise. You can hole up here as long as ya like, or as long as ya need to think about things. Goodnight to ya, George. Now get them clothes up to that girl o' yours."

"Goodnight, sir." George headed up the ladder and handed the sweater to Joan who had heard the conversation. Her face looked sweetly at it. It was a dowdy pink, and stunk of mothballs. It was, however, about the nicest sweater on the planet considering where it came from and how it was given. They put on their new duds and looked at one another, all smiles at the fashion statement. It was decided to tag-team the surveillance of the Moss house in order to get some rest. They lay together for warmth, angled so the farm was in full view. A few hours later, during George's second shift something caught the corner of a half-shut eye. As he squinted he saw the car pulling out on to the tractor path from the bush. It pulled on to the road where two figures were silhouetted in the front seat by the thin phosphorescent illumination of the approaching sunrise. They were gone, and with them, immediate danger. George dropped into an instant sleep. A little while later the light was high enough to pry its way into Joan's eyes. She kissed George on the neck, waking him.

"Are they still there?"

"No. They left just before sun up." George and Joan were warm but damp, and in need of something hot in their stomachs.

"Let's get something to eat." George got up somewhat stiffly and headed to the ladder. There at the bottom sound asleep, sitting on the floor, gun in his hand, back on the ladder, was Mr. McDonough. There were three inhalers lying on the ground next to him. He had used them to remain quiet before sleep gave him some well-deserved peace. George waved at Joan to look. She smiled affectionately.

"Guard duty?" she whispered. George nodded: The old coot had watched over them all night and managed not to cough once.

"I hear ya up there." The old farmer's voice crackled. He slowly hauled his way up to his feet. Once vertical something must have moved disagreeably in his chest and the cough began.

"You shouldn't have been out all night, Mr. McDonough." George said as he climbed down the ladder after Joan.

"Well now, George, when ya get to be my age ya might think ya *know* what ya should and shouldn't do. Or maybe at least command enough respect that citified youngsters aren't sittin' in yer own clothes judgin' ya."

George started to laugh, and Joan stepped down and hugged him kissing his cheek gently.

"Thanks Mr. McDonough it was sweet of you to watch over us."

He clearly loved Joan's attention, and when his old red eyes focused on the sweater covering the roundness of her breasts framed by the straps of his baggy coveralls, they welled up momentarily.

"Well let's not stand around here lollygagging'. Let's get in the house and make some breakfast." He turned and headed toward the door, wheezing and coughing.

"We can go back to our house... " George began.

"The hell you can!" Mr. McDonough cut in. "You slept in my barn, on my horse blankets, wearin' my coveralls and the wife's sweater. Least ya can do now is humour an old man who might like some company fer breakfast fer a goddamned change, if you'll pardon ma French. There are rubber boots for the pair of ya 'gainst the wall."

They slipped on the boots and obediently followed him out the door, down the grass tractor ramp, and over to the house. The dog that had mercifully slept in the kitchen through the night now began yapping hysterically with the sound of people outside.

Inside, the house was unmistakably the dwelling of two bachelors. The floors hadn't seen a vacuum for years. There were cobwebs and dust balls everywhere, dead flies on every windowsill, but somehow the old homestead embraced the neighbours with a wholesome welcome.

After the dog had a reassuring sniff of them all he calmed down and went back to a stinky old sofa cushion on the floor next to the stove. Mr. McDonough hauled out a cast iron skillet from the cupboard then opened their oversized fridge. They always had the best appliances going when George was a kid and the current fridge stated that this practice had made it through the financial difficulties of the times. People all have their bottom lines for an acceptable quality of life. For the McDonough's it was their appliances. The fridge was packed with food as always. The old man reached in and pulled out a package of bacon and a bowl of fresh brown eggs from his chicken coop, complete with a few feathers.

Joan's help was as readily accepted as George's offer of the same was refused. The old man loved having a woman in his home. George could see he was enjoying the smell of her, the sound of her voice, and in particular the gentle thoughts that still clung to the sweater she wore. His facial expressions manifested a mental journey that passed over territory both sweet and sad. The memories, viewed from a relatively safe emotional distance provided by the immediate task of making breakfast. George could tell the old man's memories had a strong gravitational pull that, if given another moment, could have created an irresistible whirlpool of debilitating melancholy and introspection. It was only practice, years of practice in the education of being a widower that allowed the old man to avoid their sad call.

Excited molecules of sizzling bacon and brewing coffee had no sooner hit the air than a thump landed on the floor in one of the upstairs bedrooms causing Mr. McDonough to roll his eyes.

The loud thump became a series of lesser ones that sputtered down the stairs and approached revealing Billy, in the full splendour of his dirty boxer shorts. At first he stood in the kitchen doorway with puffy swollen eyelids, scratching his testicles, trying to figure out where he was. When his brain began processing the limited information that was allowed through the slits housing two very bloodshot eyes, a slow grip on consciousness crept into his eyes. This was followed by the realization that Joan was there and he was in his boxer shorts. Shortly thereafter a tertiary cognitive stage hit him with the further understanding that he was scratching his nuts for the guests. Stage four of course required action.

"Jeezus H. Christ," he muttered and turned back to the direction of the bedrooms to put on some clothes. George had always been fascinated by the expression Jesus H. Christ. He often wondered what the H stood for. *People in the country appeared to have a more personal relationship with the Messiah than most. In other rural areas, Christ is known as Lord E. Jesus. It is through the combination of this anecdotal evidence that the full name of the saviour emerged.*

George had concluded in the last year of high school that the Messiah's full name, to those in the rural inner circle of course, was the Lord Edward Jesus Harry Christ. *"I'm Just Wild About Harry" was likely an early hymn that fell into disfavour because it was too happy-sounding for the reverent. The Lord title, of course, meant he has a reserved seat in the English Upper House (though not as good as the Queen's) in the event of a Second Coming. This "English" title of course dovetailed nicely with the Anglo-Saxon picture of the fair-haired Messiah so popular in the west. The British aristocracy couldn't have their Messiah looking too middle-eastern now could they!*

While Billy struggled back up the stairs Mr. McDonough went to the oak buffet and got out four of his wife's good china plates with the good silverware. He placed them gently in front of George at the kitchen table. "Spread these around fer me, would ya George?"

"My pleasure," George reacted, seeing the night had taken a toll on the old soul, nearly at the end of his capabilities. "Why don't you have a seat for a minute and let me get you a coffee Mr. McDonough."

"You know I think I may have to take you up on that." He wheezed and sat down on the closest chair. George poured everyone a coffee while Joan flipped the oven on and put the bacon in to stay warm. She moved on to requests for how everybody wanted their eggs as they began to crackle in the pan. Billy thumped back down the stairs, rounded the corner and went to the coffee without a word. Once he had a couple of gulps to kick-start him, questions formed like flickers of pain.

"Do you have any idea what time it is?"

"It's nearly seven o'clock," Joan answered politely, not going for the question behind the question.

"So, is that not just a little early for a neighbourly get together?"

"They spent the night in the hayloft." Mr. McDonough coughed.

"And your father spent the night at the bottom of the ladder with his gun standing guard for us." George gave the old man an affectionate pat on the back.

"What! He shouldn't be out all night. What's the matter with you? You alright, Dad? What the hell's going on here?" Billy's voice was a mixture of genuine concern and anger. But his face indicated there was an element of jealousy mixed up in there somewhere too.

"Don't tell me what I should do, Billy. See what I mean? Seniority counts for nothin' round here." Mr. McDonough coughed the words out. Joan signalled George to bring the plates over and spoke while she looked in the oven.

"Sounds to me like your son actually worries about you because he loves you, Mr. McDonough. I might be the youngest one here but I know what love and concern sounds like." The room went uncomfortably silent while the neighbours dished up the breakfast and sat down.

"Now whose side are you on?" Mr. McDonough huffed. Joan assumed a rather Shakespearean pose in her oversized coveralls, and responded in a bad English accent.

"Alas, kind sir, I am on the side of love."

The silence returned but if the old man's smile was any indication she was forgiven. Billy hoovered an egg into his mouth just before it slipped off of his fork.

"What was the occasion for a sleep-over in the barn?" He spat as he chewed.

Before George could answer, Mr. McDonough jumped in.

"Them fellas that killed Ernie and George's father tried to do in George and Joan last night."

"What?" Billy's mouth was wide-open revealing un-chewed egg and toast.

Robert Douglas and his driver Stanley had checked into a motel on the main highway. Stanley was in the next room and asleep in an instant. His snoring however resonated on the thin motel wall. After Douglas had neatly ironed his suit for the next day, he lay awake listening to Stanley's never-ending snore. He was briefly irritated then gained his usual composure by diverting his attention to the riddle at hand. Something was wrong. A more manageable thought was that some simple rationale escaped him for the moment.

Where were the nerd professor and his sweet young thing? Had they gone back to the city? Why wouldn't they take their suitcases? Wouldn't they have locked the house up? His father hadn't locked the door either; maybe it was a family failing or some bizarre rural trust thing. No they had to be around, and quite frankly one doesn't drive all that way, spending money on gas and accommodations for nothing! His cold mind was now distilling everything down to a matter of fiscal responsibility.

A couple of people had to be relieved of information and apologize in an extremely meaningful way for the trouble they were causing. This would justify the expenditure of time and energy. Douglas's final thought was in eager anticipation of solving the rest of this little riddle on a new day. He loved challenges and had never lost. He would check in with Joseph again and see how the accident victims were doing. In the last cell-phone update, Douglas was disappointed to learn one was critical and the other was stable. They were at least in a place where tidying up and death was commonplace and came easily. He had one little call to make, but thought it would wait a few hours. Sheer fatigue finally forced his cold eyes to accept the defencelessness of sleep.

24

Timing

It had been a long night in ICU. Andy had wandered down to stand watch over Martha's battered body. His mind was lost in values that had been made clear under the pressures of a life-and-death struggle.

Andy leaned over Martha and kissed her more meaningfully than he had ever kissed anyone. If she hadn't been unconscious he probably wouldn't have taken the liberty. He kept his face next to hers and stroked her hair.

The sound of the monitoring machines in ICU fell into the background when some air entered his ear giving him goose bumps – some air, from Martha's mouth.

"Nice." The word was faint but it was Martha's. Andy looked into her swollen eyes and noticed her left eye had struggled open. Relief swept across his entire being like a warm breeze.

"Thank God you're okay," Andy sighed.

"How b... b... bad?" Martha whispered. "Muh ... mm ... outh?"

"You broke your jaw. They've got it wired shut."

"Wha' else? Do I have all mm.... bits and pieces?"

"You cracked your skull, broke the femur in one leg, dislocated your shoulder, some cracked ribs, broken arm and they think there is some minor internal bleeding they are worried about, but not bad enough to open you up."

"How a ... a... bout you?"

"Just a concussion, a few stitches... Oh Martha I thought I was going to lose you. I, I uh, I've never felt like... well you know."

"What do you ff... eel like, Andy?"

"I dunno, I guess, you know, I like you Martha."

"I like you too."

"Actually, it's more than like, I think."

"Whoa."

"I'm sorry; I didn't mean to get heavy or anything. Maybe it's just the circumstances."

"No, no, important wor... w... words." Martha was in great pain trying to speak but felt the need.

"Important words?" Andy's mind was rapidly processing this new information in many directions. It took everything he had to break through the shell of his own insecurity.

"Am I important to you Martha?" Martha's very weak hand groped for his and held it to her breast amidst a tangle of IV lines, monitor wires and ID bracelets.

"You say it first, An... drew."

Andy dug down deep and found the courage.

"You mean I, I love you?" Their eyes locked.

"That was a question, Andy." Andy dug deep a second time.

"I love you Martha."

"Ff ... feel ... same, Andy.

"Me and you?"

"Me and you, ff ... funny, huh?" What Andy felt was amplified by Martha's words. He had never heard those words from a woman before. He was a computer geek with a major case of low self-esteem. The only interaction to date with females was at www.pussy/tits.com. The emotional complications of real human interaction were overpowering. He wasn't just telling some naked woman on line what to do and what he was doing to himself – this woman, who held his hand to her breast, actually wanted him without his credit card numbers. This was an overwhelming concept. And holy mackerel, he suddenly realized his hand was on her breast and yet her eyes and words were more important! This had to be love, he thought, as he cherished the privilege of holding her breast, not a virtual breast or cathode image, but a real breast and an extension of a person he cared for.

Martha, through the pain and discomfort of her battered body managed a thought that her choice was good. The circumstances certainly could have been more romantic but not any more dramatic. She wished that she could have looked attractive at that moment instead of so beat up, but the newly spoken sentiments were what she had been hoping might happen between them. The crucible of danger and death's cold breath had certainly sped the process up somewhat.

Martha had thought about the old adage that when you are not looking you don't see. Once she looked, she saw much in Andy that was attractive to her. He seemed to possess none of the bravado and machismo that she so abhorred in men. Her slightly older age and experience gave her the perception of control that her own insecurities required and he was kind of cute and attentive. She loved the masculinity of his forearms and his youthful physique. She loved the way they laughed and worked so well together and was in awe of his technical skills on-line. There was also some additional depth of character demonstrated in his willingness to do anything to help his friend Jim. There was a good man in this boy who stood before her.

Andy, for his part, was smitten with the entire package. He found Martha a little abrasive, but he liked that – it held directness he didn't possess himself. Mostly though it was Martha's womanliness that he found overpowering. He wanted to be wrapped in it. The fact that they had known each other for years and had been on-line pals made the whole thing even more powerful. He trusted her implicitly, and probably wouldn't have allowed himself to love her otherwise. She also seemed sensitive to his erotic sense of fantasy and wasn't disgusted by it. To the contrary, she made him feel for the first time in his life that he was normal and to that end she had even confided some of her own fantasies. They had talked into the wee hours openly about sexual expression even though they hadn't gone there yet. The moment was interrupted by the whisper of the duty nurse.

"Mr. Schumann, there is a call for you in the..." She noticed Andy's hand on Martha's breast and was about to scold him when she saw that Martha's one eye was open and that her hand held Andy's. She looked startled, but quickly recovered her professional persona.

"My, my, look who is back in the world of the living. Why didn't you ring for me, Mr. Schumann?"

Andy self-consciously removed his hand from Martha's breast and offered only awkward silence. The shrug that followed was the only answer he could find. He leaned over and kissed Martha. "I'll be back in a flash; the nurse probably wants to check you over." He left the curious eyes of the nurse and went to find the phone. He answered the phone dazed and distracted by the realization he was in love with someone who actually loved him. Wow the world was perfect.

"Hello?"

"Mr. Schumann?"

"Yes, who's speaking please?"

"I'm Martha's father."

"She's conscious; I think she's going to be okay." An uncomfortable silence followed, then the caller spoke again.

"Good, thank you, that is all I wanted to know." The voice was so stiff and had no southern accent. In one of their late night talks about parents Andy had learned Martha's father was quite the old southern gentleman – well, he was southern anyway. She said his drawl was annoying to her, this guy on the phone had no drawl and how did he know who Andy was? Something snapped.

"You're not Martha's father. Who are you?"

"Very good, Mr. Schumann, very good indeed. Let's just say we've *brushed* into each other before. Mr. Schumann, you're very lucky to be alive. Life can be so pleasant when one keeps one's nose in his own business. Forget Fairchild, and you might be granted a little more time for the pursuit of happiness."

The phone disconnected. Andy's bubble of lover's elation had just been burst by shards of fear. He wasn't sure whether these people would accept a laissez-faire status from him and Martha or whether they would come at them again to finish the job. The man's voice on the phone sounded oddly refined and mannerly. It contrasted so heavily with what was being said that Andy got the cold shivers. He couldn't think of what to do. He dialled a number and a groggy voice answered.

"Bill."

"Andy how's Martha?"

"She's conscious, Bill, but that isn't why I'm calling. It's my stupid life, Bill. I'm cursed."

"Easy Andy. What's going on?"

"I just received a phone call informing me that if I forget Fairchild I might live a little longer."

"These guys are just so up front and brazen with their agenda aren't they? I hate to be negative but they haven't offered you any guarantee and would you believe them if they made you such a promise anyway?"

"I know; I know; we're dead meat." Andy was totally lost.

"So..." Bill led but didn't instruct.

"So..." Andy's mind began to move in a straight path with no thought for himself. "So, until Martha can be moved, she must be under constant watch. When we can move her, we will need a plan to leave here without being observed and a safe house where we can work at getting these criminals put away."

"You'll need someone to spell you off while you sleep as well, Andy. What about her parents?"

"She hasn't spoken to her father in years. He's somewhere in Georgia, and her mother is a shrink in Boston."

"What about your parents?"

"Worse. I think they would be happy if some terrible mishap occurred. They're so afraid of any potential embarrassment, and the elders in their church are convinced I'm in league with the devil."

"Ah, the warm embrace of family and faith."

"Ha!" Andy huffed in disgust. Bill sensed the depth of Andy's turbulent family waters and changed gears.

"Leave it with me and Jim. Either we'll be there or we'll think of something better. I'll be in touch in a couple of hours. Can you stay awake that long?"

"Yeah… and Bill?"

"Yes." There was an uncomfortably long pause. "What is it Andy?"

"I have to tell someone. I want to tell the world, actually."

"What?"

"We're in love, Bill. I love Martha and she loves me. There, I've said it!"

Bill looked at his receiver with disbelief, both at the timing and the information itself.

"That's very nice, Andy, but let's see if we all can't stay alive to talk about this over a celebratory drink. Got to go."

When Bill got off the phone, Jim was in his room and bursting with curiosity.

"What is it? What's going on?"

"Martha's conscious, and Andy and Martha are in love."

"Oh shut up, no way!" A wide smile appeared on Jim's face. "There's somebody for everybody isn't there?" Jim's elation slowly dissipated and he crumpled against the wall head in hands. His "somebody" was gone. Bill patted Jim's shoulder. His sense of compassion was stronger than his homophobia. In Bill's case it was less of a homophobia than a physical revulsion to the idea of kissing another man or the deeds that follow such foreplay.

Bill just couldn't think of gay men without thinking about what went on behind closed doors. His mind always went there. He would dig his way out with the thought that much of what heterosexuals did behind closed doors disgusted him too and that's where he found his ground. He attended parties at Jim's place as a way of wearing his revulsion out. The more he saw men being affectionate to men, the more he thought he might get used to it. Things weren't going quite as well as he had hoped. He figured he needed a few more years to actually get casual with it. But, he was resigned that he would learn to see only the positive nature of affection no matter where it occurs and so in this thought he comforted his friend with a warm compassion.

"I'll put a fresh pot of coffee on, my friend. We've got work to do. Andy and Martha have been threatened again."

"What?"

Once the new threat to Andy and Martha had been explained, Jim pulled himself together immediately and was on the phone. In a matter of minutes the word was out. Jim and Randy had done a lot for the local AIDS hospice. There was a strong support network in the local gay community for survivors. Aware of Randy's death, many friends had already expressed concern for Jim's current needs and whereabouts, for that matter. AIDS had polarized a few people into becoming more conscious of some bottom line of basic human decency. There were good people who had filled a vacuum created by the fear, intolerance and ignorance of others. The religious right or as Jim called it, "the religious-righteously-wrong" were a scary bunch. The tribal Old Testament references that a man lying with a man was an abomination conveniently outweighed the love and forgiveness of the New Testament even though the New Testament contained the enlightened teachings of the man whose name they inappropriately wore like a mantle. There's nothing like some good old infallible interpretation to stir the pot. The need to speak the damnation stuff was itself cruel and revealing enough.

In essence, Andy and Martha's problem was a variation on a theme so familiar to Jim. Two people in hospital needed support that could not be provided by family. Within the hour the first of Jim's friends from the AIDS support network introduced themselves. Some were flamboyantly dressed, some hissingly effeminate and some incredibly straight-looking and conservative. The demographic had a comprehensively wide range; there were those suffering from AIDS and their spouses, a guilty parent seeking penance, a sibling seeking to understand the hidden life of a departed brother in a sadly late effort to know him better. There were those who sincerely wished to demonstrate their brand of religion through action, and those who sought absolution from ignorance past. The most amazing in the lot were just ordinary people of good heart.

All were powerfully motivated in the area of basic human compassion for their own reasons. Those reasons, granted, may have been complex and ranging from good to bad but the focus and outcome remained positive. They asked no questions, wishing only to be there for another human being in need, passing the emergency cell phone on to the next watch with little conversation.

Andy stayed by Martha's side until he couldn't keep his eyes open and returned to his own bed. The support net remained in the waiting rooms outside the ICU and Andy's ward much to the consternation of hospital staff – until they were told it was a religious watch. Amazing how much slack gets cut when one invokes the name of God.

Jim and Bill went to work, once security had been provided for Andy and Martha. They had decided on Randy's remote-controlled airplane. Such a vehicle could hover around the Peroni home for up to ten minutes at a time. The whole idea came crashing to the ground when Randy's plane was discovered to be in worse shape than remembered. Not accepting defeat they went to the biggest hobby shop in town. Granted, the noisy model airplane wasn't the best of clandestine surveillance devices, but it was the only one they had going; until they arrived at the hobby shop. While Bill was getting the low down on a confusing number of models, Jim stood at the counter looking through the glass case at motors. That's when he focused on a plastic radio in the shape of a Pepsi can sitting on the countertop. He picked it up and realized he'd just saved what was looking like a thousand-dollar investment in model plane gear. He handed $10 to the girl at the counter and became the proud owner of his own Pepsi can AM-FM radio. He went over to Bill, who was in the middle of a seminar from the salesman.

"Bill. Something urgent has come up. We'll have to come back."

Bill looked worried, and followed Jim out. "What is it?"

"This is *it*, Bill," Jim said waving his new acquisition.

"A friggin' can of Pepsi?"

"It's a plastic radio. Take the radio out. Put the line reader-receiver in with a small step-up signal transformer and transmitter. This will double our receiver radius for safety. It picks up the signal, boosts and transmits. We drop it in the gutter underneath the pole and go to the safety of a 250-to-400 foot transmitter range. The can is plastic so it won't interfere with transmission. An Ac adaptor, a laptop, an external hard-drive, and we are in business for as long as we've got memory or until a street cleaner comes along." Bill was impressed with the superiority and safety of the new plan.

"What did that stupid radio cost?"

"Ten bucks."

"I like the way you think, Jim."

Jim and Bill worked diligently through the day assembling the electronics and inserting everything into a piece of foam rubber the exact shape of the pop can. The foam had been sliced down the middle with a razor-knife and small cavities were cut to fit two nine-volt batteries, a line reader-receiver, signal booster and transmitter. The two halves of the foam were then joined and stuffed into the plastic Pepsi can. Once the end was epoxied securely and taped for good measure, they were ready for the drop at dusk. They decided to drag the plastic container on fishing line so they wouldn't have to stop in front of the Peroni house. Because the can was plastic it made very little noise. As they drove by and let go of the line, the Pepsi can slowly rolled snug up to the curb. When it finally came to rest it looked relatively inconspicuous.

They pulled into the parking lot of the little park at the end of the block. A woman in a jogging suit ran by and gave the two men a suspicious glare. Jim was busy getting his gear hooked up and plugged in. They settled in for what they thought would be a long wait.

Bill went out for a walk an hour later to hunt for junk food, startling Jim on his return when the door flew open and an assortment of chips, pop and candy landed on his lap. After ingesting every shelf life, color enhanced, freshness-simulating preservative known to man they began to doze off, surrounded by the debris field of chip bags and candy wrappers. Just as Jim's eyelids began to droop, an activity LED flashed setting off silent alarms in his subconscious. In a split second the subconscious spat the message upstairs, jerking Jim to a fully alert position. Benito had finished a late supper and was on-line.

"Well hello, Mr. Peroni," he purred.

Bill opened an eye. "Is he on-line? Is everything working?"

"Ya gotta love technology," Jim replied, eyes glued to his LCD screen. The first thing up was a live sex chat line.

"This is going to be a long night!" Bill groaned as he closed his eyes attempting to get back to some serious dozing. Jim endured for a good ninety minutes until Benito finally got off and signed off. The screen went blank. Jim thought for sure this night would not be THE night until ten minutes later the screen popped on again. This time Benito was doing business.

"First things first," Benito muttered as he saved the access codes. Everything Benito typed or saw on his screen for the next forty minutes appeared on Jim's laptop and was saved to the external hard drive and backed up on the CD writer on the floor all powered by a twelve-volt transformer plugged into the cigarette lighter. Benito sensed nothing other than a little annoyance that his system felt unusually slow and flickered every so often. Being a man of very little patience he would have Joseph look into these little glitches in the morning. When he shut down his screen flickered oddly and the shut down took a little longer than usual. "Piece of shit!" he muttered, turning out the light.

Jim waited twenty long minutes then played back the access codes and entered. He was in and he would stay in all night. After an hour of systems analysis and tinkering, he followed Ben's path from earlier in the evening to the multiple personalities that resided in the mainframe. There were at least three sets of realities when it came to the financial accounting statements that Benito's codes accessed. Not only was Fairchild keeping much from the tax department but Benito was also keeping financial data from his brother. There were a series of entries under promotional expenditures to a public relations firm that looked more than a little suspect. It was the rounded-off figures that caught Jim's attention initially. When the same stream of figures showed up in Benito's personal financial file they were not attached to the public relations firm but to a series of names. BINGO! As dawn approached, Jim went to the human resources section of Fairchild and downloaded the entire list of paid employees.

The corner of his laptop screen read 6:11 am when he dumped the final download to the CD writer. With daylight approaching and no idea of Benito's morning routine, Jim thought it prudent to power down, and woke Bill up.

"Bill, let's get out of here."

"Did you get anything useful?"

"You could say that."

"Let's get our transmitter."

"What are you nuts? Jim snapped." We couldn't pick it up without drawing attention to ourselves. Let's get the hell out of here, and leave it for the street cleaner."

"What did you get?" Bill asked.

A smug look crept over Jim's face. He just looked at Bill and broke into a satisfied grin wider than Carol Channing singing a legato "cheese." As Bill attempted to pull out of the parking lot, an unmarked police cruiser suddenly blocked his exit red lights flashing in the grill and front windshield. Bill hit the brakes and two plain-clothes officers appeared on either side of the car screaming commands.

"Get out of the car and place your hands on the roof!"

"Shit balls!" Jim said under his breath. He grabbed the writeable CD disk from his drive and reached into the side door panel slipping the disc into the dog-eared Mercedes owner's manual. He glanced at Bill and saw that he was completely frozen.

"Bill. Relax! Could be they think were just a couple of fags performing lewd acts in a public place or it's me they're after for questioning regarding Randy's death. Either way as far as they know, you're an innocent who was just making out in the park."

"Making out?" Bill's face was now horrified. His last line of homophobia was now confronted head-on. Someone, no, anyone thinking he was in a park performing sexual acts with another man was more than he could handle. To continue seeking some kind of justice for a friend he now had to accept possible wrath and scorn from two potentially intolerant cops. He was being asked to pose as George Michaels and his experience with the local police so far indicated that some were pretty intolerant. In fact, the law firm he worked for had represented a few homosexuals over the years that had been severely beaten by cops. All this flashed through his head in a split second.

"Get out of the car and place your hands on the roof!" The command came again and this time sounded even more ominous.

"Bill?" Jim looked at his friend still frozen in the driver's seat.

"Do I have to pose as a fag cock-sucker?" The words were out before he could stop them, catching Jim off guard. Bill had always seemed so tolerant. Jim never suspected there was an internal struggle.

"If you want to help me get some justice for Randy and if you want to perhaps save the lives of George and Joan and God knows how many other people these Fairchild sickos might wish to remove from the conscious world, well… yes! Unless you have some other plan, I will tell them nothing other than I ran to you after Randy was killed and one thing led to another. You'll be out in no time and might be able to get the stuff off to George. It's in your owner's manual in the door panel."

"I'm sorry for what I said Jim. If these guys brand me a fag, it will make it back to my employer. I don't know how I can live with that!"

"I repeat. Do you have a better plan?"

"No, I don't. Why would two grown men be in the park at this hour? Hell we are guilty already just through circumstance! These two look like grade ten dropouts with six weeks of police school and will probably smugly consider themselves great sleuths if we confirm their feeble-minded conclusions.

"Wow, Bill has a distaste for law enforcement officers?"

"Let's just say I've seen too much abuse of power over the years. You do the talking. I'll just act as embarrassed and as horrified as I really am."

"Okay. Here goes nothing you honorary fag you."

"Fuck off!" Bill snapped.

"Are we still friends even though I'm a fag cock-sucker?"

"Of course. This is my issue I'm dealing with!"

Jim opened the door and stood up placing his hands on the roof. Bill sheepishly followed. The officer on Jim's side looked at him mockingly.

"Might I ask what you ladies are doing in a public park this hour?"

"As you said officer it is a public place and we are part of the public so this is our place. We have a right to be here." Jim countered.

"Show me some I.D. smart ass!"

"Actually officer what he said was not inflammatory and I would suggest civility. I work for Makovitch and Davidson my name is... "

"William Munroe, 283 River Street. We ran the plates. Please don't say anything more gentlemen until we've read you your rights."

After the Miranda recitation Bill and Jim were cuffed and placed in the back of the cruiser. A tow truck was called, and Bill's Mercedes was hauled to the police compound.

If Bill and Jim stuck to their story Bill might get out and get the information to George. He had found a righteous streak in himself to work with the fag handle. He felt like a white man standing with the blacks against southern cops in a '60s civil rights struggle.

Jim, on the other hand, was wanted for questioning in the death of Randall Cousins. His might be a longer stay.

25

Lost and Found

Breakfast at the McDonough's was the most wonderful calorie-infested, cholesterol-loaded fix of bacon and eggs, toast and preserves, coffee and more coffee that Joan had ever eaten and she had to admit, it tasted great after the night she had been through.

They had been at the breakfast table for most of the morning trying to plot a course out of the mess they were in when the phone rang.

After a short hello Billy passed George the receiver. It was Ann. "Thank God, I thought something had happened to you two. I tried calling late last night and first thing this morning."

George took a quick swallow of coffee. "They came at us last night Ann We spent the night in McDonough's barn."

"Came at you? What do you mean - came at you?"

"I think they meant to put Joan and me away permanently."

"This is all so hard to believe!"

"They must be on to us somehow."

"Well that's why I was calling. Speeks and some councillors have pulled a couple of fast ones.

"What do you mean?"

"The hearing has been bumped up!"

"They can't do that!"

"Well they did and they're getting around the legality by making the last minute change at the request of the commissioner. It is under the guise of a scheduling conflict thing – and that's not all."

"It gets better?"

"Due to the commissioner's schedule, there will not be an open forum. Those who wish to speak will have to provide written requests to the city clerk no later than twenty-four hours before the hearing."

"Mmm. Pretty thorough aren't they? Reducing the chances of opposition and flushing the opposition out in the open at the same time so they can dispose of them. If they know I'm going to speak I'm a dead man for sure…"

Ann broke an uncomfortable silence. "There's more, George. Allan Thornhill's been fired from the local paper."

"Yes I know."

"Is there some bad blood between you two?"

"Apparently so, some kind of competition he's been having with me in absentia. Joan has another theory that he is in love with me."

"Allan? You know… that might explain a few things."

"How be we have that conversation later. Right now we need to alter plans to accommodate this new timetable. Can you meet us at your shop in an hour?"

When George hung up, his look said it all and Joan was already putting two and two together.

"Thornhill again?"

"Isn't he that smart-aleck newspaper man?" McDonough asked.

"One in the same." Billy interjected. "What did he have on Fairchild?"

"Enough to get him sacked."

"You know if we are seen to be in cahoots with you George, it could cost us our deal with New World Developments."

Mr. McDonough went to cuff Billy's head but Billy grabbed his hand. "I was just kidding, and besides if they renege on our deal we'll still have the farm and that first somewhat sizeable payment."

"Thinkin' 'bout money at a time like this. You're an embarrassment t'me!" his father shot back in disgust.

"I wasn't thinking about the profit as much as I was enjoying the thought of these jerks losing money to an old man and a drunk." Billy began to laugh but stopped dead, suddenly serious. "I'll drive you to town George. You don't want to be seen in something as obvious as your grandfather's Fargo. I might be a drunk but I can't abide anyone threatening my friends!"

There was nobility in his son's words that he'd not seen for some time and McDonough senior felt a welcome measure of pride unfamiliar to him. Billy was indeed a drunken fool but there was some good in him.

Before leaving, George tried calling Bill Monroe but only got the answering machine. Something was wrong but he couldn't put his finger on it. The *Sight* was useful but not overly so in the hands of the as-of-yet unskilled. He cursed himself for not honing the talent sooner. For some reason, at that moment, he remembered his mom saying that with talents came the responsibility to develop them. She said those words the day he quit piano lessons but he knew she also meant the *Sight*. His mother's death was the last straw for George and the family curse. Why hadn't his father used his damned *Sight* to prevent her death?

As George stumbled into that old territory it hit him hard. He remembered screaming that question to his father the day she died. "Why didn't you use the *Sight*?" "WHY?" His heart sank into a deep hole. He realized in a flash something of what had come between him and his father all those years. *Jesus, sweet Jesus I blamed him for my mother's death.* That thread when pulled unleashed an avalanche of thought. An angry child had turned pain into blame. The blame had grown into a learned behavioural pattern disconnected from its source by the calluses of practice. George had never thought the distance between him and his father was his fault because he had never addressed the source. He had blamed his father for his mother's death, locked it away in some cold, sick, storage bin of denial and then threw away the key. *Forgive me Dad. Forgive me.*

Billy's horn sounded out front and George snapped back to reality. He'd been standing in a daze, talking to himself with Mr. McDonough looking curiously at him. He thanked the old man for his kind hospitality and flew out the door.

What a stupid time to have such a revelation, George thought as he approached Billy's car.

"Better get in the back with Joan so you can duck out of sight," Billy instructed.

All the way into town George begged forgiveness over and over in his head. Joan looked at him with worry, given the serious pain etched on his face. He was almost in a state of shock. He was to blame for the distance between him and his father. This was territory he would have great difficulty in forgiving himself. As they pulled into town George felt... *incoming.* The hair went up on the back of his neck and it hit him quite clearly for a change. This time he knew what it was.

"Billy, do you see a dark blue sedan with a couple of straight-laced guys in suits?"

"Well... yeah," Billy responded tentatively, "they just pulled outta the motel right in front of me."

"See where they go before you drop us off at Ann's."

"Who are they?"

"The guys who came to visit us last night." George said.

Joan looked at him with raised eyebrows. "I'm impressed."

"Don't be. I didn't do a damn thing."

They followed the sedan to city hall. Douglas was now striding up the steps. George looked out of the back window and saw Douglas's face as he politely opened the door of the building for an older woman.

"The man who killed my father." The words burned their way out of his throat. Joan took a quick look then ducked back down.

"Are you sure?"

"Not the tiniest sliver of doubt." That's the guy in the dream – the cold-hearted son of a bitch who administered the lethal injection to my father!" Douglas glanced at Billy's car as they rounded the corner but nothing registered on his face as he went into the building. George had an intriguing thought: *Maybe the stalker's not used to being stalked?*

Stanley, Douglas's driver, looked a little worse for the weather as he sat stoically behind the wheel staring forward. If his eyes weren't so tired he might have seen the motel key on the dash and it would have dawned on him he was going to be savouring small town hospitality just a little longer than anticipated. He had done road trips with Douglas before but could never get used to the fact that Douglas, a hopeless insomniac, was able to re-charge in a couple of hours and expected the same of Stanley.

By the time Douglas had knocked on Stanley's door that morning, he had already been up for an hour or so and had spoken extensively with head office after Benito returned his call. Benito was not impressed that Douglas wasn't on schedule and relished the opportunity to dress him down a little. It was just plain unprofessional given the amount of money he was being paid. Douglas had hung up, angry and galvanized in purpose. But now there were new instructions that required staying in town for an environmental hearing that had been conveniently moved up. At least now the trip was making some greater kind of sense. He would have plenty of time to accomplish a number of things for his employer.

Billy dropped George and Joan off at Ann's then parked his car at the grocery store following George's request not to park out in front of Ann's. Moments later he joined Ann, Dwayne, Joan and George in the back room. Dwayne looked a little dubious about being there. After hellos and strained small talk George waded in.

"So, has Ann told you there was an attempt on our lives last night?"

"I can't wrap my mind around it, George. It doesn't seem possible," Dwayne said softly in his usual "awe shucks" manner.

"Oh, it's possible all right," George snapped. "And the men are in town; actually one is at city hall right now for some reason. My guess is he's meeting with Speeks. What can you tell me about process here, Dwayne? Even if I submit a request to make some sort of presentation, how do I know Speeks won't lose it or deny me on some technicality?"

"Well, why don't you copy every council member as well and even if the entire council is dirty I will have a record of it and table your dated and legal written request at the hearing. Speeks doesn't come in until ten o'clock, and Barbara, the secretary is in at nine. I'll deliver the request to her and ask her to make sure it goes into the councillors' mail slots before Speeks arrives."

"Could you also ask her to make no mention of it to Speeks? That could buy us a few hours," Joan thought out loud.

"Oh, by the way, this came yesterday afternoon." Ann handed George a courier envelope.

"Ann, do you have a VCR here?" he asked.

"Yes," Ann confirmed, "but the monitor is hanging from the ceiling in the store. We'll have to look at it out there."

Joan shook her head and voiced concern. "What if someone came in and saw us all together? We should be more discreet."

Dwayne grabbed a ladder, went out into the store and tilted the monitor so it faced the back room. "Give me the tape and I'll fire it up for you. Just watch from there." They all watched through the doorway while Dwayne popped the tape in the VCR and hit play. In a second, Jim's apartment was on screen. In the middle of the room Randy sat slouched on the sofa. The sound of the door being kicked open was followed by a view of a man's back passing the camera. He scanned the room thoroughly, gun ready, then went off camera to the kitchen area.

"Well, well... we have a girlfriend. Ah yes of course, the nicotine addict you were expecting." The sound was ambient but audible. The man walked back into frame, rolled up Randy's sleeve and appeared to be checking for a pulse. He looked toward the door, revealing his face, then walked swiftly out. Joan gasped in recognition. Everyone stared at Randy's lifeless body until Joan began to weep. A few seconds later, the sound of running feet could be heard approaching. The door opened, a hand appeared in front of the lens and the picture went off.

"That's the man we saw a minute ago going into city hall isn't it?" Joan sniffled.

"Yup," George responded. "Gets around, doesn't he?"

"What does that tape prove?" Ann asked. "It doesn't show him doing anything except checking for a pulse to see if that poor guy on the couch was dead."

George shook his head. "Not quite, Ann. It shows two things. Roll the tape back Dwayne and play it again."

Dwayne hit rewind and play. The man entered sweeping the room with his gun.

"Hit pause, Dwayne! Do you have a slow motion function on that remote?" George asked. Dwayne looked closely at the remote.

"Sure thing." He pressed the button and the picture crept slowly on screen revealing the man rolling up Randy's sleeve, and then rubbing his arm briefly before lowering the sleeve.

"Pause right there!" George yelled. "He wasn't checking for a pulse, Ann, look he was making sure there was no tell-tale bleeding from the puncture hole where he injected whatever it was that killed Randy. He did the same little dance with my father. If Randy died by injection in that arm, who else would know that little piece of information but the killer? Who else would want to make sure there was no incriminating residual bleeding?"

At the far end of town, in the local cemetery, shovels were scraping gouges into the dirt-stained varnish of George's father's coffin. Sheriff Williams was there with the Doc. Both stood silently as chains were secured to the coffin handles and the backhoe on the tractor. The metal links pulled straight and the engine strained until the earth reluctantly surrendered what it had just reclaimed days before. The coffin was loaded in a cube van and taken to the County Hospital morgue.

As Mr. Moss's body was removed from the coffin and placed on a stainless steel examining table, Doc Harris looked the other way. Sure he was a scientist but this was the body of his old friend. He found clinical indifference a little out of his reach that day. Ernie Dobson's coffin was also disinterred and placed temporarily in the old mausoleum cooler. Brad, an eager young man from Med-Tech Laboratories was doing a quick visual inspection of Ernie that Doc Harris had excused himself from. He would be forced to see Ernie soon enough.

"Prep Mr. Moss for a full thoracic, but cut the sleeves away please. I don't want fabric rubbing up against anything that might be on the epidermal tissue of the arms, the left forearm in particular, and cover the face please. I also want the shirt sleeves checked for any residues on the interior of the fabric." The technicians, after looking inquisitively about the request to cover the face, complied. Doc Harris slowly approached the table and lifted his friend's very dead and discoloured left arm, rotating it slightly then gently lowering it, palm up, on the table.

"Sorry, my old friend," he said softly as he pulled a large overhead magnifier into position. He scanned the arm briefly, stopping to focus on a small area on the upper left forearm, then groaned angrily at the expected discovery. There it was. A small puncture wound consistent with the mark of a surgical hypodermic needle. Doc Harris grabbed some tape and was framing the puncture when he noticed something else – white residue around the point of entry.

The door burst open and eager Brad from Med-Tech flew in. Med-Tech did all the blood work for the hospital and Brad was familiar with both the facilities and staff. "Hey Doc, we did some preliminary regurgitation on the Dobson E. files you were looking for, and there *are* some anomalies in the chemical analysis."

Doc Harris held up a hand to stop further conversation, turned to one of the technicians, and pointed to the area he had marked in tape.

"Get some close-up pictures and magnifications of this area right away, will you please? And be careful that you don't corrupt the white residue around the puncture. Now Brad, what kind of anomalies?"

"Well, we can't say exactly, yet, that's why they're anomalies, heh, heh, heh. But, where a chemical is involved, usually there are cascade effects or at least a chemical fingerprint in the body chemistry. Something, though not quite qualifying as abnormal, doesn't look right. And since you suggested potassium we are looking for any signature traces. If we have no luck with concrete signs we'll begin looking at reaction traces. But at the mausoleum this morning, I noticed a crystal on the arm of Dobson, E., so I took a sample."

"You what?"

"Should I have waited?"

The Doc shook his head and looked at Brad.

"What if you compromised the body in anyway that could damage the forensic investigation?"

"Well, chemically everything is interior so we should be alright."

"Alright what have you got?" The Doc cut to the chase.

"Well my skin is real soft, I'm always cutting myself when I shave, so I go through styptic pencils like there's no tomorrow. It beats the hell out of sticking little pieces of toilet paper on my face. Anyway, darned if on the small puncture, not the shunt punctures mind you, but on the one consistent with a high-grade injection needle, there wasn't a substance that resembled styptic pencil. It had been pretty well wiped up, but some had crystallized on the inner rim of the puncture hole. It was just a stroke of luck I had my magnifying glass in my kit or I'd never have seen it!"

"Styptic pencil?"

"Yeah it sounds too simple but to my way of thinking if you want to stop a little residual bleeding it works. Unless Dobson, E. applied it himself, I'd say someone was covering their tracks. The way I figure, if he was injected with something, like you suggested, the heart would have begun fibrillating while the needle was being pulled out so there would have been blood flow, therefore, some blood to tidy up at the puncture site."

"My God!" the Doc exclaimed. "Have at look at this for me will you Brad?" The Doc walked over to his friend's body, swung the magnifier into position and drew Brad's attention to the puncture wound on the arm.

"Well I'll be – I think you've got some on this puncture as well."

"Can you take a sample without disturbing much flesh?"

"Are you kidding me?" Brad selected a small pointed scalpel from the stainless tray and extracted a sample, placing it in a sterile sample container that Doc handed him.

"I'll get on this right away." Brad said on the move.

"How long?"

"An hour or two, it's faster if you know what you're looking for."

"What about the blood sample analysis?"

"Geeze, more like the better part of two working days."

"Any idea what else we should we be looking for?" Doc inquired, causing Brad to stop and scratch his head in earnest thought.

"This is an odd one. I mean what's going on here, some kind of potassium epidemic?"

"Looks like it, and not just in Lincoln. What we find here may be of use elsewhere."

"You got a phone in this dungeon?"

Doc Harris pointed to a glass window with a door next to it.

"Let me call the boss," Brad said, "and see if he's got any ideas."

"Maybe you could ask him whether he'd mind coming over. I'm doing a full thoracic and would like his chemical expertise. I think I'm a little over my head."

"Sure thing Doc." As Brad disappeared into the office, Doc Harris looked down at the remains of his friend and felt deep anger at such an unnecessary demise. He also felt a little nudge regarding a statistical proximity to the end of his own life. He was wondering whether or not he would meet this old friend again. A limb thumped on the steel table.

"Hey! You be careful with him!" Doc snapped. The technician at fault acknowledged with remorseful body language while he gingerly removed the clothing from the corpse with a dose of self-consciousness.

Brad emerged from around the corner. "Some guy named Moss on the phone for you, Doc."

Doc Harris removed his gloves and came to the phone.

"How are you making out, Doc?" George asked.

"There's a puncture all right, and it's where you said it would be. Now we need samples and tests to connect the puncture wound with the cause of death. Oh yes, and by the way, Ernie Dobson has a similar puncture in the same arm."

"They've bumped the hearing up to the day after tomorrow at ten in the morning," George warned.

"I don't know if we'll have anything by then, but I'll try and put a bomb under everyone. Some of the chemical tests run on their own timetable though, George."

"I understand, Doc. And Doc?"

"Yes?"

"I know this is hard on you. If it's any comfort, I believe my father's sense of justice would outweigh any immediate corporal indignities his old shell may be suffering."

"Thanks for that, George. I guess I'm just getting a little old for this kind of thing."

"You're a good man. I know why my father called you friend all these years."

"I'll be in touch as soon as I have anything."

"Thanks, Doc."

Brad got his boss on the line for a talk with Doc Harris. It was decided to halt everything until he got there, which was a full hour later.

The Doc didn't want to be responsible for inadvertently destroying any evidence. He sought further council with an acquaintance in the New York City coroner's office who immediately got one of the best forensic chemists on the conference line. Brad began an analysis of the small crystals he removed from the puncture wound on Mr. Moss's arm.

Dr. James Philpot, Brad's boss, was a no-nonsense chemist in his fifties with virtually no people skills. He was so bright that his mind appeared to move far too quickly to ever slow down enough to interface meaningfully with mere mortals. His knowledge of organic chemistry was astounding. He started out as a MD but just couldn't relate to people on a one-to-one basis. His inability to relate to other human beings had gone relatively unnoticed in the medical community but fortunately, for all concerned, he followed his bliss into chemistry.

Once the chest and abdomen were splayed open, the conference call began and the team moved methodically through a barrage of procedural protocols. Harris was a good doctor, and an adequate coroner for the needs of Lincoln. His genuine humility and ability to seek counsel made him an exceptional coroner that day. Once all the appropriate tissue samples were removed correctly, they were carted away for immediate analysis. Everyone's curiosity was piqued in such a manner that the suspected Lincoln potassium anomaly became the number one priority at Med-Tech laboratories.

Mr. Moss's body went to cold storage on the slight chance that further samples were necessary, and Doc Harris went home exhausted.

Doc's sweetheart was there at the door dressed to the nines with her pearls on. She saw the look on his weary face and knew what the events of the day had taken out of him.

She closed the door behind him and offered her usual kiss on the cheek but something made her hang on a little longer that day. Doc held her tight and absorbed a moment of refuge.

26

Guilty Until Proven Innocent

The police lock-up was everything Bill Monroe expected right down to being called a "pathetic fag" by one of the duty officers. Funny, but it didn't hurt like he thought it would. It not only made him angry at such intolerance but also conscious of the insecurity of the perpetrators.

Jim was being held for questioning in Randy's death. The police were extremely curious why Jim Grayson would run when the death of his partner appeared to be from natural causes. Randall Cousins had a heart attack, according to the coroner's report, so why were the police called about someone trying to break into the place? At first, Jim had attempted to avoid the Fairchild thing knowing the sensitivities of the information and how rough they played. Whether it was fatigue or just the end of his line, Jim blurted it out to the investigating detective.

"He didn't have a heart attack you fucking idiots! Fairchild Environmental killed him thinking he was me because I was hacking into their computer system. I have the guy who killed him on video tape."

The detective interrogating him froze for a second with an expression that said he was holding some kind of internal debate, until he suddenly stormed out of the room. Jim thought he had sealed his own coffin. About ninety minutes later, the detective returned with another man who looked even more serious and threatening.

"Mr. Grayson, my name is Albert Georgiadis. I'm with an investigations unit of the FBI. I understand you believe your friend's death was not from natural causes and that Fairchild Environmental was somehow involved. Would you mind talking to me about it?"

Jim wanted some answers before proceeding any further.

"I would appreciate it if you released my associate Mr. Monroe or at least included him in this discussion before I say a thing."

"Your associate? That's what you fags call yourselves nowadays is it?" The detective huffed. Jim properly assessed that the detective's nose was out of joint because he was being outranked by the feds. But the homophobic demonstration was irritating as hell.

"Detective whatever-your-name-is, I can't begin to guess how you solve any crimes with such a presumptuous steel-trap mind. You assume because Mr. Monroe and I were in a parked car, we were involved in some type of sexual activity. You assume based on your first wrong assumption that Mr. Monroe is a homosexual. You further assume given the results of clearly inadequate testing that Randall Cousins had a heart attack. And all of this is done with a measure of smug manly disdain in the middle of a police force that is rampant with homosexuality. Is your level of blissful ignorance hereditary or something you have to work at?"

Enraged, the detective took a swing at Jim who stood his ground, but Georgiadis grabbed the flying fist and shouted: "Get a hold of yourself detective, and bring Mr. Monroe up here, if you would, sir!"

The detective stormed out of the room slamming the door behind him so hard it shook the wall. Agent Georgiadis sat down and waited patiently in silence until Bill was brought up to the interrogation room. Then he introduced himself politely, flashed his ID in their direction, and abruptly dismissed the detective.

"That will be all, detective. This conversation must remain confidential for the time being. I will call you if I need anything."

The detective started to protest but threw his hands in the air as if to signal he wanted to know nothing, and strolled out of the room.

"So, gentlemen, might I ask how Fairchild Environmental is involved in the murder of Randall Cousins?" Bill looked at Jim with a look of disappointment then turned to Georgiadis and spoke calmly.

"You might, sir, but first if we are going to be having this conversation, please indulge me. Just what is the FBI's interest in Fairchild?"

"Fair enough, Mr. Monroe. We are investigating the disappearance of a Fairchild employee in Nebraska and... "

Bill interrupted: "That would be Steven McClusky, former waste site manager who was to testify at a hearing into environmental violations two years ago. It looked like he didn't want to do time for the corporation and was set to leak information. Funny thing that one; left a wife and two children somewhat suddenly, I might add."

Georgiadis was taken by surprise at Monroe's knowledge and the look on his face gave it all away...

George and Joan had no idea why they couldn't get a hold of Bill and Jim after leaving Ann's late in the afternoon. They had drafted the letter of request to speak at the hearing and Dwayne assured them they would make the agenda. It became apparent that a full house was needed at the hearing. The public had to know what was going on, and a public presence might make it more difficult to pull a fast one. Attendance at such hearings was usually pretty pathetic despite the seriousness and long lasting effects of the subject matter. This was the stuff of public indifference that some industrial concerns counted on.

It also didn't help that the hearing date had been changed. So far, the only way the public had of knowing this new information was a small typed single-page on the bulletin board at city hall. This, of course, was part of a well-used tactic. Whenever public process might inhibit industry, it was easy enough to make it awkward for the public to be involved. A little sleight-of-hand here, a dash of payola there, be just a little too late for the press, make it appear like it was an honest mistake and voila! No public process. It was as easy as rigging a Florida election.

The only tangible things they had going for them were the municipal zoning violation and the company's history in other states. They needed to hear from Bill and Jim fast.

In order to get a good crowd of people out to the hearing, George and Joan decided on a massive phone campaign. This would have to be left as late as possible in order not to alert Fairchild that they were going to have a big audience, or jeopardize any more lives unnecessarily.

They needed Fairchild off guard. If it looked even slightly awkward, Fairchild could cancel and have more time to prepare. George shuddered at the thought of what the word "prepare" might mean to a company like Fairchild Environmental Inc. He wondered how many more people could meet with accidents. It was hard to believe the company had come this far without any really successful prosecution. As they pulled into McDonough's farm George's heart sank – there was a dark sedan in the driveway.

"Get down on the floor you two!" Billy yelled, causing Joan and George to duck out of sight immediately. Billy had wisely determined that turning around would only cause more suspicion. Stanley turned to watch Billy's car approach. Billy began to speak quietly and a little slurred like a bad amateur ventriloquist, attempting not to move his lips.

"I'll park this thing in the barn and you two hide somewhere." Billy waved at Stanley on the way by and drove up the ramp to the barn, got out and opened the big door. He got back in the car and drove into the barn right up to the tractor, whispering under his breath.

"The driver is watching me, wait until I close the door before you move." Billy got out, whistling as he rolled the barn door shut.

"Hey there buddy!" Billy yelled. "What can I do for ya t'day?" Stanley was a little startled by Billy's big booming voice.

"Oh, we're with New World Developments."

"We?"

"Yes, Mr. Douglas is meeting inside with the owner of this farm."

"Being as I'm the owner of this farm I guess I better attend the meeting." Billy brushed by Stanley, who got out of his car and followed. Inside the house, Billy found his father with a mischievous smirk on his face forcing some leftover reheated coffee on Douglas, who looked like he was afraid to sit anywhere for fear of staining his perfect suit.

Mr. Douglas here is looking for that university big shot George and his girlfriend. You seen 'em anywhere?"

"Not for a day or two. Hello Mr. Douglas, Billy McDonough is the name." He saw Stanley peering in the door. "Maybe your friend might like some coffee. Come on in." Stanley reluctantly entered and Mr. McDonough pushed a coffee on him.

"So you're lookin' for Georgie Porgie. He sounded like he was about ready to sell his dad's place when I talked with him the other day."

Mr. McDonough was a master at delivering false information. It was how he used to fish Billy and George into confessing some wrongdoing. He'd spew some line that made the boys feel like anything they may have done wrong was nothing in the big picture. When they'd reveal themselves a little, he would spring the trap.

"Oh really. Mr. Moss is ready to sell?" Douglas inquired tentatively.

"Well, he sure as hell can't plough a field with a fountain pen now can he? No, there was never a body disliked farming' more than George. He was a big disappointment to his father. Mind you, the kind of money you fellas are offering for these old farms is generous' nuf to change even a *good* farmer's mind."

"There doesn't seem to be anyone home, Mr. McDonough. Do you know if he has any transportation other than the old truck in the barn?"

"Been over there snoopin' around have ya?" Mr. McDonough said with a twinkle in his eye. "Was a time you could shoot a body fer trespassin'."

Douglas put his coffee down and ended the conversation abruptly realizing he was being baited. "Goodness, look at the time. Thank you so much for the hospitality Mr. McDonough. I'm afraid we have other business to tend to."

Douglas began heading to the door. Stanley got there before him and opened it, as Mr. McDonough offered a parting observation: "You know, that's the trouble with you city slickers. You're all in such damn big hurry, ya got no idea when to stop and smell the roses."

"Good day to you, Mr. McDonough," Douglas said as he followed Stanley to the car. They left in a cloud of dust from the dirt driveway.

Billy sat down and started to laugh. "Why you lyin' old coot."

"Well now that's no way to be talkin' to yer father but thankie fer the thought. I doubt them fellas will be dropping back real soon, so you can get them two outta the barn. We don't have guests very often. Let's fix some dinner."

"How did you know they were in the barn?"

"Never seen ya care enough to put the car away out of the weather so I knew somethin' was up." Billy headed to the door but his dad stopped him: "I'd wait till them fellas are over the east hill before ya go out and fetch em."

Billy looked at his father. He hadn't seen him so alive for a long time, clearly invigorated by the events and intrigue of the last few days. He realized how much he admired the old man and what a disappointment he had been as a son. He was on his way down a fairly depressing line of thought when his father's voice interrupted.

"I think they're outta sight now son, go get George and Joan and I'll see what we got in the freezer."

Billy called to George and Joan who came out from behind a couple of bails of hay. Back in the house they dug into reheated lasagna and heard how Mr. McDonough had played Douglas. Billy told the story with a pride in his voice that his father lapped up.

Joan had a shower and recommended George do the same. She wanted to head over to the farm to get a change of clothes but they decided it was safer to make do for the moment right down to the borrowed socks and gumboots. George wasn't sure if Douglas and his man had booby-trapped the joint or bugged it to detect any return. It was early evening and George was going over his presentation with Joan when Dwayne called. He said Ann was worried about the hearing and couldn't relax at home, so she went back to work and was catching up on a little book-keeping when the fax machine took off on a printing spree.

"George, you better get over there. Her fax machine has been running non-stop," Billy said excitedly.

Billy took them into town and it was decided he would park out front of the bar this time and walk through the alley to Ann's.

Joan and George waited a few minutes to see if the coast was clear and then ran in. All went well except for one hitch, which revealed itself a few minutes later as they perused the material Bill Monroe and Jim had sent. The door to the shop opened and in strode Patricia Sandfield. Ann went out front to deal with her.

"I'm sorry, Patricia I'm closed."

"I saw George Moss and his sweet young thing run in here. I had a man in my shop looking for them and asking questions this afternoon. Are they in trouble with the law?"

"Oh dear." Ann seemed a little uptight which increased Patricia's curiosity. Something was wrong and the suspense was killing her.

"Just what the heck is goin' on 'round here? People hidin' in cars and sneakin' about," Patricia huffed.

George let Ann off the hook and poked his head into the shop from the back room. "Patricia, come on back here. Ann, lock the door please."

Patricia was powerless against an overwhelming curiosity that hooked her nose like a bass on a line. In the back room her curiosity peaked even higher at the sight of Joan cutting sheets from the running roll of fax paper and putting them into separate folders. She acknowledged Joan with a lift of her eyebrows. Joan glanced back with a worried look of disapproval as she continued to work.

"Well George," Patricia demanded, "what's goin' on with all this cloak-and-dagger stuff?"

"I'll tell you Patricia. Sit down." She sat in the chair tentatively.

"The story goes like this: There is a company who wants three farms. The Dobson's', McDonough's' and my father's place."

"Well, we all know 'bout that. Them folks are building executive homes and the like."

"That was the initial myth to keep public opposition to a minimum Patricia. I would have thought you, of all people, would know more than that propaganda."

"This isn't about that storage facility business is it?"

George smiled. Her reputation was alive and well.

"Right on the nose. Now here's where it gets a little scary. They killed Ernie Dobson and Dad, who didn't want to sell, and they tried to kill Joan and me. The man who came to see you was probably the hit man or whatever they call them nowadays."

"Cleaner. I think they call them cleaners now," Joan said snidely as she read the incoming info.

"A hit man? A cleaner? Oh dear." Patricia was uncharacteristically shaken.

"Do you know about the environmental hearing the day after tomorrow?"

"I certainly do and I don't appreciate the way they tried to sneak that by me. I will be attending."

"I need you to do more than attend, Patricia. And this may require you to not go to work tomorrow in case you accidentally say something. One word and someone else could get killed."

The colour left Patricia's face. "Killed? Oh dear. Oh dear me."

George filled Patricia in on how she and her particular skills could help. She seemed very suspicious at first, but when Joan threw some pages from the fax machine on her lap, her eyes popped out like organ stops, and she began to fathom the seriousness of the whole thing. She agreed to everything, in part because it made her a key person in her own mind. George certainly didn't want to do anything to jeopardize how important she felt. She was involved as a gossip in the biggest piece of gossip of her career.

As Patricia left, Ann glared at George. "What are you, nuts?" The words burst out of her mouth as soon as the door closed behind Patricia.

George shrugged and explained: "What rumours would she have spread after seeing us sneak in here after hiding in Billy's back seat? It would expose you, Dwayne, the McDonough's, Joan and me. I had no choice but to include her. She hates having the wool pulled over her eyes and that's exactly what Fairchild has attempted to do. I think she'll be fine. At least she knows who the bad guys are now."

"Doesn't matter, it's done," Joan sighed, looking up from a pile of paper. "We're going to need some legal advice on how to present this stuff in the context of the hearing. We need to speak to Bill Monroe."

George nodded agreement. "We can't set up shop at McDonough's. Things are going to get pretty intense once that request to speak is discovered tomorrow. We need a place to sleep and work."

"You're welcome to my place." Ann offered.

"I wouldn't want to bring any danger to your family, Ann."

"Well you're already here so why don't you just hole up and I'll go get some sleeping bags and an air mattress?"

"Ann," Joan asked, "would it be possible to bum a change of clothes for George and me? It's too dangerous to get our things from the house."

Ann smiled affectionately back at Joan. "Back in a flash," she said. They locked the door behind her.

While Billy and the others sat in Ann's office conspiring, Mr. McDonough stewed on chivalrous thoughts. He had heard Joan's spoken need for some clean clothing earlier in the day. Even though they had ruled out going to the house, the old man stubbornly thought "to hell" with the possibility of danger when a woman's dignity is at stake. He waited until dark, loaded his shotgun with two cartridges, stuffed a flashlight into his pocket and began what would be an arduous journey.

The terrain was going to be demanding for him. His old ravaged lungs felt like they were done in before he had even crossed his own driveway. However, his purpose was strong and he somehow willed himself to keep going. The night was overcast again leaving the sky pitch-black. He dragged his feet over the dirt driveway until his old boots fell silent on the matted grass at the edge of the field. He methodically paced himself one foot at a time, stopping every few steps to gasp for air. The discomfort was muted by thoughts of all the years he had ploughed that field and the ones around it, the good years, the lean years, the droughts and the floods. His instincts for farming were fed by a passion to play some small role in the magic of creation by planting and tending. He had never lost his awe for the power and struggle of life observed in the fragile little green sprouts that pushed their way up though clumps of heavy earth seemingly defeating the forces of gravity.

The crops over the years had become the markers of his life. The wheat years, the hay years, the corn years, and on this particular piece of God's good Earth, even the strawberry years. He remembered the sweet fragrance that came off the field when it was alive with the fruit. He heard cornstalks rustle like the petticoats of a beautiful woman, even though the dregs of that crop had been ploughed under years ago. His senses could smell and feel residual traces of everything he had ever grown there as his mind played back sounds from the roar of his tractor to the welcome clang of the dinner bell. His wife's voice whispered to him in the warm, moisture-laden breeze that cascaded down the slope from the crest of the hill. He felt the memory of her slender fingers slipping into his hand helping him across the field they had walked together so many times.

As he reached his old neighbour's house, a coughing spell rattled his loosening frame. He frantically reached for his inhaler only to realize it was back home on the kitchen counter. Mind over matter, he thought, forcing a temporary meditative calm on himself. With the eagle eye of a seasoned hunter he scanned his perimeter. The shotgun flew open with a deft flick of his wrist revealing two shells in the breach then it snapped shut as readily as it had opened. He slowly moved around the house to the side of the front porch. The breeze dropped suddenly only to hit a little harder seconds later with an abrupt shove from a passing westerly on its way through.

The air carried the smell of life and the approaching summer. The old man loved the way nature 'bill boarded' what was coming aromatically if you only took the time to smell it. It always amazed him how the smell of fall would appear in the air in the blink of an eye. Summer was always a little slower, he thought to himself: it takes longer to resurrect life than kill it.

He looked up at the windmill as it spun slowly, complaining with every rotation. His eyes squinted in a keen focus at the property. He scanned once more in a slow and methodical circle for anything out of the ordinary before making his way up the front steps and on to the porch. With one last glance over the shoulder he opened the squeaky front door and entered. The place spooked him a little in the dark so he thought he'd make it short and sweet. His hand fumbled around in his pocket until the flashlight was out, blazing a path that he followed down the hall toward the bedrooms.

"Good evening, Mr. McDonough. Kind of a long way from home, aren't you?" The voice came out of the dark behind him. The old man swung around and fired. The roar of his shotgun was followed by a smaller popping sound that sent his frail body reeling to the floor with a stabbing pain in his chest. The flashlight, still in the tight grip of his gnarled old hand, shone straight up on to the hall ceiling like a searchlight as he struggled for breath.

"Fools! Fools!" A harried voice called from the dark. McDonough looked into the black room as a rather distinguished looking figure slowly materialized into the vertical stream of his flashlight. With the light shining on his features from below, Douglas looked every bit as sinister as he really was.

"You stupid old man," he scolded. Douglas grabbed the shotgun and pried it out of the gnarled, leathery hands. The flashlight dropped, spilling light across the floor to a jumbled heap that slowly registered as a man lying on his side with the top of his head blown off. McDonough smiled. He had got one of the bastards, he thought to himself. Stanley's finger was still on the trigger of the 38 he held in his hand. When the shotgun blast hit him, his finger reflexively squeezed off the round that had entered Mr. McDonough's chest.

Pins and needles started at Mr. McDonough's feet and moved up his body. Light-headedness wafted in making the pain seem farther away. Was this it, he wondered? Would he hold her again? Would he see her and hear her? Oh God, he hoped so. What would she look like? Would she be as beautiful as the first time he laid eyes on her? Would she see an old dishevelled wreck or the strong able man she fell in love with? A welcome warmth smothered him as the room spun like a slow inviting whirlpool to somewhere nice. His expression left pain behind as it turned into a cheeky grin of anticipation.

"At long last, my sweetheart." He whispered as his eyes rolled into the back of his head.

27

Full Bloom

George suddenly looked startled and he dropped a stack of papers. "Something's happened to Mr. McDonough."

Joan looked at him waiting for more – nothing came. "What's happened?"

"I don't know. I have to get Billy."

"What if Douglas is out there?" Joan asked fearfully.

George let his mind go for a minute, then responded. "He's not in town at the moment. Lock the door behind me!" He flew out the door leaving Joan with a somewhat stunned look on her face. George knew she felt a modicum of security in the sureness of his words as he ran down the back alley to the Hot Spot bar. As he entered the back door, Al came out of the washroom licking a rollie.

"Hey, George."

"Al." George brushed by with a little too much urgency tripping Al's curiosity wire. He returned to his rollie but fell in behind George at his usual saunter to see what was going on.

The bar was as George remembered, a stinky old watering hole, an olfactory cocktail of beer, smoke and urine. Must be, George thought, that a new bar owner might be able to purchase that fragrance in an aerosol can to lend an establishment some kind of instant legitimacy.

The Biggar family had run it for years, and made just enough money from it to support the family's predisposition to alcoholism.

Some councillors had been trying to shut it down for years because it was such an eyesore, but Mrs. Biggar would have none of it. It was a free world she would cough through her beer breath and bad brown tobacco-stained teeth. It was her "goddamned piece of the goddamned American Dream."

George spotted Billy in a booth chatting up some not-so-sweet young thing, and went straight to him. "Billy something's happened to your father!"

Billy's head moved slowly. It was obvious he'd had a few too many. "What? Is he OK?"

"I don't think so."

"Jesus Christ." Billy struggled to get up from the table but could hardly stand; he was so saturated with alcohol.

Al's voice came from behind. "What's the matter with Mr. McDonough, George?"

"I'm not sure, but we need to get out there."

"He shouldn't be drivin' like that, George. Need a limo?"

"Yeah, great Al." George took Al's offer up thinking there might be greater safety in numbers anyway. They took an arm each and led Billy out into the fresh air. Al's significant other stumbled out behind them.

"Where the fuck you goin' at this time of the fuckin night?"

"Can't ya see I'm workin' Christie? I'm takin' Billy home."

"Well how the fuck am I s'posed to get the fuck home for fuck sakes?" Al had a real dilemma on his hands. He looked at George for an answer, which George didn't provide.

Al forced a grin. "I'll be back soon, honey. You wait here."

"The hell I will," Christie shot back. She stormed ahead and staked her claim to the front seat of Al's limo while Al and George stuffed Billy into the back and George hopped in after him.

"Let's get there as quick as we can, Al."

"Is he in danger or somethin', George?"

"Yeah," George said as calmly as possible. Christie swung her head around and looked at George in the eyes as straight as she could.

"Is this some of yer fuckin' *Sight* shit you got goin' Georgie?"

"I think so, Christie. I think it's the Moss *Sight* shit."

Christie looked him up and down, then something snapped.

"You makin' a fuckin' fool outta me ya fuckin' freak?"

"Christie, you shouldn't speak to my customers that way – it's unprofessional like!" George had never heard Al raise his voice before and it looked apparent that Christie hadn't, either. It threw her off of her train of thought. Actually it wasn't an entire train, maybe more like one small car... the kind you crank by hand. So, George reassessed that it threw her off her "cart" of thought, leaving her totally blank trying to remember where she was.

"I wasn't making fun of you Christie." He said, trying to smooth things over. "Actually, I thought you were making fun of me. I'm just a little worried about Billy's Dad, that's all."

Christie slowly came back on line.

"Nobody makes fun of fuckin' Christie Adams and gets the fuck away with it." She turned to Al who was shaking a little and looking remorseful. "Gimme a rollie."

"Uh yeah, okay darlin'." Al steered with one hand and reached into his pocket with the other. As soon as he touched his tobacco – terra firma, his trembling stopped. He began the sure-fingered one-handed manufacture of a cigarette for the love of his life.

"Nobody makes fuckin' fun of Christie fuckin' Adams." She muttered again as she began to sniffle a little to herself. Al now noticed her distress and glanced at George in the rear-view as if to say, "Don't ask me why she's cryin'. I'm just a guy. Chicks! Go figure!" He licked the rollie and handed it to her as the tail end of the car spun onto the dirt side road. Christie lit up and stared out the window.

Billy's eyes were fixed on George like he needed to hear everything was all right. George had no such assurances to give, so Billy opened his window and began smacking his face in an attempt to find some sobriety. A few minutes later, they skidded into his driveway and Billy, in his eagerness, jumped out before the car had fully stopped and was thrown to the ground. He got up immediately with both hands skinned a little, ripped and bleeding from chunks of gravel embedded in the dirt driveway. Undeterred, he ran into the house.

"Dad? Dad?" he yelled, running frantically from room to room. As George approached the porch Billy came running out. "He's not here. I'll check the barn." George ran with him and they looked in every nook and cranny, still no Mr. McDonough. That was when George looked at a light shining from across the field.

"Somebody's been over at my father's house."

"I'll get the gun." Billy ran back to the farmhouse and came back out moments later screaming, "It's gone! His shotgun is gone!"

Christie stumbled out of the car. "What's goin' on?"

Al emerged with a curious look. "Yeah, did you find him?"

"No, Al, he's not here," George replied. "We're going to look over at my place. Perhaps it would be safer if you and Christie waited for us here."

"Safer? Should I call 911 or something?"

"Not yet, Al. We'll be back in a minute." Billy began stumbling across the field, and George followed. Al and Christie looked at them like they were nuts and got back in the car. Al's radio went on with a blast. The local station was caught right in the middle of the Carpenters *Top of the World.* Christie cursed: "Give me a fuckin' break for fuck sakes," as Al kept changing stations, finally settling on something loud and raunchy with power guitar chords.

Running across the field wasn't any easier than the last time, and George was gasping for air when he reached the house. Billy somehow managed to keep up. Breathing heavily, they approached the front door cautiously and went in. There was nobody there. George turned all the lights on and looked around the living room. Billy searched the other rooms and came back with a puzzled look.

"What now?" He wheezed as he sat down on the couch. He was pale from exertion. As he tried to catch his breath he began looking like he was going to be sick.

"If you're going to hurl, step outside Billy."

"Okee dokee." Without missing a beat he got up, glided out to the front porch and wretched over the railing. As George's eyes followed him out the door they were caught by something unfamiliar on the wall. He looked closer at what appeared to be a series of spots. Jesus, it was buckshot in the plaster! George turned around and sensed something in the hall and approached his old bedroom. He stopped dead, looked down on the floor and smelled something, a chemical odour that had a familiarity to it. It was... Mr. Clean? George knew the smell of Mr. Clean. Joan had just been using it in the kitchen in an attempt to detoxify the cupboards. George was so focused on his sense of smell that his face looked a little screwed up to Billy who was done heaving his biscuits.

"You gonna puke, too?" Billy asked as he stood in the doorway.

"No, Mr. Clean."

"Hey, sorry, at least I went outside."

"No, not you, the cleanser, I smell Mr. Clean."

"So?"

"So, it didn't smell like this two days ago. Somebody has cleaned the floor. And look on the wall to your left. There's some buckshot in the plaster that wasn't there two days ago either."

Billy spun around and looked at the wall. "Dad's shot gun?"

"Maybe," George muttered. There was something glistening in between the floorboards. He squatted and ran his finger along one plank and looked at it. It was red.

"Blood. There's fresh blood in the cracks of the floorboards. Somebody's been shot. I think your Dad fired from here at somebody and they must have shot him back."

"Oh God, no." Billy crumpled to the floor. George went over and held him as he started to fall apart and that's when he realized the living room rug was gone. In front of the living room window the lines between the floorboards looked moist as well.

"There's more over there." George said.

"What?" Billy's tears subsided a little. He let go of George who went over to the window and reached down, running his finger along the crack in the floorboards again.

"Blood. Looks like the old bugger got a piece of whoever shot him." The smell of Mr. Clean grew even stronger. "And that wall has been cleaned, there must have been blood on it."

"Is Dad dead, George?"

George went back to the place in the hall where he felt the old man had fallen. "I, I don't know. I only know he felt... good... here."

"Getting shot doesn't feel good! What the hell are you talking about George?"

"I don't know, Billy. I'm sorry; I don't know how to read this stuff. I'm not as good as my father was at this. Let me think about it some more."

Billy wandered through to the kitchen and dropped onto a chair. He didn't even flinch when the phone shattered the silence. George walked over and answered.

"Go to a secure phone." The phone disconnected. It was Jim's voice. At last, some contact.

George hung up. "Billy, we have to get out of here."

Billy just nodded and stood up.

George ran to the bedroom, threw shoes and a bunch of things into one of the bags and turned off the lights.

They headed out the door and across the field.

"I don't think it's safe for you to spend the night at your place, Billy. We have to stick together until the hearing."

"What's so damn special about the hearing?"

"Hopefully we can blow the lid off this thing in such a loud and public manner that we might find some justice; maybe some safety."

"He seemed happy to you George? No bullshit now, I don't need bullshit," Billy sniffed.

"What I felt was a warm sense of happiness, almost... well being, no pain."

"He's dead, he must be dead. He sure wasn't happy alive."

They walked the rest of the way with no words. The radio on Al's limo blared. Led Zeppelin was roaring on a hard rock station that been playing the same songs in rotation for twenty years like some kind of musical Flat Earth Society.

As they headed to the car, George wondered why he couldn't ascertain Mr. McDonough's death. Maybe it was because there really wasn't such a thing as death per say, just change. Maybe the *Sight* was sympathetic to the infinite stream of things. Maybe the old man, as he had sensed in his father's case, was just somewhere else.

"Do you still feel your father's presence?" George asked.

Billy looked at him a little confused.

"You don't have to answer. Just think about it. And if you do sense it, hold on to that feeling and invest in it. I think it's real." They got to Al's limo and piled in the back.

"What's goin' on guys?" Al asked. Christie just swayed her head back and forth in time to the music with her eyes shut.

"We don't exactly know Al. We didn't find anything. Could you drive us to the gas station near Ten Side-road? I need the pay phone."

"Sure thing." Al was on the job. He fired the engine up and put the pedal to the metal. He kept glancing back at Billy whose shoulders would start shaking followed by a scrunched up face that pushed out a stream of tears every so often. He wondered what the hell was going wrong with the world that made people just up and burst into tears like Christie did with some regularity, and now Billy for Christ sakes! He chalked it up to El Nino or lunar cycles and lit a rollie. They roared up to the pay phone in a cloud of dust.

George made a phone call. "Where the hell have you been, Jim?"

"It's a long story, George. Andy and Martha are in hospital. Bill and I had a nice visit to jail. Listen, we are sending you some heavy stuff. I got into the mainframe with Andy's line reader."

"Wait, slow down a little! Are Andy and Martha okay?"

"Yes, a little banged up, Martha worse than Andy, but it looks like they'll be okay."

"Thank God. Now, what's this about a line reader?"

"It's a... never mind, it doesn't matter, we're almost done transmitting to the fax line you gave us."

"I know, Joan is over there now. Jim, is Bill Munroe around? We need some legal input for this damn hearing. It's been bumped up to the day after tomorrow, we..." George froze.

"George?" Jim wondered if the line was dead. The hair was up on the back of George's neck. He looked up and saw a dark-coloured late-model car heading toward town that suddenly pulled over about a hundred yards down the road.

"Jim, the bad guys are here, the guy in your video just spotted me on this damn pay phone and pulled over on the road up ahead. I'll call you back!" He slammed the phone into the cradle and hopped back into Al's limo. Christie was still swaying to the music, eyes shut. Billy's eyes were red from a major workout and the car was full of smoke.

"Al, what kind of shape is this vehicle in?"

"Tuned her up myself, George. Runs like a top."

"Do you think you could lose somebody trying to follow you?" Al's head snapped to the rear view.

"You going a little funny, George? There's no one following us."

"Not yet, Al. He's up the road about a hundred yards or so and waiting for us. He just spotted me in the phone booth and pulled over.

Billy squinted out the window and saw nothing until a passing vehicle's lights silhouetted the shadow of a vehicle on the side of the road.

Al saw it too. "So he's gonna follow us?"

"Yup."

"Why don't we peel outta here and head the other way. We can cut over Fourth Sideroad and take the old quarry road back on to highway."

"Sounds like a plan," George answered. Al looked forward, eyes glued to car up the road, assessing his opponent while he slowly rolled a smoke. George gathered that for Al's driving skills to be at their best, a rollie had to be hanging from his lips. He pulled the brim of his baseball cap down and lit up like Clint Eastwood in a spaghetti western, then without warning, the tires squealed as they fishtailed out on to the road. George looked behind them though a cloud of blue burned rubber and exhaust at two headlights that flicked on as the dark coloured car spun into a U-turn.

"Son of a bitch, he's coming after us! Nice call, George!" Billy said wiping his face. Al was deep in concentration. When they approached 90 miles an hour the car began to shake like it was going to come apart.

"Don't worry 'bout that little tremor, just need the tires rotated," Al yelled, eyes fixed on the road. Fourth Sideroad was a concealed intersection that sat on the other side of a crest in the highway. Al was hoping that whoever was following would shoot past it and have to double back, increasing the odds of losing them. Christie seemed oblivious to everything except when Al screeched around the corner on to Fourth Sideroad. She opened her eyes with a cheesed-off expression, turned the radio up, put on her seat belt and closed her eyes again swaying to the dulcet tones of AC/DC. She was such a party girl. As an adolescent George was smitten with the way she lost herself in music. She had no idea how sexy or provocative her body movement was when she entered the zone. She could lose herself, and the world around her, in dance and rhythm. George watched her, glad that music still offered her a place of refuge.

The hunter was closing in. He hadn't missed the turn like Al had hoped, leaving Al with a bit of a worried expression on his face. His car began to smell a little and George noticed the heat gauge was moving up toward red. Al flew on to the old quarry road and didn't let up. He knew every twist and turn of that dangerous snake-like dirt ribbon. Whoever was pursuing would most certainly have trouble negotiating the blind turns with a face full of dust. The distance between the two vehicles slowly increased. They flew past flashes of lateral moraine, sandpits heavily rutted by weekend dirt-bikers. Airborne over the last hill, the old wagon slammed back hard on to the dirt and twisted its way back on to the highway. By the time Al's limo approached the outskirts of town the dark sedan was nowhere to be seen.

"Nice driving, Al," George stroked. Al lifted his baseball cap up a little, grateful that the match was over.

"It's my trade, George," he chimed with an unusual amount of bravado. His adrenal glands were working overtime. His rollie had gone out, stuck to his bottom lip. He opened the window and spat it out only to roll a fresh one that Christie swiped before he could light it.

"Where would you like me to set ya down?"

"Could you drop up us off at Biggars, Al?"

"You got it."

"What do I owe you?"

"Twenty ought to cover it."

George reached for his wallet and grabbed a twenty as they pulled up to the Hot Spot. George got out and reached back in the window for Al's hand. "Thanks, buddy."

"Anytime, George." The handshake was sincere but ended rather abruptly as Al backed his smoking, overheated old wagon out on to the street. Christie opened her eyes to see what was going on. George waved thanks to her but she just went back to the zone, turning the radio down just a little. She leaned into Al's hand as he stroked her hair affectionately while steering the limo away with the other. This had the makings of a good night for Al and Christie. George sensed Al had good fortune with amorous ideas when Christie was in "the zone." The trick was to get home before she passed out.

"Why here, George?"

"We aren't staying. Follow me."

Billy followed George through Biggar's Hot Spot and back down the alley to Ann's shop where he banged on the door. A very worried Joan opened it and flew into George's arms. "Are you two alright? What happened?"

"Al gave the guy the slip on the old quarry road."

"The guy?"

"Yeah, *the* guy."

"God help us. How is Mr. McDonough?" She said after noticing Billy's spent face.

"We don't know for sure," George answered. He filled her in while Billy just stared at the walls. Then George remembered Jim's call.

"Jim called. He said Andy and Martha were in the hospital but were okay. I said I would call him back."

There was a courtesy knock at the door, then it swung open. Ann and Dwayne came in with clothes, a large air mattress, sleeping bags and pillows. "Here you go, guys," Ann smiled. "You might as well be a little comfortable." Ann was startled by the sight of Billy standing quietly in the corner. "Hey, Billy. You alright?"

"Yeah I guess so." He muttered, lost in thought.

"Billy's dad is missing. I think he was involved in some kind of shoot out at our place." George offered, breaking the silence

"Shootout?" Ann's tone was one of disbelief.

"There was evidence of blood on the floor that had been missed in a fairly thorough clean up. There was nobody there and the living room carpet was gone."

"This is starting to sound like a Scorsese film." Ann muttered with disgust. Dwayne was struck mute by what was being said.

Billy put up a bit of an argument but eventually conceded to spend the night at Ann and Dwayne's. George tried Jim again with no luck. Joan and George inflated the air mattress while she peppered him with questions about Martha and Andy. They rolled out the sleeping bags removed their clothing and crawled in, a little concerned over the whereabouts of Bill and Jim.

George and Joan lay there exhausted by the events of the last couple of days and filled with anticipation for what lay ahead. They had to stay out of sight for one more day until the hearing, prepare their case, and hope like hell Patricia Sandfield was up to the challenge of staying quiet for twenty-four hours. Their minds were busy, but they finally found a comforting peace in holding each other and drifted off.

The dream was back and once again George was conscious that it was just that – a dream. He wondered what he had missed in the first few run-throughs that necessitated a replay. The two men held his father down, the guy with the needle entered, his father struggled, and the picture fell. The syringe went into his arm; his chest screamed with the pain that now was only a twinge to George. He left his body. The formal gentleman who injected his father held the bedpost with his right hand and checked the carotid artery for a pulse. They left the room. One went out to get the car and one tripped over the rack holding the walking canes and his grandfather's umbrella sending the lot crashing across the floor. Another man broke into the living room desk and took some documents. Then they left. George didn't wake up when the men closed the door behind them. This time, he lingered in the room. So what was it and why was it so damned important to replay this scene? Maybe it was the papers the guy took from the desk. No, he already knew what they were. Just what the hell was his father trying to tell me? That was when he focused on the cane rack and his grandfather's umbrella. There was no umbrella. That was it. It was raining when the first guy opened the door and the nervous guy had taken his grandfather's umbrella. George replayed the nervous guy's voice over and over in his head until it he remembered where he had heard it before.

He woke up and looked at his watch. It was 3:10:10 a.m. and George realized that a noise in the alley had awakened him and now someone was at the back door. He whispered into Joan's ear and held his hand gently to her lips.

"Don't make a sound. Someone is outside." Her eyes opened, instantly alert from the fear she heard in George's words.

"What do we do?" she whispered nervously.

"You hide under the desk, and I'll get something to whack them over the head with when they come in." She quietly crawled out of the sleeping bag, over to the desk, and hid.

George found a snow shovel in the closet as the back door knob rattled. Whoever was at the door paused briefly, and then resumed work on the door, but this time there was a new sound. It was metal on metal – the lock in the handle was being picked! The intruder tried the door again and the deadbolt above the handle began to move. George reached down into his soul to find some anger to help him in the aggressive department. He found it sitting in the memory of the moment when he realized his father had been murdered. He was capable of killing someone then and needed that same resolve. Heart pounding, mouth dry, he knew he could kill, not for himself, but for Joan and his father. He stoked the fires of anger until the height of the flames dwarfed his own gentle nature.

"Come on in and kiss your ass goodbye," he whispered under his breath playing even farther into his new dark role.

The door clicked open; George raised the shovel over his head and swung with all his might. One blow might be the only chance he would get. The end of the shovel connected with a "thunk" sending the intruder sprawling to the floor.

"Argh! Don't hit me, Georgiadis... FBI!" the intruder moaned. George flipped the light on and saw that the end of the shovel was plastic; He realized he couldn't have killed a flea with the damn thing but held the shovel up for a threatening effect anyway.

"How do I know you are who you say you are?" George asked firmly. The man looked up and started to smile.

"What's so funny, pal?" George said with as ominous a tone as possible.

"You're standing there naked holding a snow shovel for starters. It's not something I see everyday. Now don't get me wrong, I'm not saying that you're not a fine specimen of a man. George ignored the man's levity. His nakedness didn't bug him at all and he wasn't about to be thrown off his sole purpose, which at that moment was Joan's safety.

"Answer me: How do I know you are who you say you are?"

"Because I came here with Jim Grayson and Bill Monroe. They're out front in my car."

"Jim?" Joan asked, emerging from under the desk. "Jim's here?"

Georgiadis did a double take, as Joan tried to hide her nakedness with her hands. "Am I the only one around here who can afford clothes?" he said, averting his eyes and facing the floor.

Another voice suddenly entered the room: "What the hell is going on in here?" Jim Grayson appeared and looked at George stark naked with the shovel. "Well, hello there, shovel boy."

Joan ran to him. "Oh Jim! Are you okay? We were so worried."

George reached for some pants and also grabbed a coat, which he wrapped around Joan's shoulders. Georgiadis got up from the floor holding his head and looking a little incensed.

"I'm sorry for whacking you over the noggin like that," George apologized. "Things are just a little uncivilized around here lately."

"I'm just glad it's a plastic shovel," Georgiadis replied, inspecting a little bit of blood on fingers he had just run through his thick black hair. He sent his hand back up to survey the damage and found a spot on his scalp where the skin was broken. His fingers returned for one last scan that seemed to confirm the damage was minimal.

"Close the door would you, Mr. Moss? Let's try and not wake up the entire neighbourhood." The tone was business-like, but friendly.

Jim pulled the coat around Joan in an effort to protect her dignity.

"Oh, Jim." Joan whispered. He looked at her and his lip started to quiver. They just held each other and wept. He was sharing his grief for Randy with his best friend. She was grieving for both of them. The tension of the last few days fuelled the emotional release.

"How did you know where we were?" George asked.

"We didn't. We just got an address on the fax number."

"Why the B and E?"

"Well, it was a little stupid and unnecessary of me I suppose, but we found no one out at your father's farm, or the farm next door. We came here to see if all the information they had sent was missing, as well. We feared we were too late and all the evidence might have been cleaned up."

"Oh, they do clean up, these fellows," George said sarcastically. "But there are traces of blood in the cracks between the floorboards at my father's house that you could put your forensics people to work on."

"Blood? Whose blood? I was told your father had an induced cardiac arrest."

"This is fresh blood and it poses an interesting question because there are two patches of it and some buckshot on the wall. I think there was a little bit of a showdown. One patch of blood I believe belongs to our old neighbour Mr. McDonough. The other patch must be one of the two men who have been poking around town."

"And Mr. McDonough?"

"Missing."

"Do you believe Fairchild is involved?"

"Yes, but before we continue Mr. Georgiadis, just what exactly is your interest in all of this?"

"We've been investigating Fairchild with regard to some other interstate matters. I stumbled on to Jim and Bill when they were arrested by the local police for performing lewd acts in a public place."

"Bill Monroe and Jim?"

"I said that's what they were arrested for, not what they were doing. They were involved in some illegal surveillance, the fruits of which came down the pike to you over that fax machine. As illegally obtained evidence it is of course inadmissible in a court of law but it's such good stuff I thought it might be prudent to see how far you get with it until we can secure the same stuff legally."

"We have a couple of aces up our sleeve, but we need a major strategy for this environmental hearing," George thought out loud.

"That's an understatement, Mr. Moss. Sam Johnson is a sticky guy when it comes to process. I have seen him in action. He loves to shut his opposition down on fine points of procedure; the man is a master at it."

"What exactly are his ties to Fairchild?" George had no sooner asked the question when the back door opened and Bill Monroe walked in. "Would anyone have come to get me or was I supposed to stay out in the car all night?"

"Man, are we glad to see you," George grinned.

"I'm glad you're seeing me, too. We were getting a little concerned when you hung up. So we flew all the way out here – and I don't mind saying the taxpayers are paying big time for the way the FBI likes to travel in private aircraft. I am so relieved you and Joan are okay. It's funny what awful roads the imagination travels, when left to its own devices. I had you both dead and buried."

"Thanks just the same," George smirked, "but we're kind of grateful to still be alive and kicking."

"Would it be too much to suggest to everyone that we might get a good night's sleep and pick up on this in the morning?" Georgiadis croaked with obvious exhaustion. Jim peered through tear-soaked eyes over Joan's shoulder in obvious agreement with the idea of sleep.

"You're seconds away from the old hotel," George instructed. "It's only a block away. If you don't mind velour everything, the mattresses are fairly new. Why don't you guys check in and meet us back here in the morning." There seemed to be general consensus that sleep would do them all good. They lingered for at least another hour though. There was just too much to catch up on, and some genuine mourning to do for Randy.

They laughed and cried remembering what a character Randy was. Jim recalled stories of his sensitive side as well as humorous incidents that revealed his cranky persona. Randy would acknowledge his crankiness with self-deprecating humour. This, they agreed, was the instrument that turned a grump into an interesting, lovable character. His flamboyance was priceless. His overt sexuality put many people off but was accepted as part of who he was by his friends. They finally parted company before sun-up. Joan and George returned to the sleeping bags on the air mattress and a sleep that could not have been more welcomed.

The new day began too soon and too heavy. Ann called from the emergency room at the hospital. It was Billy. She had found him face down and unconscious after he got into their liquor cupboard and consumed just about everything in it while they slept. As a precaution in the event of substances other than alcohol, his stomach was being pumped out as they spoke.

Dwayne arrived a few minutes later to take George and Joan over to County General where they all hung around Billy's bed until he slowly came to. The doctor let slip that Billy had another really close call from booze and an apparent good dose of amphetamines not too long ago. It was what he referred to as the combo platter. Billy's eyes finally opened with an expression of disappointment that revealed how much he had wanted to kill himself.

"I'm still here?" He burst into tears. George couldn't go there with him. Sure it was tragic, sad and hopeless, but there were other things going on that required attention and something snapped.

"Billy, you selfish son of a bitch! We're all hanging on by a thread here and you want to add your death to the stew?"

Joan grabbed George with serious look. "Stop!" She whispered emphatically under her breath. George looked at her with a look that said: "Don't mess with me!" and ripped into his old friend.

"Look Billy, if you want to check out because you've crossed too many lines that's okay with me. I can't begin to fathom the pain that drives you to such a place. But I beg of you as an old friend, refrain from killing yourself, for the time being at least. We need to devote our complete attention to staying alive without the distraction of having to pump your stomach out and rush to your deathbed."

"You, you don't need to do nothin' for me. Just leave me alone," Billy shot back.

"Dwayne, get me the hell away from this selfish jerk. I've got work to do!" George stormed out of the room. Joan stroked Billy's head for a few more seconds and followed out into the hall with Dwayne in tow.

Ann being the Earth-mother she was, stayed behind to hold his hand and let him know she cared.

The ride back to the store was pretty quiet until Dwayne gingerly spoke up. "Weren't you a little rough on him? He nearly died, for crying out loud."

"Probably, but he isn't supposed to die now."

"What the hell does that mean?" Joan asked, confused.

"It isn't Billy's time. Something's coming, I'm not sure what it is, but Billy's supposed to be here for it. The only hope of avoiding more distraction I thought was to ask him to stay alive for us, at least until this mess is over."

Joan looked as though she was trying to understand, but George's statement was just a little out of everyone's grasp.

They got back to the shop and tidied up the sleeping bags and clutter. Jim, Bill Monroe and the FBI guy would be joining them soon.

Shortly after nine, Dwayne headed over to the town hall with the written request for George to be on the hearing agenda. He found Barbara, the secretary, alone as he had hoped and instructed her to ensure copies of the request to speak were inserted into the councillor's mail slots before Mr. Speeks arrived. Barbara was curious, but Dwayne would only say that if all went well some fallout would hit the fan, and that some of it would likely end up on Speek's face. She quite liked the sound of that, revealing that she had her own issues with Speeks, and let Dwayne know in no uncertain terms that all would be done as he asked.

Dwayne and Ann arrived back at the shop via the hospital with a load of coffee and doughnuts for the big pow-wow. Jim, Bill Monroe, and Georgiadis arrived shortly after eleven o'clock. After greetings and small talk, they dug in. It was going to be a long day. Ann put a "closed" sign on the shop door. Dwayne dragged some folding chairs up from the basement. They sat around the stack of papers trying to figure out what they could use and what Johnson might deem irrelevant.

"What can we do with the video?" Jim began.

"Let me see it." Georgiadis responded in his usual dry manner. Dwayne inserted the video, and Georgiadis watched, shaking his head. When it was over he pronounced it interesting but not damning. George replayed it and pointed out the fact that the man in the video wasn't checking for a pulse, but in fact, was rubbing something off of Randy's arm around the probable injection point.

"Maybe and maybe not," Georgiadis responded. "The only thing we really have here is circumstantial. It's a man at the scene of an apparent cardiac arrest."

"And if we can prove it was an artificially induced cardiac arrest and what he is looking at is the point of injection?" George inquired.

"Then we have circumstantial evidence of a man at the scene of an artificially induced cardiac arrest." He responded flatly.

"And what if I can produce a fingerprint of the same man from the scene of another artificially induced cardiac arrest?"

"A fingerprint? Where?"

"On my father's bedpost."

"And the cardiac arrest, how can we prove it was induced?"

"They are doing an autopsy."

"Here?"

"Yes."

"Why didn't anyone tell me about this? I need to get some of my people here. Can you show us where the print is on your father's bedpost?"

George nodded agreement. The lawman grabbed his cell-phone and hit a number on speed dial. His voice was low and firm. His crew would arrive in a couple hours. George couldn't get his thoughts off of poor old Mr. McDonough. Worse, he couldn't seem to focus his thoughts. Suddenly, the reason became clear; His thoughts were based on a presumption that was interfering with his instincts. George had presumed McDonough was dead, but when he opened his mind, other possibilities flooded in. He couldn't get his mind off of him because his fate wasn't sealed. He wracked his brain for some sense of the man. The rest of the room fell silent, and George realized all eyes were on him.

"George. Are you OK, George?" Joan's voice was a little distant. He felt the hair up on the back of his neck.

"Mr. McDonough is alive," George whispered, fearing if he spoke too loud the *Sight* would dissipate and return him back to reality. Joan was about to speak, but he put his hand up to stop her. His mind was racing and his breathing was laboured. His breathing? No, it was Mr. McDonough's breathing. His knees went out from under him and he fell to the floor assuming a crumpled up position. George was aware that he was freaking everyone out, including Joan, but he needed to find the old man. He was still alive in a heap somewhere. George squinted his eyes then slowly closed them until he saw a small patch of light in a dark place. As his eyes re-focused he could make out what appeared to be sumac trees and something rusty in the distance to the right of a dirt path. What was it? It was round... no, it was cylindrical. It was an old rotting oil barrel. He had seen it before: He knew the place! His eyes rolled into the back of his head and his body began to shake.

"Oh God, what's happening to him?" Joan screamed. George heard her in the distance then found a path to his own speech center.

"Drrr...drive me. I've found him. Drive me." He whispered as he slowly tried to stand up but buckled over again in a pain that didn't belong to him. It was the old man's. George hobbled, bent over, to the back door where Joan stopped him.

"Dwayne will get the car, George. You can't be seen on the street. Are you sure you know what you're doing? Are you all right?"

"Yes. He's still breathing. Hurry," he whispered, his eyes half-open. Occasionally, they rolled into the back of his head. He needed to see where he was going but knew he needed to remain with Mr. McDonough. Somehow George's presence in the stream fortified the old man's connection to reality as he drifted in and out of consciousness. When he entered the "now," there was pain; it was not a place where he wanted to linger. There was happiness in his mind but only when he drifted out of the "now" to a place devoid of time. That's what George felt at the house when he stood where the old man had fallen; he must have been unconscious then.

George felt Ann take his hand and lead him to Dwayne's car as he pulled into the alleyway. She had seen George like that before when they were kids. She whispered to Joan that he would be all right and to come along. They got into Dwayne's car. Georgiadis looked at George with a face full of incredulity and cracked to Joan.

"Is this some kind of Kreskin thing?" She ignored him. The look was on both of their faces and George hadn't felt that look on him for years. He hated it. Georgiadis, Jim and Bill ran to their car, and followed.

Ann still held George's arm while Joan stared at him, her security shaken to the roots. She felt like an outsider in her own relationship. George sensed her distress, but had to remain focused to help the old man hold on.

"Where George? Where are we going?" Ann asked softly.

"Tractor path, east of dad's farm." He whispered. He felt searing pain shoot up his side as the sumac tree came into view again – the old man was conscious and suffering.

"We're coming Mr. McDonough." George said firmly. "We're coming." The pain was awful. He buckled over in agony. Dwayne flew over the roads to the farm with Georgiadis on his tail. George's eyes kept rolling while he writhed in Mr. McDonough's reality.

Joan continued to look at him in horror as they turned on to the old tractor path and drove about one hundred yards just over the crest of the hill. There it was - the rusty barrel, the sumac trees and the rotting remains of a '59 Chevy with a tail-light out. The missing tail-light – that was the place where the daylight entered Mr. McDonough's dark prison. There was a heavy rock on the trunk holding it shut. When Dwayne could go no farther, he stopped the car and Ann helped George out.

"Where is he, George?"

"The trunk. He's in the trunk." Dwayne ran over followed by Georgiadis and Joan. He hauled the rock off and the rotting trunk lid popped open. There, in a fetal position, was old Mr. McDonough. Dwayne reached in and pulled him out to a long wheeze and cough. He didn't look good.

Georgiadis intervened. "We better move quick. No time to call an ambulance. Keep him in that position! I think it might be inhibiting the bleeding. How far is the closest hospital?"

"Five minutes!" Ann replied.

"Let's move it. He's lost a load of blood by the looks of things."

Dwayne laid him gently in the back seat, then backed out onto the road. Georgiadis followed. He phoned ahead to the hospital, and emergency staff was waiting when they pulled up to the doors.

The old man was rushed away on a gurney as George climbed out of the car, slowly getting a grip on his own consciousness and looking for Joan. He turned and smiled, finding her standing right behind him with a very tentative look that said the *Sight* was finally too weird for her; in fact George was too weird for her. In George's mind she had the face of someone looking at a circus freak. He couldn't take it, not from Joan. His smile crashed and so did he. The *Sight* had come back full force and it appeared to be too much for the woman he loved. He had something else to do, so he just got on with it.

Billy was lying on his bed looking out of the window full of self-pity when George entered the hospital room.

"Back to lecture the man who can't even kill himself properly!" he slurred with fatigue.

"No, Billy. I found your dad. He's alive."

Billy looked at George in disbelief then began to cry. "I can't let him see me like this." He turned his face into his pillow and screamed a muffled scream then turned back to George with a pleading look of exasperation. "He can't know I tried to kill myself."

"He doesn't have to know a thing Billy. But..."

"But what?"

"He's not out of trouble yet. He's up in surgery for some repairs to a pretty nasty gunshot wound."

Billy swung his legs around and stood up. He could hardly stand but he had a determined face George had seen a dozen times before – there would be no stopping him. He headed for the washroom and teetered. George jerked to the rescue in a nick of time to stop him from falling.

"I'll do it myself." He swiped at the air. George let him go and he dropped to the floor but stood up again and wobbled toward the shower. A nurse entered the room and was about to rush to his side when George stopped her and shook his head as a warning to her.

"We'll be fine. He's just a little funky right now and needs to do this himself." The nurse refused to leave. They both watched him stumble to the bathroom, big bare hairy ass sticking out of his hospital gown. With the help of the rails he braced himself, removed the gown and turned on the shower.

"Call me if he tries to hurt himself." The nurse said, turning and heading back to her duties. George walked over to the bathroom to keep an eye on him. Billy hung his head in the shower stream to camouflage his tears. They weren't tears of self-pity anymore as much as they were tears for the painful road ahead of him. He, who didn't want to live, had to live to take care of a father who didn't want to live. Could anything be more screwed up? In his mind he had already come to terms with his father's death. Now he had to come to terms with his father's life again. Life could be such a stubborn old mule; there for those who didn't want it and so often taken away from those who craved every last second of it.

As the water poured over him he slowly revived and began to wash himself. George looked around for a towel and, when Billy finally shut the water off, handed it to him. Billy dried himself off and found his clothes in the closet.

George knew better than to interfere. He offered no help or words, knowing the first words between them now had to be Billy's. Finally, there was a look of acknowledgment and the first uncomfortable words sliced into the silence.

"Where did ya find 'im?"

"The tractor path by dad's place. He was in the trunk of the old Chevy."

"Cripes. What about the guy he got a piece of?"

"No idea."

"What made you think to look in the old Chevy?" He asked preoccupied with the challenge of his shirt buttons.

"Well, you know, the Moss thing."

"I thought the Moss thing told you he was happy, not lying in pain in some God forsaken stinkin' trunk."

"He was happy when he was unconscious. I don't know where he went but I sense it involved thoughts of your mom."

"Old bugger's wanted to join her ever since she died. What a rip-off! What a great big stinkin rip-off for the both of us! Why couldn't we both just die and be done with it? I don't mean to sound ungrateful but why did ya have to go and save 'im?"

"He was in pain, Billy, horrible pain when he was conscious. I didn't know if finding him was right, or wrong, I just knew what I had to do. He was in pain and I feared he would suffer for some time if we didn't get to him."

"Ya sound just like yer friggin' old man."

"Thanks." The words were out before George knew what he was saying. Billy looked at him like he was mad.

"What's up with you? You hated your father."

"I know this sounds a little pat and analytical but I think I've been hating myself all these years, Billy."

"What the hell for? You're a successful university type, livin' with a young hottie. What the hell have you got to hate? If ya want to see someone with a good reason ta hate himself, yer lookin' at 'im. I've done nothin' with my life other than cause my ol' man shame."

George went over to Billy and put his arm around him.

"I don't need yer pity George." He growled trying to pull away.

"Shut up and let me be here for my oldest friend for Christ's sake. I'm not feeling pity and I'm not trying to get into your pants you grumpy old bugger. You're just like your old man, too, you know."

"Yeah, huh." They both looked at each other and began to laugh. It was one of those moments where all was said without words. Their arms were loose around each other as they stood forehead to forehead. Words probably would only have led to other words, which would have led to posturing, which would have led to further alienation and like many times before, once the words began of course there would be no stopping them. The two of them just didn't have the energy to do that dance of verbal pride, and certainly neither one had the energy to lead.

There was contentment and humour in knowing that they both had a part of their fathers in them. It was a connection they held on to with all of their might.

Out of the corner of George's eye he saw Joan and Ann approach the door then turn around. Maybe the sight of two old friends holding each other up looked a little too pathetic to deal with. Maybe they knew it was an embrace for all that was lost and all that could never be said. There they were, two father's sons – the stubborn mule and the freak.

28

Discovery

Joseph was at his usual post in the glassed in computer and security room at Fairchild Environmental when Benito Peroni entered. Joseph stood up instantly; virtually clicking his heals to attention.

"Joseph, I meant to tell you yesterday that my home computer was acting kind of strange the other night."

"What was it doing, sir?"

"The screen was flickering and it was taking far too much time to answer commands."

"I noticed on the log file that you were working most of the night, sir. Was it like that intermittently or for your entire duration on-line?"

"Most of the night? What the hell do you mean? I couldn't have been on for any more than an hour."

"Sir, according to the log..." Joseph sat down and hit a command key. The screen lit up immediately and he typed in Benito's home terminal log. "Let's see... you were on line from 9:37 p.m. until 11:00 p.m. and then again from 11:15 p.m. until 12:22 a.m. accessing the mainframe, then minutes later at 12:29 a.m. until 6:11 a.m."

"I was *not* on-line until six in the morning Joseph. Could I have forgotten to shut my terminal down properly when I signed off at..." He looked at the screen... "12:22 a.m.?"

"Well, that's possible except you signed on again at 12:29 by re-entering your codes and entering the mainframe. Once in the mainframe, you entered your personal codes and accessed what I believe are your private files, sir?"

"I was not into my private files at that hour, Joseph. How could this be? Who the hell could have gotten in?"

"Did you have any guests at the house with access to your pin numbers?"

"Don't be stupid! I'm the only person with access to my private files! Where's Douglas? Get me Douglas on the line!"

Joseph dialled Douglas's cell number and passed the phone to Peroni. Douglas was sitting at a table by himself at the Deluxe Restaurant picking at his salad, isolating soggy croutons. "Yes."

Peroni sounded irate. "Someone's been into our mainframe and accessed my personal files, Douglas. Where are you?"

"I'm finishing up business and remaining here to ensure smooth sailing tomorrow."

"Finishing up? Nothing's finished yet?"

"We've had a few set backs, sir, but nothing I can't deal with."

"I'm beginning to lose faith in your self-confidence Mr. Douglas. Someone hacked into our mainframe. Any ideas?"

"Schumann. Andrew Schumann."

"I thought you took care of him."

"We did. He and his female companion are hospitalized. I was sure they'd be sidelined long enough for us to deal with matters here first."

"Like I said, your confidence is killing me. So how did Schumann get my pin numbers and access the mainframe from my own damn computer?"

"He must be on the loose again. He had placed a small tapping device on your line but we removed it, sir."

"Removed it my ass, you incompetent piece of shit! We need some personal property retrieved and apologies from Schumann immediately, and they better be meaningful apologies. If he has what I think he has, Mr. Douglas, your ass is grass." Benito slammed the phone down and stormed out of the room. Douglas threw ten bucks on the table, went out to his car and banged a number angrily into his phone pad.

"Joseph here."

"How the hell did they gain access to the mainframe Joseph?"

"It was from Mr. Peroni's home line – they used his own codes."

"They couldn't have gotten into his house without at least an appearance on the surveillance tapes and a perimeter alarm!"

"Perhaps not, sir. I will look into it right away."

"And send someone out immediately to check that damn pole out front again, Joseph. And if you can't find anything have all the phone lines changed anyway."

"Yes sir."

Douglas hung up and started the car. His mind was racing ahead in so many directions. He began itemizing his tasks so he could assess how to best facilitate them all. He needed to take care of Schumann and his female acquaintance after acquiring all of their illegally obtained data. Then he needed to get back to Lincoln to finish the Moss matter and oversee the hearing. Stanley, who was wrapped tightly in the Moss's rug in the trunk of the car, would keep for a couple of days before he started to stink. The only way Douglas could accomplish everything was by renting a private plane. He had located a small agricultural airport a half an hour away days before but then decided driving to Lincoln would be less conspicuous. Now that time was compressing with the hearing advanced, a little conspicuousness was necessary.

After acquiring directions to the field he managed to speak to a local gentleman who was working on his pilot's license and in need of flying hours. Douglas was a qualified pilot and this was his only way out of Lincoln in a hurry. He arrived at the small landing strip in the middle of a farmer's field ten minutes later. There were a couple of Cessna two-seaters and an old DeHaviland Beaver parked next to a small corrugated aluminum hangar. As Douglas pulled up, an eager looking gentleman in a new brown leather bomber jacket approached.

"Mr. Douglas?"

"Yes. Would you be Malcolm Howard?"

"One and the same. I've been thinking if we leave now it will take us two to three hours and change to touchdown. When were you thinking of flying back?"

"Tonight, all going well, Mr. Howard."

"I'm not rated for night instrument flying, that's the problem."

"I am, Mr. Howard. There is no problem. I will pay your full fee nonetheless."

"Fantastic. You said: "all going well," does that mean we might need a layover?"

"Possibly. In that event I will take care of your accommodations with a generous per diem and we will return at first light."

An uncontrollable smile crept across Howard's face. He was a retired banker living a dream. He and his wife had moved from New York City and settled in a piece of rural quiet. The plane was a new toy that his wife refused to play in. Like an excited schoolboy he revelled in the idea of an overnight trip with anyone, to say nothing of an actual fellow flying enthusiast. He showed Douglas where to park his car and in minutes they were airborne, soaring over life incubating in the quilt of agricultural squares below. If Douglas hadn't been in such a hurry to get airborne, he might have wandered into the old hangar and seen a small Challenger executive jet, just like the ones used by the FBI.

Lulled by the friendly hum of the engine, Douglas felt a moment of respite from life and actually began contemplating retirement himself, after observing the infectious joy in the eyes of the older man next to him. He quickly pulled back from those thoughts, unable to afford such luxury. He needed to focus on the intricacies of what lay ahead.

"What line of business are you in, Mr. Douglas?" Howard yelled.

"The P.R. business, Mr. Howard."

"What brings you to this neck of the woods?"

"Oh, I can't divulge that yet Mr. Howard, corporate secrets being what they are."

"Understand, understand." Howard let it go primarily because he was more interested in nattering about his plane anyway. By the time they reached their destination, Douglas had heard everything from the price of a replacement oil pump to the best place in the state to have aircraft interiors refurbished.

Joseph was waiting in a dark Fairchild sedan at the Durham airfield when Malcolm Howard pulled up to the small aircraft-hanger. Joseph had done his homework in more ways than one. He had ascertained there were some nicely appointed crew layover quarters in the small hanger where Mr. Howard could rest until take-off. This courtesy was already paid for, as was the refuelling of the aircraft. Howard was happy as hell to discover a mechanic working on an old Second World War Harvard trainer for the local aeronautical society and museum. The mechanic looked like Yosemite Sam with steam coming out his ears as he glared at Douglas for leaving him with such a gabby airplane nut. Douglas contained a smile as he followed Joseph to the car.

"What have you got Joseph?"

"There was a line reader we missed. It was cleverly placed behind the box and looked like standard-issue AT&T gear."

"And?"

"I'm not sure how they got close enough without being spotted. The reader had a transmitter with about a seventy-five foot radius and we're good on the porch "fish-eye" to about ninety feet."

"I need answers, Joseph. Did you bring the brief case from my desk as I asked?"

"Yes sir, in the back seat."

"Thank you, Joseph. Take me to Memorial Hospital; I have an appointment that shouldn't take long."

They drove in silence to the hospital while Joseph contemplated the technical mystery of why he didn't see anything suspicious with such a lame seventy-five-foot transmitter. Douglas was deep in thought planning a cold and quick action. He instructed Joseph to wait for him in the short-term parking lot.

As soon as Douglas was in the building he went directly to the main floor washroom and into an open stall where he dialled in the combination to his briefcase. Underneath some papers was a pair of latex gloves and a conspicuously outdated Time magazine that covered a leather flap. He undid the retainer strap revealing a form-fitting compartment that held a small Smith and Wesson, a silencer and nylon shoulder holster. He removed his jacket strapped on the holster, screwed in the silencer, and holstered the gun. In the top of the case a clean syringe and a small bottle of a clear fluid were held in place by Velcro straps. He removed a plastic sheathe from the needle punctured the rubber seal of the bottle and drew an inch of the fluid into the syringe. Carefully placing the bottle back into his case, he placed the needle back into the plastic sheathe, pocketed it and moved out. Just outside the washroom he located a pay phone and dialled the hospital switchboard. He simply said he was a florist delivering some flowers and was readily given the room number.

When the elevators opened on Andy's floor, Douglas moved with authority. He brushed right by the man standing outside Andy's room and entered. But there was nobody home.

"Excuse me sir, can I help you?" The man in the doorway looked curiously at Douglas who turned from the empty bed. Without missing a beat Douglas probed for information.

"Yes, I am with State Farm Insurance. I'm looking for Mr. Andrew Schumann to discuss his insurance claim. My God, he's all right, I hope! I was just talking to him this morning."

"Yes, sir, he's fine. He's up in ICU."

"With Ms. Martha Lewis I presume. How is she doing?"

"I understand she's coming along well."

"Oh, thank goodness. I have another patient to see while I'm here, if you can believe that, so I'll drop back."

"Do you have a card or something Mister…?"

"Thompson. Don Thompson, and actually I'm waiting for my new cards to come in. I just moved over from Prudential two weeks ago and the damn things aren't here yet. Can you believe that? I hope they're not thinking of me as temporary help. I'll stop back in an hour or so." Douglas was smooth, and gone before the volunteer could ask any more questions. He headed right to the elevator and a lab technician with a blood sample trolley, who provided directions to ICU.

In the ICU, Andy gave Martha a peck on her forehead, contemplating a few hours of sleep. He had been with the love of his life most of the night and had only grabbed a couple of hours in the morning. Being a novice in the field of love, its newness occupied him completely. Martha longed to respond without inhibition but was so beat up and incapacitated it was an exercise in frustration. The nurses in ICU were all quite abuzz with the love story. Andy and Martha were thrilled to be the focus of romantic thought, feeling like characters in a romance novel. Neither of them had envisioned such territory possible and certainly not playing the leading roles.

Douglas found a supply cupboard in the O.R. prep rooms one floor below, and emerged on the ICU floor via the stairwell. Andy only saw what appeared to be a physician in a white jacket walking down the hall as he entered the elevator and thought nothing of the unusual fact that he was carrying a briefcase. For his part, Douglas was focused on the ICU sign over the entrance beyond the elevators and thought nothing of the rather non-descript patient entering the elevator. His timing was additionally fortuitous given that the volunteer posted outside ICU stepped into the washroom two doors down as soon as Andy was out of sight. Douglas walked in and saw the nurses busy dealing with another patient and scoped the room for a chart attached to the foot of the bed with Martha's name on it – and Bingo.

Martha was drifting off when she sensed someone beside her. She opened her eyes and saw a new doctor in a surgical mask, inspecting the equipment around her. *That's odd; the nurses usually take care of the gear while the MDs just strut in, look at charts, bark orders and strut out.* She again started to drift off when she suddenly felt severe pain in her jaw and opened her eyes. Douglas had pulled the curtains around her bed and had a firm hold of the broken mandible. His eyes were cold and black in the subdued lighting of the ICU.

"My condolences Ms. Lewis on your recent accident. You might not make it, I'm afraid. Where's the information you stole from the Fairchild mainframe?" He twisted her face firmly causing her to writhe in excruciating pain. She frantically spurted out an answer.

"I ... don't know ... what you're ... talking about, we have nothing."

He twisted her face some more. "Where is Mr. Schumann?"

"I, I don't know, please let..." He twisted harder and Martha started to black out.

Downstairs, Andy strolled toward his room as the volunteer from the hospice approached. "You just missed your insurance agent."

Andy stopped in his tracks. "My insurance agent?"

"Well, you were in a car accident weren't you?"

"It was Martha's car and we haven't called anyone – oh no, Martha!" Andy took off and yelled over his shoulder. "Call security and tell them to get up to I.C.U. immediately!" Andy ran as fast as he could to the elevators and pressed the button, just as the doors closed. He ran to the stairwell, taking the stairs two at a time up three flights to the I.C.U. floor, then raced down the hall past the nursing station picking up the curious duty nurse in his wake. As Andy entered the I.C.U., he saw the curtains pulled around Martha's bed and rushed over just in time to see a man standing over Martha, preparing to inject a hypodermic needle into her IV line. "Stop!"

Douglas spun around and faced him. "Mr. Schumann, I presume. I am sorry I didn't recognize you with your new hairstyle. We were just talking about you. It seems you obtained some information the other night that belongs to Fairchild. Perhaps you might tell me where it is, or should I continue with Ms. Lewis's treatment?" He grabbed her face again just as she began coming around causing her to wriggle in pain. Her eyes, inflamed with horrified agony, found Andy.

"Excuse me doctor, may I help you?" the duty nurse inquired.

"Thank you no, nurse. Mr. Schumann?"

Andy was trembling with fear. "Leave her alone, we have nothing and haven't done a thing since you ran us off the road. I swear!"

Douglas looked coldly into his eyes and sensed a truth that no longer mattered. The immediate problem was only slightly complicated with the addition of the nurse but not unsolvable. He did after all have six bullets. He reached for the syringe plunger while his other hand fumbled with the shoulder holster.

"No!" Andy screamed. He dove through the air at Douglas sending them both to the floor as Douglas emptied the contents of the syringe into the IV line. Douglas took one quick swipe at Andy, knocking him out and aimed his gun at the nurse who was suddenly pushed out of the way by a rather bulky security guard. The guard took the silenced bullet in the forehead and fell to the floor. The nurse pressed the code blue button at the bed side before she felt a shattering pain in her chest.

As Douglas stood up, he heard people rushing towards him. He quickly assessed that he would have no time to interrogate Andy further as to who was using the line reader, so he dispassionately decided to clean up what he could. He fired two rounds into Andy who lay sprawled on the floor. He threw the syringe into a wastebasket and crouched down to place his gun in the security guard's hand seconds before two nurses and an intern pulled the curtains back and rushed in.

"Hurry, the security guard went crazy and killed the nurse and that poor young man on the floor!" Douglas advised as he stood up.

The intern and one nurse ran to the wounded nurse from the station desk, who was gagging on her own blood. The other nurse ran to Andy, then it dawned on her, the doctor who was apparently on duty wasn't tending to anyone. When she turned to ask for his help he was gone. Two more doctors showed up and quickly started to sort out priorities.

Andy who was bleeding profusely came to his senses, and began to scream: "There's something in the IV! He put something in Martha's IV!" The room spun in Andy's eyes and faded to black.

Douglas, briefcase in hand, was in the stairwell, removing his facemask, latex gloves and white jacket. He threw them off as he continued on down the stairs and back outside, disappearing into a sea of people coming and going at the main entrance to the hospital. A few strides later he was back in the car with Joseph heading to Fairchild.

"I think I know why we have no surveillance tape of the people who used the line reader," Joseph said with a slow realization.

"And your theory is?" Douglas was a little out of breath and unhappy with the forced termination of his own leads.

"We know for sure the one who put it there was that Andrew Schumann guy right? I mean, we have him on tape and no one else could have made it up the pole without making an appearance on our monitors right?"

"Yes, I think that is a relatively safe assumption. And to the question of how a reader with a fifty-foot radius could be used and evade our cameras?"

"If they weren't in our security radius they would have needed a step-up transformer and transmitter with a greater distance to a nearby receiver out of camera range."

"Fine, but how could you place a step-up transmitter without us seeing it being placed?"

"We probably saw it being placed or have it being placed on tape but didn't know what was going on. I will look at all the surveillance footage back at the office. I would imagine it was put in position the night they broke into the mainframe for fear of being discovered in daylight."

After the drive to Richmond they pulled into the underground parking lot at Fairchild. Douglas went immediately up to Benito's office and Joseph got busy screening video footage.

"Well?" Benito roared as Douglas entered.

"Well, we know it wasn't the two in the hospital."

"I don't care who it *wasn't*, Douglas!" Douglas had never seen Peroni so nervous. Douglas assessed it was well founded given the fact that the dimensions of this thing were now, obviously, a far more organized effort than they had originally thought. Peroni closed the door to his office quietly.

"So where are we? What the hell do we know?"

"Joseph may know how they broke into the mainframe using your access codes, and will have that answer for us shortly, if his theory pans out. I'm beginning to believe we may have something large after us, like the FBI."

"Those dumb fucks have been after us for years. They don't have the brainpower for this."

"Maybe they've contracted out to hackers."

"Can we confirm any FBI involvement from the guy who placed that bug on my line?"

"I'm afraid not. I was forced to accept an apology from both him and his girlfriend. Might I ask what information they could get from our mainframe that is potentially damning? It would help me to know what I'm trying to recover."

"Everything from my own personal financial records to our staff and paid acquaintances."

"So you could fall pretty hard on this one with the IRS and the feds for illegal campaign contributions and such?"

"I won't be the only one who falls, Douglas. I kept a list of your apology clients in my personal folder and the bonuses that were paid to your Zurich account."

Douglas felt as though he had the wind knocked out of him. "You what? You stupid, stupid man!" Douglas muttered losing his composure.

"Watch your mouth, Douglas! I might have been big enough to take that kind of disrespect from someone with a perfect record but you have been such a major fuck-up lately. Insurance policies, Mr. Douglas, are necessary whenever business deals go sour," Peroni added smugly.

Douglas found his own cold sense of calm dignity again. "I'm not impressed, Mr. Peroni. The insurance business as we know is based on a level of paranoia and fear of mishap. I somehow credited you with more intelligence than keeping some evidentiary trail of the human obstacles we have removed."

"We?"

"Oh yes, in the eyes of the law. You were so anxious to have something to hold over me, your personal files make you as guilty as if you had pulled the trigger yourself. The people were in *your* way, not mine! That buck, I am afraid, stops at your desk. I think the terms of incarceration for conspiracy to commit and being an accessory on all charges would be equal or greater to anything inflicted on those who simply carried out your wishes. Surely, you are not so stupid as to think this information hurts anyone but yourself? Oh dear, perhaps you are."

"Always so calm and cool aren't you, Douglas?"

"I would recommend you try to remain so as well sir. The game isn't over yet. I would further suggest we be supportive of one another in such times as these, rather than spiralling into hysteria." Douglas's voice was pretentiously calm and meant to irritate. He must have done a wonderful job because the look on Benito's face was one of blood-red fury. He was ready to vent the longest stream of expletives when his phone rang. He grabbed it and roared into the receiver.

"What is it?" He listened a moment then looked up at Douglas, slammed the receiver down and headed toward his door.

"That was Joseph. He's on to something. At least someone is earning their fucking keep around here!" Peroni breezed by Douglas and headed down the hall to the computer room, Douglas in tow.

"What have you got Joseph?" Benito boomed.

"An early 'Seventies Mercedes. Given the black smoke coming out of the exhaust I would say it's a diesel. I have run references on the model and even though there is no model lettering left on the rear of the car, given the style of bumpers, and the assumption of a diesel engine, I ran a quick search and believe it is probably a 1968 to 1970 220D. I have half of a license plate number, and with some cross referencing I should be able to get an ID." Joseph ran the surveillance video again.

"It's just a car driving by – I don't see anything suspicious." Benito huffed.

"Neither did I, at first. What caught my attention initially was that it slowed down a little while it passed your house Mr. Peroni, then it accelerated. I initially thought it was just changing gears but then I considered the idea that it could have been slowing down to drop something off. When I was attempting to tidy up the image to get a better look at the plate number, I saw it."

"Saw what?" Douglas inquired. Joseph froze the video frame and pointed to the lower quadrant on screen.

"It's a shiny object that is being dragged behind the car on a fine grade string, probably fishing line, then it is let go more or less in front of the house. You can see it clearly when it passes under the street light." He advanced the video a few frames at a time and sure enough the shiny object moved under the light at the same rate as the Mercedes. "Note how the shiny object stops moving and rolls off camera, presumably towards the gutter, when the Mercedes speeds off."

"Nice work Joseph. How long until we get some possibilities on the license plate?" Douglas said with his usual cool.

"Momentarily," Joseph replied with eyes glued to the screen. He continued attempting to enhance the picture of the rear end of the Mercedes in an attempt at unveiling more numbers from the plate.

Benito turned to Douglas, eyes burning. "Make this problem go away with a little more attention to detail than you've been showing us lately, or we're all as good as dead!" He stormed off leaving Douglas in an uncomfortable silence. The discomfort was Douglas's alone, Joseph was too busy: He would soon have the license plate number, I.D., and address – he could taste it.

29
Strategy

Georgiadis and his men had been out to the farm. A specialist from the ident-squad had lifted perfect thumb and index fingerprints from Mr. Moss's bedpost and was running an ID search via modem. They found additional prints on the desk and on the cane rack near the front door. Blood samples were lifted from the cracks in the floorboards in the hall and living room. Buckshot was removed from the entrance wall and a bullet was discovered in the plaster at the end of the hall.

Georgiadis received a call from one of his agents, who had stayed back at the hospital, and was informed Mr. McDonough was out of surgery and had already started regaining consciousness. The bullet they found in the wall had blood on it and Georgiadis correctly assumed it had passed through the old man's chest, barely missing his heart. The internal bleeding had put additional pressure on the battered old saddlebags McDonough used for lungs. He was in serious but stable condition and, like his son, a little pissed-off to have re-materialized in the physical universe.

George was the last to leave Billy, who was holding his father's receptive hand and stroking the old man's head. It was almost like they were saying the goodbye to each other they hadn't the luxury of saying. Being able to say goodbye made George jealous of Billy and happy for him at the same time. George would've loved that luxury of luxuries, to have held the arthritic time-weathered hands, and to have heard his father say: "Goodbye son, see you later." That simple act now was at the top of his list of the most valuable things one could ever hope for in this material world. Not some ultimate island paradise described ever so poetically by Robin Leach for television's *Lifestyles of the Rich and Famous*, but a simple little handshake or good-bye kiss at checkout time.

Joan and George stopped in on Millie while they were at the hospital and listened to her reminisce for a few minutes. She seemed a little better and some colour had returned to her face. Joan was unusually quiet with her though and even more so with George on the ride back to Ann's shop. George attempted to hold her hand, but gave up when he sensed her distance and discomfort in the touching of her.

He knew she was afraid of the full-blown *Sight* and busy re-evaluating everything. George's link with Mr. McDonough had taken him too far away from her reality – to somewhere she couldn't go. The expression on her face when his mind went to Mr. McDonough was awful. It held all that he had tried to escape when he had left town so many years before. The physical seizure must have looked pretty grotesque especially in the context of his other role as the key romantic figure in her life. Prince Charming had lost a little ground, with eyes rolling around and a little drool thrown in for good measure.

George found Joan's reaction reminiscent of the look on the faces of his Grade 4 classmates, two days after his ninth birthday. His mother was in County General where he would stop everyday after school. Early that afternoon, she had slipped into a coma catching everyone, his father included, by surprise. It was the first time George had ever connected to someone with his *Sight*. As his thoughts drifted to his mother, it came out of nowhere and slugged him hard. He fell to the floor next to his desk crawling into his mother's thoughts and trembling empathetically on his back, assuming her body position. At first a few kids laughed, and the teacher, Mrs. Hobgood, told him to get back into his seat. But when she saw his eyes rolling into the back of his head, she panicked and ran for help. George was on the floor; a canopy of classmates' faces hanging overhead as he lay immersed in the throes of his mother's death. They stared, horrified at the grotesque freak shaking on the floor, drifting in and out of consciousness and drooling. George felt something snap and knew his mother's connection to her body had severed.

"No! No! No! Mom! Come back Mom!" he had cried. Snickering classmates hissed down a long tunnel to him where he lay paralyzed in the enormity of what was happening. She was dead. Even though he briefly felt incoming joy as she experienced an overpowering sensation of love and wonder, she was nonetheless physically gone from him – from *his* life. He cried hysterically, gazing back up the tunnel into the classroom, unable to respond to the jeers and comedic imitations of him calling for his mom. He attempted to ask them to quit staring, but his voice was so full of grief it only made some of them stare harder while others laughed and imitated him again in baby voices.

George lay there trying to will his mother to return, insane with feelings of embarrassment and desertion. On the walls around him hung the now-hideous self-portraits they had all done in art class the day before. There, looking back at him was his own picture and he believed he saw what looked so frightening to those he used to think were his friends. He decided at that moment that they could no longer be his friends. Who would want to be seen with a weirdo, let alone be friends with one? Youth was mostly about conforming. He had lost some irretrievable ground and would be forever branded a leper in their eyes. Mrs. Hobgood showed up with Mr. Pritchard, the principal, who picked the limp, catatonic freak off the floor and carried him down to the nurse's office.

George had stopped crying and was just staring at the wall when his father arrived, face white and gaunt... his eyes vacant. They couldn't speak through the pain and when George finally found his father's pain, it swamped him like a tidal wave. Mr. Moss had been at the hospital and was caught off guard by the massive embolic stroke that took his lover, his wife, his best friend, and... young George's mother. The *Sight* had failed him when he most needed it. A random act of nature had declared its supremacy. George now knew it was his father's incredibly deep love and concern for his wife that drew George like a moth to a flame in those last few seconds of her life. It was a love George had admitted to feeling himself, all too late.

Looking at Joan in the seat next to him made him feel helpless. He knew less about her now than he did a couple of days ago. He was certainly less sure. Loving, like knowing, George understood was a non-static term, a work in progress, a never-ending process altered by the constant influx of new information. Maybe a successful life is one engaged in the slow realization of how much isn't known and how great the distance is to pure love. George felt like he was clawing his way to ignorance.

All would have to unfold as it would. He sought patience and a position of love, not fear. He could not fear losing Joan. He must love her enough to let her go if she sought happiness elsewhere.

Georgiadis arrived at County Hospital with Jim's video and a small liquid quartz screen to see if Mr. McDonough recognized the man standing over Randy's body. When the screen lit up, the old man's face slowly turned to anger. "That's the son of a bitch who shot me!" he whispered through the hissing of the oxygen tubes in his nose.

"Did you see him actually shoot you, Mr. McDonough?"

The old man pondered the question that he so desperately wanted to answer in the affirmative, but he was such an honest man he couldn't go there. "No. I guess not." Mr. McDonough started gasping for air briefly, and then closed his eyes in a concentrated attempt to calm down.

After a minute or two he continued in halting puffs. "It was too dark. He was... the one I saw... before I passed out. Maybe the one... I saw layin'... on the floor... with his head blown off... was the one... who shot me?"

"Could be. Sir, I wonder if you could say what you just said to me once more for the record and on camera. I would also like your permission to use this statement in a court of law."

"Be glad ta," the old man wheezed. Billy looked a little worried and Georgiadis gave him a sympathetic look.

"As soon as I have the statement. I'm outta here."

"Thanks. I don't know how much of this he can take."

"I understand."

The testimony was repeated and documented. Georgiadis finally had some hard evidence. If the prints were the same as the ones on the bed he was beginning to see the making of a case, though it remained an elusively circumstantial one for the moment. He would need to find the vehicle used to transport Mr. McDonough and also the whereabouts of the man McDonough claimed to have seen with his head blown off.

Just as Georgiadis was leaving, Sheriff Williams walked in. "Would somebody mind tellin' me what is goin' on around here? I understand there has been a shooting and nobody notified me. I had to find out from a County General admitting nurse by accident. I'd like to know when I was voted outta office!" He looked at Mr. McDonough and went to his side. "How ya feeling, old timer?"

"Been... better Ted."

"What the hell happened?"

"Let Billy tell ya, I'm havin' a little trouble breathin'."

Billy rattled off the facts: "He was shot in George's hallway and stuffed in the trunk of the old Chevy out by the tractor path, Ted."

Sheriff Williams took his hat off and shook his head in disgust. "What the hell is the world comin' to?" he said with an element of sad resignation. He looked around the room at Georgiadis and the gear his assistant was packing up.

"And you would be federal, no doubt? Busy workin' on somethin' that would be way over the head of a small town law enforcement officer like myself are ya?"

"I am engaged in a federal case, sir."

"And this man, this old friend o'mine here who got shot and stuffed in a trunk ta die. None of my business, is it? He's your big Jesus federal case is he?"

"He's a crucial piece of a puzzle," Georgiadis replied.

"I wonder how many others you'd like to have shot up just to make sure ya got enough pieces of your big federal puzzle before you can recognize the picture on the damn box? Sorry, I didn't get your name?"

"Georgiadis, FBI... Sheriff Williams is it?"

"Oh, I'm flattered you know my name. Do you know where my office is?"

"Yes sir I do. I guess it's time we had a meeting," Georgiadis said respectfully.

"That would be nice." The Sheriff went to Mr. McDonough and patted him on the shoulder. "Get well my friend." His tone was warm. The old man started drifting and the Sheriff took his cue to leave.

Billy looked at him as he passed. "Thanks for lookin' in on us, Ted," he said gratefully.

"Sure, Billy. Call me next time somebody shoots a family member and stuffs 'em in a trunk, will ya?" He slapped Billy lightly on the back and signalled Georgiadis with a snap of his fingers to follow. Georgiadis nodded a thank you at Billy, and retreated.

The room once more returned to a soundscape of hissing oxygen and the laboured breathing of the old man. Billy resumed his post in the chair next to his father's bed, sensing the great divide that only one of them would soon cross, and reached again for his father's hand.

Georgiadis was better than the Sheriff expected him to be. He caught up to Williams in the hall and suggested that they head to Ann's shop. Williams was shocked and actually embarrassed that even more of the people under his charge were involved in something of which he was largely ignorant. But proud as he was, he had a grasp that the whole mess was big, too big for his limited resources that consisted of a few friends with the state police and one deputy, home with the flu.

Back at Ann's shop, Sheriff Ted Williams began to absorb the magnitude of what was being prepared for the hearing. He read page after page of documentation, occasionally huffing in disbelief. He knew there were really no jurisdictional lines, where such an affront to humanity was involved. He soon lost his initial feelings of offence at Georgiadis. These Fairchild people were cold-blooded murderers. On a larger scale, their track record indicated they were poised to cause so much environmental damage that generations to come could be affected. In some ways waste was becoming a blueprint for genocide. The "Me" generation pretty well summed it all up, he thought.

The loose ends of unsolved events that looked like crimes but couldn't be called such for lack of evidence were staggering. Williams knew that Georgiadis was looking for the thread that would unravel the whole thing. It was beginning to look like the deaths of a couple of farmers, simple folk in the middle of nowhere, might be the undoing of Fairchild. Like laundering money, Georgiadis was looking for ways to have inadmissible evidence made admissible. In the best-case scenario, he might nail Peroni. In the second best case scenario, the press might help taint a jury into reaching the right verdict, if and when it ever came to trial.

The worst-case scenario, of course, would be more people getting killed and Fairchild walking free, minus a token fine for one impropriety or another. But a pre-emptive strike of public allegation might chip at the veneer and cause some impulsive behaviour. Rats run from the scent of fire and some of the smouldering material being assembled was more than allegation.

As night approached, Bill's strategy called for some new players. George sent Ann, against Joan's wishes, for Allan Thornhill who wasn't answering his phone. When she returned with him he was more than a little pissed-off.

"Wanted to gloat a little over my current unemployment status did you Moss?"

"No one's gloating – we may have the biggest story of your career."

"What career?"

"One handed to you on a silver platter," Georgiadis said softly.

"And who might you be?"

"He's a honcho from the FBI," Sheriff Williams said with a little bit of an edge.

"Oh great, the FBI. Moss, you're such an ass. It was the FBI that called my publisher and had me dumped in the first place. Like I'm supposed to be impressed the FBI is here! The lot of you can drop dead!"

Georgiadis had an odd expression on his face as everyone in the room stared at him waiting for a rebuttal.

"The FBI had Allan fired?" George asked, breaking the silence.

"Actually, it was partially my fault," Georgiadis responded gingerly. "I fear the few questions I had for his publisher tipped the scales. The publisher said he was an annoyance with a chip on his shoulder and was glad to have an excuse to fire him. Apparently Talmer, the lawyer for Fairchild, was on his case as well threatening a huge libel suit. My request was simply icing on the cake."

"You son of a..."Allan was furious. He went to slug Georgiadis but Sheriff Williams grabbed his arm. "Settle down now, Allan, or I'll cuff ya," He ordered in a fatherly tone.

Joan looked puzzled. "How did you know he was about to publish a piece on Fairchild?"

"We knew Fairchild was working on a dump site in this area and had some feelers out," Georgiadis answered.

"Feelers?" Joan pushed for a more concise answer.

"That's all I'm at liberty to say."

"You tapped my lines didn't you?" Allan snapped. He sat down so angry his face turned red. "They tapped my freaking lines!"

"Actually, no. We didn't tap your line; we were monitoring the people who did tap your phone and your computer modem." Georgiadis said defensively.

Bill scanned the room with a look of disgust on his face. "Look, I don't care who's annoying, who tapped or monitored whose line, all I know is we need a journalist on this and we need TV coverage as well. If we're going to make any of this shit stick to Fairchild's fur tomorrow, we'll have to throw as much at them as we can and in the most public way. Now Mr. Georgiadis, you say you contributed to this man's dismissal. Perhaps you could have him re-instated? Is there any way we could have his piece circulated to some larger papers as well? Do you have any contacts at the Times or USA Today or the like?"

Georgiadis scratched his brow and shook his head. "No."

Jim jumped in. "Just get him re-instated. If his publisher runs with the piece leave the rest to me. I can have this thing out on the Internet and I'm sure we can get some majors on it. The story could be real big and with national repercussions."

"And what if I don't write it?" Allan asked curtly.

"Allan, Allan, Allan," George admonished impatiently. "I thought it was just me you were mad at. Christ, you're mad at the whole world for your own shortcomings. Don't blow this, now."

Allan looked at George with disdain. But the opportunity was as plain as the nose on his face. He looked around the room and saw the

Sheriff, strangers, the FBI, wall-to-wall fax paper in piles around the room... this had to be big. "You can get me re-instated?"

"Count on it," Georgiadis confirmed, "temporarily, anyway. I don't know how much of a hate-on your publisher has for you."

Allan continued looking around the room assessing the situation and then finally spoke coldly and in a calculating manner.

"I'll do it. But I'll need to ensure it's my story. I'll co-ordinate the TV coverage. I have a friend, Kate Brandon, at Channel 7 Eyewitness News. She'll interview me. It'll be my story. Those are my terms."

The room was silent. Jim couldn't contain himself. "Why you ungrateful little prick. People have been murdered here and you, you pompous... this isn't your story, this story belongs to all of us. People are dead, you asshole! George, I think I could get someone from at least one major to cover this."

George looked at Jim, then at Allan. Allan knew time was of the essence and in his favour. But he didn't like the look on George's face. He also didn't know how vindictive George could be. It was George's call and George wanted to tell Allan to go get stuffed *so* badly.

"You feel confident you could get someone else Jim?"

"Absolutely!" He went to the phone and started dialling.

"Hang on, Jim." George weighed his options. "I think Allan's the man for the job." George faced Allan and put his hand on Allan's shoulder. "If you can get your angry little gay ass out of the closet and focus some of that anger on your work, then maybe you can start dealing with your fears and who you really are, like the rest of us have to do."

The silence was deafening. The look on Allan's face was total horror. Jim's one eyebrow went up as he looked at Allan in a different way and quietly hung up the receiver. The air was thick with anger, frustration and mostly confusion.

Allan was speechless. Joan's guess was on the money. Allan went to the desk and, when he was able to breathe again, he started reading some of the information in a daze.

The game was on. Sheriff Williams looked at Allan, then took his hat off and scratched his head – a few of his own questions had just been answered.

George nodded at Georgiadis who went out to his car to make a private call to the publisher on his cell phone. He knew he had his work cut out for him: How do you get a known asshole a job?

Jim had his laptop out in a flash, plugged in his modem and began going down his list of university alumni with ties to newspaper publishing and the media.

Bill picked up the ball and moseyed over to Allan, introduced himself and began a full-blown history of Fairchild, the payola, the missing persons and the deaths they were responsible for.

Allan's jaw dropped a few times, but Bill backed up his allegations with reams of anecdotal evidence and some of the hard facts on the pages in front of them. They began making copies of the documents Allan needed for his article.

It was just before midnight when they decided to pack it in for some rest. Allan was wired. He got his friend at Eyewitness News on the phone to ensure a camera crew and coverage for "his" piece. Most self-respecting print reporters would never share a story with TV until it had run, but Allan wanted exposure and that need served the cause. In a CNN world that harvested news almost before it happened, publicity could occasionally give a writer with the details a leg up in weekend edition publications and even in the book market.

Allan would work through the night, driven by his anger at George and his hatred of himself. George felt a little like he was taking advantage of a misfit; the man's problems ran so deep.

George's hope was that if Allan had something to be proud of, he might start to turn around. George felt no malice toward him though, only pity, and the odd reflection of self-esteem territory not so unfamiliar.

After co-coordinating tactics with Sheriff Williams, Georgiadis took Joan and George back to the Moss farm. George knew it was safe but not why. Georgiadis stayed in George's old room, gun under pillow for good measure.

Joan remained confused and distant. She would see this Fairchild thing to the end for Jim's sake, but that might be it. Before they fell asleep she only said one thing to George: "What you did for Allan tonight was good." No kiss, no contact. George was surprised at how a double bed could be such a huge place. He knew his age combined with his affliction was adding up, making his prospects a crapshoot at best. There was some critical mass developing in a pool of confusion that even the *Sight* couldn't see though.

30
D-Day

Under the early morning sky, the tarmac glistened like it was covered in cellophane. Shiny tires sliced through gathered pools of fresh fallen rain as a Yellow cab approached the hanger with the "Charter" sign emblazoned on the wall.

Douglas pulled out his wallet, flopped a hundred over the vinyl seat and told the cabby to keep the change. While the driver attempted a thank you, Douglas got out, slammed the door, and gave the sky a pretty serious once-over. The storm had passed over Durham, but visibility was not great. He found Malcolm Howard sound asleep on the cot in the pilot's lounge surrounded by boxes of really foul-looking Chinese food.

"Time to go home, Mr. Howard!" he barked."

Malcolm Howard was a little on the groggy side. He glanced down at his watch and saw it was just before six in the morning. He had finally won over the mechanic he was pestering the night before when it was discovered they had a mutual acquaintance. They got into a bottle of gin from a chute locker and ordered in the Chinese. By the time they called it a night, Malcolm had extracted enough aeronautical tall tales and various engine statistics to keep the Lincoln Flying Club going for weeks. He stood up and stretched. "Is she refuelled?"

"We fuelled her up last night."

"What's the sky doing?"

"Waiting for us, Mr. Howard."

Douglas turned and headed toward the plane. Malcolm followed.

The night had been a busy one for Douglas. Joseph had successfully identified the car as Bill Monroe's and also produced an address. Douglas had been unnerved by what he found in Bill's home. Next to the computer was an open filing cabinet. The section marked Fairchild Environmental contained volumes of material, most of it relatively harmless. That stuff didn't bother Douglas as much as what he thought they had from Benito Peroni's files, which, of course, were nowhere to be found. After a few hours of waiting in the dark he realized Bill probably wasn't coming home in time to make an apology. In the event of hidden files, Douglas decided to take no chances and rigged the gas stove with a small battery timer that emitted a wonderful little spark at the right moment. Joseph had called him with the name of Bill's employer and that would be his last stop for the night.

Breaking into the law office was easy. It was in an old Victorian house with a conveniently private rear parking lot and a limited security system. Douglas estimated he had 20 seconds to disable the alarm from the main panel, which he figured was behind a door that was either a closet or the top of the basement stairs. He had visually followed a conspicuous wire from a motion detector down an interior brick wall and along a baseboard to the closed door. Sloppy security system installations made his job so much easier. As soon as he picked the lock allowing entry, he made a beeline to the closed door and found the main panel immediately. It was an old system that offered no protection from anyone who had read the manual.

The word "security" was such a joke to Douglas; a false sense of safety propagated by exaggerated advertising. If somebody wants in, there really isn't much to it. Even with alarms, pathetic police response times usually gave someone who knew what he was doing a reasonable enough timeframe to take all the furniture, if so desired. Monroe's desk was easy to locate. It was the one with the envelopes bearing his name next to the model gull-wing 300SL Mercedes. His whereabouts presented another problem that Douglas would have to deal with on his return from Lincoln. After searching for a few minutes he was satisfied there was nothing there. Before he left, he installed a precautionary little virus with quite an appetite, in the computer terminal at Bill's desk.

Douglas was in some uncharted professional territory with too many loose ends to deal with. He was up against so many people it was beginning to feel like a conspiracy. Schumann and his little friend had been taken care of and he was hoping optimistically that Monroe would run when he heard the news.

Part of Douglas's professional cool came from his ability to remain focused when alarm bells sounded. The down side of this was that alarm bells were often tuned out to allow for calm and calculated thinking when perhaps the best thing one could do for one's self was to get the hell out of the building. Alarms were silently ringing in his subconscious. They had been pushed there, into the background, replaced with what was beginning to amount to denial. Douglas was primarily worried about Peroni, whom he now believed was unstable. He perused various scenarios for accepting an apology from Peroni on his return, after certain files disappeared, of course...

As the plane gently lifted off into the light drizzle, Douglas's mind floated to thoughts of vanishing into early retirement. The farther from the ground he was, the more freedom he felt from the annoying little ants that complicated his life. Malcolm Howard seemed content with the occasional nod or grunt from Douglas, as he waxed non-stop about planes, planes and planes. Howard knew Douglas wasn't listening but it didn't really matter. He was just reiterating new information as a method of memorizing it anyway. He had been well conditioned by his wife in the skill of dealing with the uninterested...

The day ahead needed George's full attention. He'd been awake for most of that night watching Joan while she slept; sad at the prospect of losing her, afraid to touch her. He had seen it before; people, who love each other deeply, but acquire monumentally drained tolerance levels from the little stuff. The sum of the little stuff had caused many to walk away much to the surprise of their friends and family.

After the hearing, he had no idea what his life would be like. If the hearing went badly he wasn't sure he'd even be alive in six months. Nevertheless, he thought about the futility of running from himself for so long. Allan Thornhill had provided another dot to connect in the lesson of denial for which he was deeply grateful. Learning about self comes from such strange places. The state he had entered in front of Joan, when he found Mr. McDonough's pain, felt in some ways like his own coming out. He realized how much energy he had consumed hiding what he was.

Somehow, there was no justice in it all, he thought. The altruistic goal of a couple having no secrets from one another maybe was just that – altruistic. Maybe there are things in everyone that are best kept secret. Maybe releasing personal demons onto others is about the most uncaring thing one could do. Complete honesty was looking like one of those absolutes that can only exist in dreams, not in an imperfect world unequipped to deal with the same ... particularly where love is involved. Complete honesty was looking like the battleground for the inevitable clash of the intellectual and emotional realms, the dual to the death of the spiritual ideal and the physical reality. Sure, there was less for George to hide, *but Jesus, what a price.*

He rolled out of bed to the sound of a stronger than usual wind. The windmill was awake and complaining. The skies were solid grey again and a few large raindrops began to bang away on the tin roof of the barn. Within seconds, intermittent drips grew into the conservative, steady patter of a long distance runner. It had the feel of an all-day rain. It was the kind of all-day rain that made the hallways at school dark when he was a kid. On those days, the halls smelled of rubber from shiny yellow raincoats and black rubber boots, neatly lined up outside classroom doors waiting for the warmth of small feet. At the end of the day, the cacophony of squeaky soles on the polished stone aggregate floor sounded like a flock of geese, as young scholars, clutching the latest adventures of Dick and Jane in plastic and canvas bags, ran out to waiting buses.

This new day, it was the sound of water drops on tin and the smell of Mr. Clean that filled the air.

George stumbled down the hall over the floorboards where Mr. McDonough had fallen, and put the coffee on. It was 6:30 a.m. The hearing was at 10 a.m. Council hearings were usually in the evening to allow for public attendance. The timing alone indicated obvious schedule manipulation in an attempt to avoid public participation.

They would soon know if things were going to go their way or conversely, whether they would be out-manoeuvred by Commissioner Sam Johnson. He was a crafty chairman, and if George crossed one line, he would be silenced for sure on procedural grounds, end of the round and maybe end of match. That's why Bill Monroe had drilled him so heavily on process. Still they had to kick some doors down before they could take the hearing in the desired direction. They needed visibility, an irrefutable argument and publicity to push this thing over the top and past the local level. They had to use a corrupted process to advantage.

George sat poring over the notes and sipping coffee when Georgiadis wandered in. He pointed at the coffee and George looked up long enough to signal: "Help yourself." Joan followed a few minutes later in one of Mr. Moss's old housecoats. He could see she only had her usual T-shirt on underneath, losing focus briefly in a flash of sensual nostalgia that ended when she tightened the belt.

While George reviewed his notes, the other two sat in silence staring into the murky depths of coffee mugs as though looking for mystical signs of the future in mud. Georgiadis asked if he might have a shower and Joan found him a clean towel. By nine o'clock, they had all had a turn dancing under the old showerhead trying to find enough spray to rinse the soap off.

Georgiadis sensed something wrong between Joan and George, so he feigned morning grogginess and important phone calls as a way of avoiding saying anything uncomfortable to either of them. He read their situation like the intuitive investigator he was. The silence worked out well for George; he was able to concentrate and prepare. His nerves were a little shaky so he kept trying to convince himself it was just another lecture... just another lecture. When it was time to set the plan in motion, he called Patricia Sandfield on his new improved, untapped line courtesy of Georgiadis and his team.

"You all set, Patricia?"

"Yep. I've got a chain reaction ready to go at nine like you asked. Don't you worry about my end of things, my girls are the best."

"Thanks, Patricia I knew we could count on you."

"Give 'em hell, George!"

Joan had begun toasting a couple of bagels when George got off of the phone. They sat down together for an uncomfortable breakfast of diplomacy and avoidance.

"Ms. Sandfield ready?"

"Says her girls are the best..."

"God she's actually proud of being the consummate gossip?"

"Oh yeah."

"Who are her girls?"

"I think they are a combination of the bridge club and the woman's auxiliary at the church. I'll be taking my grandfather's truck for the trip to town if you don't mind, Mr. Georgiadis."

"Not at all, George. I'll follow you though, if you don't mind?"

Joan and George ran to the barn under the same raincoat. The Fargo sat with a strange nobility that morning. Once they pulled off the tarp it shone like well-polished armor ready for battle. Such thoughts used to ring a little idiotic to George, after all, the diamond industry sold an entire world on how romantic and essential a piece of carbon was. It all came down to how much one emotionally invested in such chunks of matter. The matter itself was inconsequential, compared to what it represented. And the truck, that morning, held the warm embrace of a noble family steed about to carry its rider into battle.

George paused at the sound of a small airplane overhead. The plane registered as significant, though he wasn't sure why. He shook it off in order to remain focused and turned the key on the end of the faded blue rabbit's foot keychain. The truck fired up on the first try. As they pulled out on to the driveway, Georgiadis wheeled in behind, his dutiful face revealed in regular intervals by the slow sweep of his windshield wipers.

When Mr. McDonough awakened after a long sedated night, Billy started to explain he would have to leave shortly to attend the hearing, and stopped suddenly with a look of incredulity as old man started pulling his covers off.

"I'm comin'," he wheezed.

"Dad you're not able to walk, and you need your rest."

"Fer what? I wouldn't miss this for the world, Billy. It's a chance to see some right done, the like of which I may never see again."

The old man struggled and wheezed but was standing by his bed gasping for air with a look of determination. The duty nurse ran in and protested furiously but Billy knew the look on his father's face and what had to be done. As the nurse tried to push the old man back on to his bed Billy intervened and pulled her off.

"Please. Get us a wheelchair. There is something of great importance to him that he must do. It is worth what is left of life itself to him." The nurse looked at Billy, then the old man.

"I can't play any part in this. I would be liable if anything happened. In fact, it is my duty to call the doctor immediately."

"See what the lawyers have done to ya? They robbed ya of basic compassion. Sweetheart, I've been looking out for myself since before you was born. Nobody is responsible for me, but me." The old man huffed on the front end of a rattling burst of uncontrollable coughing.

Billy looked at his father's blood stained clothes in the bag by the bed and realized he had another trip to make first. "Dad, you wait here. I'll go get you some respectable clothes."

"Yer comin' back? Yer not humourin' me?"

"I'm comin' right back, I promise."

The old man dropped to a sitting position on the bed, exhausted. The nurse helped him recline, checked his IV line and pulled the covers up around him.

"You're both crazy if you think this man is going anywhere!" She said officiously. Billy winked at his dad who with effort managed to wink back. He went to the pay phone at the emergency entrance and called Al who showed up minutes later. Christie was upset as usual that the phone rang so early and was seriously beginning to consider having the phone moved to Al's side of the bed. Al dropped Billy off at his car, which was still parked down a few doors from the Hot Spot bar and grill.

"How's ten, Billy?" Al puffed while he put out yet another fire in his ashtray. Billy hopped out and pulled a ten from a wad of bills in his back pocket and pushed it through the inch of open window. A few minutes later, he was back at the farm where he carefully shook out his fathers Sunday best. He was granting his father a wish. It made him feel good; it made him feel sad. It made him feel some of the love he held for the old man that had been forgotten in the stress of their daily routine.

When he got back to the ward, the nurse refused to look at him. Billy was expecting trouble until he noticed a folded wheel chair outside the door to his father's room. As he grabbed it, he saw the nurse out of the corner of his eye, shake her head in disapproval. It was obvious she had placed the chair there to help. Eye contact was avoided for fear of a change of mind. She would not report them missing until they had enough time to leave the building.

Feeling like he played a roll in justice was important to Mr. McDonough. The "stuff worth living for" to him came in the form of chances to do something you thought was right, to be there for someone else or to stand up and be counted. He wanted to be there for George's father, Ernie Dobson, and... George. Billy now primarily wanted to be there for that fragile organism that held the spirit of his father.

As the Fargo entered town it was obvious Patricia Sandfield had lived up to her reputation. Despite the rain, people were filing in to the old town hall in droves. George had never seen so many vehicles in town at once. Pick up trucks abounded from many of the rural folk. Everything from old wrecks that had been molly-coddled past their prime to a surprisingly large number of late-model cars and 4WD-SUVs came from all directions.

Patricia had set up her "girls" with a saturation plan for her latest morsel of gossip. Nearly every name in the book had been called in a matter of an hour, granted, the Lincoln directory didn't quite qualify as a book as much as it did a pamphlet. Every person called was given a list of names like a chain letter. There were contingency plans for the stubborn or un-cooperative. It had been decided not to call anyone until the last minute, the morning of the hearing. This element of surprise was necessary to catch Fairchild off guard. Speeks, Johnson, and the corrupt councillors would have no time to rally their forces. The Mayor and all councillors were excluded from the phone list and were to have no idea anyone cared about the "waste storage facility" except for George's request to speak. He was included on the agenda despite strong opposition. Dwayne had played innocent and wondered aloud what all the fuss was about. It was after all a legal request and this was a democracy where "people have some kind of rights, don't they?"

A long, black limousine with darkened windows pulled up in front of the town hall. A man got out and held an umbrella for Sam Johnson in front of the opened limousine door. Sam looked a little surprised to see so many people standing in the rain looking back at him. His assistant escorted him directly to the Mayor's chambers to meet with the Fairchild lawyers and the rest of the councillors. He sent one of his assistants down to Speek's office and behind the closed doors Barbara heard a hushed conversation that began with: "What the hell is going on around here?! I thought you said this would be a cake-walk!"

George pulled the Fargo up in front of Walker's hardware. All of the parking spots within shouting distance of the Town Hall were taken. As the old Fargo did its signature sputter, an Eyewitness News van pulled up. Allan Thornhill got out with a young woman who George assumed was his friend, Kate Brandon, from Channel 7. Georgiadis stuck to George like glue after parking down the road. A couple of his plainclothes guys walked nearby as inconspicuously as possible. Joan and George shared his father's old trench coat, held over their heads like a tarpaulin against the drizzling rain.

The rain, oh yeah, the rain, George remembered. He would speak to Barbara as soon as he got there to both affirm his hunch and more importantly, use it.

The shops that should have been open were all closed. Even the Deluxe restaurant had a closed sign up and breakfast was their only real money-maker. Eggs they could handle, what they did with meat, customers knew, could be done at most glue factories. George and Joan headed up the stone steps to the front doors. The air was crowded with the healthy smell of farm folk mixed in with a war of colognes. It was a dubious bouquet of horse manure, straw, Aqua Velva, Gucci and even a whiff of the not-so subtle and thought to be extinct… Brut.

George left Joan and Georgiadis at the top of the stairs and ran down to ask Barbara "the" favour. He brushed past Speeks and Sam Johnson's assistant on his way down the stairs. Speeks gave him a suspicious look and whispered something in a snide tone to the assistant. By the time George got back upstairs there were no seats left in the hall except for the council chairs. They were told there was standing room only by a familiar face at the door.

Joan and George entered the great hall, which was not unlike a church decked out in oak wainscoting. The windows were tall and the long oak Dais with the plush council chairs was noble and sombre in appearance. The custodian had broken out the entire supply of folding chairs, one after another, as people kept pouring in. He was about done in by the look on his face. As Joan and George entered, he noticed two of Georgiadis' plainclothes men nodding to what had to be a couple of other agents who were even more dressed down for the occasion so as not to stand out in a rural crowd. Dark suits in Lincoln were the equivalent of a neon sign. As they headed down the center aisle a hand grabbed him. George looked down. It was Millie with Mr. Walker.

"Good luck, George," she whispered

"Millie are you sure you should be here? Are you okay"

"Wouldn't miss this for the world, George. Besides, I was gettin' out tomorrow anyway!" He leaned down and kissed her cheek.

"She wouldn't listen to common sense. You know what she's like when she gets something in her head," Mr. Walker huffed. Joan looked at her and gave her about as much of a smile as she was capable of under the circumstances. The look on Millie's face said she knew all was not well between the "youngsters."

Mrs. Harrison, who played the piano at George's father's funeral, sat a few seats over from Millie. In fact, all of the old-timers were out in full force. As George looked around the room he saw virtually everyone who had been at his father's funeral. His father's war buddies all signed on for a look of approval.

Allan Thornhill sat with a "this-better-be-good" expression on his face. He had been up all night, as George knew he would be, and had emailed his preliminary story. His publisher was rolling the press a day early to scoop the evening news after Georgiadis pleaded his case. Even if the publisher was into Fairchild for advertising money it appeared this could be the moment to jump ship and sell a few extra papers to boot.

An arrangement had already been made with the *New York Times*, depending on the outcome of the hearing, to run the story on the weekend, crediting both the writer and publisher. This was a big day for a community newspaper, and Jim's contacts had panned out well. He had sent Allan's piece down the computer pike the second it was done. Allan's *Eyewitness News* friend was ready to go with the sound-bite version of the piece regardless of any outcome.

It was the video of Jim's that sealed the deal for TV coverage... this was show business; a home movie of a suspected killer... yes!

As George was looking around the room to see who was there, it became strangely quiet. He realized that almost everyone was now looking at him. It was a different look than he was used to; it was a look of expectation, not one of staring at the neighbourhood weirdo. He didn't know what Patricia had told everyone, and frankly at that point it didn't really matter. Maybe they all knew that Ernie and his father were given pre-boarding assistance to the big dirt nap. Or, maybe they all knew that in the bat of an eye, this quaint farming community could turn into a toxic disaster that would infest the land and the ground water for generations to come. In the recesses of George's mind he recognized a residue of anger at some of those people who had made cruel jokes about him behind his back, now expecting him to do something for them. He was grateful for guidance from somewhere that stopped him from lingering in such negative places. His own consciousness resonated again with the example of Allan Thornhill's anger and what a colossal waste of time it was. Anger was irrelevant, the ultimate waste of time, the long detour to love.

For the first time, George felt that he was being allowed to be one of them, and irony of ironies, he was at that junction *because* of the *Sight*. George sensed Patricia had painted him as some kind of heir apparent to his father's throne. However, his motives were far too selfish to put him in his father's shoes, which he thought might always be a little too big for him anyway. He mostly wanted justice for a dead man who he missed terribly. He was seeking some kind of absolution for years of being less than he could to a good human being who was deserving of better than he got.

Fairchild was prepared. There was a table full of lawyers and spokespersons shuffling papers, an overhead projector and a screen sitting off to one side for what Bill and Jim guessed would be a wonderfully prepared sales pitch. They were all going to be sold on fabulous new environmental technologies and community benefits.

Dwayne came out of nowhere with a couple of folding chairs for Joan and George. "I stole these from the Mayor's cupboard."

"Thanks Dwayne. What's going on in the Mayor's chambers?"

"Johnson is giving Mayor Barnes hell for not knowing there would be such a turn-out. Your name is being thrown around a little. They know something is up. I told them the whole town thought you were a little weird and were probably here out of curiosity for what you might have to say. That seemed to settle them down a little. The head honcho from Fairchild seems confident they have an offer only an idiot could refuse... that's about it."

"Thanks for everything, Dwayne," George smirked, "particularly the part about me being weird."

"It worked, George. Besides, you are weird and I'm grateful for it." His honesty made George smile as he watched Dwayne head back into chambers. A terrible but familiar cough entered the room and George swung around hardly able to believe his eyes.

Billy pushed his father down the far aisle near the front and locked the chair wheels into place. The old man looked at George with a squint, broken by a tense wink. They locked eyes as he gave George a proud nod. George was so deeply moved that his eyes started to well up. It was like seeing his parents in the audience at a school play. There, for him.

His thoughts now embraced the idea of how some of these people were indeed extended family. Many had enriched his life without any kind of acknowledgment. George began looking around the room and acknowledging almost everyone. As he unloaded his briefcase, Joan helped him sort everything out on one of the folding chairs and caught him by surprise when she put her hand on his.

"You'll do well, George." She kissed him on the cheek. It was cold and confused, it was all she had, the words sounded prophetically singular. She went over to the far wall and stood with Jim.

Bill Monroe, who sat in the front row a couple of feet away, came over to see how George was feeling. "If you need anything or fall off of strategy I'm right here. I put what we went over last night in point form for you." He handed George a piece of paper.

"Still nothing from Doc Harris?" George asked.

"I spoke with him ten minutes ago and he said the lab results were due any minute."

"Down to the wire huh?"

"You can say that again."

"Thanks, Bill."

"Good luck." He returned to his seat in front of Al and Christie. Christie looked sort of pissed-off and curious at the same time. Pissed-off for being up so early, but curious about something that looked like it could be important.

Speeks scurried out of the Mayor's chambers and joined his assistant Barbara at a small steno desk off to one side of the council chairs. Moments later, the councillors began to file in. Ned Patterson led the procession, perspiring as usual. Behind him was Katherine DesChamps, a pristine looking woman of forty or so years. Her hair was pulled back tight into a bun. Her dress was fairly snug revealing a pleasant enough shape. She ran the small camera and photo shop next to the Deluxe Restaurant. It had been a feed store when George was a kid, and had sat vacant for many years. Mr. Walker, as owner, must have given a sigh of relief when she showed up interested in the place.

Dwayne was next, trying to be cool, but his honest face gave him away. He had an uncertainty in his walk for what lay ahead. He looked at Ann who gazed proudly back at him, converting his insecurities to purpose. His stride changed and he appeared to walk a little taller in her love and approval. The fourth Councillor, Edward Ellison, was an older distinguished-looking gentleman, who took over Lincoln Insurance Brokers from Doc Harris's late brother-in-law. He had the air of a decent man. He had left a larger company and salary in the city for something with less stress. The Mayor and Sam Johnson entered the room as though they were finishing a rather jovial conversation. This, of course, was a technique of Johnson's when a potentially serious situation needed a little diffusion. Enter happy and laughing and you look like a good guy going about his work in a positive fashion with nothing to hide.

Mayor Don Barnes was a pompous little man with a huge butt that forced his suit jacket to flap at the back when he walked. He was doing his best to look officious and important. Sam Johnson on the other hand just reeked of power and importance without effort. His suit was impeccable. There wasn't a white hair out of place on his perfectly coifed head. He had a physical presence that gave the illusion of a big man even though he was of average height. He stood straight behind the Mayor's center chair, and smiled elegantly at the room. The Mayor leaned over his chair and shuffled the same few papers a few times in an attempt to look like he was giving the taxpayers their money's worth. Finally, he tapped his microphone.

"Good morning ladies and gentlemen. I will be relinquishing the chair today to a gentleman who is no stranger to many of us. His distinguished political career spans close to forty years as a senator, and now he is continuing his service to the people of New York as commissioner of the New York State Department of Environmental

Conservation. Mr. Johnson is here in answer to a personal invitation from me. His knowledge of environmental law will be most helpful to us as we try to work through the proposal before us today. Ladies and gentlemen: Senator Sam Johnson."

There was an embarrassingly small amount of applause: Patricia had apparently been a little too thorough. The Mayor moved over one chair while Johnson took the Mayor's seat. He sat down reviewing the papers before him, ignoring the room. Keeping everyone waiting in silence appeared to give him an infusion of power to overcome the cool reception. He looked up and smiled in a very disarming manner at everyone.

"Thank you, Mayor Barnes, councillors, ladies and gentlemen. It is very encouraging to see so many out this morning despite the weather. In my position as commissioner for the Department of Environmental Conservation it is a joy to see such interest in the democratic process. Public involvement is a major element of the Uniform Procedures Act. We are here today to determine how the application before you may or may not suit the needs or wishes of your community. This, of course, will play a role in the final application for a state environmental permit. The application will have to be in accordance with federal standards as set forth in the Environmental Protection Act and undergo an assessment of environmental impacts. So as you can see, today is a small but important part of the whole process.

Today, your councillors vote on the issue of community impact and whether or not the town of Lincoln supports the application by..." Johnson stopped and made like he was searching his notes for the name of the applicant to feign impartiality. He cleared his throat and shuffled papers then spoke haltingly to further the illusion. "Yes, ah here it is: The application is by New World Developments a division of Fairchild Environmental." He turned to the table of suits and looked over his reading glasses. "I take it you folks are here on behalf of the applicant?"

A rather studious looking young lawyer smiled and stood.

"Yes sir. I am Jacob DeVries, from Helmut Talmer and Associates, legal counsel to the applicant. I am joined by two other members of our firm and several representatives from Fairchild."

"Thank you, Mr. DeVries. And we have a request to speak from one resident, a Mr. Moss I believe."

George stood and awkwardly acknowledged Johnson. "Yes sir, that would be me."

"Perhaps, Mr. Moss, you might like to get the ball rolling."

It was just as Bill Munroe predicted. George would be asked to speak first as a way of offering Fairchild a chance for a rebuttal to anything he might say. It was a tried and tested method of silencing a public voice. The public would raise questions and then be hobbled by

NIMBY (Not In My Back Yard) accusations. This reduces a broader issue to a selfish individualistic and small-minded one that can be more easily squashed under foot. This is further accomplished by methodically countering opposition with flashy, biased and often very flawed statistics. By the time the bogus statistics are revealed for their worthlessness, it is usually too late. The last nails in the coffin of these debates would be to accuse those residents speaking on behalf of the community as being ignorant of new technologies and calling them tree-huggers or radical alarmist environmentalists who think the end of the world is near. Industry had painted the word "environmentalist" as a negative term. Martha's sarcastic response to such posturing had always been: "Environmentalist – one who wants clean air to breathe, clean water to drink, and non-toxic soil to grow food. That's a lunatic all right!"

George looked Johnson in the face and smiled. It didn't really matter in this case who went first but Bill had suggested a move to let Johnson know they were familiar with the song and dance.

"Mr. Commissioner, thank you so much for your consideration. These gentlemen have gone to a lot of trouble to bring overhead projection and other educational materials. Perhaps it would be prudent for me to be more educated in the details of their proposal before offering any comments."

Johnson's eyes converged into a laser beam in George's direction.

"It is common practice to let the public have their say first as a courtesy, Mr. Moss."

"I understand sir, but perhaps in this instance common sense might be better than common practice. I would rather speak as an informed member of the public than in a position of ignorance. And I'm sure you meant no disrespect to the public interest by referring to my input here today as merely a courtesy. I know how much the Commissioner believes in public participation and process. So perhaps we can offer our guests from Fairchild Environmental a little Lincoln hospitality with the opportunity to speak first."

"As you wish, Mr. Moss." Johnson went back to the papers in front of him in order to regroup. His face showed nothing, but George knew a fire raged within. The Mayor glared at Moss briefly but corrected himself after he realized there were so many eyes glued to him. Johnson's serious face could be misconstrued as one deeply involved in the papers and procedures in front of him; except for the fact he knew everything about this proposal. How dare some local yokel mess with his formula for ramming projects through! George felt an acquired disdain for real democracy from the man. For him democracy had probably become the ultimate time-consuming, pain-in-the-ass exercise in pluralism. This disdain for the masses helped forge a stance of superiority. How dare anyone from the ranks of the great unwashed, question the full time politician. He knew what was good for them.

Johnson may have been a good man with ideals and values at one point in his life, but now, as an older man he ironically needed and craved the respect he had sold away a piece at a time. Though he commanded the trappings of respect wherever he went, he knew the rotten pulp underneath that veneer. Johnson finally looked up and had once again found his disarming smile.

"Mr. DeVries you have the floor."

Jacob DeVries stood and smiled pleasantly. "Thank you, Commissioner Johnson. Mr. Commissioner, Mr. Mayor, councillors, ladies and gentlemen of Lincoln: Fairchild Environmental is a conscientious member of many communities in North America. We are making new inroads in the fields of reclaiming and recycling. We have devised new methods of extracting useful chemicals from forms of waste that before we came along were dangerous hazardous materials with no effective form of disposal. With some of the leading edge technology we are developing, the world is becoming a safer and more environmentally friendly place in which to live. It is our wish to partner with you on an exciting new project that can bring millions of dollars to your good town of Lincoln."

The pitch was strong and DeVries was a good point man. He had geological surveys and financial tables spelling out a rosy future for Lincoln. In the middle of a wonderful explanation of tonnage royalty fees George felt a hard cold sensation that made him shudder. He turned around and saw *him* enter and stand at the back against the wall. His appearance was impeccable; his face cool and collected. He saw George staring, but avoided eye contact while feigning interest in the presentation. When George moved his head back toward the front of the room he felt his eyes follow, so he turned again, catching him off guard with a smile. The confusion on his face was a sight to behold. While Jacob DeVries continued with the sermon, George could feel Douglas's mind trying to find some reason for why some guy he had never met was smiling at him. What was going on? Jim noticed *him* as well and turned his face away quickly so he wouldn't be recognized.

When DeVries was finished his presentation, of some thirty-five minutes, it brought about a smattering of applause. It was a good convincing sales pitch. The stuff about money to a community center and continuing tariff fees went over better than the incredible sounding advances in new technologies. George scanned the room for Doc Harris but he still wasn't anywhere to be seen. Sam Johnson did some more paper shuffling then spoke.

"Thank you, Mr. DeVries. You've made an excellent proposal and I applaud your thoroughness. Mr. ... ah Mr. Moss, you have the floor. Please state your name and address for the record before you begin."

George scanned the room full of old familiar faces again. Georgiadis leaned against the back wall in the corner offering a somewhat reassuring nod. Douglas stared with a curious look still wondering: "Why the smile?" but chalked it up to some kind of ignorant, rural friendliness. As George stood, he turned to face Joan and wished he had not. Her face held no encouragement like Ann had offered Dwayne; there was only confusion, doubt and a trace of conditional love, conditions that were not presently being met. George had to look away in order to focus thoughts and face Johnson.

"I am George Moss, and my family farm is on Ten Sideroad. One could say I have a vested interest here today because our farm is part of the bargain. But as it turns out, I have more of a vested interest here as a citizen in a democracy and this wonderful thing we call democratic process. So where to start, how about at the beginning? Item one, citizens of Lincoln, has to do with our own council. One might ask: Whose council is it?"

"Mr. Moss, I must interrupt! I would ask you to deal with the proposal at hand here not some personal issues you may have with your council!" Commissioner Johnson was playing his hand.

"Commissioner Johnson, the Uniform Procedures Act requires us to encourage public participation. I see nowhere in the Act, which I have a copy of here, that requires us to head public participation off at the pass."

"How dare you sir, I was merely attempting to keep this hearing focused!" Johnson huffed and puffed but was starting to suspect he might not be able to blow the house down.

George had to go easy on him. They needed the process to continue as a hearing for the press and for the town. "I apologize, Commissioner. Before I continue let me assure you that all my comments will be completely relevant to the issue before us today and underlined with factual evidence rather than opinion."

"Thank you, Mr. Moss, proceed." It was as Bill Munroe said – in this public forum, Johnson needed to hold his head high and be shown respect. If he felt his neck was on the public block, the hearing would fall apart. George had to dance a little with him, as Bill had advised.

"I was wondering whose council this was? My question was a simple one, sir, and so is the answer. It is our council. These men and women work for us, and today they speak for us when they vote on the issue at hand. They were voted into office to represent our interests and uphold the trust we place in them," George said evenly, pausing briefly.

"Let's address one of the reasons we are all here today," he continued. "We are here in part because the zoning of the land in question is favourable to Fairchild's plan. Why is it favourable you might ask? The last time I looked, the property in question was zoned agricultural land, not commercial. Well, ladies and gentlemen, the zoning was changed – and by your council. This zoning change was not posted for public consideration. Do you know what this means? This means the zoning change was in violation of the law." The room began to hiss and there were a couple of derogatory shouts at council. George ploughed on and the unrest quieted down.

"Zoning laws were designed to protect the public from back-room deals, to ensure public participation in the development of its own surroundings. Our representatives in this regard not only failed to represent us but have shown contempt for the laws that protect us by changing this zoning without public posting.

"Mr. Moss," Mayor Barnes cleared his throat." Please I can explain. This was an administrative error that…"

"Commissioner, do I have the floor here or has this hearing process changed to an interactive free-for-all, on the fly?"

"Do you not think the Mayor should be allowed to offer you some explanation, Mr. Moss?"

"Oh yes, Mr. Commissioner. I believe Mayor Barnes has much to explain."

"Give 'em hell, George!" Old man McDonough's face was red and he began to cough from his outburst. The crowd mumbled in response. Johnson was not about to lose control and banged the Mayor's gavel loudly. "Please, ladies and gentlemen, I will have Order! Now, Mr. Moss, are we going to allow Mayor Barnes a word?"

"Actually, Commissioner Johnson, we are not and for very good reason." George approached Johnson and placed four papers stapled together in front of him.

"The Mayor has forfeited his right to speak here today," George stated forcefully. "He's been driving a nice new Cadillac for the last six months leased from a leasing company in Richmond, Virginia."

"There's nothing wrong with that, Moss!" The Mayor shot back.

"Well now that isn't exactly true, Mayor Barnes. Because the payments for this car come from a promotional fund in a company called TLC INC. The Lease Company Inc. is owned by one Benito Peroni. Mr. Peroni also owns New World Developments, which is owned by Fairchild Environmental." The room began to hum with disapproval. Jacob DeVries swung around and whispered angrily at one of the Fairchild executives who shrugged his shoulders. It was clear they weren't all in the loop. Mayor Barnes turned beet-red and began a sorry excuse.

"They have my post-dated cheques, Mr. Moss. There is nothing illegal going on here. I have no knowledge of anyone making my lease payments for me." Barnes was embarrassed. His face gave him away. Johnson shook his head in disgust. He wasn't disgusted that the Mayor was on the take; just that he was so clumsy at it.

"The legalities are not for the commissioner or me to decide, Mayor Barnes. I am only concerned with this hearing and the public interest. I would say there is adequate justification to have your voting privileges revoked today for what appears to be an apparent conflict of interest whether intentional or not sir."

"Mr. Commissioner, this is... " Barnes knew he was baked.

"Highly irregular, Mr. Moss," Johnson interrupted. He had obviously not scanned the second page yet. Page two was the pre-emptive strike Bill had suggested.

"Commissioner Johnson, if you would please, as chair of this hearing look at all of the documents in front of you, I am prepared to live with your ruling on the matter." Johnson's expression was puzzled. He flipped over the first page and looked up at George with a stern expression. Page two was a deed of ownership for a large parcel of property near Aspen. Johnson had purchased the property for $15,000 and the vendor was, low and behold, New World Developments, which had purchased the same parcel for $2.5-million the year before. Page three was a record of numerous trips made by Johnson to the Caribbean and Europe paid for by New World Developments. Page four was a personal e-mail to Benito Peroni from Johnson assuring environmental assessment approval with a copy of the assessment documentation post-dated and signed by Johnson. The game was rigged and he had rigged it. It was the moment of truth he had feared most of his life. He reached for some water for a suddenly dry throat and wondered why George, his executioner, was not blowing his cover. He knew the hearing now belonged to George, but was appreciative he wasn't about to be embarrassed publicly... yet. A dignified façade apparently was as Bill suggested, all the man needed, in fact it was all the man had become. He moved effortlessly to accommodate his new situation.

"Mayor Barnes, given this documentation I believe it is in the public interest to suggest that until such time as you are cleared of any conflict of interest, you should, out of respect for your constituents, withdraw yourself from any active role in these proceedings."

"But sir, I..."

"Mayor Barnes, please." Johnson stopped him dead. The Mayor stood up and snorted back to his chambers. The flap of his suit jacket bounced audibly. There were only a couple of snickers. As comical as he appeared, the abuse of their trust brought only sad disappointment. Most of the people in the room couldn't believe that one of their own could betray them so.

"Mr. Moss, do you have any other conflict-of-interest issues with your council or can we proceed?"

"One very obvious one, sir. Ned Patterson of course as the real estate agent for New World Developments, a division of Fairchild Environmental, has already profited from this proposal through the sale of two farms. He also stands to make more income should the remaining property be sold. Actually, I cannot understand why his obvious conflict-of-interest would not have been brought up before now."

"Are your circumstances as Mr. Moss describes, Mr. Patterson?"

"Well I uh… well I suppose so, Mr. Johnson, uh Mr. Commissioner, sir." Ned's tail was between his legs. "Should I uh…?"

"Yes, you should Mr. Patterson." Ned stood and headed to the Mayor's chambers, misery loving company.

"Well, Mr. Moss, if you lose anyone else here I am afraid you will not have a quorum. Are there any further conflicts we need to know about?" George nodded in the affirmative and the room started to hum with hushed whispers. George approached the Commissioner and handed him some more documentation. He looked at the papers in front of him, shook his head and then looked over at Katherine DesChamps whose pristine expression was replaced with a flushed look of horror. She quietly got up and walked past everyone on her tiptoes. Her intentions were somehow very clear to George. She was leaving the meeting and the town. The humiliation of betraying her friends and neighbours for the small sum of money she had recently paid Mr. Walker was too much for the good side of her to live with. She had recently bought the building she had been renting. The exact amount of money she had paid was equal to a photographic service fee invoiced to TLC Inc. It was in the books as advertising and promotional costs. The only problem was TLC Inc. didn't advertise for public business. It was involved in leasing arrangements for "employees" only.

"Let the record show that Ms. DesChamps has a conflict of interest due to a business relationship with TLC Leasing, a division of Fairchild Environmental. It would now appear we have lost our quorum and cannot proceed, Mr. Moss." The Commissioner's look was hopeful. He briefly thought George was dumb enough to snooker himself until he saw the look on George's face.

"Not quite so, sir. Under the provisions of our own town constitution…" George handed him a copy, "…in times of emergency our Sheriff has the elected authority to act as Mayor should our Mayor be unavailable."

"This is hardly an emergency, Mr. Moss."

"Oh, I beg to differ sir. I would call the betrayal of public trust an emergency of most grave importance and the issue before us here today, one that could have repercussions for generations. This is an emergency that demands immediate public consideration."

"Is the Sheriff here this morning?"

"I am, sir." Ted Williams replied with his usual no-nonsense tone of authority.

"Would you please join us up here so that we might have a quorum?"

"Yes sir, I would, sir." Williams strode authoritatively up to the chair vacated by Mayor Barnes and sat down.

"Now, Mr. Moss, can we proceed."

"Thank you, Commissioner Johnson." George looked at the next item on Bill Monroe's agenda. It read: "Fairchild is asking for our trust and to be a member of our community." The floodgates opened.

"Ladies and Gentlemen, Mr. DeVries eloquently asked us to trust a wonderful, environmentally concerned company called Fairchild Environmental. Why even its name suggests an environmentally friendly predisposition. Fairchild Environmental wants to be our neighbour. They want to contribute to our community and profit share. We've heard their propaganda, how they work with communities all over America and Canada. We've heard how their new processing techniques extract useful chemicals from toxic wastes. We have heard about a new treatment for the toxic leachate produced by dumpsites that can reduce environmental impacts. To Mr. DeVries credit some of what he says is true, to his shame much is not."

"Who is this company that wishes to be our best new neighbour? Who are these people who seek our trust? And let's face it; the trust issue here is central to this proposal because what they are proposing today can affect generations to come. Let's look at the record of those who seek our trust. There have been twenty-nine environmental violations in sixteen states. These are only the ones we know about." George placed the documentation in front of Johnson. "On at least three occasions, illegal dumping of toxic wastes has occurred in public landfill sites not designated or equipped for it. Our new best friends, as I have just pointed out, turned good people on our council against their own neighbours. These people who would ask for our trust have apparently tried to rig the game. They even had many of you seriously thinking about the new community center and tariff fees that would benefit our town for years to come. In essence they have tried to buy you as well."

George paused, then continued: "In two other cases, one in Texas and one in Georgia, the towns involved after five years of dumping have yet to see a cent in tariff fees. This pattern hardly brings the word trust to mind does it? And when the environmental damages are obviously severe and people start to die, the company will, of course, declare bankruptcy and we the taxpayers will be stuck with the clean-up bill. This is not a new pattern."

"Commissioner, if I may?" DeVries had an excuse ready.

"Mr. Commissioner," George asserted, "I have no problem with Mr. DeVries speaking when I am through. I would however like to continue my train of thought uninterrupted."

"You may continue Mr. Moss." DeVries sat down and looked at Johnson with a glare that said it all. They had done this dog-and-pony show before. His was a look that said he was not as innocent as George had initially thought.

"Thank you, sir. I won't be much longer, Mr. DeVries, I promise. To continue on the issue of trust, Fairchild has had reporters fired from major papers around the country who have looked into their affairs. How could they do this? Well, by advertising, of course. Become a major benefactor and editors will be asked to turn a blind eye by publishers. Too much money is at stake! Here are sworn statements from three journalists whose investigative research into Fairchild was halted by their editors and led to their dismissal. Our own Allan Thornhill was fired due in part to threats from Mr. Helmut Talmer, whose firm represents Fairchild today. Should we be asked to trust someone who undermines one of the only safeguards of democracy, the freedom of the press? Oh, this freedom we all think we have is getting more fragile by the minute." George looked around for Doc Harris and began to stall.

"Business interests have subverted our own democratic process. From the legal lobbies in Washington all the way down to the financial benefits provided to local councillors, our democracy and our rights are being bought a brick at a time. Of course, only a tree-hugger would say something nasty about a publicly minded company that employs thousands. They are here for our economic good, aren't they? Our economic good, yes that's what we all buy into, isn't it? Doesn't matter what mess we leave future generations. Our current economic good overrules everything doesn't it? We don't want to ruin an economy that is more precious than life itself, do we?" He was running out of material when Doc Harris entered the room with a sad look on his face. He looked at George and nodded a slow yes; it was time to cut to the chase. George breathed deeply and went for it.

"And what happens when our new "friends" can't get what they want? Well, they simply remove the opposition, don't they, Mr. Speeks?" The room looked at Speeks. "I, uh, I don't know what you're talking about," he said squirming in his seat.

"Let me help you. " George continued. "Bad enough you are still an employee of Fairchild Environmental, sir, while posing as the town clerk." George threw the documentation on the desk in front of Johnson who looked gravely ill. "Bad enough you have placed wiretaps on phones. But that is, after all, your specialty isn't it, Mr. Speeks? And when you're not tapping phones you're holding the legs of people like Ernie Dobson and my father while some even-sicker individual injects them with potassium to induce cardiac arrest."

"Mr. Moss," Johnson said, ashen-faced, "this isn't a court of law. Perhaps your charges would best be presented in that forum."

"Oh, they will be, I'm sure, Mr. Commissioner, but I am still really addressing the issue of the trust we have been asked to give this company!"

The room was stunned. Speeks began to shake and tears steamed down his face. "You... you have no proof," he dribbled.

"I didn't think I had proof either, but I had a little help from the rain this morning didn't I?"

"I don't know what you mean."

"Barbara, could you get me Mr. Speek's umbrella." Barbara moved down the side aisle and handed it to George.

"Interesting umbrella, just like one that sat in the stand at my house the night you helped to kill my father; you know, the night you knocked them all over?"

"How could you know...? Lies, it's all a pack of lies, that's my umbrella."

"Is it, Mr. Speeks? Allow me to show you something about my grandfather's umbrella." George unscrewed the handle and produced a small pocket-knife.

"That proves nothing. That's my knife."

"It wouldn't prove anything except for some reason my grandfather's name is on *your* knife. I bought it for his sixty-fifth birthday and had it engraved myself. You are a murderer Mr. Speeks. You murder for your employer! Your fingerprints are all over the canes and the rack that held them in my father's house. Your prints are well known to law enforcement agencies because of two convictions for illegal wire taps." The tears on Speek's face increased as his shaking grew more noticeable to the entire room.

"I didn't kill anyone it was... it was... "

"Oh, I know you didn't actually pull the trigger, Mr. Speeks. It was this man wasn't it?" George held up a picture, extracted from Jim's 8mm video, of Douglas standing over the dead body of Randy Cousins.

"I had to co-operate, he...he would have killed me if I didn't." Douglas made a slow casual move to exit but suddenly the two undercover agents dressed as locals countered. They had been standing on either side of him and held his arms, while two more sitting in the seats in front of him jumped in and assisted cuffing his hands behind him. Georgiadis moved in, pulled Douglas's gun from his shoulder holster and signalled his men to remove Douglas from the hall. The room was electric with shock and disbelief. McDonough senior smiled at George and reached up to slap Billy on the shoulder. Sheriff Williams reached for the walkie-talkie on his belt.

"Sheriff Williams here. Could you send me in a couple of troopers? I am indisposed with another civic duty at the moment." Within seconds two state troopers appeared at the door. The murmur in the room increased to the point the sheriff had to shout to be heard.

"Down here, gentlemen." The troopers approached the Sheriff who didn't bother getting up. Read that weeping, sorry excuse for a man his rights and take him into custody for me, will ya?" Speeks' rights were read to him as he was escorted out of the room crying. "I didn't kill anyone I swear. It wasn't me!"

When the doors swung closed the room went quiet again and all eyes were once more on George. DeVries hissed at the Fairchild suits in disgust. "Find yourself new counsel, gentlemen."

Sam Johnson looked around the room and tried to wrap things up. "Well, I guess you finished what you came here to do Mr. Moss."

"No sir, I haven't. I could give you the evidence of proof, that my father and Ernie Dobson were murdered. Doctor Harris has been working round the clock and has such proof. But this proof as you stated belongs in a court of law. Doctor Harris if you would be so kind as to give the documentation to Sheriff Williams, he has been expecting it." The Sheriff was caught off guard. He thought for sure that George would have asked for the evidence to be given to Georgiadis. Williams would take it to Georgiadis himself but his people needed to see that he was in the loop. The Doc handed him a folder. He thanked the Doc and looked at George with gratitude for the courtesy.

"Commissioner, I believe we have one more relevant task before us. Our representatives have to vote on the proposal before them. It is after all the heart of the matter, the reason we're all here." He turned and faced Dwayne, Edward Ellison and Sheriff Williams.

"Gentlemen, what you do here today is important. As we speak, this proposal has already been fast-tracked through the back door of the environmental assessment process and false documents have been filed in compliance with federal standards as set out in the National Environmental Protection Act. What we have here is the proverbial done deal. It will, hopefully, unravel when the events of this hearing hit the news. We the people of Lincoln need to be on the record. We need to state very clearly that we do not want this proposal. We find it flawed and have hard evidence of those flaws. I have a document, prepared by a legal advisor, which I would like you to read. Then as a council, if it so pleases you, I would like it considered as your official statement on this matter. It contains the correct language and volumes of data regarding infractions of the Comprehensive Environmental Response Compensation and Liability Act by Fairchild Environmental. This document will be forwarded to all appropriate governmental agencies. This small town can send a loud message to the nation today that public process cannot be sold, well... not in Lincoln anyway. Our lives and the lives of our children depend on it."

"This is most irregular, Mr. Moss."

"Yes, it is, Mr. Commissioner. So we should *make* it regular, shouldn't we? Sheriff Williams, I would ask you first to propose a motion to consider this document in keeping with proper procedures of governance. I further request copies be available for public consideration and that after public input you set a date to review this document publicly and vote on whether to send the attached letter and form."

"You are very thorough, Mr. Moss." The Commissioner's tone was one of resignation. He would not try to head them off again on any technicalities. They were using them all.

"Democratic, I believe might be the word of the day," George responded.

Sheriff Williams wasted no time. "Councillors, as acting-Mayor I propose a motion to consider this document for two days and to return here for a public discussion and council vote."

"I second the motion, Sheriff Williams." Dwayne responded.

"All those in favour?" The three men raised their hands.

"What about copies for the public, George?" Williams asked.

"They will be handed out at the end of this meeting Sheriff." George answered, sending Ann and her boys into motion. Commissioner Johnson looked around the room.

"It would seem we can adjourn this public forum if you are through Mr. Moss..."

"I am finished, sir. But our councillors could vote on the Fairchild proposal as tabled here today," George said cutting him off.

"Councillors?"

"I move we reject the Fairchild Proposal as it stands." Dwayne said with new-found confidence.

"I second the motion." Ellison responded.

"All those in favour?" Sheriff Williams chimed in with a smile. He looked at the other two whose hands were in the air. "The motion is carried. The town of Lincoln rejects the waste facility as proposed by Fairchild Environmental."

"This meeting is then adjourned if that's all right with you, Mr. Moss?" the commissioner asked snidely.

"Fine with me, sir," George replied. Johnson banged the gavel down and the town hall burst into spontaneous applause, whistles and whoops. Joan came over and gave him a rather limp victory hug then went to Jim who looked like he had just crashed. It was the end of a long road for him and time to deal with the grief that had been placed on a back burner. Monroe came over and patted George on the back.

"Kept your cool George. You should be a lawyer."

"Couldn't have done it without you Bill, thanks."

"Don't thank me. I'm higher than a kite over what just went down."

The room began to flush out. Many folks came over to shake the hand of the prodigal son to say "thanks," and "job well done," and such. Some said nothing. They just offered a look of approval. Ann and her sons handed out copies of the petition.

Commissioner Johnson was hounded by the *Eyewitness News* reporter but huffed his usual "no comment!" as he made a hurried exit to the safety of his limo. The reporter then turned the lights on Allan Thornhill who gave a well-informed synopsis of the event.

Barbara came over and shook George's hand. "I had no idea, Mr. Moss, I had no idea." After a few words, Dwayne left for a victory celebration with Jim, Bill and Joan. The Deluxe was just opening its doors to what was looking like a very promising business day. George said he'd follow in a few minutes. He just wanted to sit alone for a moment.

George sat holding his grandfather's "rain stick" as he used to call it and screwed the top back on after inserting the knife. He had an overwhelming sense of his father's presence.

"There you go." He said to him under his breath. The unspoken transmission of response was immediate. "No, there you go George."

Ann finished with the petitions as the last few people made their way out. She poked her head back in and called to George. "You heading to the Deluxe?"

"Yeah, I'll be along shortly." She mouthed an "okay" with a concerned face, then left with her sons.

George sat in the empty hall, feeling… empty. The purpose he had held for days was gone. Reality dropped on him like a wet blanket. A short time ago, he lived happily in denial with a woman who didn't really know him. He longed for that place and time. He longed for the days when his father's existence in the world helped hold up his floor, his security. It was a new world now and one he had to get on with. He needed to hew a few timbers to shore up a new reality.

The caretaker entered, overcome with the number of chairs he had to put away. He gave a loud sigh, hiked up his pants and started noisily folding them up and placing them on the trolley. George sat for a few more minutes trying to find his father, but the clatter of chairs ruined the attempt and the afterglow of victory.

As he stood to leave, a wave of dizziness swept over him and he had to grab the back of his chair to stop from falling. A slow realization entered his consciousness.

"Oh no." He shook the dizziness off and ran out. On the front stairs of the town hall, people were trying to congratulate him again and shake his hand. He tried to be as polite as possible but time was of the essence. He saw Billy's car and ran toward it but more people intervened in celebration and congratulation. As he finally got closer he could see Billy in the driver's seat looking at his dad who looked back at him from the passenger seat. George opened the back door and got in. People passed by and waved shouting hellos and thanks. Ten minutes seemed like an hour, but finally the street cleared and they were on their own.

George's face cracked. "I'm so sorry, Billy."

"He's gone, George. I just put him in the damn car and when I walked around and got in he was gone, just like that."

George leaned forward and gripped Billy's shoulder. "He loved you, Billy."

"I know, I know. He didn't want to sometimes, but he was just too damn warm-hearted for his own good."

"He's happy, you know."

"Aw, come on, George, he's fuckin' dead." Billy sobbed.

"Did you see his face in the town hall? He was in his element. He was there to see some bastards pay the piper. God, he loved his revenge. No it was bigger and sweeter than that – he loved justice. Look at his face, Billy. He died happy and I can tell you he is happy."

"Oh, screw off with your *Sight* right now George. Just be my friend will ya? My daddy's dead, for Pete's sake, I'm gonna miss the old coot. He was all I had." George reached round with both arms and held Billy's shoulders from the back seat. It wasn't long before they were both crying. They cried and cried until Billy started to laugh.

"Christ, look at him will ya?" Billy said, sniffling a little. "He looks so fuckin' happy."

Mr. McDonough had the sweetest and most mischievous look. Maybe he had seen her at the moment of his death. Maybe she was there waiting for him just like he thought she would be. God, George hoped those feelings were true. George and Billy laughed and cried and laughed and cried, two old friends, hanging on to the fragrance of sweet, precious memories.

31

Life

A couple of days later came the uplifting experience of another funeral. The faces were mostly the same as those in attendance at George's father's service, and the words from the young interim minister were mostly the same for yet another person he never knew. The casket was even the same model; a plain poorly stained, highly varnished piece of veneer-laminated, crappy plywood. The new taillight on the hearse was a deeper red than the older more weathered one on the other side.

Mr. Brown wore his professional mask of sympathy as he hovered around the ceremony making sure everything ran smoothly. The similarities to George's father's funeral made George painfully aware of life's play, re-enacted by the constant influx of new players in the key roles. As the Bard had said: "All the worlds a stage and all the men and women merely players." When he read those words in high school they meant nothing to him, but in his new reality they held a profound sweet-sadness. The realization that his grief was a pain known to millions over thousands of years, didn't diminish the importance of his own experience, it simply marked a significant point of the journey that connected one and all to each other and infinity.

Some folks in the crowd made their way over to console Billy, who stared off somewhere unable to say much, while his mind burrowed within, looking for what George hoped he would find – a reason to be.

The reception at Ann's was real unpretentious country warmth. Some ladies at the church had cut the crusts off of triangular little tuna and devilled ham sandwiches, which were placed on paper plates next to carrots, celery, pickles, butter tarts, cookies and coffee. George and Joan had followed Billy, who sat in the back of Brown's limo with Ann in the role of the comforting surrogate sister through it all.

As they got out of the Fargo in front of Ann's house, Allan Thornhill caught up. "Why, George?"

"He was old, Allan, it was his time."

"No, no, no, you dime-store philosopher! Why did you give me the leg up with the story thing?"

"Just wanted you to have one good thing to say about me and maybe yourself as well, Allan. You did a great job. I understand the *New York Times* is running your piece in its entirety?"

"News travels fast."

"Small town."

"Yeah."

"I'm sure you'll get some good offers out of this, Allan."

"Got one this morning."

"Good on ya."

"Thanks, George. There I've said it. I have thanked you."

"You're welcome, Allan. Now focus on what a talent you have instead of who else you might think is responsible for your failures."

"I knew I couldn't get away without the mandatory lecture."

"You bring out the orator in me, Allan."

"You are such a condescending jerk Moss, but thanks anyway."

"Pleasure, Allan, on both counts. Good luck."

"Thanks, man," Allan said as he headed to the reception.

"Asshole!" Joan hissed under her breath.

"Yup, will be until the day he dies. It's just nature's way of preparing us for his loss."

Inside, Billy was already into the booze and would soon begin to get loud and obnoxious. Ann answered the phone, plugging her free ear in an attempt to defeat the babbling brook of support for the bereaved. After settling in to an enthusiastic if somewhat brief conversation she called Joan over. It was Jim. Workload, an anxious client, missed deadlines and his own need for the company of his dear friend and colleague all conspired against George. Joan would work at Jimmy's for a couple of weeks before heading back home to Canada and George knew she needed to go alone. They found out from Dwayne there was a train in an hour, and Joan thought she might as well try to catch it.   George drove her back to the farm to get her things, then on to the station where they stood, wordless, until the passenger cars came to a halt in front of them.

"Come home soon," she said. "Soon" when combined with the other 90 per cent of her unspoken communication took on the extended meaning of "not right away." George kissed her forehead and stood on the platform hoping she might look back but knowing better. As the mighty diesel engines rumbled off into the distance, a deafening silence poured back in like water assuming its rightful level after being so rudely displaced by the ugly sound of technology. George stood motionless, not knowing what to do until he tugged on the rabbit's foot and keys to his grandfather's Fargo in his pocket.

By the time George returned to the wake, Billy was royally drunk. Some stragglers sat singing around Ann's piano while old Mrs. Harrison played "Goodnight Irene." Billy's foghorn voice dominated the pack with what had been one of his father's favourite tunes. He sang and sang till the room was empty, and old Mrs. Harrison could play no more. Ann's son took him home in Mr. Brown's funeral car. It was a ride he insisted on, part of the Lincoln death ritual that ended when the door opened and he pathetically staggered into the house.

Upstairs in his father's bedroom, Billy sat on the edge of the bed looking around at the few meagre personal possessions left by a simple farmer. His shoulders began to shake in a painful awareness that ruthlessly pierced the anaesthesia of alcohol: he was alone.

George kicked around Lincoln for a few weeks, getting into a little maintenance at the farm and finding, much to his surprise, that he quite enjoyed the rewards of some physical labour. Nonetheless, he wanted to get back to school; he had an article to write; a little research to do at the McMaster University library; he was after all a teacher, not a farmer. Being surrounded by the promise and potential of his students was a drug. At the same time though, the farm held too much for him to part with and he thought it might provide a place to come and hide from time to time. The great divide between Canada and the U.S.A somehow got smaller in the events following his father's death

Billy offered to keep his eye on things and do a little basic upkeep for him, and reluctantly agreed to Ann and George's demand to become a card-carrying member of Alcoholics Anonymous. Ann thought he signed on to the meetings as some kind of penance for his failures to his father. She and George hoped that with a little luck, one day, he might embrace such an investment for his own benefit, but the road ahead would more than likely not be a smooth one…

It was a couple of neighbourhood dogs that drew Sheriff Williams to the sedan parked behind the town hall. He checked the plates over the cruiser computer and TLC leasing came up as the owner. As he got out for a closer look, the foul stench of rotting flesh warranted a look in the trunk. When the ropes were undone, poor Stanley's folded corpse was extracted from the Moss's living room rug. It had held Stanley like the funereal blankets of a sacrificial Inca child since the night Mr. McDonough's shotgun caught him off guard. Fortunately, the blast of lead shot had left one good side profile that his devastated parents could barely identify the afternoon they were ushered into the morgue. No one seemed willing to rub any salt of negativity into open emotional wounds and so there was no talk of the charges that were laid posthumously in the attempted murder of Mr. McDonough.

Sheriff Williams and Georgiadis' team went along with Stanley's parents' mantra that he was a good lad who got mixed up with the wrong people. This was repeated over and over to anyone who would listen and it would be all they would have to hang onto for the rest of their lives. In fact, it was probably the only answer to the question that would haunt them to the relief of their own graves. Why?

George's father and Ernie Dobson were finally re-interred after federal officials confirmed the lab work and the Doc's conclusions. After the backhoe left, Doc Harris stayed at the gravesite with George to share a few thoughts over his father's remains. It was a meaningful moment of closure – spoken cherished memories from a lifelong friend – mortal lyrics to the gentle song, *The Whisper of God*, which sifted through the old spruce trees. George joined the Doc and his wife for dinner the night before he left Lincoln. They seemed to be moving into the role of adoptive parents with the genuine comfort and concern they offered. George was happy with that thought and had no difficulty in promising to visit as often as possible.

Early the following morning, George got out of bed in time for a thorough farewell stroll around the farm. The country air was fresh, exhaling the fragrant stuff of life through the blades of the ever-complaining windmill. In the barn, he sat in the Fargo for a few minutes before finally covering it over gently with the tarp. When he was finished packing and staring at the walls, he sat out on the porch on the new swing, until a plume of dust like the tail of a comet revealed Al's green wagon in the vanguard. The tail continued down the road when the comet severed itself with a hard right into the driveway.

"Hey, buddy," Al said, hanging out of his window as he pulled up.

"Hey, Al." George threw his bags on the back seat and hopped in the front. As they headed down the road, George craned his neck around to see the farm until it disappeared into the hills like a ship into the sea. He opened the window to let the smell of new life wash over his face and soothe the depths of his soul.

"Al, would you mind driving through town on the way to the station?"

"Not at all, George." Al steered his old wagon with his usual dexterity while manufacturing a rollie and lighting up. The town was unusually quiet that morning, which suited George fine. He didn't really want to see anyone; He just wanted to wade uninterrupted into the memories of a little boy walking hand in hand with his parents down the main street. Yeah, that weird little Moss boy with the weird father and beautiful mother. Not bad folks, the Mosses, "just a little funny upstairs, if ya know what I mean. Got some kind of spooky ESP thing. Not to say there isn't somethin' to it all mind you, they's bin right too many times to pay no mind to!" George heard the chatter play like an old record while the shadows of those who stared as they passed by were confronted by Mrs. Moss with her outgoing: "Hello, beautiful day!" Mr. Moss would tip his hat while the little Moss boy turned to observe everyone's reactions with embarrassment. Mostly, they would smile uncomfortably at the boy then exchange the hushed whispers that at long last, would haunt him no more. The embarrassment, the insecurity, the denial was gone, cast off like an outgrown, moulted skin.

George's mind jolted back to the present as they arrived at the station, to an unusual number of cars in the parking lot. When he climbed out of Al's limo he realized what was going on. Al sent him on ahead while he grabbed the luggage. Ann and Dwayne, Barbara, Sheriff Williams, Billy, Mr. Walker and Mildred, Christie Adams, Doc and Mrs. Harris, et al, stood there quietly as he climbed up the three steps onto the platform. Ann came over and opened with a kiss.

"Don't be a stranger," she whispered in his ear. Millie hobbled up for a hug. "Your Daddy would've been proud for what ya done fer us."

"I'm no saint, Millie. I did it for myself."

"Oh, I know, George, you are your father's son, as far as the saint part goes anyway." She smiled an odd but knowing smile.

"I always wondered why he spoke so affectionately of you, Millie," he whispered in her ear. She didn't seem to mind that George knew, but nothing would ever be said in reverence to the dead. He hugged the old woman and kissed her tenderly on the top of her head. One by one they said their good-byes. Christie gave him a half-hearted hug but was unusually silent. Patricia Sandfield had kind words. Her gift of gossip was the stuff of local legend; she was now elevated in status as the head of a state-of-the-art communication network that saved a town.

Many years ago, George felt he had left Lincoln as an outcast, but really he had left an ignorant fool. To those people he was and always had been, one of their own. "Weird? Well hell yes," but one of their own nonetheless. He was learning to acknowledge the honour and responsibility that comes with such kinship. He climbed on the train and looked back at them all, so fragile, so flawed, so human, and so - his. Yes, he was proud to say, he was one of them.

"Come home soon George. This will always be home you know!" Ann yelled.

"Don't you fuckin' ferget it, Moss!" Everyone swung around to see Christie Adams. "What? What the fuck are ya fuckin' starin' at me for?" Some shook their heads, some smothered laughter. Mrs. Harris of course made like she hadn't heard a thing while Al just put his arm around his sweetheart and offered her a freshly rolled wet rollie with his spare hand.

"Thanks, Christie!" George yelled back. She looked around at everyone as if to say, "See, I'm George's fuckin' friend too, ya dick weeds!" Christie, dear sweet, Christie, the poet laureate of Lincoln, one overly experienced face that sank back into a Norman Rockwell painting of simple townsfolk waving goodbye to a friend. That image stabbed George's consciousness like a needle, carrying an antidote that overwhelmed any remaining residues of insecurity that had consumed him for so long.

George had decided to go to Durham first for the gratitude that needed the sincerity of physical manifestation. On his arrival there, he took a cab over to Durham Regional Hospital, to visit Andy and Martha. It may have been their sheer desire to see their love come to some kind of fruition that got them through not one but two attempts on their lives to say nothing of multiple surgeries.

The doctor who had entered the room when Douglas fled had heard Andy's alarm about Martha's IV. He pulled it out milliseconds before the potassium would have entered her bloodstream. In hearing the story George had finally found the worth of measurements in milliseconds – they can hold the difference between life and death. Five hours after extensive surgery, Andy had emerged hanging onto life by the thread of Martha's worry. Had he been wounded anywhere but a few feet from a surgical team, he would not have survived.

Andy and Martha's feelings for one another were so genuine and brand new as to warm many a cold heart. When George arrived and asked directions to their rooms the receptionist responded with a twinkle "Oh, you'll find the lovebirds in room 306." The hospital had finally given up and put them in the same room. The separate room thing became a hazard because they would all too often be found crammed into one bed much to the detriment of their battered bodies. So a co-ed room was the answer – two beds pushed together, allowing hands to be held and faces caressed as needed. In a few days, they would be returning to Martha's where the door would be locked, curtains drawn and the answering machine would earn its worth fending off all inquiry from the outside world. They had some serious catching up to do in the wonderful joy and discovery of love, in private!

Jim, Bill, Andy and Martha were praised glowingly, in most media reports on the unravelling of Fairchild Environmental. Monroe decided to return to law school with a senior partner at the office paying the ticket! The notoriety was good for the firm along with the money to be made in a fluffed-up reputation of fighting for the public interest.

Bill would be staying in Randy's old apartment while he fought with a new culture in insurance companies that preferred negotiation and legal action to paying out any claims. This practice saved such companies millions of dollars annually as clients who couldn't afford lawyers were coerced into accepting twenty to fifty percent of what they were due. What Bill's insurance company hadn't bargained for was his free access to legal representation from the firm he worked for plus his connections with the media. It would take perseverance but the house that Douglas's gas explosion had demolished would be properly rebuilt by an insurance company that would actually live up to their own policy, even though they had to be shamed into it by bad press.

While Fairchild stocks plummeted, Speeks cried like a baby to plea bargain for his own sorry comfort. Douglas was denied bail after being identified by Andy as the man who had killed a security guard and attempted to murder Andy, Martha and an ICU nurse. Benito Peroni's bail was set at one million dollars, which he had no trouble producing. Georgiadis felt the federal case was iron clad and that both Douglas and Peroni would do life sentences. It all looked wrapped up neat and tidy until the van pulled up at the side entrance of the courthouse after the bail hearing.

In preparation for his court appearance, Douglas had asked his lawyer to bring him his good black suit from his apartment. Of course there was nothing in the pockets and it passed inspection. On the way to the courthouse, Douglas calmly chatted with the guard while removing two pins from the satin lining in the left arm of the jacket. The guard was quite impressed with the apparent wealth of his prisoner and falsely convinced that the only crime such a man was capable of was the stock manipulation Douglas claimed was his downfall. They were discussing the minimum-security prisons where white-collar criminals did their time while Douglas opened the lock to one of his handcuffs. He quickly closed it again, having learned the workings of the mechanism.

The guard saw nothing as Douglas played up the spoiled gentleman role to the point of appearing almost effeminate. This, off course, was all designed to help the guard underestimate him just enough for the element of surprise Douglas would need when the time was right. Douglas surveyed his surroundings, noticing the doors of the prisoner transfer van could only be opened from the outside. Clearly, the van interior was not the place to make his move.

At the end of the bail hearing Douglas was led to the side of the building where the transfer van waited with the engine running. Exhaust tumbled on to the pavement as Douglas clumsily stumbled his way down the concrete-steps, manacled hands chained to manacled feet. Douglas exaggerated that last stumble and as he hoped, the guard reached under Douglas's arm to steady him. That's when he made his move. His one hand seemed to defy the limits of the chains as it reached into the officer's holster. The move was so fluid and fast that the guard didn't know what the pain in his side was until he realized he had been shot and fell to the ground with a stunned expression on his face. Before he passed out he saw the white-collar wimp was free of the handcuffs he'd locked properly and double-checked.

The second guard took a bullet between the eyes before he could respond. The driver, hearing the shots, got out to see what was going on and saw all three men on the ground. Douglas, while acting wounded and writhing in phoney pain pointed down the alley and shouted: "That man shot us! Get him!" While on the ground he successfully undid one of his foot manacles and was on his feet before the driver's brain had processed all the incoming information. When it registered that the prisoner had pointed down the alleyway with a free hand that should have been manacled; it was too late. As he turned around he took a shot in the left knee that shattered the joint causing him to drop in a wave of nausea. He managed to reach for his gun and looked back up toward the prisoner, but Douglas was already in the van and driving out on to the crowded street.

The van was found two blocks away parked neatly in front of a meter – handcuffs on the seat, foot manacles and chain on the floor next to the accelerator. Douglas had disappeared into the unsuspecting crowd like a businessman on his way to the office, which was exactly where he was going. Five minutes later he resurfaced at the back entrance of Fairchild where he entered his code into the touch pad and the door clicked open. On the way to his office he passed a bewildered looking Joseph who came out of the operations room looking a little suspicious.

"You're out Mr. Douglas? I take it things went well for you?"

"Thank you, Joseph, yes; fortunately the law has accommodated me for the time being." He strode into his office and locked the door. The room bore the telltale signs of what Douglas assessed as a fairly clumsy search by the FBI. They had gone through the clothes' closet and desk drawers but had not twigged to the wall safe.

Douglas found the rather innocuous looking calculator where he left it in the top drawer of his desk, typed in the numerical sequence and hit the add key. The large Rubens painting began to move sideways slowly revealing the safe. After dialling in the combination, he swung the door open, stepped over the sill and walked in.

He placed bundle after bundle of hundred dollar bills into a large nylon gym bag then opened a mahogany humidor from the shelf in front of him. Underneath a layer of expensive Cuban cigars he slid a false bottom off to one side. There in a slender compartment lay a few false drivers' licenses, passports in different names as well as valid credit cards in the names of various Fairchild employees. He gently pulled on the gold-plated handle of a small drawer until it was fully extended and reached underneath to peel off a loose piece of duct tape. Stuck to the tape was a safe deposit-box key. Douglas removed it and placed it carefully in the inside pocket of his jacket, then reached up to a wall hook and removed a shoulder holster that cradled a Smith and Wesson 38 with a silencer.

On the floor just inside the safe, he found the attaché case he had used the day he visited Andy and Martha in the hospital. Upon opening it he reached in for a rather beat up wallet he thought might come in handy on a rainy day. He opened it and pulled out a credit card, driver's license and a pilot's license in the name of one Malcolm Howard. Affixing his own image to the documents would mean one more fifteen-minute stop, but the sky he believed was his ticket to freedom and this little item just might come in handy. He was about to close the door when a smile came over his face and he re-entered the safe one last time. A few seconds later, he emerged with two additional items – a syringe, and a small vial of clear fluid that he placed in the bag. The safe was closed and Douglas had one final look around his office, to bid it all a silent farewell. He closed the office door quietly behind him and stopped in on Joseph.

"Joseph, have you informed anyone of my presence here?"

"No, Mr. Douglas."

"Thank you, Joseph." Douglas reached out for Joseph's hand and squeezed it with great force for an uncomfortable period of time, while looking deeply into his eyes. He finally nodded a reluctant acceptance of Joseph's word, turned and disappeared out of the door. Joseph grabbed a Kleenex from the counter in front of him and wiped the sweat from his brow. He had read about the charges against Robert Douglas and though he never really wanted to believe the papers, in that moment he knew he had gazed into the eyes of a man who had just mentally flipped a coin for his life. If he had lied, Joseph knew that Douglas would have seen it in his face and killed him on the spot. Joseph grabbed the newspaper he had been reading that morning and went directly to the want ads. It was time for a change. The bow of the ship he was on was well under the waves and the stern would soon slip into the silent depths of receivership.

By the time Ben Peroni arrived home from Talmer's office, the news of the daring escape of Robert Douglas was on every channel. He watched the TV with an ominous feeling of foreboding as the bodies of the two guards were loaded into ambulances. The one surviving guard was quoted as saying that it had all happened so fast that he wasn't sure if there was an accomplice or not. Benito turned the television off as his wife entered the room. She noticed how pale and agitated he was: He was scared and she knew he had good reason.

"Do you think Mr. Douglas will come here, to our house?"

"Don't worry, I'm leaving. I wouldn't do anything to jeopardize you or the children."

"Where will you go?"

"The less you know the better. I will be in touch." Ben stood and kissed his wife, then went to the hall phone to call for a company car. Mary was already carefully folding a few things for him and placing them lovingly into the leather Gucci bag her husband always took on business trips. When he entered the bedroom she turned her head away in an attempt to cover her tears.

"Oh, Mary, don't be so dramatic, everything will be fine!" By the time the bag was packed, the car was waiting outside for the short drive to the local airport. He looked at the mother of his children and kissed her with the all the affection he had in him. "Tell the kids I love them."

Peroni headed out the front door and into the waiting car. He had chartered a small executive jet with some regularity as the company grew, and his secretary had already called ahead to make sure there was a plane ready and the standby crew would be there in half an hour.

As the car pulled away a disturbing thought entered Benito's mind: watching his wife crying on the front doorstep, Peroni thought she looked like a widow. He stared until his own eyes began to water forcing him to turn away. Had he looked back a split-second longer he might have seen the small rented Toyota that pulled in behind the Fairchild limousine and followed at a safe distance. When Peroni called Joseph to order increased security around his house, he learned of Douglas's visit to the office, causing a shudder to course through his bones.

It was a relatively nice day with scattered cloud cover as the Fairchild limousine pulled up to the charter building. The Lear jet was fuelled, engines running, ahead of schedule. Benito Peroni entered the office and slapped down his corporate Visa to cover the $8,000 charter fee. A very deferential young female employee, in awe of Peroni's power, escorted him out to the plane. She was so patronizing, it was all that Benito could do to suffer her company in the short walk to the steps of the jet. As soon as they reached the plane, Peroni turned and cut the employee off in the middle of a load of conversational drivel.

"Thank you for your assistance and good day to you." Benito entered the Lear and barked at the co-pilot to close the door and get underway. He settled into his leather chair and held a stiff single-malt Scotch by the time the Lear pulled out on to the runway. The young employee feeling unjustly snubbed, spoke quite audibly as she waved goodbye with a broad smile to the passenger who wasn't looking. "And fuck you too."

"I beg your pardon?" The formal voice came from behind her, causing her to spin around, her face flushed with embarrassment.

"I am so sorry sir I…"

"Please, no need to apologize. It is I who should be apologizing for sneaking up behind you. Brad Jackson's the name. I would like to rent a small plane for the day; it's such a glorious day for flying." The young woman looked at the bearded gentleman in front of her in the expensive leather jacket and slacks.

"I trust you have all necessary documentation Mr. Jackson?"

"Yes, of course," the gentleman replied. "My, that was a handsome Lear that just left. How much would one of those charter for?"

"Depending on the length of the trip and the in-flight services, anywhere from four to ten thousand, Mr. Jackson."

"Goodness gracious. Where is it off to today?"

"Denver."

"Nice way to travel if you have the money! Excuse me, I'm going to get my wallet from the car, can I meet you inside in a minute?"

"Certainly, Mr. Jackson." The young woman headed back to the building and Douglas walked to his rented Toyota with no intention of returning. He had learned all he needed to know and would be looking at small aircraft in another location, somewhere like Denver perhaps.

When Peroni arrived in Denver, he was met by a limousine that delivered him to his favourite getaway and some peace of mind. It was a small house on the outskirts of the city and he was quite sure no one knew about it. The house was rented by Fairchild Environmental for a rather attractive-looking woman, who was moving through the corporate ranks in leaps and bounds – a testimony to her talent. She was at the door holding a couple of drinks and not wearing much of anything when Peroni arrived. The fear for his life only heightened his sexual drive and so a few hours of lust became the corporate agenda of the day.

After his American Airlines flight touched down, Douglas rented another car with phoney I.D. Benito was right, no one knew about the house or his affair with the Fairchild employee, but nonetheless, Douglas had all the information he needed. Peroni loved steak and this would be his Achilles heal. He had often spoken of his favourite restaurant in Denver that served a forty-ounce porterhouse. They say red meat can kill you and never was the saying so true as the night Peroni pulled up to Morton's Steak House in a new Lexus driven by a rather attractive-looking woman.

Douglas had been patiently watching the restaurant for three days and sat quietly in the parking lot looking through the large rear views of his rented Lincoln Navigator. He immediately recognized the woman from personnel files that he had gone over many times with Joseph in routine security checks. "Hmm, employee relations," Douglas muttered dryly under his breath. As another car came down the street, Douglas held a digital camera out of the window and snapped a picture of the couple embracing before heading to the restaurant arm in arm. He pulled the camera back in the window quickly when Peroni turned, startled by a flash of light that he mistook for the headlights of the approaching car.

Douglas allowed them what he thought would be enough time to get comfortably seated then followed. After palming a hundred- dollar bill to the hostess, Robert Douglas was taken to the seat of his choice, the booth next to Benito Peroni. His slicked back newly dyed black hair and beard did not reveal him to Peroni's casual glance as he approached. It was probably the cowboy hat obscuring the eyes that was the cleverest part of his disguise: Douglas in a cowboy hat? Now what could be more out of character? Once seated, Douglas reached into his pocket and prepared his little surprise underneath the table before putting it in his pocket. He ordered dinner and casually waited for opportunity to arrive. About forty minutes later, Ben got up and went to the men's room.

"Ah, well done, sir, I am just finished my dinner." Douglas muttered under his breath. He waited seconds then followed Peroni who was standing at a urinal when Douglas walked through the door. The jab in Peroni's buttocks startled him causing urine to dribble down the front of his trousers. He turned to Douglas and recognized the cold eyes and the syringe immediately.

"You!" The sight of Douglas was not as bad as the searing pain that began to rip across his chest causing Ben to drop to the floor. Douglas smiled at him and said with uncharacteristic crudeness: "Rather appropriate isn't it? You being found, having just pissed yourself and with that rather pathetic little prick sticking out of your trousers."

"How did you?"

"Don't trouble your mind with such Earthly thoughts Mr. Peroni; you have no need of them. By the way, I'll send this picture of faithlessness to Mary." Douglas stroked Peroni's head almost affectionately as he showed him the screen of his digital camera that displayed Benito embracing his mistress.

"You fuck, I'll..."Before the sentence could be completed Peroni's sweaty face, frozen with hatred, thudded onto the cold tile floor.

"You'll nothing of the sort, you stupid little man." Douglas said as he patted him on the head and pocketed his camera. He had finished all of his business with Fairchild Environmental. Exiting the men's room he walked directly to the hostess at the reception table.

"I beg your pardon but there is a gentleman in the washroom who appears to have had a heart attack. Do you know CPR?"

"Oh, dear." The hostess called a waiter and the two of them rushed to the men's room. Douglas kept on walking.

It was twenty minutes later, according to airport flight records, a man with identification in the name of Malcolm Howard received runway clearance and lifted off into a clear night sky in the used single engine Cessna he had purchased two days before. The lights of Denver twinkled magically as he banked the plane and levelled off in a southerly direction. It felt good; in fact it surpassed the feeling he had anticipated since his flight with the real Malcolm Howard. The white-capped Rockies looked in through the passenger window and would keep him company for the first leg of his journey.

It was time to settle down, and enjoy all the money he'd been secreting away for years. He reckoned he could live his days in Mexico like a king. Little did he know it would be a couple of short years in the quiet haven of his luxurious villa near Manzanillo before the fog of remorse drifted in. Much like a soldier forever haunted by the faces of his dead buddies, Douglas, in retirement, had a little too much time on his hands for contemplation and his dementia began to conjure such thoughts and images. He would never know the peace he thought he was retiring to, only the faces of people contorted in agony that awakened him nightly. They were mostly good people, he thought, good people whose lives he had snuffed out for money from a man he despised.

He searched for some kind of justification for his actions that he would never find, a peace that would always be just out of reach. A sadness grew deeper and the more he fought it the deeper it grew, reducing him to outbursts of tears. The tiny seed of good that hid within him began to root in the mixed up soils of his disease. An insatiable need for forgiveness accompanied by an even greater thirst for self-worth began to grow into a dark depression. He would stop strangers on the street and beg for their forgiveness only to get a momentary grip, then crumble into tears, stop another stranger and repeat the cycle.

Life produced a questionable mercy for Douglas. By the time a few tests revealed the worst fears of his cognitive mind, full blown Alzheimer's wasn't far behind. Douglas' maid had already persuaded him to sign virtually everything he owned over to her. He would live for a time wandering in his own locked room, until being admitted to a seedy Mexican facility where patients had an alarming number of incidences of malnutrition and abuse resulting in premature death.

Back in Richmond, Helmut Talmer watched helplessly while the value of his shares in Fairchild evaporated into thin air. Procedures were underway to have him disbarred. He had tried to silence freedom of speech, freedom of the press, and public interest with law fashioned into a contemporary offensive weapon. The fortune he had traded his soul for disappeared into the thin vapour of stock market rumour and bankruptcy leaving him with close to nothing, according to the press. When Bill read some of the latest news to his friends, it was Jim who wondered what it would feel like to know "you had sold your soul... for nothing!"

But Talmer, ever the clever lawyer, had so manipulated the press over the years that the stories of his financial ruin were actually well planted and quite exaggerated. He had tucked enough of a personal fortune away to live well. The disbarment proceedings were an inconvenience that he thought he could delay long enough for a few big pay cheques from a company that was buying up all of Fairchild's assets at bargain prices. He was still on a sizeable retainer and using all his knowledge of his former employee to benefit his new employer. He was after all, a lawyer. He believed his position like any other was arguable. If he was disbarred he would no doubt appeal

Sam Johnson realized his worst nightmare in no longer being granted even the thinnest façade of dignity. After Benito Peroni's death, information of Sam's corrupt, money-grabbing, political life seemed to spring forth from the bowels of the Earth. One trickle led to another until the flow turned his life into an overwhelming quagmire. Even his doorman scowled at him with contempt. His wife stood bravely by him for the first month, but then the pictures surfaced of Sam in a compromising position with some young "hottie" on a Fairchild golf vacation in Bermuda. When his wife left him, he just sat in his penthouse afraid to go out, buzzards swarming and criminal charges pending. He dove into a bottle of Valium, before the charges were actually laid, and never made it back into the conscious world. He had over-invested in a pride so disconnected from reality, that the real world had become unliveable. He was an alien creature suffocating in the atmosphere of a hostile environment.

32

Life Goes On

The return to Canada held an odd sensation for George. It was as though the air somehow became lighter as the train crossed the border. The conflicts facing an America re-evaluating everything from the separation of church and state to basic human rights were inescapably overbearing at times.

Sure, Canada had its own problems but there did seem to be an air of greater tolerance and moderation. It even had an opposition party whose soul purpose was to split the country, if that wasn't tolerance and real democracy at work, nothing was. The end-run was a greater sense of well-being than George felt in the country of his birth, but as an American he still had an ingrained faith in the promise that America held for itself and the world.

The *Sight* continued to grow as George prepared for the fall term. He knew enough to lock himself in the bathroom when he felt a strong episode coming on in order to keep it from Joan and the rest of the world; a bit like some kind of personal hygienic practice. He didn't mind when the *Sight* invaded his consciousness, other than some minimal fear of embarrassment. He was learning how to handle it, which felt much better than the denial approach of his past. He was learning how to look and act normal while engaging in what was perceived as the abnormal.

While the *Sight* itself astounded him on occasion, he was also aware that in the vessel of human weakness and imperfection it was all too fallible. He often wondered if his father knew of Ernie Dobson's murder. His inability to believe anyone could kill such a good man may have blocked any information to the contrary. Belief was a powerful thing and an integral part of both human greatness and human frailty. His father's own bias had more than likely stopped him from imagining the unimaginable in Ernie's demise. Bias like religious dogma remained obstacles in the evolution of the human being, he thought. So much growth stopped daily at those barricaded doors.

George was beginning to think accessing the *Sight* was an odd mix of art and science much like music. The greatest technical prowess was powerless without inspiration and a natural gift. Things appeared with great clarity to composers of music on some occasions, and on others, hours of painstaking effort went unrewarded. In one moment an idea could appear brilliant and feel so utterly stupid the next. He had often wrongly interpreted what he had convinced himself to be true. Flaws of the user aside, the *Sight* could also realize an incredible power when animal, intellect and spirit occasionally phased into harmonious synchronicity. In such times of clarity it soared like a beautiful melody and he was in awe of it.

George hoped there might be a better understanding of the spiritual realms. There was far too much anecdotal information on a worldwide scale to dismiss. A consciousness separate from the organic brain was finally beginning to be seriously studied and documented in near death and out-of-body experiences around the globe. It was painfully ironic that a world still capable of buying into myths of virgin birth, infallible prophets and the like, could not make allowances for its own spiritual possibilities.

Things between Joan and George improved slowly. Her reserved manner, a residue from the images of the invalid she saw in Lincoln had lost some edge. Their sex life resumed, as powerful a force as ever, providing a measure of healing at times, a refuge for two weary souls seeking oneness, that stubborn minds often interfered with. Love remained despite being occasionally burdened with a lack of surety. It had taken George so long to realize who he was, that the discovery of self at times was a chip on his shoulder – a like-it-or-lump-it mentality.

The laws of physical survival so often overshadow the laws of forgiveness and love, the stuff of spiritual survival. The biggest piece of George's well-being and survival however had been revealed back in Lincoln. He had been thinking about it and processing it and now felt its closeness. He couldn't tell anyone and the need to find some release caused him to go out and buy a blank book that he scribbles into everyday. He locks his office door and sits at his desk for an hour then tucks it away tenderly in his bottom drawer.

Bequest

One entry held words he hoped might be of use to someone else...
some day: *Joan is pregnant but I cannot tell her even though I long to
share this new wonder with her. My knowledge, if revealed, would of
course marginalize her own sense of being and worth. She must find out
herself and I will do my best to act surprised. It will not be hard or
insincere to invest in such joy or her magnificent ability to nurture this
new life. I didn't go looking for the data concerning Joan's pregnancy;
somehow it came looking for me back in Lincoln. It took me a long time
to figure out what those visions were all about. I know I will have a
beautiful daughter who will have soft dark hair like her mother. I also
know why I built a swinging seat on my father's porch. It will be her
favourite place, for a time, where she will sing songs in a little voice, so
sweet and soothing the ears of two doting parents. I had the old tractor
towed away and started the sandpits for horseshoes at the side of the
barn before I left. I know we will spend time there, laughing.*

*I am grateful for having been allowed to stand above my own time
line, as painful as it was, for those brief flashes. I have seen my place as
a link in an infinite chain and not the end of it, which helps to diminish
some of my own selfishness, though sadly not all of it.*

*Joan will want to name our little girl after her mother and this
newborn Moss will have the Sight. My daughter will be the first woman
in generations of my genetic line to have this talent and it will be
interesting to see what nuance her gender brings to its expression. I will
do my best to help her incorporate this blessing into the fabric of her
being while refining techniques of camouflage to protect her from those
who fear the unknown... what they can't or don't wish to understand.
Maybe she will need no protection in this new millennium from the wrath
of ignorance... wishful thinking? Probably. I guess ignorance will
always be. It is how we learn the joy and pain of discovery in connecting
the dots found in the metaphors that surround us, recognizing something
of ourselves in people and situations we find offensive.*

*This Sight is my gift to our child as it was my father's to me and his
father's before him. It seems these talents bestowed upon us by our
parents are as much burden as gift. Even the celebrated or embraced gift
can be a source of sacrifice and suffering. This can be seen in the parent
who spends their last penny on the best skates for a potentially talented
child, or in extraordinarily talented individuals, tortured by the idea they
can never be loved for themselves, only their talent.*

I have never loved my father more than since his passing. Every once in a while I still find myself uncontrollably sinking in the loss of his physical presence. I can feel sadness approaching like a warm moist fog. Sometimes, I am able to ignore it or avoid it, but other times for no good reason I walk right into the painful mist for a good stiff dose of it. I try to stay away from the darkest thoughts, seeking now mostly the positive memories. There is more of the man there.

We speak daily when I am alone. I don't know exactly where he is but I can say it gives me great comfort to talk to him. I feel incoming love from a source that I think I can identify as him. I have no evidence that would please science, just what I feel, in a world that values only measurable units for commercial purposes.

I kissed Joan at the breakfast table when I left for school. She is probably getting ready by now. This morning she has an appointment with her Doctor where she will find out the wonderful news of the sweet little life that grows in her womb. I will sit by the phone at work and let my mind wander to warm places while I wait for her call. I will think about the way she used to purr and lean into me when I kissed her goodbye in the morning and how I might nurture that sense of well being into her presence again. The powerful memory of it fills me with such a longing for that wonderful flash in time when in another's eyes I could do no wrong. Yeah okay, maybe that statement is a little rich – but at least allow me the idea that there was a time when I was somehow more palatable to the woman of my dreams. I will find some of what I seek. The possibilities are assembling into something good in front of me. If I can follow what truths I feel, I can be more than I am, which might hold more appeal to this remarkable woman I love.

I am slowly learning an unwavering sense of hope and love that I believe is the ultimate gift my father left to me... his true bequest.

Manor House Publishing Inc.
www.manor-house.biz
905-648-2193